Praise for

A
FINE
IMITATION

"When a restless Park Avenue socialite has an affair with a mysterious French artist, her world suddenly topples around her. The beautiful Vera Bellington has secrets of her own, and flashbacks to a former friendship and her years at Vassar threaten her social standing and reputation in this story set in glamourous 1920s New York."

—Harpersbazaar.com

"In her debut novel set in Prohibition-era Manhattan, Brock sets out to explore those feelings of unrest both in society and in the life of Vera Bellington, a pedigreed beauty whose insulated world has become a whirlwind of alcohol-fueled social events and nights spent alone while her husband roams."

—*Atlanta Journal-Constitution*

"Brock's introspective characters, satisfying sub-plots, and unexpected—but justified—twists elevate the novel from a period romance to a suspenseful peek inside high society's gilded cage."

—*Historical Novels Review*

"Told from the inside of the gilded cage, *A Fine Imitation* explores one Manhattan socialite's growing realization that who she's been brought up to be is increasingly at odds with who she is. Although set in a rarefied corner of the early twentieth century, this lush, incisive debut novel explores the universal choice between doing what is right versus what is expected."

—Miranda Beverly-Whittemore,
New York Times bestselling author of *Bittersweet*

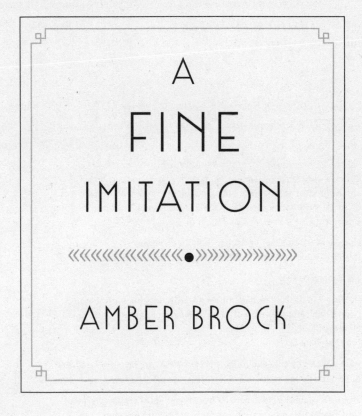

A
FINE
IMITATION

AMBER BROCK

B\D\W\Y
BROADWAY BOOKS
NEW YORK

Copyright © 2016, 2017 by Amber Leah Brock Player
Reader's Guide copyright © 2017 by Penguin Random House LLC

Published in the United States by Broadway Books, an imprint of the Crown Publishing Group, a division of Penguin Random House LLC, New York.
broadwaybooks.com

BROADWAY BOOKS and its logo, B \ D \ W \ Y, are registered trademarks of Penguin Random House LLC.

Originally published in hardcover by Crown Publishers, an imprint of the Crown Publishing Group, a division of Penguin Random House LLC, New York, in 2016.

Library of Congress Cataloging-in-Publication Data is available upon request.

ISBN 978-1-101-90513-5
Ebook ISBN 978-1-101-90512-8

Printed in the United States of America

Cover design: Elena Giavaldi
Cover photographs: (woman) Condé Nast Archives/Corbis; (skyline) E.O. Hoppé/Corbis

10 9 8 7 6 5 4 3 2

First Paperback Edition

For my mother.

For my husband.

For the girls.

Men, it has been well said, think in herds; it will be seen that they go mad in herds, while they only recover their senses slowly, one by one.

—CHARLES MACKAY

« | »

If she had to guess, Vera Longacre would say that most of the girls at Vassar College knew her name and could pick her out of a crowd, even if she could not do the same for them. Her peculiar brand of celebrity came without any effort on her part, much like the money, the houses, and appearances on the society page. Very few of her fellow students could claim to know her personally, and a still smaller group would be able to identify her favorite foods or pastimes or which room in the dormitory was hers. But almost everyone knew Vera's face well enough to whisper and nod discreetly in her direction as she glided past them on the quad. She sometimes felt like a walking magazine cover, with her name above her head in place of a title.

Not that she didn't have a social group. In her first two years, she had selected a couple of girls of adequate means and manners, with whom she ate dinner and studied from time to time. The classroom, however, was a sacred space for her. When the instructor lectured, she preferred to be out of danger of distraction. She found the third row of the classroom the perfect compromise. Freshman year she had made the mistake of choosing a seat too close to the professor's podium, and sophomore year had taught her the back of the room made it difficult to hear over the whispers of less inspired classmates. Now, as a senior, she had found the perfect balance. Close enough to hear well, not so close that the professor would expect her to answer every question.

Vera liked to arrive a few minutes early. On that morning, she walked into the classroom in the Main Building to find only three other girls giggling in the back row. The auditorium-style seating sloped down to a lectern and desk at the front of the room, and three large windows at the back provided far more light than the new electric bulbs overhead. Once she had chosen her third-row seat, she opened her textbook to the assigned reading. She skimmed back over the paragraphs, then found her attention drifting to the plates, which showed richly colored prints of a set of neoclassical paintings. Who could read endless pages of dry description when the paintings were right there to be devoured?

A satchel thunked down beside Vera, but she did not bother to look up. Her two closest friends did not share any of her classes, and she didn't care for small talk. She flipped the page to a new painting as the girl in the neighboring seat let out a huff.

"If you ask me, the problem with the neoclassicists is all the lounging," the girl said.

Vera looked up to find a pretty girl with hair as black as her own, though her eyes were blue instead of Vera's brown. A playful smile lit up the girl's round face.

"I mean, look," the girl continued, gesturing at the plate on the page. "Every single figure here is draped against a marble wall or slumped against a column. Surely one of those painters must have known the ancient Romans or Greeks could stand and sit like normal people, don't you think? Just look at how this woman is flopping around."

"I . . . suppose." Vera could not think of a better answer to such an absurd observation. "It is part of the style, though."

The girl tapped the paper. "Oh, it's always part of the style. Anytime they're doing something silly-looking it's part of the style."

"How would you have done it, then?"

The girl pulled the book from Vera's desk and inspected it. She waved her hand again, dismissing the painting in front of her. "I don't know. Wouldn't it be much nicer if it looked like real life? If it had real detail?"

"Like a photograph?"

A grin spread on the girl's pink-cheeked face. "Exactly. See? You understand. With their eyes all rolled to the gods like that, it looks like they're having fits. The worst thing is how lazy it is on the artist's part. Making a person look real is far more of a challenge."

Vera stared at the girl. At least she wasn't talking about the weather. "I'm sorry, have we met before?"

"I don't think so, why?"

Before she could prepare a more polite answer, Vera said, "Because most people introduce themselves before barging up to complain about women in neoclassical paintings having fits."

The girl's eyes widened. Vera thought for a moment she would get up and leave, but instead she laughed. "Then I'd better introduce myself. I'm Bea Stillman. Please, never, ever call me Beatrice."

Vera's brows shot up. "Stillman? I'm surprised we haven't met before now. I didn't know there were any Stillmans here."

Bea shook her head. "Not those Stillmans. Related, though. He's my father's cousin. We left for Georgia before he left Texas." She sat up straighter. "We're the Atlanta Stillmans."

The mention of Georgia explained Bea's breathy cadence and drawn-out vowels. "I must say I'm surprised," Vera said. "Why come so far north?"

The girl toyed with her bracelet. "I was at Agnes Scott, in Decatur, but my parents decided the New York set would be a good influence for me. Fewer pearls, more diamonds. Though I don't know how good your manners are after all." At Vera's frown, Bea leaned forward. "You haven't introduced yourself yet."

"Oh." Her stern look relaxed. "Right. I'm Vera Longacre."

"Of course I knew there was a Longacre among us," Bea said with a wry tone.

Vera turned to fuss in her bag. "Yes, that's me."

Bea paused at Vera's tightened expression. "Oh, now, don't be that way. That's not the first time you've gotten that reaction, is it, Rockefeller?" Her softened pronunciation of the final *r* made it sound closer to "fella."

Vera's features loosened into a smile. She adopted the tone her mother and her friends used to speak to the wait staff at the club. "We are not the Rockefellers, goodness."

Bea played along, lifting her nose into the air. "Don't like the comparison?"

"Certainly not, darling." Vera leaned in, lowering her voice to a hush. "New money."

The girls laughed. The room had filled as they were talking, and now most of the rows were occupied. The instructor walked in, set her briefcase on the desk, and turned on the slide projector. The slight, gray-haired woman's voice bounced around the oak-paneled room for about five minutes before Bea started scribbling on a scrap of paper. She passed the note to Vera.

Are you a senior?

Vera wrote *yes* and passed it back. After further scratching on Bea's part, the scrap returned.

I'm a junior. I live in Josselyn. You?

Ignoring the note for a moment, Vera put on a firm listening-to-the-teacher face. When she felt her point was made, she wrote *Strong Building.*

Bea didn't write back for a good while. At last, the paper returned to Vera, with a new line.

You ought to get moved to Josselyn. We have showers.

Vera wrote back, *Josselyn wasn't built when I started here.*

Bad luck. Do you have a beau?

This question took Vera by surprise, and she missed most of the discussion about the sculptor Canova as she chose an answer. Finally, she put *yes* on the paper and slid it back down the long desk.

Bea glanced at the paper and pursed her lips dramatically.

That took a while to write.

I didn't want to miss any more of the lecture.

But you sure didn't look like you were listening. Who is he? Is it forbidden? I simply love forbidden romance.

It's not forbidden.

You can tell me. I'm good at keeping secrets.

Not now.

Vera thought for a moment after this and added: *It's not a secret.*

When the professor dismissed the class, Bea stood and exhaled hard. "I must say, you have me in suspense, Vera Longacre. Why don't you come with me and tell me all about your scandalous love affair?"

Vera laughed. "It's not a scandal. It's the exact opposite of a scandal, as a matter of fact."

Bea scooped up her books, papers, and pen in one messy jumble with one hand and hooked her elbow through Vera's. "Well, come with me and tell me your deadly dull story anyway." She shot a look out of the corner of her eye. "I may as well say it. I wasn't planning to like you."

"Oh, no?"

"That's why I started talking to you." Bea led Vera down the stairs to the exit.

"You started talking to me because you thought you wouldn't like me?" Vera asked.

"That's right. I like to pick a serious-looking girl and say a few shocking things, to see how fast she moves to another desk."

Vera nudged Bea with her shoulder. "That's horrible."

"It is, but I'm starved for entertainment." She rolled her eyes and drawled out the word *starved*. "Anyway, you didn't move desks. You sat right there and said something clever." Bea released Vera's arm as they entered the hallway. "I'm afraid this means we have no choice. We simply must be friends."

Vera studied the odd, lively girl beaming in front of her. Papers dripped from the clumsy stack in her arms. Bea's careless stance sent a shot of affection through her. Perhaps it was that carelessness that drew her to Bea. There was none of the social posturing Vera was so accustomed to. The girls she typically socialized with were so afraid of saying the wrong thing, they hardly spoke at all. Bea wasn't a breath of fresh air, she was a balmy gust.

"If we must be friends, then I guess we ought to go to lunch together," Vera said. "Would you like to?"

Bea nodded, and the two headed off, trailing paper all the way.

« 2 »

The two-and-a-half-minute elevator ride from the penthouse to the lobby of the Angelus building was more than enough time for Vera Bellington to contemplate ways out of her weekly Wednesday lunch with her mother. What if she called to say she was ill? What if she got into the Packard waiting downstairs and directed the driver to a different restaurant? What if she got into the Packard, went to the usual restaurant, but sat at a different table and said nothing to her mother? She could pretend to be a stranger. *Terribly sorry, you must have me confused with someone else.*

Well, they would lock her up, no question about that. Her mother and Arthur would conclude Vera had lost her mind at last, and would spare no expense in finding her the best facility in which to go insane. Going to another restaurant was no solution, either. Her mother would simply come to the penthouse of the Angelus looking for Vera, and then there would be hell to pay. Feigning illness would also mean an unwelcome visit. Her fanciful options exhausted, Vera went out to the curb to meet the car. She did not have to say a word to the driver. He knew where to go for Wednesday lunch.

Her mother was already seated in the Tea Room at the Plaza

when Vera arrived, at their usual table. Lorna Longacre was a slender woman with steel-gray hair coiled in a knot at the back of her head and remarkably smooth skin for her age. This was, in part, because she refused to frown, citing the wrinkles such a disagreeable expression would cause. Of course, she did not smile much either, which probably had the same helpful effect.

Vera slid into the floral cushion of the chair with a quiet greeting, but her mother kept her gaze trained on a group of girls passing by the window. Something between disgust and satisfaction pulled on her face, as if insects had invaded and she looked forward to the pleasure of stamping them out one by one.

"What are you looking at?" Vera asked, as the waiter spread a napkin onto her lap for her.

"The clothing some of these—well, you can hardly call them ladies, can you? The skirts on them. Can't decently call them skirts, either. Up to their knees. More like bathing costumes." Her mother sniffed and turned her attention to Vera. "If you had dressed with so little sense at that age, I'd have thrown you out."

"Which is why I would never have done such a thing, Mother. Good gracious." Vera peered at the menu, though she always ordered the crab cocktail with sliced tomatoes.

Her mother shot her a pointed look but did not comment. "And that short hair," she continued. "Though it's not just silly girls doing that now. Do you know, the ladies at the club have convinced themselves it's appropriate for women of their age? Petunia Etherington came in the other day with it chopped straight off at her chin." Vera's mother clicked her tongue. "Imagine."

The two ladies ordered their meals, and Vera squeezed a lemon into her tea. They sat looking around the room for a moment in silence, before taking up the usual set of questions and answers that served as their script for these lunches.

"How is Daddy?" Vera asked.

Her mother picked an invisible thread from her jacket. "Forever with his horses. I'm always half surprised he doesn't offer me a sugar cube and try to brush me when he comes in."

"When is the next race?"

"Not for ages. The next is Saratoga. I hope you'll come with us. I'll call your girl and have her put it on your calendar."

Vera nodded. "Did you go to the opera this weekend?"

"It was *La Traviata*."

"Mmm. Daddy hates that one."

"I went with the Stanfords." Her mother took a sip of tea. "She tried to hide it, but Eleanor wept like a baby at the end. Honestly, in public."

"It is a lovely opera, though." Vera inclined her head at the waiter as he set down their plates.

"Weeping in public is for infants and funerals, darling. And even then it should be done discreetly." Her mother lifted her fork over her chicken salad. "How is Arthur?"

The question should have been a throwaway one, but Vera's throat tightened at the mention of her husband. Thirty years of conversation with her mother had taught her better, but her response was out of her mouth before she could stop herself. "Mother, when Daddy was working . . . away a lot . . . did you ever get lonely?"

Her mother set her fork down on her plate and glanced around. "I hope that's a unique way of telling me you're having a child."

Vera looked at her hands in her lap, her face burning. She would have been better off confessing an urge to strip naked and dance around the restaurant than to admit something like loneliness to her mother. She struggled for the words to explain herself and settled on something close to the truth. "No, nothing like that. Nothing out of the ordinary. But Arthur has so many late nights, more trips away. It's been a bit difficult."

Her mother snapped her fork back into the air. "What did you think marriage would be like? Besides, lonely people are people without anything to do. Don't you have your charities? Your friends? Good heavens, if we expected our husbands to provide us with our only company we'd all go mad." She narrowed her eyes. "Have you been reading those romances again? Those silly things will rot your brain."

"I'm sorry, Mother. Forget I said it."

"Yes, let's." Her mother took a sip of water. "Oh, I have something to occupy you. There's a painting I'm thinking of buying, but I want you to take a look for me first. One of my friends from the club introduced me to a dealer, and he says he's got a Dutch master. He's selling at an amazing price. I'm afraid the price is a little too good."

"Have you seen it yet?"

"I haven't." Her mother pursed her lips. "How much did your father and I pay for you to go to Vassar? We may as well get some use out of your studies, don't you think?"

Vera knew not to take the bait on that line of inquiry. "When do you want me to go?"

"Are you free tomorrow? The dealer phoned this morning, I told him I didn't think you had anything pressing."

Vera stifled a groan. She did have a luncheon with the ladies in her building, but her mother did not make requests. She mandated. "Who is he?"

"Fleming somebody. He's apparently a French dealer with an established gallery in Paris. He's just opened an offshoot in the city to better cater to his American clientele. I'll give you the address. He's a few blocks from here."

Vera tried frantically to think of some way she could redirect her mother's interest. The idea of traipsing through the city for a Dutch master her mother would not even really appreciate was not Vera's idea of an afternoon well spent. "Surely his Paris gallery would have a better selection if he's just setting up here. Why not wait until you're there next?"

Her mother shook her head. "No way of knowing when that will be. Your father won't go with me, and I certainly won't travel alone. Unless you'd like to go with me?"

An hour in a local gallery seemed a less daunting prospect than a month in Europe with her mother, and Vera agreed to go see the painting. After they finished their meal, her mother wrote the gallery's address on a card. They walked out onto the sidewalk to wait for their drivers to bring their cars. Her mother's arrived first, and she waved a few fingers at Vera from the backseat. A hint of worry still lingered in her eyes, indicating she had not forgotten Vera's confession.

« 3 »

After their first lunch together on the day they met, Vera and Bea ate together nearly every afternoon. At first, Vera had alternated between her usual lunch crowd and Bea. Once, she invited Bea to eat with her group, but the blend had not been a harmonious one. All Ella Gregory and Lillie Huntsfield could do was stare, and Bea had pronounced them "dull as flour, but with less taste." After that, Vera adjusted her schedule to come in late enough that she and Bea missed her other friends entirely. The dreariness of her more appropriate friends could not compete with her new, vibrant friend from the South. Unfortunately, her lively lunches made dinner with her old crowd seem even more tedious. No one in her right mind would choose polite small talk and inquiries about her academic progress over Bea's naughty asides.

Dinner seating was naturally trickier to navigate, since the evening lacked the casual atmosphere of lunch, and class schedules could not be blamed for interrupting the standing social appointment of the regular table. One night, emboldened by imagining what her new friend would do in her situation, Vera strolled through the dining room right past Ella and Lillie, nodding a greeting but saying nothing. The girls gave her stony looks but would never have dreamed of challenging Vera's choice. She wove her way around the square, white-clothed tables to take a seat beside Bea.

"Not sitting with the Opera Board tonight?" Bea asked, a smile playing at the corners of her mouth.

Vera spread her napkin in her lap and scooted her wooden chair closer to the table. "They have each other. I thought you could use some company, too."

"Maybe they do teach girls up here manners after all." Bea leaned in and spoke under her breath. "You couldn't take it anymore?"

"Not for another minute." Vera laughed. "Your parents may have sent you up here for the good influences of the North, but you've been a bad influence on me, Bea Stillman."

"Impossible. Girls like you are incorruptible." Bea poked at the sliver of roast beef on her plate.

"I don't know about that."

"You'd rather be corruptible? I knew there was a sinner lurking inside you. Maybe now you'll tell me more about your summer romance." A familiar gleam brightened Bea's eyes.

Vera wanted to reply that Arthur's pursuit was hardly a romance, but she stopped. Of course, technically, it was a romance. He wouldn't have visited her so often last summer if he hadn't had marriage on his mind in some way. So why did Bea's description seem so ill fitting? "Maybe I will," Vera said at last. She had held off this discussion through weeks of lunches; it was probably time she gave her friend more than just a passing detail.

Bea turned, eyes shining. "Finally. What does Arthur look like? He must be handsome. Is he rich?"

"He is terribly handsome," Vera admitted. She ignored Bea's last question, leaving a discussion of Arthur's financial situation for a more private conversation. A maid appeared at her elbow, and Vera nodded. As the maid spooned green beans onto their plates, Vera tried to keep her voice low until the woman stepped away. "Tall, with dark hair. Not too slender. He's about ten years older, and very sophisticated."

Bea wrinkled her nose. "You sound like you're describing a building. What are his eyes like? His lips?" She drew out the last word with
relish, and Vera's cheeks warmed.

"Goodness, does everyone in Atlanta talk like that in public?"

"Just me, as far as I know. Aren't you lucky I came your way?" Bea
chewed thoughtfully on a green bean. "So, dark hair. Tall. Promising
start."

Vera fixed a hard gaze on her food. "His eyes are lovely. They're pale
blue, like crystal."

"Like forget-me-nots?"

"More silvery than that. I've never seen eyes like his."

"Now, that sounds like something a lover might say. Much better."
Bea offered a quiet clap.

Vera glanced at the neighboring tables. "Do you have a beau?" she
asked quickly.

Bea laughed. "You've seen the reaction I get from girls. Can you
imagine what men think of me?"

"You're pretty, outgoing, smart . . . I'd think your beaus would be
tripping over each other."

"If I meet a man I like, I'll have you write me a letter of reference.
My own mother wouldn't be so complimentary."

"I don't know. It sounds like you get along well with her," Vera said.
Bea had described a soft-spoken, sweet woman with a wicked sense of
humor that belied her poise.

"I do. Most of the time." Bea shrugged. "But never mind her. What
do you and Arthur do together? Hopefully more than sit in the parlor."

"He took me to the soda fountain," Vera said, with a hopeful lift in
her voice.

Bea sighed. "I was hoping for something more interesting than the
soda fountain."

"Well . . . once we took a walk on the beach. He even took his shoes
off." Vera laughed at the memory, but the look on Bea's face suggested
the thought of a barefoot Arthur was not as funny to someone who
didn't know him personally. Her laugh died away.

Bea placed a hand on Vera's arm. "As long as you like him, that's the important thing. He sounds . . . he sounds very nice."

"I do like him," Vera said. She really did. There was something so solid about Arthur, like an anchor in rough waters. What better man to marry than one she could depend on? He might not be exciting, but Vera reassured herself there were qualities in a husband more important than being exciting. Anyway, as long as Vera stayed friends with Bea, she doubted she'd have to worry about a lack of excitement in her life.

« 4 »

The knots that gathered in Vera's shoulders during every visit with her mother began to untangle as she headed home after lunch to the Angelus building. Her husband, Arthur, had built the Angelus in 1919, intending to make the other luxury properties springing up on Park Avenue look like tenement housing. He may not have shamed them to that extent, but there was no question that the building dominated the block, as he and Vera dominated the society within the building. Four golden angel statues topped the roof, their wings tucked, and they glared down at Vera as she left her car and went into the lobby.

She nodded a greeting to the elevator operator as she stepped on, and he took her up to the twentieth floor. She let herself into the penthouse, her low heels clicking on the green marble floor of the foyer. A tall, silver-haired man in a dark suit came in at the sound. His long nose and pinched face always put Vera in mind of an eagle, fixed on some prey in the distance. She removed her gloves, and he accepted them with a nod of greeting.

"Good afternoon, Mrs. Bellington."

"Hello, Evans. Has my husband phoned?"

"No, madam."

She did not know why she had asked. Still, arrangements needed to be made in case he did come home. "Please let me know when you hear from him. I'll need to be sure Gertrude times dinner for his arrival."

"Yes, madam. Would you like me to bring up some wine for you and Mr. Bellington?"

"He'll want a bottle of the cabernet, will you fetch that? Not the '02, the '07." Vera brushed a hair from her forehead, then checked her chignon to make sure there were no other escapees. Everything in its place. "Oh, and please send Marguerite to my room," she continued. "Tell her I want to change into the black silk with silver beading for dinner."

"Yes, madam."

"Thank you, Evans. That will be all for now."

Evans bowed slightly, then turned and went back through the door to Vera's right, which led from the foyer to the servants' rooms in the rear of the apartment. The three other huge oak doors on the semicircular foyer led to the library, the dining room, and the drawing room, and above them rose a dual staircase that led to the private areas of the home.

Vera took the right-hand staircase up to the hall, her steps muted by the thick red rug that ran up to the second floor. The door to the bedroom she shared with her husband, when he was not out of town for business, was the fourth one on the left. There were six bedrooms in all, although Vera toyed with the idea of turning the conservatory into a seventh; they never used it, after all. But then they hardly used the other bedrooms, either. Though they entertained regularly, they did not have overnight guests often.

The master bedroom held a huge brass bed, and one wall had a floor-to-ceiling window with a spectacular view. Off the main room were Vera's dressing room, Arthur's dressing room, and a black-and-white marble bath. Inside the bathroom was a claw-foot tub Vera had purchased in France before the war, an item she was especially proud to have found. She went into the dressing room and sat on the stool at the vanity. While waiting for her lady's maid to bring her gown, she began removing her few items of day jewelry.

In the moment of solitude, Vera's conversation with her mother pushed its way back to the front of her mind. She wished she had not mentioned feeling lonely, but then *lonely* was not the most precise word. Her mother had been right; there were her so-called friends, there were charities. Though her mother failed to mention that most of Vera's time spent on charitable causes was limited to writing checks. The constant stream of dinner parties, teas, and luncheons meant Vera rarely had any time not occupied by other people. Arthur's work had kept him away from home throughout their marriage, so that was nothing new. Other women she knew had become mothers well before Vera's age, but the time never seemed to be right for her marriage to transition naturally to a family, so she had waited. Still, she wanted more from her husband, and more in general, and lately the need tugged harder at her. So perhaps the word she wanted was not *lonely*, but *neglected*. Or isolated. She wondered what her mother would have thought of that.

The maid, a slight girl with wispy blond hair, slipped into the room. She held the dress Vera had requested. "Good afternoon, madam."

"Ah, Marguerite," Vera said. "Thank you."

Marguerite hung the dress from a bar on the wall, spreading the sleeves to avoid wrinkles. "How was lunch?"

"You've met my mother."

The girl allowed herself a small smile. "Would you like me to arrange your hair for dinner?"

Vera patted her dark bun and adjusted a white enamel comb. "No, thank you. It still looks lovely. I will ask you to look at my calendar, though. I need a few hours set aside tomorrow to run to a gallery for my mother. It may mean calling Bessie Harper about the luncheon."

"Of course." Marguerite helped with the small buttons at the back of her neck, and Vera shimmied out of the yellow dress before pulling the black one over her head. The maid zipped her up and handed Vera a pair of black heels to slip on.

"Thank you, Marguerite, that will be all for now. Oh, and will you please tell Evans I'll be in the library? For when my husband phones."

After Marguerite closed the door behind her, Vera sat on the stool once more and began to pick through the jewelry she kept in a lacquered box on the vanity. Dismissing a pair of ruby earrings, she chose understated diamond studs and decided against a necklace or bracelet. Arthur thought it distasteful for a woman to wear a lot of jewelry at home. He really only considered a display of jewelry appropriate for the theater or dining at a restaurant. He would never chide her directly, but a well-placed remark a few days later might indicate his true feelings.

When she was satisfied with her outfit, Vera left the bedroom and went back downstairs to the library. She liked the cozy feel the wood paneling gave the room, and the phonograph made it the perfect place to enjoy a pre-dinner cocktail. Her favorite paintings from her collection also hung in that room, and she enjoyed the opportunity to admire them as she relaxed after the day's social visits. A colorful pastoral landscape hung above the piano. Beside the fireplace, a portrait of a sad-looking young man in Edwardian garb. Near the tall window, a few delicately posed ballerinas.

There was even a portrait of Vera herself, done right after she and Arthur moved into the Angelus. She sighed as she crossed to the liquor cart. The portrait was her least favorite, and she frequently thought of taking it down. It was unlikely anyone would notice if she did. She was convinced she was the only one who ever so much as glanced at any of the works that graced the walls, but she could spend hours looking them over, standing close enough to see each brushstroke, each gradient of color. No matter where she found herself, a well-chosen piece had the ability to make her feel more at home. She was of the opinion that good art lent a kind of dignity to everything.

Evans would have mixed her a drink if she had used the bell to summon him, but she preferred to pour her own. She placed an opera recording on the phonograph and had just lifted the crystal decanter when the phone rang in the distance. Her pulse quickened, but she continued mixing her cocktail, waiting for word that the call was for her. After a few moments, Evans stepped in.

"Madam, Mr. Bellington regrets he will be unable to dine at home this evening. He has an important meeting with clients."

Vera's heart sank. The question *Again?* bounced against the inside of her mouth, but she did not let it out. The butler was hardly the man to bring into her personal troubles. She brought her gin and tonic to her lips to give herself a moment for composure. When she finally spoke, her voice remained pleasingly calm. "Thank you, Evans. Please tell Gertrude we'll only need one plate tonight."

"Yes, madam. Will you take your dinner in the dining room?"

She hesitated. The thought of eating at the long table by herself for one too many nights in a row, with no sound but the scrape of her fork on her plate, was daunting. "You know, on second thought, I had a good bit to eat this afternoon," she lied. "I'll call if I want anything."

The butler inclined his head, then left the library. Vera, cocktail in hand, sank into a maroon leather chair. Around her the music swelled, accompanied by the occasional clink of ice in her glass, as she studied her paintings, alone and hungry.

« 5 »

Vera startled at a knock on her dorm room door. She hadn't expected company, and had even hung the placard on the door to indicate that she was studying. She slid a ribbon between the pages in her history text and stood, smoothing the loose strands of her hair back. The person on the other side of the door, still determined to ignore any wish for privacy, turned the knob.

"Vera, are you there?" Bea popped her head into the room, her blue eyes shining.

"Yes, you ninny, what did you think the 'studying' sign was about?" Vera dropped back into her desk chair.

Bea frowned at the front of the door. "Oh. That. I didn't notice." She stepped into the room, holding a silver tin aloft. "I had an important delivery to make."

Vera accepted the tin and pried the lid off. A dark, sugary smell burst out from the soft-edged squares inside. She closed her eyes and drew in a breath. "You lovely dear. I have been thinking about fudge all week."

Bea lolled on Vera's bed, her legs dangling off the side. "Why else would I have brought it? You haven't been thinking about it, you've been delivering entire sermons on it."

"Because it's heaven." Vera took a bite, letting the chocolate melt on her tongue. The sweetness seemed to curl through her mouth and into her chattering brain, pushing away the names and dates she'd spent the past hours trying to cram in. She let out a sigh.

"That good, eh?" Bea sat up. "Maybe I ought to have kept it all for myself."

Vera held the tin out of Bea's reach. "Well, you didn't, so now you'll have to share."

Bea laughed. "And by 'share,' you mean I'll get the crumbs left when you're done."

Vera ate another chunk, then pointed at Bea. "Why aren't you studying?

"I'm a natural genius, didn't I tell you? I don't study for anything."

"And the essay for English?"

"How did you know about that? You're not even in that class."

"Ella Gregory mentioned it after dinner a few nights ago. Have you started?"

"I will soon enough. Don't you worry on my account."

"I won't."

Bea lifted a piece of stationery from the bedside table. Her eyes widened. "Ooh, is this a love letter?"

Vera rolled her eyes. "It's a letter to a friend from finishing school. But she's married and living in England now."

"Married already." Bea clicked her tongue. "Lucky duck."

"You wouldn't say that if you could see who she's married to, or where she lives. She's in a broken-down estate in the middle of nowhere. Wouldn't you prefer to be here?"

"Sure, but wouldn't you like to have it all settled?" A flash of annoyance crossed Bea's face. "I'd like to have it decided, so I don't have to wonder anymore."

Vera took the letter back from Bea and placed it on her desk. "It is settled for me, as far as I know. I've got Arthur. At least, I expect I'll have Arthur. A whole summer of coming to the shore every weekend and escorting me to the soda fountain isn't nothing, even if Daddy did put him up to it. I'd say if he doesn't propose when I'm home for Christmas, he never will." A little thrill ran through Vera as she thought of Arthur down on one knee, his cool blue eyes pleading a bit. She would never admit, not even to Bea, that she had practiced saying yes, had imagined him sweeping her into his arms for the first time.

Bea's dry tone put a momentary end to the fantasy. "Ah, yes. The terribly un-scandalous, un-forbidden Arthur."

"I know you're only joking, but he is a nice man at heart, even if he isn't quite as lively as you." Vera held out her wrist, which was encircled by a thin gold braid. "Look, he sent me this, isn't it pretty?"

Bea inspected the bracelet. "It is . . ."

"What?" Vera pulled her arm back.

"I don't know. It doesn't . . . look like you. The one your father gave you is much more your style."

"Of course Daddy knows me better. I'm sure Arthur's not used to buying jewelry."

Bea's smile was a white flag. "It's a beautiful bracelet, really. And Arthur will have years to get to know your style, won't he? Did he send a note with it? Where are you hiding his love letters? You know I really want to see those."

"He's written a few times, but hardly what you'd call love letters. They might as well be telegrams. For all of his good points, he's no poet." She giggled. "'Dearest Vera, stop. How is Poughkeepsie? stop. Business is fine, stop.'"

"'Can't stop thinking about you, stop.'" Bea laughed. "But then who cares if he's romantic? That's not the point, is it? He's disgustingly rich. That's all I need from a husband."

Vera sat on the bed beside Bea, her back against the wall, and elbowed her. "You don't want a little romance in your life?"

A wicked smile curved up the side of Bea's face. "I'll have loads of romance, of course. But who needs a husband for that?"

Vera glanced at the open door. "Honestly, Bea."

"I'll have to marry someone as rich as Arthur, and then we can live in the same building. We'll patronize the same charities, serve on the same boards, and you'll always have me around to bring you candy and say shocking things." Bea settled against the wall and laid her head on Vera's shoulder.

"You don't think you'll go back to Atlanta? Not that I want you to."

Bea pursed her lips. "Atlanta has lost its charms for me. No, I'm planning to stay here, if you'll have me."

"We'll make you into a real New Yorker. I'm sure Arthur has some friends. Shall I play matchmaker?"

"Sweet of you to offer, but I've got a cousin at Yale, remember? Some of those boys are downright gorgeous. Then again, who knows? If that doesn't work out, I might be interested in taking my chances with Arthur's friends." Bea lifted her head, turning to admire a postcard Vera had pinned to the wall. "I love your room. I ought to do mine up."

"Maybe your room is all done up, and you just can't see it under all the mess," Vera said.

"Then we'll never know, because the mess is there to stay, sadly."

Vera looked around, trying to see what her room must look like to someone who didn't spend hours every day there. On the walls, she displayed cards, prints, newspaper articles, and ticket stubs from museums she loved. Fragrant sprigs of dried lavender and rosemary, picked over the spring months and stored carefully in her trunks over the summer, ringed the window. The room was smaller than a maid's room at her summer house, but she would never have been able to decorate her expansive suite in her home in the city the way she did here. Even when she removed nearly everything for one of her mother's infrequent visits, her mother still complained of the clutter. Still, there wasn't much about Vera's college experience that didn't wrinkle her mother's nose. She could not abide the dining room, even when it was emptied of gossiping young women. The quad had been declared "too airy," the classrooms "musty," and she had no intention of going to the art gallery on the fourth floor of the Main Building at all. Even with her mother's dissatisfaction, which had begun the minute Vera mentioned going to college in the first place, Vera loved every moment. She dreaded the coming May. Graduation would make the whole experience disappear like a dream.

The snap of the fudge tin lid next to her brought Vera out of her reverie. She watched Bea select a piece with a slight smile. If what Bea said was true, and they both married men of good standing, Vera could have a reminder of her college days with her in the city. Maybe a bit of fun, too. Maybe she should talk to Arthur about a friend for Bea.

"Come on," Bea said through a mouthful of candy. "Let's go to Sunset Lake. This might be the last of the really warm days we get." She caught Vera's peek at the desk. "Studying can wait. You've got all day tomorrow. Let's go."

Bea stood and grabbed Vera's hands, pulling her off the bed. With a guilty glance at her books, Vera followed Bea out.

« 6 »

Vera awoke to find Arthur's side of the bed cold and smooth. When he got home after she went to bed, he would usually sleep in one of the spare rooms rather than disturb her. She found him at the table in the dining room, dressed for work in a tweed suit. When she saw him like that, with his broad shoulders and black curls, she thought how formidable he must look to any rival. Like a nobleman visiting from the age of chivalry. He turned his ice-blue eyes from his newspaper to her when she entered.

"Good morning," he said. His mahogany-dark voice commanded attention, even in the noisiest room.

"Good morning, dear. Long night?" Vera settled into the chair next to him and pulled her dressing gown tighter over her chest.

"Very long. Negotiating contracts with the Wilhelm group."

"I hope you at least ate a little something."

He smiled, but quickly turned his attention back to the financial page. "I did, thank you."

"I worry about you being out so late." She leaned in, hoping to catch his gaze again. "That's the third night this week. And tomorrow you're off to Chicago . . . when does your train leave? I could go down to the station with you, we could have a little lunch before you go."

"I wouldn't think of it. Interrupting your schedule like that."

She reached for a piece of toast and took a small bite of the corner. "It's no trouble."

He turned the page. "I have some notes to review for the meeting. Some other time."

She did not want to risk being a nuisance by pressing him. They ate the rest of the meal in silence, except for the brush of the paper on the table and the rattle of china. After his second cup of coffee, Arthur excused himself, kissing her lightly on the top of her head before going. The cool tang of his aftershave hovered above her long after he had departed. Vera closed her eyes and took a deep breath, enjoying the tingle of the scent in her nose.

After the driver took Arthur to work, he returned for Vera. Her schedule had been open that morning, allowing her to get the gallery visit for her mother out of the way before lunch with the ladies. She gave George the directions, and he maneuvered the Packard into the flow of traffic.

When they arrived, Vera almost missed the entrance to the gallery. The door was narrow with no awning, wedged between a large bank and a restaurant patio. She was within two feet of the entrance before she could see the small black sign. The white lettering read M. FLEMING: FINE ART, the only clue that she was in the correct place. Though she knew the signage must have been temporary while Fleming was setting up shop, the place had an air of exclusivity. One had to know the gallery was there to find it.

She pushed the door open to reveal a long room with shining hardwood floors and a few framed paintings on the right-hand wall. The smell of lacquer and the gleaming white walls gave the old building a fresh, renovated feel. A pretty, dark-haired woman sat behind a desk against the left wall, and she stood when Vera entered. A quick shock pinched Vera's nerves. She wanted to turn and walk right back through the door, but she stood still, willing herself to look calm. The woman looked just past Vera's shoulder, her eyes indifferent.

"May I help you?" she asked.

"I'm looking for Mr. Fleming," Vera said, her voice measured. "Is he in?"

"He is. May I tell him who's here?"

Vera waited a beat. "Mrs. Arthur Bellington. I'm here on behalf of my mother."

The woman cocked an eyebrow. "Of course. Please, make yourself comfortable." She crossed the long room to a door in the back wall and disappeared.

But Vera now felt deeply uncomfortable, a slow heaviness settling in the pit of her stomach. She distracted herself by examining the room. A handful of sculptures stood in a tight crowd in the corner, as though they were deep in conversation. Vera stepped closer to one of the paintings, a still life with a white vase of daisies on a gingham tablecloth. Nice, clean lines. Competent, but nothing notable. The display work must have been intended for the casual shopper looking to decorate the walls of an office or bank. More valuable works would be kept in the back, viewed by request only.

A sound from the far corner of the room startled Vera, but it was not the woman who had greeted her. A man emerged alone, as short and round as his gallery was long and thin. His mustache obscured his lips, and he had combed what was left of his hair over his scalp.

"Can I help you?" he asked, smoothing the strands of hair with his palm.

The flat sound of his vowels surprised Vera. She had expected someone with a gallery in Paris to be French, but this man was New York by way of the Bowery. Still, you never knew where the connoisseurs would come from these days. "Are you Mr. Fleming?" she asked.

"I am." He adjusted the small spectacles he wore on the bridge of his nose. "Mrs. Bellington, was it?"

"Yes. My mother, Mrs. Joseph Longacre, sent me to see you about a painting."

His face lit up. "Yes, Mrs. Bellington. I'm sorry, I should have known. I spoke to your mother again this morning." He thought for a moment. "Bellington ... is that the Angelus Bellingtons, by any chance?"

"Yes." She could not be surprised. Arthur's reputation always preceded her.

"Well, welcome. Nice to meet you." He offered her the hand he had been using to slick the hair on his scalp. His palm glistened in the beam of light from the single window. He must have imagined that the pomade gave him a sophisticated polish, but failed to realize it would come off on everything he touched. Vera took the tips of his fingers in hers and let go quickly.

"The painting Mrs. Longacre asked about is in the storage room. Just arrived, but I've had it framed." He started for the corner he had appeared from, waving at her to follow him. "Good walnut frame. I can add it into the price."

"Yes, well, she may want it redone. Who does your framing?" She did not really want to go with him to the back if that was where the woman from the desk had disappeared to, but she followed him anyway.

"I got a guy, all framing is done in-house. Back here, watch your step." Fleming led her through a door in the back wall. The woman was nowhere to be seen. The room had a high ceiling, like the gallery, and was divided into smaller areas by low plywood partitions. On the far wall, a door opened up to the alley, letting in sunlight and fresh air.

Fleming stopped in front of a canvas, which was covered with a large piece of brown cloth. "Here we are," he said, pulling the fabric off. "Fantastic, isn't it?"

Vera stepped closer, inspecting the work. A blond girl sat at a table composing a letter in a shaft of pale light. She was in three-quarter profile, and the shading in the background made objects against the far wall difficult to distinguish. The use of shadow and light was spot-on. The painting looked a bit worn, but the texture and richness of detail were apparent. "Vermeer? I've never seen this one before," she said.

Fleming beamed. "It was lost, very few records of it. Turned up in the south of France after the war. Painted around 1667, by my consultant's guess. "

"I see." Vera studied the girl's skirt. The painting's composition did suggest Vermeer. And yet . . .

Wood clattered behind Vera, and she jumped. She turned to the source of the noise, which had come from behind one of the plywood partitions, but saw nothing. Had the woman from the front been watching them? Fleming also turned to the sound, a deep frown darkening his features. He stepped between Vera and the space where the sound had come from, plastering on a cheery smile.

"Sorry, that's my framer. I told him if he breaks one more, he's out of here." He clapped his hands together. "So? Should I wrap it up for Mrs. Longacre? Where would she like it delivered?"

Vera glanced at the painting again, then started for the door back to the gallery. "Thank you for showing me. I'll tell her I saw it."

He blocked her path. "But what did you think?"

"Excuse me?"

Fleming looked at her over his glasses. "I need to know if she wants to buy. This is a very special piece. I have a number of potential buyers lined up. If she wants the painting, she'll have to jump."

She shook her head. "I have to say no. I don't think my mother will be buying. Sorry to have wasted your time."

"But why not?"

Vera cleared her throat, unwilling to have this discussion. "Surely you know."

"I promise you, Mrs. Bellington, my consultant in Paris would know if this wasn't the real McCoy. He's an expert." Fleming extended a hand back toward the front room. "Would you like to see the letter from the gentleman who sold it to me? The Duke of Aarschot, he has such a good eye. Fascinating man. Knows more about Vermeer than Vermeer's wife did, I'd wager."

She smiled, cold and tight. "And I can assure you, I know a few things myself. So sorry, I really must go. I'm late for an engagement."

He made a few false starts, then let out a sigh of genuine pain. "Okay. But she's missing out."

"I'm sure one of your other buyers will be delighted to take her place." Vera turned for the door. "Good-bye, Mr. Fleming."

When she walked out onto the sidewalk, she found her car idling at the curb. The driver held the door open for her, and she got in, relieved to have left without seeing Fleming's secretary again. She pushed the woman from her mind to concentrate on what had bothered her about the painting.

Once she was alone with her thoughts, the error was immediately clear. Though almost every detail was immaculate, down to the choice of scene and subtle flecks of color in the shadows, the blue was wrong. Vermeer's blues were deep and bold, and had a quality that could be detected even after centuries of fading or mishandling. This blue was too high, too light. A robin's-egg blue, not cobalt, and it could not be attributed to anything natural like sun damage. The painting had been aged to perfection, so it did not look new, and the difference was subtle enough to fool a less trained eye. Most of Fleming's customers likely only cared that the art they bought matched the drapes in the sitting room and sounded impressive. And the forgery was pristine, done by someone with deep knowledge. Even a gallery owner could be forgiven for missing the error, especially since Vermeer himself was such a mystery. She would be hard-pressed to prove the painting was a forgery, so the thought of reporting it to anyone made no sense. Someone would no doubt be made very happy by the painting, no matter what its origin.

Once she had settled the matter of the painting, the face of the woman at the desk intruded on Vera's thoughts once more. She recognized her instantly, of course, as she had the other times she had spotted her around the city. Once at a museum, once at a restaurant. Most recently she had been at an auction, clinging to the arm of a well-dressed gentleman twice her age. The brief conversation in the gallery had been the first time she and Vera had so much as acknowledged each other in all those coincidental meetings, however. Their polite back-and-forth at Fleming's had finally allowed Vera to get a good look, to see that her hair was still as black as Vera's, her eyes still a vibrant blue. But some of the pink had faded from her cheeks, and time had chilled her warm demeanor.

Vera had honestly not expected to have any occasion to exchange words with her again. Not with Bea Stillman. Not after the heartbreak that had passed between them on that cold November weekend so many years ago.

VASSAR COLLEGE, OCTOBER 1913

Vera crossed the quad, the early fall air tempting her nose with the smell of leaves and smoke. She mentally rehearsed the terms and definitions for the day's test, even though she'd been over them a thousand times since rolling over under her quilt before dawn that morning.

Bea ran up and fell into step beside her. "Honestly, if they're going to insist on having these classes every day, I'm not sure I'll be able to keep this up."

"Don't be silly," Vera said, her mind still on vocabulary. "It's your junior year. They had classes at Agnes Scott. You're used to it by now."

"Used to something and delighted by something are two entirely different states." Bea yawned, stretching a hand over her head. "I want to show you something after class."

"It's not another passage from *What a Young Woman Ought to Know*, is it? I hate to spoil the fun, but I already knew most of those things." Vera tossed a wry look over her shoulder as she slid down the aisle to her preferred seat.

"No, it's not that." Bea dropped into her seat, letting her books scatter across the desktop. She turned to beam at Vera. "I made you something."

"What?"

"It's a little trifle, really a little nothing. Can you come by my room?"

Vera smiled. "Of course. We'll go right after class."

Vera labored over the test, ink smudging her fingers as she wrote, crossed out, and rewrote. She couldn't help but notice from the corner of her eye that Bea wasn't taking the same approach. Bea filled in the blanks on the right side of the page, one after the other, with an air of something like boredom. Vera took care not to read the answers themselves, but she saw that the first letter of each word looped and swirled with embellishments under Bea's pen. Vera forced her attention back to her own test paper, wondering whether Bea was concentrating harder on the artistry of her penmanship than the accuracy of her responses.

Vera left the classroom with the same washed-out-and-emptied feeling tests always gave her but had confidence her time studying had paid off. Bea talked the whole way to her dorm, though she never said a word about the test. In her room, she took Vera's hand and guided her to the desk chair.

"Now, close your eyes," Bea said.

"This is a lot of ceremony for 'a little nothing,'" Vera said, but complied with the request.

"You can't see anything?"

"Nothing at all."

Bea ignored this, placing something feather-light in Vera's lap. "Now, open!"

Vera opened her eyes to find a scroll of paper tied with a rose-colored ribbon. She pulled the ribbon off and unrolled the page. A gasp escaped her. "Where did you get this?"

Bea sank, satisfied, onto the dress-covered bed. "I told you, I made it."

"You never did. How did you . . . Bea, it's remarkable."

The drawing on the paper was so vivid, so clean, it looked as though someone had taken a photograph of the *Bon Ton* magazine cover it was meant to mimic. And yet, it was sharper somehow, each line so even and resolute it seemed one of them might slice right through the thin paper. The girl's black hat and bright yellow coat looked like they would be starchy and stiff under Vera's fingers, though she knew they would only be smooth paper. She had seen Bea's doodles and sketches in the margins of her notebooks, and of course they had discussed their favorite works and artists in class, but Vera had no idea Bea had such genuine talent.

"You did this from memory?" Vera said when she found her voice.

Bea waved her off. "No, Catherine Allston had a copy of the magazine in her room. She let me borrow it."

"This is beautiful. I love it. Thank you."

"I'm so glad you like it. It took me positively forever, but you were so upset when the other got torn. I wanted you to have a replacement. Though if Catherine were tempted at all by treats, I might have gotten the real thing off her."

"I like it better than the real thing, truly." Vera traced a line with her finger. "You should have gone to art school, Bea. Somewhere with a real studio program. Why didn't you?"

A cloud crossed Bea's face for an instant, then was replaced by a smirk. "Are you trying to say you wish I hadn't come to Vassar?"

Vera laughed. "Of course not. But you're very good. You must have studied drawing more seriously at some point."

The brightness in Bea's eyes dimmed. "Oh, Vera. None of it matters anyway, does it?"

"None of what matters?"

Bea cocked her head. "None of . . . this." She gestured to the books piled on the desk. "School. College."

"Of course it matters," Vera said, the words clipped. "We ought to do our best."

Bea sat quiet. She picked at some lace on the bedspread, no longer meeting Vera's eyes. "I always thought all your studying, all that work . . . I thought it was like your room. Everything where it belongs, even the right answers in the right spaces. That you had to do well because it was who you were. Because it was expected of you." She looked up, the corners of her mouth pulled down. "But it's important to you, isn't it? That you learn it. That you know it."

Vera studied the drawing spread across her skirt. "It isn't to you?" She knew the answer before the question left her mouth, but she didn't know what else to say.

"Well, we're going to be wives, aren't we?" Bea said, her voice falsely bright. "It's not as if we're planning to be teachers or curators. We don't have to do any of that." She scooted to the edge of the bed and took Vera's hands. "We'll have our lovely lunches in the city and dinner parties and trips to the shore. We'll have big households to manage. That'll be far better, won't it?"

"But I know you get good grades, I've seen them." Vera plowed through Bea's sunny version of their future, more curious than ever about the disconnect between Bea's sloppy study habits and her good marks.

"Please don't worry about it." Bea dropped Vera's hands. "Let's just say I have a system."

The answer clicked into place. "You're cheating?" Vera asked. Bea opened and closed her mouth. When she didn't answer, Vera said, "Tell me the truth. You wouldn't cheat, would you?"

"Don't be cross with me. I never meant it to be a lie. When we first met, I assumed you knew, and then it got harder and harder to tell you. So I didn't. Everyone does it," Bea said, her voice taking on a pleading tone. At a hard look from Vera, she held her hands up in defeat. "Not everyone, no. But who's it hurting? Not you. And I don't go for top grades, just enough to keep me here."

"But how?"

Bea examined her fingernails. "Girls who've taken a course give me old tests, old essays. I make them things in exchange. Drawings, that sort of thing. I give Professor Harrison an essay he's probably accepted ten times, and he gives me a B. It's easy enough."

"Why even come to college then?" Vera asked.

"To make friends. To have a good time before I'm an old married lady." Her answer rang false to Vera, but Bea did not elaborate. "Speaking of which, I have another surprise for you." Bea leaned forward, a hopeful gleam in her eyes.

"I don't know if I can take another surprise."

Bea blinked hard and leaned in. "Please, Vera, you're not surprised. You must have known I couldn't be doing as well as I am. You've dressed me down more than once for leaving an assignment to the last minute."

Vera had to admit that was true. She'd seen Bea's study habits—or lack thereof—firsthand. Had she really been willfully blind? It was a distinct possibility, and one she didn't like pondering. Still, she didn't want to fight with her friend about something she knew she wouldn't be able to change.

"And you did like the first surprise, right?" Bea tapped the drawing.

Vera's shoulders relaxed. "Yes."

"All right then." Bea sat up straight, her eyes shining once more. "You'll love this one, I promise you."

Vera looked around. "Is it in this room? Do I have to close my eyes again?"

Bea lowered her voice to a hush. "Get ready, Miss Longacre. I'm bringing you some boys."

« 8 »

Seeing Bea at Fleming's gallery rattled Vera for days. Thoughts of her old friend continued to pop up, unwelcome, as Vera attempted to get through tea with the ladies in the Angelus or one of her charity meetings. Lunch with her mother had been the most trying. Vera ate much more than she normally did in an effort to keep her mouth full. She feared if she did not, she would blurt out Bea's name. Any attempt to explain that to her mother would have been a horror Vera could not contemplate. That was one name her mother would never want to hear again.

Alone at night, however, Vera wondered what Bea's life had become. She had not expected Bea would be working, least of all as a secretary. Vera had always hoped for the best for her former friend, despite everything. When Vera had seen her those few times in the city, she'd seemed in high spirits, at least from afar. She'd liked to imagine Bea enjoying a glamorous nightlife, juggling suitors and dancing at clubs until the hour Vera herself sat at the breakfast table. She'd consoled herself with those daydreams. Now she knew better. Then again, perhaps Bea had changed and liked secretarial work despite her college talk about wanting to settle down. She could have chosen a different life. Vera thought about going back to the gallery, this time to begin a real conversation. Begin again with Bea, their girlish mistakes behind them.

But no matter what stories she'd told herself before, dark thoughts settled into Vera's mind, a fog that would not clear. Vera knew Bea's skills. The beautifully copied *Bon Ton* cover might have been years in the past, but Bea's presence in an art gallery, only steps away from a fake Vermeer, could not have been a coincidence. Vera was not going to upend her own life simply for a chance to reconcile with a woman who might be involved in criminal dealings.

With concentrated effort, Vera forced herself to abandon thoughts of Bea after a few days, as she had done every time she saw her old friend before. About a week after her trip to the gallery, no longer so preoccupied with Bea or the forged painting, Vera dressed and took the elevator down to 17B with Arthur for a dinner party at Clarence and Ida Bloomer's. She linked her arm with his.

"Have you steeled yourself?" he asked, a hint of amusement in his voice.

"For another description of Ida's new curtains? The greatest mercy would be for them to actually arrive, so that she can show them to us instead of trying to describe the exact shade of red."

"At least you don't have to spend your evening trapped in a corner by Clarence. He may be the host, but I'm the one entertaining him."

Vera always felt a little bubble of hope rise in her in these moments of camaraderie with Arthur. They tended to agree on the tediousness of evenings like this, even if neither of them could think of a graceful way out of them. As they rode in the clattering car, Vera took in the musky, slightly medicinal smell of her husband's pomade; the scent of it always reminded her of their courting days. She wondered if she had seen more of him then than she did now, despite living in the same apartment. She could feel the crispness of his suit jacket under her gloved fingers. Perhaps when they got home that evening she could coax him out of it, unbutton his starched white shirt, and slide her hands down his bare chest. The thought of it left her light-headed, and she gripped his arm tighter. She let her mind wander, imagining his warm breath on her neck, until the creak of the elevator door opening interrupted her reverie.

The butler let them into the apartment, and Ida immediately descended on them. The wobbling feather in her headband made the plump woman look like one of the cooing quails Vera's father kept for hunting at his lodge in Vermont.

"Arthur, Vera, so glad you could make it," Ida said. "Please, come in, cocktails are in the drawing room."

Vera stifled a groan. The invitation had plainly said, "Cocktails at 7, dinner served at 7:30," which was the very reason she had taken until seven twenty-five to leave her own apartment. Fashionably late was forgivable. Delaying dinner seating meant additional nattering conversation about nothing and, to Vera's mind, ought to have been punished with a firing squad. She did not know why she had expected anything different. Too many invitations arrived with times printed on them that had no relationship whatsoever to the actual times observed. She straightened her shoulders and followed Ida into the drawing room, her arm still linked with Arthur's.

A man in a white jacket, hired for the occasion, presented Vera and Arthur with martinis, and they started toward a little circle of guests near the window. Vera took the first cool sip of her drink, grateful for the enterprising people bringing liquor over the borders from Canada. A more effective Prohibition law would have made cocktail conversation unbearable. Clarence, Ida's husband, was describing problems with his newest hotel to a less-than-riveted Julius and Poppy Hastings. Of course, Vera considered, Julius's slack expression was probably more closely related to the dotage of age. A tiny, wrinkled sack of a man, he generally had to be woken several times even before the soup course. His wife, as vibrant and lurid as the flower from which she took her name, could easily have been mistaken for his daughter or an extravagantly dressed nursemaid. Though Poppy was Julius's third wife, married after his seventieth birthday, their union had still managed to produce two little girls. Vera wondered how they fared with a nearly senile father, but she supposed it was all they had ever known.

"Ah," Clarence said, catching sight of Arthur and Vera, "welcome. How are you both this evening?"

Arthur took a deliberate sip of his drink. "We're well, and you?"

"I'm well, but Ida has been in such a frenzy over this party of hers. I told her, 'Ida, it's not as if the royal family is visiting, you give these damned parties once a month.' But you know women." Clarence raised his bushy blond eyebrows.

"Quite," Arthur said. He turned to Vera, and the corner of his mouth twitched just enough for her to see. She mirrored his expression, in a show of solidarity.

Freed of the responsibility of general greetings, Clarence launched once again into his description of the failings of his new hotel's architect. Arthur listened, and Julius leaned in their general direction. Poppy laid a hand on Vera's forearm as Bessie Harper walked up to join them. Bessie, an older woman with springy gray curls, was lean and lanky. She reminded Vera of one of the cranes from Arthur's construction sites, but with a cocktail swinging from her hand instead of a wrecking ball.

"Did you hear?" Poppy asked in a rapturous hush. "Caroline Litchfield's nurse up and quit yesterday. Walked right past Caroline and out the door, never to be seen again. She's got her hands full now, no one to help with the boys. Ida said Caroline's maid had to keep them tonight." Poppy attempted a sympathetic tilt of her head, but her green eyes gleamed.

"It's so good of you to keep up with the maids, Poppy," Bessie said, with a hint of earnestness in her expression. "And Ida, too. Without you, whatever would we do for conversation?"

Poppy bit her lip. She never seemed able to sort out which of Bessie's comments were compliments and which were slights. Vera took a long drink of her cocktail to stifle a laugh. She excused herself and stepped out of the cloud of Poppy's too-sweet perfume, then crossed the room to where the Kellers stood. After accepting Martha's kiss on the cheek, Vera joined another plodding conversation, this one about the garden planning at the Kellers' weekend house. The list of flowers and their varying levels of sun tolerance was dull, but still preferable to Poppy's tawdry gossip.

At last, a maid appeared and rang a small bell to begin the dinner seating. The crowd moved into the dining room, and a few white-jacketed waiters showed people to their seats. Vera took her seat, between Walter Litchfield and Clarence. Arthur sat across from Vera but was listening to Ida's explanation of the menu, and Vera could not catch his eye.

Tomato soup came out first, followed by a pickled beet salad. Vera had never cared for beets, so she cut a few pieces and shuffled them around to give the appearance of having pecked at them, then enjoyed a glass of wine. Next were oysters, then olives, all washed down with more wine. By the time the waiters brought out the roast, the conversation was well lubricated and quite a bit louder. Vera tuned out Walter's bellowing on her right and focused on her husband across the table.

"You know, Arthur," Ida said, "I must confess, I had a bit of an ulterior motive in sitting you beside me tonight."

"Oh?" Arthur speared a piece of beef with his fork and glanced at Vera, who suppressed a smile.

Ida wagged a chubby finger at Vera. "Oh, nothing naughty, Vera, don't you worry."

"Not at all," Vera said. She could not picture plump, graying Ida attempting to seduce Arthur. "I'm intrigued. Please, continue."

"Well, I take a little swim every morning in the basement pool. On my doctor's advice. And the pool is lovely, Arthur. It's one of the main reasons Clarence and I bought here, from you, instead of at 863 Park. But the walls are so drab, all that plain white." Ida let out a tinkling laugh. "And this morning I had an inspiration. Why don't you have someone in to paint them? As the building's owner, I thought you ought to be the one to do the hiring."

"Did you have a particular color in mind?" Arthur asked in a dry tone. Ida rapped him lightly on the arm, and he startled.

"Not a color, silly," she said. "A mural, like the ones they're putting in all the public buildings these days. Something really fine."

Clarence had turned his attention to them. "I think it's an excellent idea, Arthur. Surprised you didn't think of it in the first place."

"Think of what?" Walter asked from Vera's right.

Clarence leaned over Vera and shouted, his breath heavy with the smell of wine. "A mural. For the pool. Ida's idea."

"Oh, marvelous. Yes, just what the building needs," Walter said, punctuating his approval with a gulp from his glass.

"And Vera knows all about art, don't you? She's the ideal person to tell us what we need." Ida fixed a slightly swimmy gaze on Vera.

"I studied art at Vassar, but my concentration was the Spanish masters. Murals are not really my area," Vera said.

Ida waved a hand. "That's perfect, isn't it? We want something classic. Don't want one of those daffy modern things in our building."

Bessie piped up from down the table, her drink sloshing dangerously. "Oh, yes. Wouldn't want anyone thinking of us as modern."

"Quite right, Bessie." Clarence elbowed Vera. "Not one of those fellows who puts a toilet in and calls it art. A real artist."

Poppy, who had caught wind of the conversation, joined in. Her eyes shone with a dreamy look. "It should be someone European, shouldn't it? Someone who studied in Rome or Paris?"

"There seems to be a consensus then," Arthur said, without a glance in Poppy's direction. Vera was surprised he was still listening. As the conversation bubbled around him, he had continued calmly eating.

Ida gave a little clap. "Wonderful! Oh, I am delighted. Vera, do you know anyone who could do it?"

Vera's eyes widened. "I'm sorry, I don't really know any muralists. My dealer—"

"Fine, fine. You can help with the selection, then, can't you? Tell us if we've got a good one, or if it's one of those toilet fellows," Clarence said.

Bessie winked at Vera. "You heard the man. Absolutely no toilets in the building from here on out."

"I know a gentleman, serves on one of the museum boards or another," Clarence continued. "I'll phone him first thing tomorrow. Have him put the word out."

"And the artist could live in, couldn't he?" Poppy said. "A sort of artist-in-residence? Isn't 2A open?"

"It is, isn't it, Arthur?" Ida asked.

"The unit is empty at present, yes." Arthur offered a tight smile. "We'll see how it all works out."

With that decided, and a few more excited chirps from Ida and Poppy, the diners resumed their meal. Vera noted with a glum look at the clock that it was only eight thirty. They still had dessert and cordials, and the men would certainly have cigars in the library while she suffered through another hour in the drawing room with the ladies. So she was relieved when Arthur stood at the end of the meal and announced his regret that he and Vera would have to leave early.

"Oh, no," Ida cried, her chest deflating. "You can't stay for just a bit longer?"

"Very sorry, but I've got to stop in to the office this evening. Big meeting on Monday," he said.

A cold shock went through Vera, but she kept her expression cool as she took his arm. They accepted a chorus of good-byes, then went out to the elevator. Vera waited until they were back in their own foyer to speak.

"The office, Arthur? It's Saturday night." Her voice came out harder than she wanted.

He lifted his chin. "I'm well aware what day it is. What does that matter?"

After ten years of marriage, she knew the difference between a trip to the office and simply leaving, but pushing him could make him shut down completely. She at least wanted a chance at living her daydream from the elevator. "It's so . . . late," she said at last, trying to sound more concerned than unhappy.

"I'm aware of the hour, too. You know I have to work late."

"Will you be home at all, then?"

His face was unreadable stone. "It all depends on how much I'm able to get done."

"I see." She pulled at her gloves, nearly ripping a seam in her haste.

Evans stepped in. If he had heard the exchange, or felt its meaning, it did not show in his face. He took Vera's gloves.

"Evans," Arthur said, "call down for the car, please. And that will be all this evening. Unless you needed something else?" He turned to Vera.

She exhaled hard, defeated. "No. Thank you, Evans."

"Very good." The butler left, the soft leather soles of his shoes against the marble the only sound in the foyer.

Vera stared at Arthur a moment longer, trying to will the courage to say what she knew about where he was really going. But courage failed her, as it always did, and she turned for the staircase. She called a soft "good night" over her shoulder and gritted her teeth against the ache in her chest. Why had she allowed herself to hope that their glances, their friendly words, would translate into what she had imagined in the elevator? A few jokes about tiresome company did not mean that evening would be any different than the countless evenings before.

«‹‹●››»

Vera forgot about the mural idea until two weeks later, when Evans led Clarence Bloomer into her library.

"Clarence, how are you?" She gestured to the chair near her, and he sat. "I'm sorry, we weren't expecting you. Evans should have told you Arthur is out."

"No, dear. I'm here to see you." His tawny mustache broadened with his grin. He dug into his coat's breast pocket, retrieving an envelope. "I've spoken to my friend, the one on the museum board."

"Your friend?" Vera took the proffered envelope. Peeking inside, she saw it held a letter and some photographs.

"Yes, the man I mentioned at dinner. He put the word out about our little mural project, and a man in Paris says he knows someone perfect for the job."

Vera had assumed the residents would forget about the artist idea, but she did not dare say as much to Clarence. "Of course, the mural. Who does he have in mind?"

Clarence's eyes sparkled. "He's quite new, but I'm assured he'll be one of the best known in the world in a few years. Hallan is his name. Emil Hallan. Studied at one of those very old schools, you know."

Vera cocked her head. "Hallan? I've never heard of him."

"As I say, very new. Young fellow. He's in Paris now, but he's willing to come to the city. Says in the letter he's only just started with murals, but he's completed at least one, so he's got some experience with larger works. There's a photo in here, and a few of some of his other paintings. I don't know art. They look good to me, but I wanted your expert opinion."

Vera pulled the photos from the envelope. "I'm sure I don't—" Her breath caught in her throat. Even in black and white, she could see the subtle use of shading, the careful arc of the brushstrokes. His style was undoubtedly modern, with sharp geometric lines, but he somehow blended a modern edge with a heartfelt tenderness that leapt out of the photographs. One suggested a woman, kneeling over a child in a low cradle. Another was a stand of trees, like the edge of a forest, but they looked to Vera like proud soldiers. A few at the edges were battered, but those in the middle stood strong. She wanted to look at them forever, examine every nuance. She could not imagine how incredible the paintings must be in person. Clarence's friend was right. Whoever painted these was clearly finding his style but had the potential to be among the greats.

She flipped to the last picture, then paused. The last was a beautifully done mural highlighting the musical arts. Swirling rivulets grew into streams and then near the bottom took the shapes of cellos, flutes, a kettledrum. But something was wrong. The styles of all four works were so similar, she could not think how to put her hesitation into words. But something inside of her insisted that the mural was not the work of the person who painted the other pieces. The raw emotion of the first three paintings, the tangible mix of despair and hope, was lacking in the mural. She had the strangest notion that if she could have seen the originals in color instead of the black-and-white photos, she would have been able to point out the difference. But how could she explain the subtle disparity to Clarence when she could not describe it inside her own mind? She allowed herself another glimpse at the first paintings, and her heart ached to know who had made them.

Clarence's smile drooped into a frown. "Is something wrong? I told you, I don't know the first thing about—"

"He's very good." The words escaped, riding her breath, before she knew they were coming. Heat rose in her cheeks as she thought of the rush of emotion the paintings had inspired. She felt as though Clarence had walked in on her dressing. She shoved the photos and letter back into the envelope. "They're—he's a good candidate, I suppose."

Clarence's expression brightened once more. He took the envelope from her. "Excellent! Oh, from the look on your face I was afraid they were terrible. But they're good, you say?"

Vera calmed her expression and patted her hair. "Very nice. Fine work."

"I'll write him back today, then. Thank you, dear."

After a few more pleasantries and a reminder to have Arthur phone him, Clarence left, chest still puffed out with the triumph of his find. Vera sat for a long time in a haze, still thinking about the photos. She wondered what sort of man could paint such haunting pieces. He would have to be educated, refined. The sort of man who felt deeply and did not hide it. The sort of man who could not abide coldness or indifference. A man who would not toy, who would say things honestly, and without reservation.

An uneasy tremble went through her as she remembered the photo of the mural. But then, she chided herself, a mural was a different medium altogether, and one she knew little about. Perhaps an artist's style had to be adapted for work on such a large scale. She supposed that her recent brush with forgery had left her on the alert. The postmark attested that the letter and photos had indeed come from France. Besides, she could not bring herself to care whether the pool room twenty floors below had a mural or not. The only interest she had in hiring the artist was that it might mean the arrival of someone with whom she could possibly have a real conversation.

《《《●》》》

Since bringing the artist in was Ida's idea, the other ladies named her head of a newly created "Mural Board," and she threw herself into plans for the big arrival. She roped Vera into helping her furnish 2A and make travel arrangements for Mr. Hallan, since Arthur would be the one writing the checks. The Mural Board agreed that $10,000 plus the cost of travel would be a fair price for what might take several months to paint. Vera suggested the room and board serve as a sort of deposit, with the money paid upon completion of the project. The artist would have comfortable accommodations within arm's reach of his work, and deferring the payment would ease the concerns of anyone wary about hiring an unknown. If they did not like his creation, they would not have to pay.

The maintenance staff and the chauffeur's lounge occupied most of the second floor, so 2A was a modest two-bedroom apartment. From what she had seen of his work, Vera determined that Hallan would appreciate clean lines and delicate touches of color, and she furnished his rooms accordingly. She and Ida bought a six-person dining table, since he would hardly be expected to entertain much, and hired a housekeeper to cook and clean for him. The two women debated about whether or not he would need a valet. Vera thought not, since the girl would be perfectly capable of keeping up with one man's calendar and wardrobe, but Ida thought he should have at least two servants. Weary of arguing the point, Vera allowed Ida to have her way. They booked a second-class passage on the SS *Leviathan*. Vera assumed that since she did not recognize his name, he would not necessarily be accustomed to first-class travel. With the apartment furnished, servants hired, and the ticket purchased, there was nothing to do but wait.

Mr. Hallan sent Arthur a letter of introduction and thanks for the post, but Arthur handed the unopened envelope off to Vera. She studied the gliding letters, as thin and delicate as spider webs. Hallan explained that he had attended the Ecole des Beaux-Arts in Paris and included a letter from one of his instructors there, who gushed about Hallan's talent. That much, however, had been obvious to Vera from the photographs.

Two weeks before the artist was scheduled to arrive, the Mural Board met in Vera's library to discuss who ought to go pick him up. She thought one of the men should go, but as Hallan was scheduled to arrive in the middle of a weekday, the other women quickly voted that down. They were certain none of the men would be willing to interrupt their workday to go down to the docks.

"As head of the Mural Board, I feel I should certainly be there to welcome Mr. Hallan," Ida said, her hand fluttering to her chest.

"I ought to go," Caroline Litchfield cut in. "I'm the head of the Welcoming Committee, and he could be considered a new resident."

"I want to go," Poppy Hastings said.

"Why should you go?" Vera asked.

Poppy's cheeks colored. "I speak French."

Vera pressed her lips together for a moment, summoning all her patience. "He speaks English perfectly. Or at least he writes it. If we crowd the car with a delegation, there will be no room for Mr. Hallan, to say nothing of his trunk."

"We could take two cars." Poppy's voice lifted with hope.

"Why only two?" Bessie Harper asked, in her usual dry tone. "We could all arrive in separate cars. Give him a grand welcome. Let him know he's meeting the upper crust."

A faint line of confusion appeared between Ida's brows. "I suppose that would be grand . . ."

Vera cut in without giving Ida a chance to decide if Bessie was serious. "I really don't think that's necessary. We'll all have a chance to meet him. He'll be working here for a while. Besides, the night after he arrives I'm having a dinner party. He won't have been here more than a day, and you'll all have met him. Then Ida's having cocktails, and didn't you mention a luncheon, Caroline? You'll be positively sick of him before two weeks are done." She pulled her shoulders back and spoke in her most authoritative tone. "Ida and I will go. That will be plenty of welcome."

Caroline nodded. "Of course."

"I suppose," Poppy said, deflated.

"Be sure to take an extra car or two, just in case," Bessie added.

After the ladies left, Vera lingered in the library. Why had she said she would go? Ida ought not go alone, but Vera had not really meant to volunteer herself. She was as anxious as the others to catch a glimpse of the artist, but she felt as if there were a hand on her shoulder, pulling her back. She thought again of the paintings in the photographs, and stood to pour a drink. What if he was not the man those paintings made him seem to be?

《《《●》》》

With a knot of apprehension in her chest, Vera climbed into the backseat of a car with Ida two weeks later. Though Vera looked out the window as they cruised through the city, her mind was too clouded with a jumble of thoughts to notice much. At the docks, they waited in the car while the driver took a sign with Hallan's name on it and went down to retrieve him.

"In that letter he sent your husband, did he say how old he is?" Ida asked.

"You know, I don't think he did."

Ida sighed. "I don't suppose he said what he looks like. No, he wouldn't, would he?"

Vera tugged the band of her thin silver watch. "You'll see him soon enough."

"He must be a young man, don't you think? If he's just starting to make a name for himself. And to think, our building will have his first major work." Ida tittered. "We'll say, 'Oh yes, it's an original Hallan.' And then you know 863 Park will have to have one."

Vera fanned herself. "Hmm. Does it seem a bit warm in here to you?"

"Are you feeling well?" Ida asked, leaning in.

"I need a bit of fresh air. I'm going to step out." Vera opened the car door to a blast of the sour sea air only found near docks. She stood by the side of the car, scanning the crowds for the driver and fighting the trapped feeling the cramped car gave her. The hot air did not help revive her.

All the drivers looked the same in the sea of cars and people, with their black hats and white gloves. At last she saw Ida's driver step into view, followed by two porters lugging a trunk. Behind them was a tall, long-limbed man in a tweed suit. Ida must have been watching out the window, because as soon as the driver appeared, she leapt from the car and stood beside Vera. Ida beamed, but Vera could only stare.

The porters loaded the trunk onto the back of the car, and the driver slipped them some coins. Ida all but thrust herself at the auburn-haired young man, whose mouth lifted into a slightly baffled smile.

"You must be Mr. Hallan," Ida cried. "What a pleasure to meet you. I'm Ida Bloomer, head of the Mural Board." She turned, holding out a hand to indicate Vera. "And this is Vera Bellington. Her husband owns the Angelus."

Vera cursed Ida's ridiculous and improper introduction but kept her face still in a well-practiced expression of coolness. Hallan greeted Ida, then turned to Vera. His face was all angles, like his paintings, but with a loose, friendly grin that softened his features. His eyes were striking, the color of heaven in a children's illustrated Bible, all faded blue-green and glorious. She could have inspected them as she inspected the paintings on her wall, each little glint and shift in shade. She caught herself and looked away.

"Hello, Mrs. Bellington. Pleased to meet you." He held out a hand, and she hesitated. She could not politely refuse such a gesture, but that same phantom grip that had pulled on her shoulder before held her back.

"How do you do?" she said, forcing her hand forward. He gripped it, and her cheeks grew warm. She gestured to the car, ready to go home and be done with the pleasantries. "You must be exhausted. Let's get you to your apartment, so you can settle in."

"How was your journey?" Ida asked as she and Vera climbed into the backseat.

Hallan took the seat up front by the driver. "There was a bit of rough weather on the third and fourth days, but otherwise it was lovely. It's a beautiful ship. And the food was wonderful."

"So glad you enjoyed it," Ida said. "You know, Clarence and I were thinking of taking a trip on the *Leviathan* next spring. I do love Europe in the spring. Don't you, Vera?"

"Hmm? Oh, yes. Just lovely." Vera looked out the window.

Ida chatted with Hallan the whole way, occasionally pulling Vera into the conversation for a word or two. She concentrated on listening, trying to place his accent. He had a clipped British accent, very posh, that sounded to Vera like the ones she had heard among the better families of London. Nothing of the aristocracy, but certainly something one would hear at a fine restaurant, and not from a waiter. Every once in a while a hint of something else would creep in at the back of his throat, a sort of hard, brushed sound, like something scraping metal. But it was fleeting and always disappeared before Vera could identify it.

« 9 »

A week or two had passed since Vera had exploded with questions at Bea's declaration that she would somehow be delivering boys. Uncharacteristically stoic, Bea had refused to answer, saying only that Vera should be on her guard. Despite this warning, Vera hadn't thought to be on guard as she slept in her bed.

The doorknob turned, and the sudden click woke Vera. She sat up. The stream of thought that blared through the fuzziness of sleep said there must be an emergency in the building. But Bea, not the dorm matron, appeared in the crack of light from the hall. She slipped into the room, fully dressed, and crept to Vera's bed. A tingle of relief ran down Vera's spine.

"Goodness, I thought the building was burning down," Vera said. "What on earth are you doing?"

Bea's cheeks were flushed, and her breath carried a faint sting. "Get dressed. We're going out. Oh, and do something with your hair."

"My hair? It's the middle of the night."

"It's not really the middle, more like the beginning. You go to bed earlier than my grandmother." Bea opened the wardrobe and began to paw through the skirts inside. She pulled out a royal blue one. "Ooh, this one is killing."

Vera rubbed her eyes and slung her legs out from under the quilt. "Don't use slang."

"Listen to you. Even half asleep, you're still a walking rule book. Here, let me pin your hair. Oh, and have a sip of this." Bea pulled a flask from her purse and held it out to Vera.

Vera reached for the flask, and warmth hummed through her chest before she even took a drink. Her mind grew sharp, now she was wildly awake. "Where are we going?"

"To meet the boys, of course. I promised you boys. I deliver on my promises." Bea fished combs out of the box on the dresser and started arranging them in Vera's hair. "It's my cousin—he goes to Yale—and a few of his pals from the rowing team. You'll like them."

Vera laughed nervously. "My mother would die if she knew I was doing this. Really, she would fall down dead."

Bea turned Vera by the shoulders to inspect her hair. "Don't tell me you're afraid to go."

"Not at all. Let's go." Vera pressed her fingertips to her mouth. In her excitement, her voice had gotten a bit loud. Both girls sat still, waiting for a creak in the hall or a voice from downstairs, but the building was silent. Vera moved toward the door, but Bea held her back.

"Don't forget these," she said, holding Vera's shoes. "You are ready, aren't you?"

Vera's face warmed, though her smile didn't waver. Her blood sang in her veins. She put on the shoes and followed Bea out. The night air tingled with chill, and Vera was glad she had brought her coat.

"This way," Bea said, weaving through the shadows to avoid the quad, lit brightly by the moon. They snuck across the lawn to the gravel road, where a Ford sat. In the car, Vera counted three shadowy forms. Bea got into the front seat, and arms reached out to help Vera into the back.

"Took you long enough," the boy in the driver's seat said. He turned the key, and the car roared to life.

"Be nice," Bea said, with an exaggerated wag of her finger. "You're in the presence of ladies now."

The boy snorted. "I don't know your friend, but if you're a lady, then I am."

"Maybe I should introduce you," Bea said. "Vera, this is my cousin, Harry Morton. Harry, this is Vera Longacre."

Harry turned his attention from the bumpy drive to the backseat. "Longacre, you say? Well, now. It is nice to meet you."

"I think she prefers to be called Vera," Bea said, her tone dry. "I just wanted you to know you're in polite company."

"Looks like I'm in society," he said.

"Don't listen to him, Vera." Bea faced Vera after a hard swat to Harry's arm. "Introduce your friends, Harry, don't make Vera think you were raised in a barn."

"The goofy mug on the far end is Gene," Harry said. "The one breathing all over you is Cliff."

Vera turned to the boys sharing the seat with her. Gene looked like a cornstalk, tall with gangly limbs and tufts of light blond hair. He shot Vera a toothy grin and waved. Cliff was a handsome athletic type, with red waves and a somber affect. He nodded at her.

"Pleased to meet you," she said. She scooted up to the edge of the seat to get close to Bea's ear. "Where are we going? You never did say."

"To the lake. The boys are building us a bonfire." Bea pointed to the fork ahead in the road. "Harry, that's our left."

Harry obediently steered the jostling Ford to the left.

"Is this your car, Harry?" Vera asked.

"It is indeed. A congratulatory gift from my father for my excellent grades last year. Father knows I like the newest toys, but this was a surprise," Harry said.

Concealed by the darkness, Vera raised her eyebrows. If Harry's family had bought a college-age boy his own car, that told her everything she needed to know about their wealth.

Gene leaned over Cliff. "So, Vera, how do you like Vassar?"

"I like it very much."

"Are you a junior like Bea?"

"A senior."

"And do you study anything in particular?"

Vera groaned inwardly. This was turning into one of those conversations she had with her parents' friends. The patronizing guesses at what her work must be like or what they actually do at women's colleges would come next. And the gentlemen always liked to get in a little dig about the higher education of women in general. A glance at Gene's smiling eyes made her more sympathetic, and she pushed back her reluctance. "I've concentrated on art history. The Spanish masters mainly, but Vassar has a wonderful program. The instructors give a thorough grounding in all the major movements and European schools."

"I took an art history class," Gene said, "but I'm afraid I was hopeless at it. Couldn't tell any of the paintings apart. You must have a good eye."

"I don't know if I can say that, but thank you," Vera said. "What do you study?"

"Finance," Harry piped up from the front. "Same as all of us. Same as anyone with good sense."

"I thought you studied law," Bea said.

"Never got the hang of all that Latin," Harry said. "Might as well do something in a language I know."

"Are you claiming to know English now?" Bea asked with a snort.

"Better than you lot from Georgia." Harry drew out the vowels in the word with gusto.

"I'm betting I know finance better than you."

Now it was Harry's turn to let out a grunt of derision. "Not likely. I saw how you spent your parents' money at Agnes Scott."

Even in the dim light from the windshield, Vera could see Bea's angry glare. Harry wisely said no more. Vera was curious to know what Harry had meant by that, but did not want to receive the type of look Harry had gotten by asking.

They puttered along through the countryside, their chatter turning amiably to classes and teachers. Vera noticed Cliff didn't jump in to add to the other boys' funny stories, but it wasn't as though he was falling asleep. He sat, silent but alert, his eyes mostly on the road. She wondered why he had come at all if he didn't want to be friendly.

Harry pulled the car into a clearing and cut the engine. They had arrived at the edge of a lake, and despite the brightness of the moon shimmering on the water, Vera struggled to see the boundaries in the wooded darkness. The smell of pine lit up the night air as they walked to the fire pit at the shore. Four large logs encircled the pit, evidence that they were not the first to use the site for that purpose. A pyramid of new wood stood ready, and Vera guessed that the boys must have come by before picking them up at school.

She settled on a log beside Bea, and the three boys made a show of getting the fire going. If Cliff had been reticent in the car, he was not now. He strode around, instructing the other two and shooting glances at Vera and Bea.

"He's divine, isn't he?" Bea asked in a quiet voice, her cheek nearly touching Vera's. "Don't worry, if you want him, he's yours. He is a thing of beauty."

Vera had to admit that Cliff was handsomer than she'd been able to see in the shadows of the car. The new flames of the fire made his auburn hair look even redder and lit up his square jaw. Arthur popped, unwelcome, into her mind. Though she found Arthur handsome, he'd never provoked quite the same warmth in her chest she got when she looked at Cliff. She turned away to keep the heat from rising into her face, where Bea would easily read it.

"I guess you've met him before?" Vera asked.

"Harry's parents have a place at the Cape, I've met him there a couple of times."

"Is Harry 'those Stillmans'?"

"No, he's my cousin on my mother's side. His mother grew up in Atlanta, though you'd be hard-pressed to get her to admit it these days. She's even mostly gotten rid of her accent."

"So Harry and Cliff are school friends?"

Bea nodded. "Since freshman year. I think Harry's good for Cliff. He'll introduce him to the right people. Get him moving in better circles." Bea noted Vera's surprise. "Cliff's not destitute or anything, but his family's not 'society,' you know? Of course, I don't know that much about him. Hard to get him talking, and I've tried."

"I bet you have."

"You know I have. But maybe you're the one to make him come out of his shell."

Vera guessed that if Bea couldn't tempt him, with her curves and flashing blue eyes, then he would not start telling his life story to her skinny friend. Still, when he finished with the fire, it was Vera he sat by. Bea passed her the flask, and Vera had to turn away from her devilish look. Vera took a nip, then offered the flask to Cliff.

"No, thanks," he said. He took a small glass bottle from his inside pocket. "Brought my own."

"How clever," Bea said. "Then you don't have to share."

"I don't mind sharing," he said. He drank a bit of the brown liquid.

Before Bea could make another crack, Vera jumped in. "So, Bea tells me you're all on the rowing team?"

Gene sat on the log nearest the three of them. "That's right. Unstoppable and unbeatable."

"I imagine that takes a lot of energy," Bea said, undaunted by Vera's glare.

"I guess so," Gene said. "No more than any other sport."

"What do you say, Cliff?" Bea said. "Do you have more energy than the average boy?"

Before he could answer, Vera tried again. "Bea tells me you summer with Harry's family, Cliff. Does your family have a house on the Cape, too?"

"No, nothing like that. We've only got one house." He peered at the fire, then stood. "Excuse me. I ought to get more kindling, or we'll lose the flame."

He walked away, his steps crunching through the carpet of leaves surrounding the logs. Beside her, Bea struck up a lively conversation with Gene, punctuated by an occasional quip from Harry. But Vera's head swam with the alcohol's drowsy warmth, and she was content to sit quietly, watching the dark spot where Cliff disappeared into the shadows under the trees. She had the passing thought that she ought to have fewer houses, but she brushed it away. It was a silly thing to wish for, and she smiled a little at her own embarrassment.

« 10 »

Though Vera held a party to introduce Hallan to the building the evening after his arrival, it seemed everyone had already bumped into him by the time dawn broke on his first full day at the Angelus. One by one, the ladies called on Vera, ostensibly with a question or the need to borrow some trifle. Mostly they just bragged about having met "the artist." Poppy said she ran into him in the elevator, and Vera supposed she had ridden the elevator up and down all afternoon hoping to catch a glimpse of him. Caroline Litchfield said she saw him in the hallway, but Vera could not fathom any reason for her to be on the second floor at all. Bessie Harper, true to form, was the most brazen; ignoring etiquette, she had simply knocked on his door. The women buzzed with excitement, almost floating above the chairs Vera offered.

Though the invitation clearly stated, "cocktails at 7:30, seating at 8," people began arriving as soon as the clock read seven twenty-five. Vera had Evans direct them into the drawing room and waited until the exact time on the invitation to enter. Arthur followed shortly after. Hallan arrived late.

He stood in the doorway, and the room immediately broke into applause. He smiled, but his brow knitted almost imperceptibly. Vera walked over to greet him, and he gave the room a little nod of acknowledgment before stepping to her side. His dark suit made the bluish hue in his eyes more prominent, and he had tamed his hair into a sharp part. Vera thought it fortunate that he knew how to dress himself appropriately for a formal dinner party. There was no knowing what kind of savagery a working artist might be accustomed to.

"Good evening, Mr. Hallan. So kind of you to come," she said.

"How are you this evening?" he asked.

"Very well, and you?"

"I'm well. Thank you for hosting, I'm looking forward to meeting everyone." He scanned the room. "Well, everyone I haven't met yet."

"In that case, let me introduce you to my husband." She turned and laid a hand on Arthur's sleeve. He disengaged himself from his conversation. "Arthur, I'd like to present Mr. Emil Hallan."

The men shook hands, and Arthur drew himself up to his full height. "How do you do? I received your letter, of course."

"Glad to hear it," Hallan said.

"I'm sure my wife has inquired about the suitability of your accommodations."

Hallan glanced from Arthur to Vera, then back again. "Oh, the apartment is excellent, thank you."

Arthur took a sip from his highball glass. "When do you plan to begin work?"

"Very soon. Haven't made it down to the pool yet. I'll need to get a sense of the size of it, do some sketches, that sort of thing." Hallan turned to Vera. "I was hoping you could take me down there tomorrow morning. Would you?"

Vera gave a pinched smile. "So sorry, I have an engagement in the morning. I'm sure Ida would be delighted to show you, though. She is head of the Mural Board, after all." She beckoned to a waiter with a tray of drinks. "Would you like a drink, Mr. Hallan?"

He took a drink from the tray. Arthur returned to his group, and

Vera stepped to the side to allow others to approach the artist. But Hallan, instead of circulating, stayed close to her.

"I'm sorry," she said, allowing a hint of irritation into her voice. "Would you like me to introduce you to anyone?"

"I've met a good number already, actually. In the halls and the like." He lifted a hand to the crowd. "These people certainly aren't shy."

Vera studied her drink to avoid his gaze. Something about the focus and energy in his eyes, the candidness in his manner, made her unsteady. He was too comfortable with her, as though they were old friends. "No, I suppose they aren't," she finally managed.

"It's a bit strange, isn't it?" he asked under his breath, leaning in.

"I beg your pardon?"

His face was so close to hers she could smell his shaving lotion. "The applause, the fuss. A Mural Board? It's not what I expected."

Vera pulled on the pendant of one of her canary diamond earrings. "Everyone is excited, that's all."

"And you?"

"Me what?"

His eyes gleamed. "Are you excited?"

Vera's lips parted, and she clamped them shut. When she spoke, her voice came out like the blade of a knife. "I'm generally a calm person by nature. If you'll excuse me, I ought to check on the kitchen."

She left the drawing room and downed the last of her cocktail. If this was how the artist was planning to behave for the entirety of his stay, she did not know how much of his company she could tolerate. What was he thinking, asking her if she was excited? What was that in his tone? Was he actually flirting? With her husband standing not two feet away? Surely not. She stepped into the kitchen and took a deep breath to restore her composure.

When the cook confirmed everything was running on time, Vera sent the maid out with the dinner bell. The party progressed to the dining room, and the guests found their seats. Vera was glad she had put Hallan three seats away, between the matronly Ida Bloomer and the reedy Bessie Harper. The distance was a relief. Poppy Hastings was likewise too far away to enjoy a chat with the artist; a good thing, since she had been on the point of salivating over him when Vera had returned to the drawing room.

Vera congratulated herself on having planned and timed the meal perfectly. The chilled caviar melted like ice, and the sole that followed was still steaming. She would have to commend Gertrude on the perfect presentation of the artichokes, and the chicken had just the right amount of herb seasoning. The only tiny hiccup was when Julius Hastings bellowed an order to a servant who passed away at least two years before, but that sort of thing could be forgiven at his age. Otherwise, everything flowed as Vera had planned, until the waiters brought in the cordials.

Hallan stood and clinked his fork to his glass, silencing the party. "Good evening, everyone. I want to thank you again for my appointment as your muralist. I'm delighted to begin work on the project very soon."

There was light applause around the table, which he waved off with a gracious nod before continuing. "I do have a request to make, and I thought it easiest to make it when we are all assembled together. I must ask that all keys to the pool room be turned over to me, and that no one enter the pool until the painting is finished."

Dull silence greeted this statement, followed by a rumbling murmur that increased in volume. After a stern look from his wife, Clarence Bloomer stood.

"I understand artistic temperament and all that," Clarence said, "but my wife has to take her daily exercise in the pool. Doctor's orders."

Hallan nodded. "I know it will be an inconvenience, but I really cannot proceed without privacy while I work. I never let anyone see my work until it's done. I'm afraid I must insist."

The murmur resumed, and Clarence took his seat. Kenneth Harper leaned in to Vera, speaking under his breath. "Yes, you know, I've heard of that with artists. Don't like anyone seeing a work in progress."

"I suppose," Vera said. She looked back to where Hallan stood, but turned away again when she found his eyes fixed on her.

Arthur stood. "We've paid for the man's passage and lodgings. We should indulge his conditions for work as well, don't you all think? You'll have the keys tomorrow."

"Thank you." Hallan turned to the others. "You won't be disappointed, I promise you."

Caroline Litchfield leaned across the table, eyes gleaming. "How delightfully eccentric. Don't you think so, Vera?"

"Quite unusual." Vera accepted a glass of sherry from the waiter at her elbow. A few seats down, Arthur turned cold eyes on Hallan, who chatted with Ida. If the artist felt the stare, he did not acknowledge it.

《《《 ● 》》》

Hallan got the keys the next day. Vera assumed he must have put them on a ring, because every time she saw him at a social engagement after that, his pocket jingled as he walked around. And there were many social events. Everyone in the building seemed to want to throw a cocktail party or a dinner in his honor, and Vera wondered when he would find time to do any painting at all. Not that they would know if he was. She passed him making a sketch once, out on the sidewalk, as she waited for the car to take her to Wednesday lunch with her mother. A railing blocked her view of his drawing paper, so she could not satisfy her curiosity about his subject. She worried he would tie her up in conversation if he saw her, but he was so engrossed in his work that he never looked up.

At the many social functions, however, he felt free to approach Vera, and did so earlier and earlier each time. The first welcome event after Vera's dinner was a cocktail party at the Bloomers'. When the excitement of redoing her living room had waned, Ida Bloomer had purchased an authentic Egyptian sarcophagus. Everyone had gone

mad for Egyptian artifacts and decor after the discovery the previous year of King Tut's tomb, but Ida's passion surpassed them all. A
recent fashion show highlighting Egyptian style had further increased
her ardor. Her celebration in honor of the artist would be her second
Egyptian-themed party since March, and this time she would have the
sarcophagus as the focal point.

Vera dutifully put on a gold and black dress and her large blue
scarab pendant. She asked Marguerite to darken her eyes with kohl
and to weave a gold ribbon into her elaborate hairstyle. Arthur refused
to dress up for theme parties. Costumes were, in his words, "for children." He met Vera at their front door in a plain black suit.

Even the most enthusiastic of the other men seemed to have tired
of theme nights as well. When Vera and Arthur entered Ida's drawing room, all except one of the men were dressed in suits. Clarence,
however, sported a huge golden headdress that matched Ida's. Vera
imagined it was one of two concessions he had made to the theme.
The other had to be the swoops of sapphire- and ruby-colored fabrics
hanging over the party, and the painted wooden panels with hiero-
glyphics that stood beside the tall windows.

She kept a healthy distance from the sarcophagus but still had a
clear view of it despite the guests milling around. It stood propped
in a glass case in the corner of the room. A few lightbulbs had been
placed around the base that illuminated the metal accents and made
the item even more difficult to ignore. It looked like an overlarge statue
of a man, complete with a painted-on face, but with the feet fused into
one unit. The dull black eyes stared out at no one in particular, and the
hands were crossed over the chest, one gripping some sort of crook
and the other a staff. Clarence must have found inspiration for his own
headdress in the blue and gold adornment atop the head. Vera could
not shake the disquieting knowledge that a person could fit right inside the sarcophagus, never to come out again. Being across the room
from the thing was not enough. She finally turned her back on it, but
found herself face to face with Hallan when she did.

"Mrs. Bellington," he said in a pleasant tone.

"Mr. Hallan. How do you do?"

"Very well, thank you. And you?"

She reached for a glass of champagne from a gold tray nearby. "I'm well."

"I'm disappointed we haven't had much of a chance to talk," he said.

"You have so many people who want to talk to you. I don't expect you to spend much time with me." She took a sip of her drink. When she lowered the glass, she noticed he was inspecting her eye makeup. Her hand flew to her face. "Did my makeup smudge? It smudges so easily."

"No, no," he said. "It's just . . . it makes your eyes look so striking."

Her chest tightened, and she turned her head. Another of his comments, so casually familiar. "All the women are wearing it, Mr. Hallan," she replied, her voice liquid silk. "I think you ought to go be struck by someone else."

He grinned. "You're so quick, aren't you? With an answer?"

"Would you prefer questions?"

He took a sip of his drink, his eyes sparkling over the rim of the glass. "There, you see, that's exactly what I mean."

Ida called out an invitation, and everyone except Vera and Hallan moved to admire the sarcophagus on the other side of the room. Vera shifted from one foot to the other, unwilling to cross to the artifact but reluctant to continue with Hallan. Unperturbed, he nudged her gently with his elbow and spoke in a low voice.

"What do you think of this sarcophagus thing anyway?" he asked.

She took a drink of champagne. "I think it's distasteful, the whole business."

"I don't suppose you've told Ida that."

"Of course not."

"Is anyone still inside it? It's empty at least, I hope."

"It is. Ida was devastated when she found out. She was hoping for a real mummy." Vera shuddered. "It's ghastly. Why would you want a coffin in your home? Particularly a used coffin. Never mind the body. Dreadful. Like inviting misery."

He nodded. "I'm inclined to agree. Let the dead lie."

Something in his expression darkened, though his tone remained light. The bell rang for dinner and spared Vera the need to reply. She nodded slightly, then went to join Arthur as he entered the dining room.

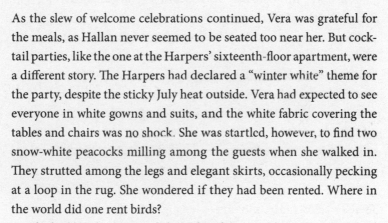

As the slew of welcome celebrations continued, Vera was grateful for the meals, as Hallan never seemed to be seated too near her. But cocktail parties, like the one at the Harpers' sixteenth-floor apartment, were a different story. The Harpers had declared a "winter white" theme for the party, despite the sticky July heat outside. Vera had expected to see everyone in white gowns and suits, and the white fabric covering the tables and chairs was no shock. She was startled, however, to find two snow-white peacocks milling among the guests when she walked in. They strutted among the legs and elegant skirts, occasionally pecking at a loop in the rug. She wondered if they had been rented. Where in the world did one rent birds?

She had barely registered the sight of the two birds when she heard the jingling behind her, like a bell on a cat. Hallan's key ring. Indeed, like a cat, he seemed to have a predilection for seeking out the one person in the room least inclined to entertain him. Vera turned, putting on her coolest expression.

"Mr. Hallan," she said. "How charming to hear you again."

He shrugged. "I had to come say hello to the most important woman in the building, didn't I?"

"I think you're expected to greet every woman. And every woman's husband." She took a martini from a nearby tray.

"I already have. I've met everyone in this building at least a hundred times, and yet every night there's another fete in my honor."

"Everyone wants the chance to host you. Talk to you more, get to know you."

He stepped in closer. "I'd rather talk to you, if that's all right."

Vera edged toward the fireplace. For some reason his ease always served to make her less at ease. "I can't imagine what about."

He cocked his head. "Why, art, of course. Just today Ida told me you studied art at university. I can't believe you didn't tell me that before."

"It never came up," Vera said. "I'm not in the habit of boring people with my biography."

"But it wouldn't bore me." There was a playful glint in his eye. "I'm a painter, after all. What did you study?"

She glanced around the room, hoping to find someone to pass Hallan off to. Poppy Hastings took a hesitant step in their direction, and Vera waved a bit with her fingers. Poppy's eyes widened at Vera's cheerful smile, and she braved a few tentative steps toward them.

"Oh, I'm sorry, Mr. Hallan. It looks like Poppy wants to say hello to you." Vera lifted her chin. "She already knows about my education, so I won't drag the conversation down with that. Besides, I need to go ask my husband something." She nodded at Poppy. "Good evening."

"Good evening, Vera," Poppy said. "Emil, I need your advice. There's a painting I'm thinking of buying . . ."

Vera suppressed a laugh at the thought of Poppy discussing the nuances of fine art. At least Hallan could be counted on not to deliberately embarrass Poppy. He was far too flirtatious for anything of the kind.

She found Arthur standing with a group, deep in discussion, and decided to join them. Clarence Bloomer held forth about an employee he had recently caught stealing tools from a work site.

"I knew better," he said, wagging a finger at no one in particular. "Can't trust the Krauts. Dirty thieving lot. Should never have hired one."

"Now, Clarence," Bessie Harper broke in. "No need for that kind of talk. They're not our enemies anymore, are they?"

"Not our—?" His nostrils flared. "Not our enemies, eh? Tell that to my sister's boy. Tell that to all those boys—"

Ida placed a hand on his arm, her face reddening. "Dear, now is not the time." Clarence stormed off, and she smiled weakly at the others. "The war still gets him so agitated, you know."

After Ida left to follow her husband, the others cast awkward glances around. Bessie was the one to break the silence.

"Well, I was sick of talking about the Germans then, and I'm even less interested in talking about them now." She held up her glass. "I need another. Excuse me."

Vera turned to go for a fresh drink herself, but froze after a single step. Hallan stood a few feet away. For the first time since she met him, his cheerful demeanor had vanished. He stared at the group, his mouth a hard line. She wondered what his experience with the war might have been, if he had been in Paris then. But as soon as the thought formed in her mind, the look disappeared, and his good-natured smile returned.

《《《 ● 》》》

At home, Vera and Arthur undressed in their respective dressing rooms. As they climbed into the massive bed, she asked, "He's a bit odd, isn't he? The artist?"

"Aren't they all?" Arthur rolled over onto his side, his back to Vera.

"I suppose. But there's something strange about him."

"Like what?"

"He's not very mannerly."

"Does that matter? Look at Poppy Hastings. If manners mattered that much, we'd have no one to associate with."

"Well, with all these parties, he's growing a bit tiresome."

"Then let's not attend the parties."

She balked. "We can't do that. It's an affront to the hostess. I can't go to one party and then not go to another—"

Arthur sat up. "I've offered you a solution. Wouldn't you prefer having fewer of those things to go to?"

When Vera spoke again, her voice was quiet. "He's got such an odd way about him. And . . . he's very fresh, Arthur."

"You're an attractive woman. I'd be surprised if he didn't notice you." Despite the kindness of his words, Arthur kept his gaze from hers. After a long moment of silence, he turned his back again, pulling the blanket up over one shoulder. "Something strange about him, I agree. Try not to let it worry you. I'll stand closer next time. He won't come sniffing around if your husband is nearby."

Vera rubbed his shoulder slowly, but he laid a hand on hers.

"Those parties are exhausting, aren't they? And I've got an early morning," he said, his voice slightly muffled in the pillow. "Good night, darling."

Vera lay in silence on her back but could not sleep. She stared at the crack where the curtains had not been drawn together, which revealed a glimpse of the radiant city lights. All she could think of was how this was the first night her husband had been in bed with her for weeks, and yet he did not even kiss her good night.

Vera enjoyed the first hour or so chatting with Harry, Gene, and Cliff. The more Bea passed her the flask, however, the heavier Vera's eyelids got. She wished she had put on her watch before she left, as the climbing moon was little help determining the time. The others seemed to gain steam from the liquor and conversation, their words and laughter echoing louder off the trees and shimmering water. For once, Bea allowed Vera her silence, naturally becoming the center of attention. When Bea stood up to demonstrate a popular new dance step with a flushed and clumsy Gene, it was Cousin Harry who pulled Vera back into the fold.

"So, art, eh?" he asked. "What are you planning to do with that? Gonna put yourself a nice collection together someday?"

Vera fidgeted with the collar of her coat. "Oh, I don't know. I can't say I've thought about it much."

"No, guess there's not really any need to, is there? Might as well study something you enjoy." When Vera looked away, he flagged a hand at her. "Don't be like that, I'm saying I'm jealous. You girls are lucky. Four years of good times, maybe a little studying, and then some guy comes along and sets you up right. Pretty thing like you, you deserve it."

"Why art?" Cliff's voice cut through Harry's stumbling.

"Pardon?" Vera said.

Cliff did not look at her, but continued to stare straight into the fire. He took a drink before repeating his question. "Why did you choose art? Instead of literature or music or something like that, I guess."

"Oh." Vera paused. "I've always loved art, ever since I was a little girl."

Cliff nodded. "Anything in particular you like about it?"

"I . . ." Her cheeks flushed. She glanced at Harry, who had turned his attention to Bea's dance lesson with Gene. Vera dropped her voice. "Promise you won't tease me?"

"I never tease."

"All right." She sucked in a breath. "Art is . . . it's like a window into someone's head. The only chance we have to really see the world through someone else's eyes. A glimpse of another time, another place. A taste of another life, in the past, one photographs can't reach. The camera lens is so cold . . . art has to come through the hands. And it's beautiful. Even when it's ugly or sad, it's beautiful." She had rehearsed the words many times in her head. As she spoke them for the first time, her stomach twisted. She pushed the toe of her shoe into the dirt. "I suppose that's not terribly original," she added, "but it's how I feel."

Cliff studied the firelight glinting off the bottle in his hands. "But then if you were the only one who felt that way, there wouldn't be so much art to enjoy, would there?"

Vera nodded, pleased he hadn't scoffed at her. "You're right. That's true." She shifted a bit, and her arm brushed his sweater. A tickle ran down her spine.

A hint of a smile appeared on his lips. "More interesting than finance, that's for sure."

"Then why are you studying that?" It was not the kind of question Vera would normally ask, but Cliff's closeness and blunt way of speaking made the words seem less invasive. Her sips from the flask had likely helped her find the courage, too.

"I study finance because I know the way the world is." He traced the lettering on his bottle with a finger. "Money makes things easier. If I understand it, I can make things easier on myself."

Her social training whimpered from the back of her mind that she ought to steer the conversation to a safer, more polite topic. Instead, she said, "Money doesn't always make things easier."

"From where I'm sitting it does."

"And where are you sitting?"

"In second class." He glanced at her out of the corner of his eye, then shook his head. "I'm not trying to upset you—"

"You're not upsetting me."

He chuckled. "I'm glad to hear that. Look, my family's not poor. My father's done very well in the textile business. But that's not the same thing as what Harry's got. Or what you've got, Miss Longacre."

She didn't bother to ask him what she had. She knew. "The name comes with a lot of things other than money."

"Houses, cars—"

"Yes, all those things. But they're just things. And then there are the rules. The endless rules. Wear this, say this, don't say that." She heaved out a breath. "I'm lucky, but you're lucky, too."

He turned to her fully now, his smile playful. "Yeah?"

She grinned. "Yeah. You could take off tomorrow, couldn't you? Go anywhere you like."

"So can you," he said. "Money buys tickets. Really good tickets, if I'm not mistaken."

"It's not the same." She hesitated. "I'm not in charge of my life. I don't get to choose."

He squinted into the distance, considering her words. "I hadn't thought of it that way."

A queasy feeling washed over her. "I don't mean to make it sound like I'm a prisoner or something. It's—there are expectations, that's all."

He offered her the bottle. "But you got to choose art. Out of all those other subjects. That's something, at least."

"I did. I got to choose art." She took a drink.

"There you go. That's a start."

His statement rang with finality, but she didn't want the conversation to end. She struggled through her watery mind for another question. "So, your father is in textiles?"

"Why, do you need fabric?"

She nudged him. "I thought you said you didn't tease."

"I don't, I don't. But you did sound like you were at a garden party just then."

She lowered her voice. "I want to know more about you."

"Do you?"

"Yes."

At that precise moment, Bea dropped down beside Vera, winded from her exertions. "And what are you two being so secretive about?"

"Not secretive." Vera's face flamed. Bea leaned in to whisper as Cliff turned back to the boys.

"Got him talking, did you? I knew you could." Bea's eyes danced with the glow of the fire.

"Could we go back? This has been fun, but I'm exhausted," Vera said. That was only part of it. She was confused, too. Cliff's assessment of money, of her life, had appealed to her when it normally would have irritated her. She liked his certainty. Most important, she liked that he had listened to her. Even from the outside, he seemed to have a perfect read on her world.

"Sure." Bea turned to Harry. "Will you take us back?"

"Aw, but it's early," Harry said.

Bea stood. "Early in the morning. Come on, let's go."

The boys put out the fire, and the group trudged back to the car. Vera's weariness caught up with her as they rumbled over the back roads toward campus. Her head drooped, and she straightened her back.

"Here," Cliff said in a low voice. He patted his shoulder.

She hesitated. Aside from taking her hand to help her into and out of his car, Arthur had never touched her at all, and he was her current best prospect for a fiancé. She shouldn't be so forward with any boy, least of all one of dubious background whom she'd only met a few hours ago. But then again, she shouldn't be sneaking off campus and drinking by the fire with him either. Or saying the things she'd said. She thanked him quietly and rested her head on his shoulder, enjoying the scent of cold air and smoke that lingered on his coat.

The campus gates were in sight when Cliff whispered again. "Vera, are you awake?"

She murmured a low "yes."

He looked at Gene, who snored quietly beside him. "You really want to know more about me?"

She lifted her head off his shoulder and nodded.

"May I write to you?"

Still floating on the alcohol and the freedom of their conversation, she nodded. She pushed away the hazy thought of Arthur. Letters from Cliff wouldn't hurt anything, as long as she was discreet about them. After all, she was the kind of girl who snuck out at night, she thought with a tingle of excitement. She could choose.

« 12 »

Vera made her way to yet another afternoon tea, although she was thankful the group was limited to the ladies. A break from Hallan's attention was welcome. Then again, the artist might as well have been present, since he was all any of the other women wanted to talk about.

"He's simply the most interesting man," Poppy said, her teacup rattling in its saucer as she gestured.

"He is," Ida agreed. "Did you know he once did a painting of a landscape entirely in shades of blue, just to see if he could use the different hues that way? Fascinating."

"It's not all that unusual for an artist to—" Vera began.

"Well, blue is his favorite," Poppy said. "I asked him. He said no one ever asked him that before."

"No one ever asked an artist about his favorite color before?" Bessie asked, widening her eyes a bit too much. Vera held a hand to her lips to hide a smile.

Poppy plumped her bobbed curls. "No one. Not a soul. He seemed very impressed."

Vera waited for a pause in the conversation and chose the wording of her question carefully. "When do you think he works?"

Everyone turned to her, like hawks on prey.

"What do you mean?" Ida asked. "Why, he works all day. All day and all night. He must."

"But he's always at parties and the like," Vera said. "I've run into him coming into the building from being out all day."

"He's probably buying supplies. Paint and ... brushes," Caroline said.

"But he never has any carrier bags with him," Vera replied.

Ida sat up straight. "He must have them delivered. Anyway, he's working, I'm sure of it. At the party the other night he said he'd chosen his subject."

Vera tried to ignore the dreamy look in Poppy's eye at that statement. "I did see him sketching once. I suppose I'm only curious because we know so little about him."

Caroline laid a hand on Vera's. "You worry too much, my dear. And didn't we get a letter from Clarence's friend, the man from the museum? With photographs of his work?"

"Yes. Clarence showed them to me." A prickle ran between Vera's shoulders at the memory of the photos.

"Well, then." Caroline smiled triumphantly, as if that statement cleared everything up.

Vera stirred her tea. "I wonder if someone shouldn't peek into the pool room, that's all."

"Nonsense," Ida said. "As the head of the Mural Board, I say we ought to honor the conditions he set out."

"There, the head of the Mural Board has spoken," Bessie said. "Do you really need a higher authority than that?"

"Thank you, Bessie," Ida continued, puffing out her chest. "If we go in there now, who knows how it might affect his work? Or worse, he may leave us with a half-finished product. You don't want that, do you?"

"No," Vera said. She plastered on a smile. "Never mind me." She glanced at the clock. "Oh, dear, it's getting late. I'd better dash."

"But Bertha hasn't even brought the cakes out," Ida said.

"I'm very sorry. Prior commitment. With my mother." Vera stood.

"Quite all right. Marshall will see you out." Ida rang the bell for the butler, but the other ladies remained seated. A strange silence settled over the room after a few abrupt good-byes, and Vera knew with absolute certainty that as soon as the door closed behind her, the artist would no longer be the most interesting subject of discussion. Her better judgment said that leaving so suddenly was a misstep, but even talking about Hallan was beginning to wear on her. The relief would be worth whatever temporary price she paid as the day's topic of gossip.

《《《●》》》

An advertisement in the paper reminded Vera that the Metropolitan Museum of Art's Italian Renaissance exhibition would close in a few weeks. She had already been twice since it opened in late spring, but she wanted to see everything one more time before the pieces were sent back to their home museums. Fortunately, she had nothing on her calendar that day. After she dressed, she had Evans call for the car.

She left the building so rarely. Apart from lunch with her mother and the occasional evening at the ballet or long weekend in Montauk, most of her engagements were on the floors below her penthouse. Rain drummed on the car window as they rolled through the city streets, and Vera peered up at the crowd of buildings that reached ever higher into the gray clouds.

The driver pulled up to the curb in front of the museum and ran around with an umbrella. He and Vera walked up the stairs together, and he kept her safe from the rain until she got to the main entryway.

"Thank you, George." She swiped at the drops on her pale blue skirt.

"What time would you like me to return?"

Vera glanced at her watch. "Shall we say two o'clock?"

"I'm sorry, your husband has a lunch engagement. He'll need the car."

"How about four?" *Better too much time than too little*, she thought.

"Yes, Mrs. Bellington."

The driver left, and Vera stepped inside. The swooping ecru arches of the entryway soared above her, with an elegance befitting the treasures the building held. All museums seemed to have an undercurrent of the same smell, whether they held art or artifacts. That faint, dusty scent of history, of important things preserved with reverence. If Vera could have bottled it and sprayed it around her home, she would have.

As she made her way to the Italian exhibition, her short heels clicking against the stone floor, she dug the catalog describing the pieces from her purse. She had penciled notes about her favorite items in the margins, and she wanted to do the same for the paintings, which she had neglected in favor of the sculpture on her last visit.

When she entered the first room, a couple already stood in front of one of the paintings. She pretended to fuss in her purse for another moment, allowing them to move on. Vera wanted solitude with the art. She would have liked to be completely alone with the paintings, but so far fortune had never afforded her that luxury.

The exhibit began with the Florentine school, mostly portraits with a religious work or two thrown in. By the time she had viewed the first few paintings, the couple had moved on to the next room. Vera paused at the portrait of Giovanna Tornabuoni, by Ghirlandaio, and squinted at the inscription on the cartel. She took out her pencil to note the Latin in her catalog and saw that it was already translated there.

As she debated with herself whether or not to write out the Latin anyway, someone stepped into the room. A little flare of annoyance tickled her chest, but she could not rightfully begrudge someone being in a public place. She concentrated her attention on the portrait once more, studying the vibrant gold tones of the lady's gown and the way they played with the deep red on the decorations on her sleeve. The reddish-brown twists of the elaborate hairstyle united the warm hues.

She sat in a straight-backed pose Vera herself had held many times, and Vera felt a sympathetic twinge along her spine.

"She's beautiful, isn't she?"

Vera whirled around, holding in a gasp of surprise at the familiar voice. Hallan stood behind her, dressed in a light brown suit with a cheerful red bow tie. His grin climbed up one side of his angular face.

"Sorry, I didn't startle you, did I?" he asked, taking a few slow steps toward Vera.

"Not at all. I heard you come in, I just didn't realize it was you." She held her chin in the air. "Taking a day off, are you?"

He looked at her appraisingly. "You do that a lot."

"What, take the day off? I don't work."

"No." He lifted his nose in imitation of her stance. "Lift your nose up. Do you like looking down at me?"

Heat tingled in the back of her neck. "Really, Mr. Hallan, the things that come out of your mouth. Do you relish being impolite, or is it some accident of nature?"

He held up his hands. "Forgive me. I had no intention of being rude."

"Intention or not, you have an awful way of saying the wrong thing."

He nodded. "That's probably true."

Vera turned back to the painting. "Anyway, you won't be paid if you spend all your time running around the city."

Hallan stepped beside her to look at the portrait. "Not running around the city. And to answer your earlier question, not exactly taking the day off. I got a bit stuck, you see, so I decided to consult some of my betters." He leaned in to the painting, and his voice took on a breathy, dreamy tone. "I love what he does with the colors here. So warm. Feels like she's alive, doesn't it?"

The sudden change of topic unsteadied Vera. "It's . . . it's lovely."

"So rare for the time, that portrait in profile. Normally they're looking at us. What do you think she's looking at?"

Vera twisted one of her earrings. "I couldn't say."

With one hand, Hallan traced the arc of the woman's back in the air. "Ah, but you see the light, the way it falls on her dress? And the shadows, here in the folds? I think she's looking out the window."

"Oh." Vera peered at the shadows he indicated, and saw immediately what he meant. "So she is."

"Who wouldn't? She was in Florence, wasn't she? Have you been there?"

"No, I never have."

Hallan did not take his eyes off the portrait. "Too bad. It's lovely. All pinks and oranges, and great shining domes. If I were stuck in the house, modeling for a painting, I'd be staring out the window, too. Look, the corner of her mouth, lifted . . . her eyes wide, alert. She looks hopeful."

Vera stared at him, speechless. The prolonged silence as she watched him examine the painting must have caught his attention, because he straightened up and turned to her with a questioning look. She struggled for words.

"You let every single thought you have come out of your mouth, don't you?" she asked slowly. "You don't hold anything back."

"And what's so wrong with that?" he said.

"One should always think before one speaks."

He chuckled. "Another lesson in etiquette from Mrs. Bellington. Don't tell me you don't sometimes wish you could say whatever's on your mind?" He raised an eyebrow. "It would make those little cocktail parties much more interesting."

A laugh threatened to bubble up. "I'm sure I don't know what you mean."

"I'm sure you don't." He held out his elbow. "Come on, we don't want to stand here all day."

She hesitated a moment, then slipped her arm through his. They walked on, passing a Madonna and several more portraits. Hallan stopped at one, leaning close as he had done with the Ghirlandaio.

"I want to paint like this," he said, in an awed whisper. "So soft, so gentle. Human. Living."

Vera did not speak at first, afraid to break the spell the painting had on him. "So why don't you?" she asked in a quiet voice.

He stepped back with a shrug. "Everything now is all modern, lots of hard lines. Geometric figures. I'm a product of my time. But I still keep some of that yielding in there. At least, I try."

A group of people came into the room. Vera gestured to a bench against the wall, and she and Hallan sat together. "I know," she said. "I saw the photographs you sent."

"You did? How?"

"Clarence showed me." She picked at the hem of her glove. "They wanted my opinion, since I studied art."

"That's right. Which you refused to tell me about." He pressed his lips together, but the smile broke through anyway. "So? What was your opinion?"

She shifted in her seat. "I'm sure that hardly matters."

He cocked his head. "You didn't like them."

"Quite the opposite." She met his gaze, and warmth flooded her cheeks. "They were lovely. Really extraordinary."

His face grew serious. "That's very kind of you. Thank you."

Vera turned back to the wall of paintings, reluctant to continue that thread of conversation. "Yes. Well. They were the reason we gave you the job, weren't they? How is the work progressing?"

"I've got an idea, it's taking shape. I want to be sure to capture the spirit of the building. Got to get the mood just right. It will take a while, you know. It's a big project."

She smiled. "So it really must be a secret? Or maybe you're trying to kill the ladies with suspense."

"It will be a wonderful surprise. Provided it doesn't kill anyone, of course." He stood and offered her his hand. She gripped it and stood, and their fingertips brushed as she drew away.

"Shall we see the rest?" Her voice was tight and about a note too high.

"Let's."

They strolled through the rest of the exhibit, occasionally remarking on the paintings but not making much conversation. From the exhibit hall, they went on to the regular collection. Vera might have excused herself to go through the museum alone, but she was enjoying Hallan's company so much, she hardly noticed as the time passed. Each time she checked her watch, she convinced herself she had a few minutes more than she really did, that her driver would circle the block if she did not appear outside at four on the dot.

She was checking the time once again when Hallan remarked on a certain shade of pale green in a textile by William Morris, and how it was the same color as the curtains in his bedroom.

"I thought you would like those," she said. "Something subtle."

"You decorated the apartment?"

"I did."

"Makes sense." He shot her a sidelong look. "Nothing subtle about Ida Bloomer. Or Poppy Hastings, while we're on the subject."

She broke into a wide smile as she glanced around the room.

"What are you doing that for?" he asked. "If they're anywhere in the world, they're not in an art museum."

She shook her head. "Really, Mr. Hallan. That's terrible."

"It's worth it. Got a smile out of you." He looked at her pointedly. "That might be the first smile I've seen from you. Real smile, that is."

At the mention of it, her smile cinched up into its usual slim line. She glanced at her watch. "I'd better go. My driver will be here soon."

"Right."

She knew she ought to offer him a ride back to the building, but she could not bear the thought of the whispers that would ensue if they arrived in the same car. To make him walk back in the rain would be almost cruel . . . but, then, he had come in dry, he must have had a dry method of travel. He shoved his hands in his pockets and looked at his shoes. The softness in his eyes as he looked at the Ghirlandaio flashed in her mind.

She took a step closer. "Won't you—may I offer you a ride back to the building? I have a car coming."

"Well, you know, I think I may stay a bit longer, get a look at some of the other exhibits," he said at last.

The tightness in her chest relaxed, and the words rushed out a little too quickly in her gratitude at his discretion. "Wonderful. So much to see."

"Yes." His eyes met hers. "Thank you for a lovely afternoon."

"You're very welcome. It was nice running into you."

When Vera walked out of the building, she noted that the rain had stopped, though wet cotton clouds still hung in the sky. The driver waited for her beside the car, and he opened the door for her. As they pulled away from the museum, it seemed to her as if the hand she had felt holding her back since she had first gone to the docks to meet the artist was loosening its grasp. She very much wished it would not.

$$\langle\langle\langle \bullet \rangle\rangle\rangle$$

Arthur walked into the bedroom a little past six, just as Vera stepped out of her dressing room. She smiled brightly.

"I didn't know you would be home for dinner. What a nice surprise." She secured her earring and sat on the bed.

He sighed. "I won't. I only came home to change. Business meeting at the Plaza with some men from Chicago."

Her shoulders drooped. "That's too bad. I feel like we haven't had a moment to ourselves in so long. You're always out so late."

"You know I'd rather be here than with those blowhards from the Real Estate Board."

"Of course. I know. I worry you're working too hard."

He walked into his dressing room and spoke louder so she could hear him. "You don't need to worry about me."

Silence hung heavy as he finished dressing. A few minutes later he stepped out, in a darker evening suit. He had slicked back his curls once more, and the smell of his hair treatment tickled Vera's nose. She stood and crossed to him, placing her hands on his shoulders.

"Please, can't we make plans to have dinner together? Out some-where, perhaps." She slid her hands down his arms, the fabric of his jacket cool and starched under her fingers. One hand drifted up to his jaw. "Or you could be late to your meeting. They'll wait for you, won't they?"

He stared at the wall behind her. "These gentlemen came a long way, they shouldn't have to wait."

Vera's face burned as she jerked her hand away. She sat on the bed and let out a hollow laugh. "I have to, though, don't I? I always do."

"What's gotten into you? Why are you talking like that?"

"Because I miss you. I miss . . . well, it's been so long . . ."

Arthur adjusted his cuffs, the lines on his face betraying his weari-ness. "Don't you think I know that? This is the way it has to be."

"But I'm your wife," she said, her voice rising. "I want to be with you."

He stepped closer. "Then you will have to wait." Each word came out flat.

She swallowed hard and looked away once more. Saying anything else would only hurt her cause. She did not know why she continued to try in the first place. The last time they had shared the bed for any-thing other than sleeping was a distant memory. Vera had excused him countless times, as he had excused himself, with any convenient explanation. He was too tired, work had him agitated, he had an early morning—and those were for the times he was home at all. She might have wondered if age had taken its toll on her beauty or figure, but the mirror told her otherwise. Besides, there had never been a time when he seemed compelled by her. He was clearly proud to have her on his arm, but that pride never became passion. She tortured herself won-dering what might be tempting to him. Perhaps he preferred blondes, redheads, curvy girls. She could only conclude that whatever inter-ested him in a woman, it was not her. At last, to appease herself more than anything, she concluded that the famous male appetite must be a modern myth.

Arthur went back into his dressing room for a final check in the mirror, then breezed past her toward the bedroom door. Before he crossed the threshold he stopped and turned.

"Have Evans make a reservation. For Wednesday night. Somewhere with a good steak. But not earlier than eight, please."

Then he left.

« 13 »

Vera struggled to keep her thoughts on the lecture, but they kept drift-ing back to what was coming that afternoon. Or, rather, *who* was com-ing. Who was on the way at that very moment. She looked out the window, hoping for some sign of an unexpected hurricane or a well-timed war that would make the roads unusable. But these thoughts came with a stab of guilt. She shouldn't wish for devastation to serve her own ends, especially not with the idea of preventing her own mother from coming to visit.

Her mother had visited before, though never with such short no-tice. The letter had come on Wednesday with the news that her mother had taken a room in Poughkeepsie for Friday through Sunday. Vera spent all Thursday evening taking her decorations down. Under the dried flowers and postcards she'd pulled from the walls, she had bur-ied the two letters Cliff had sent her so far. Still, she almost feared her mother would sense them stowed in their box under the bed.

She must have sensed something, anyhow. Her mother usually came at the start of the year or the end, and never without warning. Had Vera said something in one of her letters that gave off the whiff of her recent misbehavior? Surely not. They were the usual routine de-scriptions of her schedule with wishes for her mother's good health thrown in before the signature. The only new information was mention of Bea, but never in a way that her mother could disapprove of. She had even taken care to give Bea's full name, knowing her mother would associate "Stillman" with the right circles, and maybe even approve.

Her mother would definitely not approve, however, of Cliff, no matter how Vera couched their correspondence. Though Vera had felt a looming sense of regret from the morning after she'd agreed to the letters until she received the first one, they turned out to be entirely innocent. Cliff had made good on his promise to tell her more about himself, but had not taken any liberties or written some silly love note. She didn't know why she'd worried about that, given his quiet seriousness by the lake. His letters did reveal a more talkative side, one with a quick, dry wit and a headstrong confidence. He talked of growing up at his father's side in the family's factories, how his father had made him sweep up loose fibers from the concrete floors to teach Cliff the value of a solid day's work. Cliff planned to use his Yale finance education to help his father expand the business. His ultimate goal was to relieve his father of his seventy- and eighty-hour workweeks, though he'd never told his father that plan. He knew his father's pride would prevent him from accepting that kind of help, if he knew the real reason behind it. Cliff joked that the only way to keep his father from wearing himself out completely was to grow the business beyond the point where his father could manage it all alone.

Vera found Cliff's devotion to his father and the closeness of their relationship disarming. She'd always considered herself close to her father, but only in learning about a father and child who were practically inseparable did she realize how little she saw of her own. With her father, she always mentally added the caveat "when he's home," but Cliff simply followed his father to work and beyond. She supposed that was a luxury boys had with their fathers that girls simply didn't. Anyway, her father always brought her back gifts from his travels, and wasn't that a clear signal he was thinking of her the whole time?

It was no wonder Cliff had said to Vera at the lake that money buys better tickets; he wanted to travel. She expected dreams of European tours, but he went further. He wanted to hike the mountains in Nepal, visit tiny villages in remotest China, take a boat down the Nile. He wanted more than the kind of luxury travel to the usual museums and restaurants Vera's circle was accustomed to, though he tactfully avoided saying so in an explicit way. He wanted to "uncover the world." The idea made for a romantic picture of an adventurous soul, and Vera spent an afternoon in the library leafing through *Scenes from Every Land* and imagining what trips like those would be like.

Of course, Cliff added at the end of one of these written daydreams, *these are not the kind of trips a man makes alone. I'd like some company, a gal who understands why I need to see it all.* The mention of female companionship was the closest he ever came to writing anything inappropriate, and Vera felt the idea was so obvious it could hardly be read as an overture to her. Her own letters to him were equally chaste. He asked about art, and she discussed her favorite pieces and what drew her to them. She listed her favorite songs and books, and told what she hoped were funny stories about her professors and fellow students. Sprinkled in were descriptions of her trips to Europe, in the hopes they would inspire him as he made his own plans someday.

The friendship they were striking up via their letters was so wholesome, only the most stern mind would disapprove. This was precisely why Vera would not tell her mother, who was the possessor of just such a mind. What Vera could not reconcile with herself was why she was keeping the letters a secret from Bea.

"What's got you off in the clouds today?" Bea asked as they walked in the quad after class.

Vera sucked in a deep breath and hoped her voice didn't shake. "My mother's visit."

"Is that all? She must really be something."

"She is. I hope it's all right if we don't see much of each other this weekend. Entertaining her requires all my attention."

Bea frowned. "I'd be happy to help you keep her busy. We could take her into town. Go to the shops, get all dolled up."

"Don't use slang," Vera said absently.

"You don't have to remind me every time I use it," Bea said.

"Yes, but you don't have to use it at all. It doesn't sound refined. If you get used to using it now, you'll never get rid of it. Then how will you sound making a speech to the Museum Board or welcoming guests to your dinner party? Like a silly college girl, that's how."

"Don't snap at me." Bea stuck out her tongue. "Save it for your mother."

"You don't understand. Your mother sounds lovely. Mine's . . ." Vera clamped her mouth down on the words. Even with no chance her mother might hear, Vera couldn't criticize her out loud. Part of her knew she shouldn't criticize her mother at all. "She only wants what's best for me. It just feels as though I never quite please her."

"Are you sure you don't want some company? I'm very good with parents," Bea said.

"It's simpler to deal with her on my own, really. The offer is much appreciated, though." The bell tower chimed behind them, and Vera gasped. "I'd better go. She'll be driving up any second."

"Good luck." Bea's voice still wavered with concern.

Vera mustered a smile. "I'll come by to see you Sunday, after she's gone."

Bea nodded and walked off toward her dorm. Vera couldn't admit to her friend that she wasn't confident Bea wouldn't let slip something about their nighttime trip with the boys. Bea was too lively, too talkative, and Vera's mother was a skilled hunter. When she wanted to ferret out a secret, she did. That was one good reason not to tell Bea about the letters from Cliff. It didn't take an expert to get a secret out of her. On the off chance her mother ever did cross paths with Bea, that would probably be the first thing Bea let slip.

Vera took a deep breath and headed for her own building to drop off her books and freshen her hair. She called a greeting to the girl at the desk as she entered the foyer. A resonant voice stopped her before she reached the stairs.

"If you insist on carrying such a heavy load, you'll have arms like a sailor before you know it."

Vera's heart sank. She turned and pasted on a look of delight. "Hello, Mother. Your train must have gotten in early."

Her mother rose from the chair where she'd been waiting and looked Vera over from head to toe. "I decided not to bother with the train. Always so cramped, and you never know what sort of element you're riding with. Franklin drove me."

"Of course. Well, I'm so glad you could come this weekend. Have you checked into your room yet?" Vera shifted the books in her arms in a vain effort to make them look less heavy.

"I haven't. I thought you might like to go with me. We can have a nice dinner in town. I expect you haven't had a decent meal since you arrived." Her mother's eyes narrowed at the sight of Vera's hair. "Who dresses your hair, darling? You look as though you've been laboring in the field. I don't know why you wouldn't let me send Paula with you."

Vera's cheeks warmed. "Mother, I've told you. No one here has a maid. We do our own hair in the mornings."

Her mother sniffed. "Yes, well, I can certainly see that. Never mind. Go put your things away and come with me. I'll take you to the salon before dinner."

Vera took the stairs step by plodding step. She wished there were some way to make the trip to and from her room last for days. Then when she came back down, it would be Sunday, and her mother would be gone. Where she had wished before for a storm to impede her mother's progress, now she hoped for nothing but clear skies. A disaster now would trap her mother there with her, and the thought was too much to bear.

« 14 »

The first thing Vera did the next morning was to give Arthur's instructions about the dinner reservations to Evans. The thought of dinner out with her husband elated her, but she had two whole days and a night to fill until then. For once she was sorry to have a blank spot on her calendar. Lunch with her mother and preparing to go out would occupy her tomorrow, but this day stretched out in front of her, full of empty hours.

She dressed and had Evans call for the car to take her shopping. She was not a great shopper, as most of the women in the Angelus were, but it was a pleasant enough way to take up some time. Though most of her clothing was custom made, she liked the doting saleswomen at Bonwit Teller.

She rode the elevator down, considering whether she should have crackers and pâté in the library or have Gertrude lay out a more formal late lunch when she returned. The operator slid the elevator doors open, and she took a step out, only to find Hallan talking to the doorman. She stopped short.

"Hello, Mrs. Bellington," Hallan said with a smile. "Something the matter?"

"No, nothing. I was lost in thought," she said. "Are you going out?"

"I am. Thought I might go see a matinee. I was talking to Joe here about where to go."

Vera turned to the glass doors of the lobby. "The weather is dreadful."

His grin widened. "Don't have to worry about that inside the theater. Besides, aren't you going out, too?"

"Right. Of course." She clenched her jaw and brushed past him, heading for the door. "I hope you enjoy the show."

"I'm sorry, I didn't mean to tease you. Have you seen *The Hunchback of Notre Dame* yet? That's what I'm planning to see," he called after her.

She turned back, suppressing a sigh. "I haven't. Sorry."

"Well, it just came out, didn't it? Silly question. But . . . do you like the pictures? I mean, would you like to go? I hate to go alone."

She glanced at the doorman, who studied a list on his desk. "I don't know . . ."

"We had such a nice time at the museum. And I'd love to talk art with you a little more. Hard to do that at the dinner parties."

A prickle of irritation ran through her. She did not want the doorman to get the wrong impression from Hallan's description of their accidental meeting in the museum. The doorman never lifted his eyes from his stack of papers, however, and her annoyance faded. A strong desire to go with Hallan surprised her. Besides, her afternoon still yawned before her, diversion free. A movie would be half a day's worth of distraction. And, despite her self-consciousness about the museum, she had to admit there could be no scandal about an outing so public. "Yes, thank you," she said at last, with a nod.

Hallan's lips parted for a moment before he was able to respond. "Really? Thought it might be harder to convince you."

She ignored his incredulity, afraid her certainty would waver. "Shall we take my car? It's ready at the curb."

"You sure it's no trouble? You didn't have plans?"

"Nothing pressing."

"Wonderful."

Vera and Hallan hurried out to the sidewalk, where the driver waited with the door open. They slid into the backseat.

"So sorry to spring this on you, George," she said, placing her umbrella on the floor far from her shoes. "I've had a change of plan. My husband doesn't need the car at all this afternoon, does he?"

"No, madam. Where may I take you?"

She turned to Hallan. "Do you know where it's playing?"

"Joe said something about a 'Rialto'?"

"To the Rialto, please." She settled back in the seat as George pulled the car into the lane.

Hallan shifted to face her. "Is that one of those picture palaces?"

"It is. It's lovely, like an opera house." She smiled a little to herself. "I was never allowed to go to the pictures when they first came out. My mother would sooner have seen me cleaning coal out of a grate than at one of those nickelodeons. But now they have the Rialto, the Strand . . . it's almost like real theater." She paused. "You don't have many of them in France, do you? Or in . . . I'm sorry, I'm not sure exactly where you're from originally."

He looked out the window, gazing up at the towering buildings. The glass reflected the familiar gleam in his eye. "France will do fine. It's all the same over there anyway. There were some of those grand places, but the war shut most of them down. The ones that weren't bombed. More than a few smaller places to see a picture, though."

Vera studied her gloved hands. "I'm sorry. I wasn't thinking about the war."

"Well, I'm looking forward to seeing the Rialto, anyhow. And the picture. How often do you go?"

"Not very often. We're more regular at the opera, the ballet, the symphony, that sort of thing. When we go out at all."

"Arthur must not approve of the way you look at Valentino, then?"

She swallowed a laugh. She would rather have been upset at his frankness, but she knew too many women whose gaze lost focus when talking of Rudolph Valentino. "I don't care for Mr. Valentino, actually," she said.

"Mmm. Me either." Hallan shot her an amused look.

"Why did you choose this movie in particular?" she asked. "Are you a fan of the novel?"

"I haven't read it," he said. "But I saw the poster yesterday when I was out for a walk. Thought it looked entertaining enough."

"Not a reader, then?"

"Never said I wasn't a reader."

"Then what do you read?"

"Poetry, mainly."

"Poetry, you don't say. Any particular favorites?"

"I've always been partial to Gerard Manley Hopkins."

"I'd have pegged you as a Byron man, myself."

Hallan laughed. "Byron's not bad. 'She walks in beauty . . . '" He motioned to Vera with a wry look. "In my experience religion is a safer topic than women."

"Is that so?" She picked at her skirt. The corners of her mouth rose. "You'd never know that to talk to you."

"Well, talking *to* women is a different thing altogether than talking *about* women, isn't it?"

"I'm sure I don't know," she replied in a mock-haughty tone.

The car glided to a stop in front of a boldly flashing sign made up of hundreds of colored bulbs. Above the doors, between the second and third floors, a sign proclaimed RIALTO in blazing white lights. As they stepped out, Hallan craned his neck back, eagerly taking in the sight. Vera told her driver when to return and followed Hallan toward the entrance. He went to get a better look at a poster, and Vera stepped in front of him to the box office.

"Two orchestra, please," she said. She pushed the money across the counter, and Hallan spun on his heel.

"Now, just a minute. I'm not going to let a lady pay," he said with a frown.

"My pleasure. You are our guest, after all." Vera accepted the tickets from the smiling girl behind the glass.

Hallan offered his arm. "And what does 'best society' think of a woman paying a man's way into the theater?"

She looped an arm through his elbow. "I expect they think less of a woman going to entertainments with a man who is not her husband," Vera said, careful to keep her tone light.

"I'm sure a midday picture show with a neighbor is no stain on your virtue." He squeezed her hand in the crook of his arm and dropped back into a more casual tone. "I'm glad you agreed to spend a bit of time with me. I'm looking forward to talking more."

The two stopped to give their coats to the attendant at the cloakroom and Hallan left his hat. They stepped down the thick-carpeted stairs to the middle of the house and took seats a few spaces away from the next people over. Vera was pleased to see that they were among the very few people in attendance, and most of the others appeared to be middle- or lower-class women sitting in the balconies. Hallan and Vera practically had the orchestra to themselves.

"I don't think we'll have much time to talk. I'm not sure how people behave in theaters in France, but in New York, it's considered very bad manners to converse during a show." Vera held her skirt down in the back so it would not wrinkle when she sat on it.

"No, of course. Naturally." Hallan surveyed the intricately molded ceiling and painted wall screens. "I'll have to convince you to have a drink with me after, so we can make up for our silence during the show."

The house lights went down before Vera could make a retort, and she flushed. It was kind of him to invite her to the pictures, but she had no intention of going anywhere else with Hallan that day. She hoped he would not press the issue.

The orchestra started up with a booming tune that Vera thought a little too energetic for the afternoon. A piano solo followed that was much more to her taste, rolling and cool. The newsreel showed footage from the Frontier Mine explosion in Wyoming. Vera had already seen photographs in the paper that turned her stomach, so she feigned attention in the beading at the hem of her sleeve. Hallan had his eyes on the painted ceiling and the elaborate carvings at the edges of the screen. She was not sure if he was simply engrossed in the decor, or if he, too, lacked the stomach for the disturbing scenes of the devastation.

At last, the screen lit up with the opening credits. Then the cathedral at Notre Dame appeared. Probably a replica, Vera reasoned. The film must have been made in California; all the pictures were these days. The likeness to the original cathedral was astounding. Crowds spilled into the town square below it, filling the screen. On a balcony, the hunchback finally stepped into the light. A shock went through Vera that seemed to travel from her eyes to the tips of her fingers. She knew enough about the book to know that the monster was meant to be hideous, but she had not expected the actor to look so grotesque. Perhaps a disordered wig, a small shuffle in his step . . . but this man had a bulging, unblinking eye and lumps disfiguring the shape of his face. Joy lit up his features briefly as the bells tolled behind him, but his smile quickly fell away at the revelry of the people below him. He bared his ragged teeth at the crowd assembled in the square. Even though they were far below, the people recoiled. The hunchback began to move his twisted legs, stumbling across gargoyles as he made his way back into the cathedral.

Vera leaned over, ready with a whispered question about the actor for Hallan, but the expression on his face stopped her. His eyes were lit up from within, glowing with the same radiant joy that had shone when he examined the paintings in the museum. The flickering light of the film cast shadows on his face, accenting his high cheekbones. Vera turned back to the screen, her question abandoned.

As she grew more accustomed to seeing the features of the hunchback, she settled in to the story. The gorgeous and virtuous Esmeralda, played by Patsy Ruth Miller, met the dashing Phoebus, and their inevitable love story began to unfold. But it was increasingly clear that the monster loved her as much as Phoebus did. The hunchback saved her, even at his own peril, and destroyed his master for her sake. She would never choose the monster, would she?

Sadly, she had no such choice to make. The hunchback was stabbed in the final struggle and crept off to die as Phoebus and Esmeralda embraced. The monster's sacrifice meant Esmeralda was freed from any obligation to him.

Vera's throat constricted. An uncomfortable stiffness ran up her back, and she had the urge to run out of the theater. She pulled a handkerchief from her handbag and patted her temples as the lights came up dimly over the house. Hallan stood and held out his hand, still blinking away the awed look on his face.

"I didn't know you were so enthralled by the pictures," Vera said, standing.

"It's always been a bit of a dream of mine to go out west. To California. See the studios." A smile twitched on his lips, but it was not the usual clever smirk. He looked more like a child anticipating a gift. "It's just a new kind of art, isn't it?"

She picked her way up the steps with a short laugh. "Art? I should say not."

"And why not? Didn't you feel something in there, when that poor creature died? Or when the lovers embraced? That's all art does. When it's done well, it makes you feel, touches that part of you that's human."

She had a difficult time arguing with that. But the pictures were more like a party trick than any of the wondrous works she had seen in her life. She prepared to defend the classics. "You can't compare—"

Vera's voice faltered as they turned the corner and nearly walked into a woman. The sight of Bea's familiar blue eyes sent a tingle through Vera's extremities, and she instinctively turned her gaze to the floor. *Not here*, she thought. *Not now.* She prayed Bea would not speak to them.

Bea looked from Vera to Hallan and back again. Her eyes widened and her forehead creased for a split second. Then her expression went slack again, and she passed without a word. Vera realized she had dug her fingers into Hallan's forearm.

"Is everything all right?" he asked, his voice taut.

She glanced up to find his face ashen. He must have taken her reaction to be embarrassment about him, instead of the truth, but he looked disproportionately concerned. "I should get home. I just thought of something I need to do," Vera lied.

He held out their claim tickets as they approached the coat check window. "I see."

Vera pulled on her coat, grateful he did not press further. "Hurry, I'm sure the car is outside by now."

She braced herself for the spitting rain that had seen them into the theater, but instead found the sky aglow. The few clouds that still hung near the horizon were the most extraordinary dark orange, which cleared to pinks and yellows higher in the sky. Though Hallan seemed as eager as Vera to depart from the theater, they were both caught by the scene. Finally, he turned to her.

"Wow. Beautiful," he said.

"It is," she said. She extended a hand toward the car sitting at the curb. "Shall we?"

《《《●》》》

Back at the Angelus, Hallan got off the elevator on the second floor, and Vera rode the rest of the way to the penthouse alone. Her stomach had hardened, weighing her down from the middle, but she could not understand why. The movie had been wonderful, and Hallan had behaved like a true gentleman the whole way home, nothing like his usual foolishness at the parties—more like he had been at the museum, thoughtful and quiet. His face came into her mind again, lit by the glow of the movie screen, his eyes bright with abandon. Even a few unhappy seconds of seeing Bea should not have outweighed the rest of the day. It was not the first time she had seen her in town, and even when the sightings came so close together, she had never felt this heaviness afterward.

She took in a few slow breaths as she entered the penthouse, handing her gloves and hat to Evans.

"Would you like some dinner, madam?" he asked. His steady, deep voice calmed her.

"No, thank you." She looked at her watch. Six fifteen. "I'll be in the library if my husband phones. Will you have Gertrude slice a lime for me?"

"At once."

"Thank you."

In the library she switched on the phonograph, and a sweet, mellow tenor filled the room. She poured herself a gin and tonic, glad no one was around to see how light she had gone on the tonic, and drank the whole thing in a few long swallows. She poured another just as Evans arrived with a china plate, lime wedges gleaming in a neatly arranged fan in the middle. He closed the door behind him after she thanked him. She squeezed one of the limes into the fresh drink, its juice dispersing in a curling cloud through the crystal liquid. The second drink emptied nearly as quickly as the first. Her third would go down more slowly, but still with grave intent and purpose. She wanted to feel the liquor's effects, and soon.

Glass in hand, she strolled around the library, admiring her paintings. Though her education had favored Velázquez, Goya, and El Greco, the penthouse was a museum of the European greats, known and forgotten. The landscape over the fireplace by an Italian master. The portrait of some lovely Renaissance noblewoman by a Frenchman favored by the court of her time. The cold lines and warm sentiment of the pastoral scene, complete with a shepherd and his love, by a Dutchman whose name Vera could never pronounce exactly right. She recalled the thrill of finding and acquiring each one, sorting through each gallery or auction until she found the one piece there she could not ignore.

She ran her hand along the curved back of an oiled wood chair. Where the Ida Bloomers of her acquaintance had reproductions, Vera had the real thing. She stifled a little laugh at the idea that the quality of one's chairs could be measured by how many important derrieres had graced their seats. And then there was the delicate rug, hung on the wall so that no shoe would ever actually touch it. What country castle had that come from? She could not remember at the moment.

The ice from the third drink rattled in the glass, and Vera poured another to accompany her to the drawing room. She had chosen more delicate fabrics for the sofa and chairs in this room, and light, lacy curtains. Her head swam as she inspected the glossy surface of a mahogany end table, and she chased the feeling with another hard swallow from her glass.

In every room it was the same. Three marble statues in the dining room, found in Rome, now served as a largely ignored backdrop to her dinner parties. Hand-woven lace covered the low table in the study, displayed to show only that Vera possessed such a thing. A carved wooden box from the seventh century stood proudly on the desk in the bedroom, but held nothing.

When Vera returned to the library to refill her glass, her gaze lit on a vase in the corner. It sat on a tall table with a thin support and round top about the size of a dinner plate, which existed solely to hold a vase of that kind. From the vase's fluted top burst a spray of huge blooms and greenery, arranged by someone with talent and skill. The white flowers hung heavy on their stems. The day before the vase had held long stalks with tiny yellow flowers, and sometime before that, feathery pink blooms. Like everything else decorating the penthouse, the vase tended to go unnoticed. Despite that, the housekeeper went every day to the flower market, bought a handful of flowers, and placed them with care in that vase before Vera came downstairs in the morning. Every night, after Vera went to bed, someone would toss them in the wastebasket so that the vase would be ready for new flowers in the morning.

The same tight feeling from the elevator squeezed Vera again. She edged closer to the vase, as if it were alive and could suspect what might happen. The crystal was etched with a swirled design that bit into Vera's fingers when she lifted it. She held it up to eye level and turned it to watch the light glint off it. The voice on the phonograph, now a soprano, soared behind her. She raised the vase above her head, still studying its intricate design. Then she brought her arm down and hurled the vase to the ground. The glass shattered on the hardwood floor and showered the room with splinters of glass, waxy petals, and broken stems.

Vera took a step back, her mouth falling open at the mess before her. The gin haze fell away in a white-hot blast. What could have possessed her to do such a thing? She set her glass on the table and rang the bell for the housekeeper with a trembling hand.

Sarah opened the door to the library a moment later. She let out a cry and rushed to Vera's side.

"Are you all right, madam?" Sarah asked. "You're not hurt, are you?"

Vera pressed her shaking hands against her skirt. "I bumped into it, and it fell. I wasn't paying attention . . ."

Sarah had the good grace not to let her gaze wander to the glass on the table, still holding a crushed lime wedge. She took Vera's arm and led her to a chair.

"Are you sure you didn't get cut? Let's take a look. May I?" Sarah turned Vera's arms over, revealing the unspoiled white undersides. She took Vera's chin with a thick, matronly hand and inspected her face. "There, you seem to be all right. I'll clean this up and make you a nice cup of tea for your nerves."

"No, thank you. No tea."

"Yes, madam."

Vera stayed in the chair, taking hard breaths until Sarah returned with a broom and a large pan. She swept the crunching glass into the pan, then pulled out a sack for the flowers. When she had finished, she turned to Vera with a worried look.

"Now, don't go walking around without your shoes on. There's likely to still be some little bits there."

"I'll be careful," Vera said in a small voice.

Sarah turned to leave, but Evans stood in the doorway. She shuffled past him with the clinking bag as he nodded at Vera, his expression calm as ever.

"Madam, you have a visitor," he said.

Vera stood. "What? Who would call at this hour?"

"Mr. Hallan. Should I tell him you've retired for the evening?"

Her vision seemed to narrow to a point, the edges blurring. She sank back into the chair. "Did he say what he wanted?"

"He said he had something to give you."

"Send him in."

Evans came back in a few moments later with Hallan following. Vera stood, and Hallan's eyes widened in alarm when he saw her face.

"Are you all right? You look pale," he said, after the butler left.

"Yes. Perfectly fine, thank you. Evans said you had something to give me?" The words trembled slightly, and she gripped the back of the chair, as though that would help steady her voice.

"Well, yes, but I . . . it's not so important. I can come back another time." He held out a small leather-bound book. "It's the poetry I was telling you about. I thought you might want to have a look for yourself."

She accepted the book, turning it over in her hands. The corners were scuffed, and many of the pages were dog-eared. A scrap of paper stuck out of the middle, and she opened to the marked page. Hopkins, the poet he had mentioned on the way to the theater. A poem called "Spring and Fall." *What heart heard of, ghost guessed . . .*

Why did Hallan do this? Why did he sometimes act like the worst kind of cad, then sometimes like the gentlest friend? To confuse her? To mock her? The empty, useless woman, in the house full of empty, useless things. A horrible feeling welled at the back of her eyes, and without so much as a tremor in her lip to warn her, she burst into tears. Her shoulders shook as she held the little book in both hands, unable to keep the sobs from pouring out.

Hallan let out a surprised noise. "God, Vera, what's the matter?"

She could not answer. He passed her his handkerchief, and she pressed it to her mouth. The fresh scent of his cologne on the cloth only made her heart sink lower. He placed a hand lightly on her back, guiding her to the sofa. They sat together in silence, except for the occasional whimpers she could not stifle.

"There," he said, in soft, low tones. "There now. Will you tell me what's the matter? Why are you crying?"

She searched her tumbling thoughts for any reason to offer him, anything that would sound feasible. As she did so, the thought occurred to her that even if she had wanted to name the true reason, she could not. She did not know why she had smashed the vase, and she did not know why she had wept at the offering of the book. All she could do was shake her head at him, still gasping with tears.

He stood and crossed to the nook beside the fireplace, and Vera cringed. Above a low wooden cabinet hung the portrait of Vera, wearing a long, silky black dress. She stood with her back to the viewer, looking over her shoulder, with diamond-studded earrings dangling down to her shoulder.

Hallan studied the painting, then turned back to her. "Do you paint?"

Vera tried to control her breathing, still fighting off the last of the crying jag. "Do you mean . . . did I paint that?"

"No. Just curious if you paint. As much as you love art, I would assume you dabble." His voice was as casual as that of someone on the street asking directions. He pointed to the crystal carafes on the beverage cart. "May I pour myself a drink?"

She nodded. The pounding of her heart had slowed, and only a few warm tears trickled down her cheeks. She dabbed at them with his handkerchief. "I don't paint."

"I find that surprising." He sat on the chair near the sofa and took a sip from the glass of whiskey he had poured. "You never wanted to give it a go?"

"I did try, years ago. When I was a girl." She drew in a shaky breath. "I wasn't very good."

"It's like any other pursuit. It takes practice." He sat forward. "Can I tell you how I paint? My process, I mean?"

She nodded again. At last she had the opportunity to find out what might really be going on in the pool room. If he said something ridiculous, surely she would recognize it as a lie.

He gazed into the distance. "For me, the color is what's vital. I can have an idea, a picture in my mind, but I have to choose a core color as a place to start. To set the mood, if you like. And then I build the other colors and the rest of the composition around that. That's when it begins to really take shape." He glanced behind him to the portrait of Vera. "If I were going to paint you, I certainly wouldn't start with black. That's why that painting is all wrong, you know. Not that you don't look lovely in it. But you must admit, it's wrong."

Unsure how to respond to that, Vera asked, "What color will you use in the pool room? Have you decided?"

"I have."

"Will you tell me?"

"You'll see. And I think you'll understand when you see. You more than anyone else."

"Why me?"

"Because you understand art, of course." Worry flickered across his face. "Are you feeling any better? I'm glad to see you've stopped crying at least."

And she had stopped crying. He had distracted her with the talk of painting, and she had not even realized it. She twisted the handkerchief in her hand.

"Yes, feeling much better," she said. She was not, not really, but the embarrassment of having lost her composure in front of the artist, coupled with the thought of what a fright she must look after such a scene, engulfed her, and now she wanted nothing more than for him to leave. She stood. "Thank you for the book."

Hallan hesitated, then glanced at the door. "You're welcome. I hope you enjoy it."

"I'm sure I will."

He stood. "May I ask you one thing?"

"Yes?"

"What color would you choose? Right now. If you had to."

She sighed. "I told you, I don't paint."

"That doesn't mean you can't choose a color."

She met his gaze, staring deep into those blue-green eyes. "Orange. Like the sky outside the theater."

"Orange." He rubbed his chin, then inclined his head. "I think that would do nicely, yes."

He put down his half-finished drink and turned to go.

"It was the monster." The words surprised even Vera herself.

Hallan took a step back toward her. "Excuse me?"

Vera pulled in a wavering breath. "The monster. In the picture today. I just . . . felt, well, awful for him, I couldn't stop thinking about it. He loved that woman, but she didn't love him back." She forced a light laugh. "What a silly thing to be so emotional about."

He shook his head and walked slowly to the door. "I felt rather sorry for him myself. Good night, Vera."

The driver brought Vera's mother back to campus on Saturday morning, though Vera had tried all through dinner the night before to discourage her from spending the day at school. She suggested the china shop, the lace and embroidery house, even the theater. Her mother could sometimes be tempted by a play, and a popular one had just opened in town. When her mother stepped out of the car that morning, Vera made one last effort.

"Really, town is far more interesting than campus," she said.

"Nonsense," her mother said. "It's a lovely day. I think a stroll around that little lake would be refreshing."

Vera pulled her coat tighter. "But isn't it chilly? Do we really want to walk around in the cold?"

"I am not old, nor am I infirm," her mother said, in a tone icier than the day could ever be. "Besides, if we were in town we'd be out in the air, wouldn't we?"

"Not if we were in the playhouse. It's really—"

"Goodness, Vera. Is there something illicit happening at this school you intend to prevent me from seeing?" Her mother's eyes narrowed.

"Of course not. I only wanted to make sure you had a nice visit, that's all." The truth was she couldn't bear her mother's scornful remarks about every detail of the campus and its inhabitants. Each criticism chipped away at Vera's own enjoyment of her sanctuary, until she could see only the faults her mother saw. She especially didn't want her mother employing this process with Bea. The more time they spent at school, the more chances they had to run into her. If Bea said anything out of line, the dissection would begin. Inflicting her mother on her sweet and lively friend would have no good outcome.

"I'm sure a day here will make for a perfectly acceptable visit. If you're going to be a good hostess, you must allow your guests to choose what suits them, and not wear them out with suggestions." Her mother turned to the driver. "Franklin, please return for us at five o'clock. We'll have dinner in town. Hand Vera the lunch basket, will you?"

Vera took the basket from Franklin, grateful that her mother didn't have plans to eat in the dining room. The man climbed back into the car, and Vera watched her last hope of keeping her mother in town drive away.

"We'll have a nice picnic on the lake," her mother continued. "I want to talk to you, that's what this little visit is about. Lead the way, please."

With a tightening grip on the basket, Vera started for the lake. If her mother had gone to all this trouble just for a talk, the topic must be serious. Vera thought of the letters under her bed, with Cliff's boxy handwriting on the small pages. Her mother couldn't know about the letters, could she? Vera begin mentally preparing a defense for the correspondence, an explanation of its perfect innocence that her mother would immediately disregard. And why shouldn't she? Even if the letters themselves were innocent, the way she'd entered into an acquaintance with Cliff was not.

All the way down the path, Vera checked the faces of the other girls. A boisterous interruption from Bea would be even less welcome if her mother wanted a private conversation. But Bea was nowhere to be seen. Vera calmed herself with the thought that she could count on

Bea to stay in bed asleep for a good portion of the morning, and maybe the afternoon, too. She did love to sleep in on the weekends.

At the lake, her mother pointed out a bench, and she and Vera sat. The sun shimmered off the gold and red leaves, and a light breeze sent ripples across the water. Of all Vera's protests, the weather was the weakest. The day had turned out idyllic.

"I have something important to discuss with you," her mother began, "and I see no reason to be less than plain about it. Arthur has spoken to your father and made his intentions clear. He plans to propose to you when you're home for Christmas."

"I see." Vera felt light-headed with relief. Her mother didn't seem to know about Cliff or the letters, or that would have been the first thing out of her mouth. *Cliff.* A proposal from Arthur would mean the abrupt end of the letter writing, no matter what its intent. Vera reminded herself quickly that Cliff was just a friend, and they hadn't known each other long. He hadn't even asked her if she had a beau. "What did Daddy say?" she asked, though she knew her mother's opinion was the only one that would matter.

Her mother's jaw tensed. "Well. He always did indulge you too much. He says he approves, but it will be your decision. But I came here to make sure you understand fully what you're doing if you accept him."

"But I thought you liked Arthur. Don't you?"

"He's a good man, and he can give you the type of life a girl like you should expect. That's important. But it's also important that you are aware you will be trading the Longacre name for a name that means much less."

Vera let the words roll around in her head. Her mother had never indicated any hesitation about Arthur before. "I know he's not from an old family, of course. But those sorts of things don't matter as much these days."

Her mother pressed her lips together tightly. "They may not matter to some. I still think a legacy is essential. Arthur seems to understand that, too. After all, if he gets you, he gets an attachment to this family. Don't think he hasn't considered that. What you can do for him in society."

Vera scanned the lake. She had realized Arthur's interest in a girl ten years younger might not be entirely romantic, especially given that they had almost nothing in common. Mutual attraction was a possibility she'd preferred to consider, especially since she found him so strikingly handsome. And love could grow from attraction, couldn't it? From time and closeness. Above all, she wanted to love whoever she married and be loved by him. Her parents' relationship hadn't given her much hope on that front. Though neither her mother nor her father had been inclined to discuss their courtship, Vera got the impression that it had been less of a choice and more of an inevitability, dictated by social rank and like-minded parents. Rather than discouraging Vera, it had given her the motivation to make a better match for herself. She had seen couples, even those likely thrown together as her parents had been, who had learned to enjoy each other's company. Who had found common ground. She was willing to work for affection, even if her mother and father had not.

The warning implicit in her mother's words gave her pause. They suggested a consideration of Vera's future happiness, an acknowledgment that her mother had spent time weighing the advantages and disadvantages of the match. Of course she would be thinking about the connections the marriage would make, but her mention of "society" suggested she was contemplating more for her daughter. That maybe they wanted the same things for Vera's future.

With this in mind, Vera ventured a question she might not otherwise have dared. "Are you saying you think I should wait for someone else? Someone with a better family name?"

"I thought of that, but there's no knowing. Could you wait? It's possible you might make another match. You turned out quite pretty, not that I think that concerns Arthur much."

Vera felt herself deflate. Didn't her mother think Arthur would find

Vera attractive? Was she truly only a name to him? She'd never ask, and her mother didn't give her time anyway. Her mother took in a deep breath and continued.

"It's not worth waiting for a name and squandering the opportunity before you. As much as I don't like it, I knew you'd likely have to choose someone who'd made his own fortune. That's the way things are going nowadays. I'm just grateful he's no robber baron or war profiteer. At least he made his money the proper way, there's something admirable about that." Her mother sighed. "There's no sense in going round and round with it. I've done enough of that in my head. And I came here to discuss it with you in person, because I need you to understand what accepting him will mean. I don't want you thinking of marriage as some fairy tale. You've always had romantic notions, but life is not like one of your novels." Her mother's pause prompted Vera's hasty response.

"Of course not, Mother. I understand."

"Taking everything into account, I do approve of Arthur. Your father approves of him. If you want to accept him, I see no reason not to."

Vera's gaze went to her ring finger. The idea of a sparkling gem on it did give her a little shiver of excitement. She imagined herself at Christmas, Arthur sliding the ring on, maybe giving her a kiss. Then Cliff's face, lit by firelight, floated into her mind. She pushed the thought of him away. No matter how enlightened her mother was on the subject of a man making his own fortune, Cliff could never even compete with someone like Arthur for a seat at her mother's table, let alone marriage to her daughter. His letters were sweet, but she would have to end them before Arthur made his offer. Vera knew the right answer. "I think I should accept Arthur," she said, though the words came out more heavily than she meant them to.

Her mother nodded. "At least it's settled, and I won't have to worry about you anymore. Of course, there will be no need to come back for spring term. We'll have to plan the wedding."

Vera whipped around to face her mother. All thoughts of men

and proposals evaporated at the prospect that she might not return to school. "But I have to finish the year, it's my last. There's the senior dance, and senior weekend . . . not to mention graduation."

Her mother's features darkened. "I am not asking you, I'm telling you. There's no way to properly plan a wedding like this through letters. You'll stay home, and that's final. If he'd proposed to you earlier, you wouldn't be sitting here now." She shook her head. "I'd have liked a nice winter wedding, but summer it is."

"Then why don't we have it next winter?" Vera said, her voice growing shakier. "That would give us plenty of time to plan—"

"Stop that this instant." Her mother pressed her hand to her forehead. "I really cannot stand these theatrics right now. Can we have a civil conversation, or should I go home?"

Go home, Vera begged in her mind. But she knew the threat was idle. If she wanted to keep from leaving on Sunday with her mother, Vera would have to stay in her good graces. She could always revisit the discussion about spring semester at Christmas. Or, if all else failed, she could appeal to her father. No need to upset her mother further now. "I'm sorry, Mother. I do appreciate you advising me. Why don't we have some lunch?"

Her mother nodded, her lips still a thin line. But she accepted the sandwich Vera offered, as well as the cup of tea poured from the thermos. The conversation even steered toward the more genial topic of wedding gown styles, which visibly calmed her mother. Vera let herself think she would survive the day, until she heard a bright voice behind them call her name. She and her mother turned to see Bea, taking long strides down the path to the lake.

"Who is that?" her mother asked.

"Oh . . . that's my friend. Bea. Bea Stillman." Vera gave the last name as much emphasis as she could.

"The Stillmans don't have a daughter your age."

"Oh, she's not from the city. She's a cousin, from Atlanta."

Her mother frowned. "What did she do to get sent up here?"

Vera's face went hot with indignation. "She didn't do anything. Her family wanted her to benefit from the society here."

"They have plenty of society down south. I think she'd benefit more from a hobble skirt and the recommendation not to shout at people."

Vera ignored the wheels turning in her mother's mind and leapt off the bench to meet Bea on the path. "Why are you running? It's not like you have to catch up to us."

Bea laughed. "I can't run in front of your mother? She must be worse than I thought."

There was no polite way to avoid it now. Vera would have to introduce them. "Come on," she said, her tone harsher than she would have liked.

Vera's mother stood as they approached. Her features were placid, and her lids drooped slightly. The expression might have looked like boredom to an untrained eye, but Vera knew her mother already found much to dislike about Bea.

"Mother, may I present Bea Stillman. Bea, this is my mother." Vera wrung her hands in front of her.

"What a pleasure to meet you, Mrs. Longacre," Bea said. "Vera's said so many lovely things about you."

"How nice that I can count on my daughter to speak well of me," Vera's mother said.

"But then not every mother can say that, can they?" The corner of Bea's mouth inched up the side of her face, and her eyes sparkled.

Vera forced out a laugh. "Oh, Bea. Don't be silly."

"I've so enjoyed getting to know Vera," Bea continued. "She is just a living doll. And such a good influence. Though we do have our share of fun."

"Is that right? I'm delighted to hear it." Vera's mother gave a smile that was more a baring of teeth. "What sort of fun might that be?"

"Don't worry, we don't get into too much trouble." Bea laughed. "Mostly because no one catches us."

Vera's mother dropped what little pretense of graciousness she had. "Is that right? Vera, what sort of things have you been getting up to?"

"Nothing, Mother." Vera's stomach threatened to send her sandwich back up. "Bea is joking. She loves to joke."

"She's right," Bea said, blanching. "I'm sorry, I didn't mean to concern you."

"Believe me, you do not concern me." Vera's mother drew herself up. "Vera, bring the basket. We're going back up to call the driver. A day in town does sound good after all."

Vera tossed the remnants of lunch back into the basket and hurried in her mother's wake. She turned to look at Bea, who mouthed "sorry" and offered a small wave. Vera did not wave back. She couldn't believe Bea would be so insensitive. For a moment, Vera wondered if Bea thought her mocking comments might actually charm Lorna, but Vera angrily dismissed any charitable explanation of Bea's behavior. Was Bea trying to get her in trouble? No, Bea was just Bea. Incorrigible. At least Vera had had the sense to keep the letters from Cliff to herself. A bad afternoon could have been a disastrous one.

« 16 »

When Marguerite came in with the breakfast tray, Vera's eyes stung and watered. A sinking sense of embarrassment flooded through her, but she tamped down the hazy memory of her day at the movies and the unfortunate episode with the vase. Instead, she focused on that evening's dinner with Arthur. Something in what she had said must have gotten through to her husband, and she needed to concentrate on making the most of her opportunity. She could not waste time fretting about the nonsense the night before. She lay in bed for so long planning what she would wear and how the evening would go, she nearly forgot it was Wednesday, and had to rush to dress for lunch with her mother.

Despite her delay, she hurried enough that she arrived at the restaurant right on time. She ordered her crab salad and tomatoes, and she and her mother began their usual run of questions and answers. When the meal arrived, however, her mother surprised her with an unexpected change in topic.

"Tell me, how is the mural project coming along?"

Hallan's face leapt to Vera's mind, and she nearly dropped her fork. "Oh. It's coming along well, I think." She had been forced to mention the mural to explain why she had to miss lunch the day Hallan arrived, and her mother had latched on to the project. She wanted to know everything about the artist: where he came from, where he studied. Vera had been grateful to have the Ecole des Beaux-Arts as an answer, since she knew very little else. The lack of information only encouraged her mother's interest, and she inquired about the mural's status every time they saw each other.

Her mother's lips tightened. "You don't know? You mustn't speculate, Vera. You either know or you don't."

"He arrived and he's begun painting. That's all I know, Mother."

"Still? You haven't seen the work?"

"No. He asked to work in privacy. No one is allowed in the pool room until the painting is complete."

Her mother took a bite of salad. "Sounds like an artist. Have you spoken to him more? You hired him, you have a right to know how it's progressing."

"I haven't had much of a chance to talk to him." Vera kept her eyes on her tomatoes.

"I'd like to meet him. Remind me of his name . . . Emil . . . ?"

Vera fought the rising panic at the thought of her mother and Hallan exchanging pleasantries. "Emil Hallan."

"Unusual name. Hmm. You'll have to have us over and invite him."

"Yes, I will." Vera prayed her mother would forget that little notion but knew her mother's bear-trap mind would not allow for such a reprieve. As her mother moved into a story about the latest ballet she had attended, Vera mentally calculated how many people she would need to invite to dinner to put a suitable distance between her mother and the artist.

That afternoon, Vera and Marguerite went through nearly all of Vera's dinner dresses, as Vera tried to choose the one that might appeal to

Arthur most. She chose a sapphire satin gown with silver beading, a long multi-strand silver chain necklace, and a headband with silver scrolls. Marguerite pinned her hair into an elaborate chignon, and Vera hung large diamond teardrop earrings in her ears.

At last, she made her way down to the car. She had chosen the Crystal Room at the Ritz and could easily have walked the few blocks, but she did not want to arrive mussed or dirty. When she went in, the maître d' led her to her requested table by the window. She settled in to wait, resisting the urge to consult the mirror in her small beaded handbag. She did not have to wait long. A white-gloved waiter came over after a few minutes.

"Ma'am, there's a telephone call for you," he said.

She felt a sharp pang of dread. "For me?"

He nodded, and she rose to follow him to the front desk. The maître d' handed her the receiver, and she pulled it to her ear.

"Arthur?" she asked.

"Yes, it's me." He sounded reluctant to admit it.

"Where are you?"

"The office."

A little thrill of hope ran through her. "Oh, are you running late?"

"No. I'm afraid I have to leave for Chicago tonight."

"What?" She had the sudden impulse to bash the receiver on the brick wall beside her.

"Yes, the deal is in danger of falling to pieces. I hoped there would be a later train, but I have to leave from the office this instant to make the last one. I hardly have time for this call."

She turned away from the maître d'. "But Arthur," she whispered.

"I am sorry, truly." His voice was heavy and hoarse. "Leaving you alone like this, it's terrible . . . but it was unavoidable. When I get back, we'll plan something else. A whole evening—dinner and a show, if you like. How does that sound?"

She swallowed. "Very nice. Of course. Safe travels."

She handed the phone back to the maître d' and walked in a daze back to her table without even realizing she was doing so. The waiter appeared at her arm, jolting her back to her senses.

"Has the gentleman been delayed?" he asked.

"Oh. Oh, no. He's not coming," she said. The words stung coming out of her mouth.

"Will you still be dining with us?"

Why not? she thought. Better than going back to her empty apartment in her fine clothes. "I will. May I have a glass of Bordeaux, please?"

The waiter's eyes widened. "I'm sorry . . . no. The . . . the law, madam."

She forced a laugh. "No, of course. So silly of me. Sparkling water will do."

"Right away."

Vera stared at the plate in front of her as silverware clinked against china under the quiet chatter and laughter of the other diners. She did not even notice when her drink arrived, and when the waiter asked what she would like to eat, the only thing she could think to order was steak. Then a voice cut through the cloud surrounding her, but not the waiter's.

"Vera?"

She looked up. Hallan stood by the table, dressed in a well-cut black suit.

"My goodness. Mr. Hallan," she said, a little breathless. "I certainly didn't expect to see you."

"I can tell by the look on your face. I didn't know eyes could get that wide without falling out entirely. Are you waiting for your husband?"

She straightened her shoulders, resisting the urge to lift her chin. "He was unavoidably detained."

"That's a shame." Hallan gestured to her dress. "He shouldn't miss seeing you like this, you look stunning."

Vera grabbed her glass of water. "What a thing to say."

"I think the thing to say is 'thank you.' It was meant to be a compliment."

She relaxed a bit. "Thank you."

He glanced at the empty chair across from her. "If your husband isn't . . ." He caught himself, then started again. "I don't want to impose, but may I join you?"

"You're not meeting someone?"

He smiled faintly. "No, actually. I was walking by and saw you through the window. I thought I ought to say hello."

"How kind of you." She looked up at him. He had tamed his unruly reddish waves into a neat part. First the museum, now the restaurant. If she did not know better, she might wonder if he was following her around. But surely he would not have expected her to be on her own. She was not the type of woman to dress up and dine out alone. "Are you sure you're not meeting someone? You're dressed so nicely."

"I was planning to meet up with some friends later on, and I thought I'd have a bite to eat before." He looked around the dining room. "Well, not here, of course. But since we're both here, I'd be happy to keep you company."

She thought again of Arthur's regretful words and eager promises on the phone. Chicago, indeed. She wondered who had made their dinner plans so easy to discard. What hotel or apartment he might be staying in for the next few nights. What kind of cheap scent he would come home reeking of. She deserved a little company if her husband was determined to ignore her. And maybe if he heard Vera had had dinner with another man, the thought might awaken a little jealousy in him. Besides, Vera did not want Hallan's most recent memory of her to be the emotional spectacle in her apartment the night before. Perhaps she could make clear that she was not typically given to such outbursts.

She smiled up at Hallan. "Please, I would love for you to join me."

His blue-green eyes shone, and he sat across from her. "Wonderful, thank you. So, what do you recommend here?"

"The steak is very good."

He pointed at her glass of water. "Wine is out of the question?"

Her mouth lifted in a half smile. "I'm afraid so."

"So strange. As I was leaving, half my friends told me, 'there is no alcohol in America.' The other half said, 'America is floating away on alcohol.' I come here, your building is awash with it. But we go to a fine restaurant and—" He shook his head. "No, we have to pretend it doesn't exist. Interesting situation you find yourselves in."

"This is your first time in America, then?" she asked.

Hallan looked out the window. "Yes."

"And your accent leads me to believe you are not originally from Paris." She leaned in. "For all the conversations people in the building have had with you, no one ever seems to recall you saying much about your family, or where you're from."

He shrugged. "I find people prefer to talk about themselves rather than listen."

"I'm listening. Tell me about yourself, Mr. Hallan."

He turned to her, and they held each other's gaze for a long moment.

"What's there to tell? I studied art at the Ecole des Beaux-Arts. I paint." His words had the air of being both carefully chosen and practiced.

"I know that. Where are you from? Who is your family?"

He squinted a bit, and his mouth ticked up in amusement. "I'm not in the habit of boring people with my biography."

Her own words from the party. She would have been irritated, but there was something refreshing about chatting with someone so sharp. "I see. Very clever."

"You know, I could ask the same things of you," he said. "I don't know where you were born. I don't know your family."

"But I am not a stranger from abroad."

"You are to me."

"You've been in my home. I'm hardly a stranger."

He sighed. "Why do you care? You hired me to paint, I'm painting."

"I'm curious," she said.

"There are some things I'm curious about, too."

"Oh?"

"Is this why you were crying the other night? Because he leaves you alone?" he asked.

Vera opened her mouth, but no words came out. She ought to express outrage, to get out of her chair, fling her napkin to the floor, and walk right out. But instead she stared at the place setting before her, unable to lift a finger. Hallan dropped his head and exhaled hard then stood.

"I'm sorry, I didn't mean to upset you. I shouldn't have asked something like that. Come on, let's get out of here. I'll take you somewhere I can buy you a proper drink."

Vera took a sip of her water. "You really do say so many things you shouldn't."

"At times," he agreed. He held out a hand, and she noticed that, despite an obvious effort to scrub them, there were traces of blue paint at the cuticles. A soft sky blue. In her mind, that hand traced the arc of Giovanna Tornabuoni's back in the air. Those eyes gazed in wonder at Esmeralda dancing on the screen in the movie house. To her surprise, she took his hand and stood.

"Let me call my driver," she said.

"It's a nice evening, let's walk."

"I still need to call and let him know not to come back for me. We're not going too far, are we?"

He smiled. "We can always take a cab."

"Oh. Right."

She called George and told him not to bother returning to the restaurant, and asked the maître d' to put the bill on Arthur's account. Then she and Hallan strolled out onto the sidewalk. She took his arm, and Hallan led her confidently off to the left.

"Where are we going?" she asked.

"Fun little club. They have music and a show, then dancing after. Plus real drinks. Does that sound all right?"

"Of course." Vera's stomach tingled. She wanted to write the sensation off as hunger, since she had left her steak behind. But she knew it was anticipation. She had heard of these places, and Arthur went frequently with business associates. They were not the sorts of places men took their wives, though. Other ladies, yes. Wives, never.

They turned the corner onto the next block. Ahead of them, a man sat on a blanket. In front of him was a sign that said VETERAN: PLEASE HELP, GOD BLESS, with a can set out for coins. The sight of his face, red, raw, and pockmarked, sent an involuntary crawl under Vera's skin. Part of his leg was missing, and he had tucked the excess trouser material under the stump of his thigh. Hallan spotted him at the same moment, and he halted. He stood still for so long Vera began to worry, but she did not know if speaking to him would make whatever reaction he was having better or worse. At last, he let go of Vera's arm, dug into his pocket, and put money into the can.

"Thank you, sir," the man said. The skin around his mouth was tight and shiny, and the words came out muffled and hard to distinguish. Hallan only nodded and continued on.

Vera threw some coins into the can. "Thank you for your service," she said, unable to look the man in the eye. He called a "thank you, ma'am" to her as she walked past.

She caught up to Hallan, whose gaze was stony. "It's so terribly sad," she said. "Some days it feels so far behind us, and some days it's everywhere, isn't it?"

He did not respond. She took his arm again, and they walked a few blocks before she could feel the muscles under his jacket relax. Though she wanted to ask if he had served, she thought mention of the war might darken the evening. Perhaps the war explained his reluctance to talk about his life. She did not want to cause him any heartache after he had been kind enough to want to show her a nice time in the wake of her disappointment. She supposed the question was an empty one anyway. He was more likely than not to have been a soldier.

She remembered well how empty of men the city had seemed throughout the war. During that time, her thoughts would occasionally drift back to the young men she and Bea had sat by the lake with. How many of them had gone? Had any of them come back? She might not recognize them. She had never heard from Cliff again after that autumn. What horrors might have followed their sweet exchange of letters? The war may have damaged him as it had damaged the man sitting by the street that night. She glanced back over her shoulder for one more look before they turned the corner and left him behind.

Hallan led her into a sleepy little shop, and they walked to the back wall. There, hidden near the corner, was the door to a staircase leading down to a corridor with brick walls. As they entered, it was quiet, but the sound of muffled music and laughter increased as they continued. At last they came to the other end, where a huge man stood in front of a barred metal door.

"Password?" The man's bristly mustache barely moved as he spoke.

"Dempsey," Hallan said. The man nodded and pushed the bar away, then opened the door. Smoke and noise billowed out into the corridor, swooping over Vera and Hallan. The urge rose in her to turn and run, but she gripped Hallan's elbow harder and they stepped into the club.

If her mother disapproved of the skirts some girls wore in the streets, the dresses in the club would have sent her to an early grave. Vera had slips that covered more leg, and rather more chest as well. She felt as if she had walked in wearing Queen Victoria's wedding dress instead of her blue dinner gown. The earthy smell of damp brick carried an undercurrent of sweat and drugstore perfume. Vera worried the scent would sink into her clothes and hair, letting anyone she passed in the Angelus on her way home know that she had been somewhere she had no business being.

She wanted to tell Hallan she had to leave, but the wailing of the trumpet and the riot of conversation meant she would have to yell it, and she did not particularly want to announce her discomfort to the room. More familiar with his surroundings, he nodded to a nearby table. But before they could cross to it, a woman nearby let out a shriek that temporarily rendered every other sound in the club inaudible.

"Emil!" The woman leapt into their path and threw her arms

around Hallan's shoulders, jolting Vera to the side. "Lucy, come here, this is the artist I was telling you about."

"Hello, Jenny," Hallan said, disengaging himself.

Jenny raised a painted-on eyebrow. "Ooh, and he brought high society with him. Is this one of the people from the building?"

Before he could answer, another woman, clad in a slinky silver dress with clattering beads, tottered over in pin-thin heels. "Is this the artist?"

"That's what I just said." Jenny rolled her eyes. "Lucy is a little dim."

Lucy slapped Jenny's bare shoulder. "I am not! Don't listen to her." Lucy looked Vera up and down, her dark red lips drooping into a frown. "I thought you said he was single."

Hallan laughed. "Ladies, let me find my friend a seat." He directed Vera to the empty table, and the other two women promptly dropped into the available chairs across from her.

Vera leaned in and lowered her voice. "You've certainly been quick to find your way around the city. How is it that you already know passwords and girls after only a few weeks?"

"I know someone who moved to the city several years ago. The same friend who mentioned the Angelus mural to me. Had some good recommendations about nightlife."

"Who? Someone I might know?" Vera asked.

He shrugged. "I doubt it. Word about the mural made its way around the art world pretty quickly. I was just the lucky one you hired."

"So," Jenny said, adjusting the straps of her shimmery green dress. "You're from the building where Emil is doing his painting?"

Vera sat up, putting on her best cool expression. "I am."

Jenny pursed her lips. "A real rich lady, huh?"

A smile flickered on Hallan's face. "That's not very polite, Jenny."

Vera leaned in to him again. "You're enjoying this, aren't you?"

His lips brushed her ear as he spoke. "I'm going to enjoy watching you eat her alive. Come on, you're not afraid of this girl, are you? You're not afraid of anyone, from what I've seen."

Vera sat up, a new confidence rising in her chest. She fixed her stare on Jenny, who wilted slightly.

Lucy laid a hand on the table, oblivious to Vera's glare. "You know, I'm always so curious about what rich ladies do all day. Me, for example, I'm a telephone operator. I gotta do it, I got no choice. But I've always had something to do. You don't work, do you?"

Jenny took a drink from a passing waiter and took a long swig from the glass. Her eyes narrowed in challenge. "Yeah, what do you do all day?"

Vera did not answer right away. First, she pulled off her gloves and settled them in her lap with her purse, as she had been taught since girlhood to do. Then, she reached across the table and lifted Jenny's drink from her hand. Vera drank its contents in one smooth gulp. She placed the empty glass in front of the startled girl.

"Rich ladies drink," Vera said.

Hallan laughed and clapped his hand on the table. "Looks like we're ready for another round. Allow me."

Jenny and Lucy declined, casting glances back at Vera as they fled for the safety of the other side of the club.

"I don't think that's what they were expecting," Hallan said.

"It seems you have quite a knack for attracting an interesting sort of lady," Vera replied.

"Somehow they find me. So? Another drink?"

"Gin and tonic, please." Vera wrinkled her nose. "Whatever that was smelled like perfume and tasted worse."

Hallan waved over a waiter and ordered two cocktails. The gin was harsher than what Vera was used to. But then, Arthur got all of his liquor brought in from Canada. The stuff they were serving in this club might have been made in the back room. Still, it was recognizably gin, and she enjoyed the looseness that came with finishing the drink.

They watched a few acts, the first a trio of dancing girls and the second a dewy-eyed soloist. A black horn player wailed through a raucous set, each note blazing. When the stage shows were done for the evening, people trickled onto the dance floor. The tempo slowed with each song, and couples draped themselves over each other, swaying to the music. Vera was finishing her second cocktail when Hallan stood and extended his hand.

"Would you like to dance?" he asked.

Vera nearly choked on her drink. She set the glass on the table and glanced around the room. "I don't think that's a good idea."

"No one knows you here, believe me. And you can't have a night out without dancing, can you?"

"It's only . . . I don't know many of the popular dances. I haven't been out in some time."

He gestured toward the musicians. "This is a waltz. A girl like you, I know you can waltz."

"You're not going to give me any peace until I agree, are you?"

"No, sorry to say."

Vera sighed and started to put on her gloves, but he slid his warm hand into hers to stop her. An electric tingle ran up her arm.

"You don't need gloves," he said. "Let's go."

She stood and they wound through the tables to the dance floor. He wrapped an arm lightly around her waist, and she placed her arm on his shoulder. At first, she held her back stiff, but she relaxed at his confident lead.

"You're a good dancer," she said. "So, I've discovered that you know how to behave in polite society, even if most of the time you choose not to. And now I can tell you've been trained to dance."

He pressed his cheek to hers. "Is that enough to satisfy you?"

The hair on the back of her neck stood at the feel of his breath on her ear. She knew she ought to pull back, but she did not. "I still don't know anything, not really."

"Ah, but you've seen my art. That's all there is to know. The whole truth about me is in those paintings." He pulled back and searched her face. "Look at that, you've got some little freckles on your nose. 'Glory be to God for dappled things.'"

"Oh, goodness. I thought I powdered those."

"You did. But this close I can see them."

"Wretched things."

"I like them. Shows you're actually real."

Heat rose in her cheeks. "Why would you say that?"

"Everything about you is so cool. So still." He laid his cheek on hers again. "You're a beautiful icicle."

Vera cleared her throat as the song ended. She took a step back, disentangling herself from his arms. "I ought to get home."

He squeezed her hand. "Indulge me. One more dance."

"No."

She crossed back to the table and picked up her gloves and purse. He followed, taking hold of her elbow, but she spun around.

"Mr. Hallan, I don't know what you are trying to do, but you ought to know I'm not like the silly girls you meet at these places. I am a married woman."

"But you had fun tonight."

She blinked hard. "That's quite enough. I'm going home. Would you be so good as to come up to the street with me? I need you to hail me a cab."

"Vera, I didn't mean any harm—"

She strode to the metal door that led to the brick corridor. He followed, and they exited onto the street together.

"Will you please listen to me?" he asked.

"I've heard enough, thank you."

He threw up his arms in frustration and turned to hail a cab. The yellow and black car pulled up to the curb, and Vera climbed in. She moved to close the door, but Hallan blocked it.

"You're not going to let me share your cab? We're going to the same place," he said.

Vera scooted over, and Hallan got in. He gave the address, and the cab started off down the street.

"I'm sorry if I caused offense," he said under his breath.

"And yet you continue to find new and inventive ways to do so."

He reached into his breast pocket and pulled out a flask. "Here."

"I've had enough, thank you," she said.

"Consider it my way of making amends."

She took the flask and drank. The liquor was smooth and fragrant. "Better than the swill in the bar," she said, passing the flask back.

"I thought so." Hallan took a drink, then returned the flask to his pocket. "If I promise not to say anything to upset you, will you do one more thing with me?"

She regarded him from the corner of her eye. "I very much doubt that's a promise you can make good on."

"You said it yourself. I can behave when I want to."

"What is it you have in mind?"

He grinned. "I want to see the city."

"Absolutely not. I'm not going anywhere but home this evening."

The cab pulled up in front of the Angelus. Vera opened her purse, but Hallan slipped some money to the driver first. They stepped onto the sidewalk, and Hallan gestured at the top of the building. The enormous angel statues stood on the building's roof, announcing the grandeur of its residents to anyone passing on the street.

"There. I need to see what the city looks like from up there." He turned to her. "Will you go up there with me? I'll be a perfect gentleman, I swear it."

"You can go on your own. The doorman has a key, he'll take you up there. Though I doubt it's locked."

"I'd like to go with you. Have you ever even been up there? Don't you want to see what it looks like?"

"It's not that far above my apartment. I can see from the window."

"It must be different, with no walls or ceiling. Don't you think?"

Vera craned her neck back. The two angels they could see from where they stood were illuminated by spotlights and shone golden against the dark sky. He was right; she had never been to the roof. She dropped her gaze back to Hallan and pointed at him.

"If you say so much as one word out of line, I'm leaving."

"That's fair."

She looked up again as they walked to the entrance. "Well, we can't take the elevator. Someone might see us ride up together."

"At this hour? Does it matter?"

"You never know."

"Then we'll take the stairs."

Vera looked at her feet. "Twenty flights of stairs in heels?"

"Take them off."

"I'll ruin my stockings."

He bit down on a smile. "You'll buy more."

Vera paused. "You are the most stubborn man I've ever met."

"Possibly." He pushed the door open and allowed her to pass through. They turned left and walked into the dimly lit stairwell. She slid her shoes off and handed them to Hallan.

"The least you can do is carry them," she said.

"The very least." He gestured at the stairs. "After you."

"Wait." She stuck out her hand. "I need another drink if I'm going to go all the way up."

He gave her the flask again. She drank, swallowed, took a deep breath, and then drank again.

"Ready?"

She nodded. They started up the stairs. She knew under normal circumstances her calves would have been burning within a few flights, as she so rarely walked any real distance. But the alcohol had a nice mellowing effect. Instead of pain, she only felt the alcohol's warmth.

At last they went through the door and onto the roof. A bracing blast of cool air hit Vera's face, and she gasped. The roof itself was nothing special, mostly odd gray squares of utility machinery grinding away. But the city beyond was a shining, glittering crush of gems. Electric lights beamed up into the night sky, casting a halo over the buildings standing sentry around the park below.

"It's marvelous." She turned, but Hallan was not looking at the view. Instead, he had gone over to one of the angel statues and stood examining its face. She walked over to him. "Is this what you came to see?"

"All of it, really. Who did the statues?" he said.

She dropped her gaze. "I don't know. Someone my husband found. They were his idea."

Hallan studied her. "Let's sit down."

A few feet away, some wooden folding chairs had been set out, probably by workmen in the building who came up to the roof for repairs. Hallan and Vera sat, and they passed the flask again.

"Those lights," he said. "I still can't believe those lights."

Her head hummed with the liquor, and with the beauty of what lay before them. "Neither can I, really," she said. "When I was a girl I don't think it was this bright. I don't remember it glowing like this."

His brow furrowed. "I really don't mean to make you angry, you know. I want to get to know you. I want you to like me."

She thought of several sharp retorts but held them back. "Plenty of people like you. Why are you so worried about me?"

"Because I like you."

She let the words ring for a moment in her ears. "I meant what I said, Mr. Hallan. I'm married."

He shook his head. "I don't mean anything like that. But talking to you in the museum . . . I enjoy talking to you. When you're being yourself. When I can see through the chink in the armor."

She gave him a sidelong look. "You're certainly given to a romantic turn of phrase, aren't you? 'Beautiful icicle.' 'Chink in the armor.'"

He smiled. "I'm just being honest."

She patted his hand. "You've got plenty of admirers, you don't need me. What about Poppy?"

"Too bad about that. See, the thing is, I've never liked poppies. Daisies, maybe. But not poppies."

"I see. You're in luck, though."

"How's that?"

"Poppy isn't her real name."

Hallan rested his elbows on his knees, eyes widening. "Is that so?"

"Yes, she—" A giggle escaped Vera's lips, and she struggled to keep a straight face. "She only calls herself that because—"

"You may as well tell me, you've gone this far."

"Her real name is . . . Hildegard."

He whistled. "God, that is bad."

"Isn't it?" Vera laughed, and the sound echoed in her ears. Light, playful. Her throat nearly ached with it. She realized she had not laughed, really laughed, in such a long time. She pressed her fingertips to her lips and turned to Hallan, who watched her intently. His own cheerful expression had become more serious.

"Lit up and bright," he said in a low voice. "That's how you always ought to be. Lit up by a thousand lights, like you are now."

A few strands of hair had come loose from her chignon, and they danced in the breeze. She tucked them back before standing. "I believe it's time for me to retire. Good night, Mr. Hallan."

He stayed in his chair and watched her walk to the stairs, calling "Good night" just before the door closed behind her.

« 17 »

It took Vera less time than she imagined it would to forgive Bea for upsetting her mother. In fact, once her mother had gone, the whole incident gave them both a good giggle. Bea had even reenacted the confrontation, taking the role of Vera's mother. She nailed the intonation and withering stare perfectly, as Vera pretended to grovel at her feet.

Bea drew herself up to her full height, sticking her nose into the air so far Vera couldn't see her eyes anymore. "Believe me, youuu do not concern meeee." She collapsed on Vera's bed, a mess of laughter.

"That's pretty good," Vera said, shifting from groveling back into a sitting position on the floor. "You'd think you'd known her all your life."

"I have," Bea said. "There are a dozen women like her in my mother's circle, and all of them look at me like I've been rolling in the mud."

"She did have a good reason for visiting," Vera said, unable to keep her news to herself for a second longer.

"Oh?"

Vera toyed with the hem of her skirt, her cheeks straining with the effort of holding in her smile. "It seems Arthur has had a word with my father."

Bea sat up. "Is he . . . ?"

"He's going to propose at Christmas," Vera cried.

Bea shrieked and sprang off the bed, grabbing Vera in a hug. "You lucky thing. Are you going to accept? Of course you are, he's so rich. And handsome. Oh, you're terrible, how could you wait so long before telling me?"

"I think you're more excited than I am," Vera said, trying to loosen Bea's grip on her arms.

"Then you need to get more excited. You're not going to wait until he asks to start planning, are you?"

The thought of planning reminded Vera of what her mother had said about leaving school for good after Christmas break. She decided not to mention it to Bea, in the slim hope that she could still get her mother to back down on that point. Besides, the news might dull Bea's enjoyment of the moment. Vera was grateful for Bea's enthusiasm, which helped to lessen her own emerging worries. Hearing her mother's reservations about Arthur at the lake had made Vera wonder if accepting him was the right decision after all. Still, she didn't think turning him down would be right, and what alternatives were there? Not Cliff, despite the fact that his most recent letter had asked when he might see Vera again and gave other hints that he did not think of her in the same friendly way she forced herself to think of him. He would never be an acceptable suitor in her mother's eyes, no matter how much Vera found herself growing to like him. So Vera had resolved to keep her letters cordial and chaste. But she did not stop writing him, nor did she mention Arthur.

"It wouldn't hurt to start thinking about the wedding," Vera said. Bea launched into a list of dress shades, materials, and styles, as Vera stretched out on the rug and relished the glow of her friend's enthusiasm.

《《《 ● 》》》

The next afternoon, Vera was in the library hunting for a book she needed for a report on the Spanish Golden Age. Someone had evidently put the book back in the wrong spot, as the librarian assured her it was not checked out, so Vera resigned herself to searching each row until she found it.

"There you are." Bea appeared at the end of the row and bounded toward Vera. "I've been looking all over the building for you."

"Shhh," Vera said. "This is a library, you know."

"Yes, and you're the only one in here. It's the weekend, you shouldn't be in this old tomb."

Vera laughed. "I know this doesn't mean much to you, but I have work to do."

"It's been ages since we did anything fun." Bea slumped against the shelves.

"That's not true," Vera said. "We went to that shop last weekend."

"You know what I mean. Real fun. Yale boys." Bea's eyes gleamed.

A wave of heat ran through Vera's stomach at the thought of seeing Cliff again. The idea thrilled her, but she knew her resolution to keep romance out of their relationship would be tougher to stick to if he were really there in front of her. Not just his blocky handwriting on a page, but his strong jaw, his wide shoulders, the waves of his auburn hair. That would be harder to resist. Still, she should tell him about Arthur, and she had been putting off telling him in her letters. Wouldn't that be the sort of news to give him face to face? She could explain better, tell him what he'd really meant to her. Then, Vera assured herself, they could say a proper good-bye, much better than some cold letter. She kept her composure as she answered Bea, despite the battlefield in her mind. "So this is a bid to get me to sneak out again? Because I don't think I need to tempt fate."

"But I have a plan. And soon you'll be engaged. I've been thinking about it since yesterday, and I need to treat you to a grand finale of unmarried life."

Vera knew what she ought to say, though her heart leapt, betraying her. Immediate agreement would make Bea suspicious. "No. Absolutely not."

"Don't say that yet. Look at you, you're intrigued, I can see that you are."

"Only about what your diabolical mind has come up with this time."

Bea smiled. "It is a good plan. Don't you at least want to hear it?"

Vera sighed. "All right. I know you won't rest until you tell me."

"You won't be disappointed." Bea made a big show of clearing her throat. "I'm taking you to a Yale football game. For the whole weekend."

"I repeat: absolutely not. We'd need letters from our parents, and you know my mother would never agree."

"Let me worry about that. I'll get the letter. There's more than one way to skin a cat, you know." Bea took a step toward Vera. "If I can get us letters, will you go?"

"But we'd need a car, a room . . ."

"I've thought of all that. Harry can drive us. And there's a girls' boardinghouse in town. It's for teachers, but my friend lives there. She said no one would care if we stayed one night." Bea elbowed Vera. "I bet Cliff would like to see you again."

Vera turned so Bea could not read her expression. Did she know about the letters, or was she just teasing? If she knew something, it was unlike Bea to be coy. Vera decided to play it safe. "I'm not going to be silly about some boy. Especially not now."

"Then don't come for him. Come for me." Bea took Vera's hands. "Please? Say you'll think about it. I swear your mother would never have to know. And you deserve to do your last year of college in style."

"There's no way my mother would be involved?" Vera asked.

"Not at all. She'd never hear the first word about it. I can get letters, the dorm matron would never call her to question them. Plenty of girls go on weekend trips."

Vera pursed her lips. "Fine. I'll think about it. But that's all. No promises. And I want to see these letters before we take it any further."

Bea squealed and clapped. She ignored Vera's shushing and said, "You'll be glad we did this. I know you will."

Though she didn't really believe Bea would be able to produce letters good enough to fool the dorm matron, Vera also had a little flicker of hope. Besides the opportunity to meet up with Cliff again, she'd never gotten to go to a football game, and she realized the days when that sort of thing might be possible were growing ever fewer. Everything shrunk before her: her remaining life at college, her days of taking chances, and her time to have any kind of relationship with Cliff, friendly or otherwise. Bea was right. Vera deserved a grand finale to all of it.

« 18 »

NEW YORK CITY, AUGUST 1923

Vera woke late the morning after her trip to the roof with Hallan. Her head throbbed a bit but did not hurt nearly as bad as she expected. Her stomach was not even a little bit wobbly. She guessed all those dinner parties, with course after course of alcohol, were good for something. Still, she asked Marguerite to draw her a bath and ignored her breakfast tray in favor of a glass of club soda and a cool cloth for her forehead.

After dressing, she had Marguerite phone with regrets to the luncheon she was scheduled to attend at Caroline Litchfield's, and also instructed her to tell any callers that she was ill. Vera had no desire to leave the apartment, though it might have provided some distraction from thoughts of the artist and her two strange evenings in a row with him. But she relished the idea of running into him even less. Avoiding him would not be too difficult. The social functions in his honor had finally slowed, and she might not have to see him again for a good long while if she prepared carefully. She decided to spend the morning in the study, where she could read and take care of her correspondence.

She had just reached the foot of the stairs when the doorbell rang. Evans appeared, and Vera slipped behind the open study door to watch.

"Good day, sir," Evans said.

"Hello, yes, I'm here to see Mrs. Bellington."

Hallan. A thousand curses rang through Vera's head. Of course he would have no qualms about walking right up to her door.

"I'm sorry, sir. She's not well."

"I'll bet she's not," Hallan said with a short laugh.

"Pardon?"

"Never mind." He took a pencil from his vest and scratched something on a card. "Will you give her this?"

"Yes, sir," Evans said.

Vera heard the front door close, and she rushed to a chair. A few moments later, Evans appeared with an ivory calling card in hand. He gave it to her, then left. The front of the card read, in bold block letters:

EMIL HALLAN
ARTIST-IN-RESIDENCE
THE ANGELUS
PARK AVENUE

Vera rolled her eyes. One of the other ladies must have had them made up for him. She flipped it over to see what he had written. Hallan's wispy letters read:

> *"They say, best men are moulded out of faults,*
> *And, for the most, become much more the better*
> *By being a little bad."*
> *That's the Bard. Suspected you might be indisposed to-*
> *day, but thanks for a lovely night anyway.*
> —E.H.

After a moment's deliberation, she ripped the card in half and tossed it in the wastebasket.

《《《 ● 》》》

Three days after Vera's night out with Hallan, Marguerite woke her with the breakfast tray and the rather surprising news that Arthur was in the dining room having his coffee. Vera dressed and asked the maid to take her food in so she could join him.

He sat reading the paper at the end of the table and barely looked up when Vera walked in.

"When did you get home?" she asked, settling into her place.

"Late. Didn't want to wake you."

"Productive trip, I hope? How was the train?"

"Yes, it was all fine." He folded the paper and laid it by his plate. "Terribly sorry again about missing dinner the other night. I hope you weren't too inconvenienced."

"Not at all." She tried to keep her voice cheerful. "As you said, work comes first."

"So it does."

He retrieved his paper and they sat together in silence. Vera spread jam on her toast and took a bite, but it settled in her stomach like a rock, so she concentrated on her tea.

Arthur put the paper down again. "I nearly forgot. You'll need to look at your calendar."

"Oh?"

"Yes. Your father phoned. He and your mother want to take us to Abide Away for a weekend before the weather changes."

Vera nearly jumped with delight. Abide Away was her parents' summer home in Montauk, and a weekend there would allow her several guaranteed artist-free days. There was the added bonus of getting her husband out of the city, where they could spend some time together in the place where they had courted. They could have a nice dinner out, maybe, just the two of them.

"What a lovely idea," she said. "We could go next weekend. I don't have anything that would keep me here."

Arthur rubbed his chin as he thought. "Nor do I, come to think of it. I can always take the car back if something comes up at the office. You can ride back with your parents if need be."

Even that caveat could not dull Vera's excitement. The ocean might still be comfortable for bathing, though the water was never warm enough for her taste. At the very least she would get a little sun. She mentally moved through her closet, trying to decide which dresses she ought to take, barely noticing that Arthur had continued talking.

". . . so you'll need to ask that Hallan fellow," Arthur concluded, raising the newspaper once more.

A cold chill trickled down the back of Vera's throat. "Ask him what?"

"If he's available. Your father says your mother wants to meet him. Thought it would be nice to show him a weekend at the beach, or something on that order."

"She can meet him here, in the city. There's no need to take him out of town. It should be a family trip, don't you agree?" Vera's pitch rose as the words came clambering out.

"She's *your* mother, Vera. If you don't want him there, tell her," Arthur said.

Speaking candidly to her mother was the last thing Vera wanted to do. She thought of creating an imaginary event that would prevent her from going, but that would never work. Nothing on Vera's calendar would be crucial enough that it could not be rescheduled. Besides, her fellow residents in the Angelus were her primary social sphere, and once some of them heard that Vera and Arthur were off to Montauk, they would all certainly have to go, too. Throw the artist into the plans, and half the building would be empty by Friday morning. There would be no engagements left for Vera to hide behind.

Vera sat down that morning to write an invitation to Hallan, but after four or five false starts, it became clear she would not get the wording right. She thought of having Evans phone. She could not imagine what Hallan would think, after her two odd evenings with him, if she invited him out of town for the weekend. The conversation was not one she wanted to have face to face. However, if she spoke to him herself, she could make it evident that she did not want him there. She could dissuade him from accepting the invitation, something Evans or a properly written note would not do. With that in mind, she rode the elevator down to the second floor and knocked on the door of 2A.

She expected his valet to answer, so she almost gasped when Hallan himself flung the door open. His eyes lit up.

"Vera. I was hardly expecting you. Come in, please," he said.

She pulled her shoulders back. "I can't stay. Where's your man?"

Hallan frowned. "Who, Michael? Why do you need to see him?"

"I don't. But you shouldn't answer your own door. That's what he's there for."

He stared at her, then shook his head. "All right, noted. Please, come in. Let me get you a cup of tea."

"No, thank you. I just came by . . ." She could not get the words out. "I wanted to—or really, my mother—that is—"

He laughed. "Whatever it is, it can't be all that bad. Maybe you need something stronger than tea, you're flushed."

"No," she cried, as she thought of the influence alcohol had had on their other interludes. "No. Nothing, no tea, thank you."

"At least come in. Sit down."

Her unsteady knees begged her to agree. And sitting would allow her to get her thoughts together. "Yes, all right."

She followed him to the sitting room, which remained as tidy as she and Ida had left it the day before Hallan arrived. In fact, everything still looked as if Hallan had never moved in. There were no photographs on the mantel, no letters on the desk. No personal touches of any kind. And no art supplies. No sketches. No easels.

"May I ask you something?" She took a seat on the couch, and he sat in the chair beside her.

"Of course," he said.

"I didn't expect to find you in. What time do you start work each day?"

"Usually after lunch. I don't work well in the mornings." He sat against the back of the chair. "You sound concerned. Don't worry. You'll get your money's worth from me. Is that what you came for?"

"Ah, no." She clasped her hands together in her lap. "My mother has taken it into her head that we all need to go to Montauk together, and she wanted me to invite you."

"Your mother?"

"Yes, I've been keeping her up to date about the mural project since we had the idea. She's curious about you." Vera paused. "My mother has a great deal of influence in the city, and she doesn't like to feel she's been left out of any interesting developments, especially in my life. She likes to be . . . involved."

"I see. This Montauk. It's a restaurant?"

Vera stared. "No, it's a town on the shore. My parents have a summer home there, we'll make a weekend of it. My parents, Arthur and me, and you."

Hallan thought for a moment. "I'd love to meet your parents. And to see what a vacation looks like for the Bellingtons. Yes, wonderful. Tell your mother I'd love to go."

"I really don't think you should go, Mr. Hallan. Don't you have work to do?"

"It will keep. No one's given me a deadline, have they?"

Vera pursed her lips. "But my mother . . . she's a formidable lady."

He gestured to Vera. "She'd have to be."

"Yes, well, I'm afraid you might not have . . . compatible spirits. A weekend can be longer than it seems."

"I think I can handle it, thank you. Tell her I'd love to come. When do we leave?"

She hesitated. "Friday morning. But if you change your mind—"

He leaned in, eyes shining. "I won't."

"Fine. I shouldn't impose anymore. I'm sure you have a lot of work to do." She stood and took a deep breath. "I hope you understand that it's better not to mention our outings to my mother. The museum and dinner. I wouldn't want her to get the wrong idea."

He nodded and rose. "About the other night . . . surely you can stay a little while. We never got to speak."

She looked out the window. "I'm sorry, I really can't stay."

"Did you get my card? I came by, but your butler said you were ill."

"I got your card. Thank you for calling."

He let out an exasperated sigh. "Well, are you feeling better at least?"

She turned back to him and spoke slowly. "Yes. Much."

He took a step toward her, but she walked past him.

"Shall I show myself out, then?" she asked.

"Of course not, I'll walk you out."

She went to the door with Hallan in her wake. He opened the door, and she stepped through.

"Good day," she said.

A wicked gleam appeared in his eye. "Tell your mother how much I'm looking forward to this weekend. What a treat, a few days at the shore."

Without another word, Vera spun on her heel and went for the elevator, her mind buzzing with the many ways he could make trouble in a house with her mother and husband.

《《《●》》》

The following Friday at ten a.m. sharp, three gleaming cars pulled up to the front of the Angelus. As soon as Poppy heard about the trip, she had arranged to go with her two children to their cottage at Fort Pond Bay. Poor Julius was down with a cold and not able to travel. Walter and Caroline Litchfield had also decided to go with the group, along with their boys. Since Walter and Vera's father golfed together occasionally, Vera's father had invited them to stay at the house as well. Ida

Bloomer had an opera board meeting she absolutely could not miss, so she had been unable to go, much to her dismay. Bessie Harper declined to join the party, concerned about the effect the sea air would have on her curls. Vera secretly wondered if Bessie was more worried about sand in her martini.

Vera climbed into the car with Arthur, grateful Poppy had insisted Hallan ride with her and the children. Three hours in the car with Hallan and Arthur together was really not the start the trip needed. The other two groups crowded into their cars, and the procession drifted through the city streets.

The height of the buildings descended as they moved out of the city. The sky seemed to Vera to grow brighter, the air cooler and more mobile, and even the weight on her shoulders lightened. Though she did not relish the thought of whatever troubles awaited her this weekend, she always loved going to the summer home and the feel of hot, white sand under her bare feet. There were plenty of distractions at the shore, and surely she could put distance between herself and Hallan where necessary. Once her mother had her fun dissecting him, she would move on to other prey, which again made Vera glad to have Poppy along. She would certainly do or say something that would prove a useful distraction.

They passed through the village, with its cozy inns and dance hall. Vera made a mental note to have one of the servants go to town to buy her a magazine. The only place she ever allowed herself to read fashion magazines was on the beach. At the edge of town, the land beside the road yielded to grassy fields, and then finally to white pebbled driveways that led to neighboring estates. Poppy's car would have turned off at Fort Pond Bay to go to her cottage, but they had to follow to drop the artist off at Abide Away. Despite Vera's protests, her mother had insisted Hallan stay with them. After all, she had been the one to issue the invitation.

At last, they drove up to a rustic-style wooden gate and down a long paved path. Before them, Abide Away rose up against the teal sky. The house's dark wood exterior had been weathered by the sea air, and square red brick chimneys rose high above the two-story building. Vera's parents waited in rocking chairs on the wraparound porch as she and Arthur stepped out into the crisp, salty air. The other cars pulled up, and their occupants exited as the house's staff raced to take luggage inside. The group ascended the stairs, and Vera's father and mother came forward. Hallan hesitated at the foot of the stairs, taking in the size of the house as the flurry of greetings took place on the porch.

"Vera, darling," her mother said, taking Vera's hands. "I hope the drive wasn't too difficult."

"Not at all, Mother. The traffic was lighter than usual, actually."

Her mother nodded at Hallan, who had started up the steps. "I suppose that will be him, then. Hmm. Look at that hair. What an Irish spectacle."

"Actually, he's English, Mother." Vera said this with more confidence than she felt, though his accent seemed to make his origin clear enough. She held out an arm, and Hallan crossed to where they stood. "Mother, may I present Mr. Emil Hallan."

"How do you do?" Vera's mother said.

He removed his hat and nodded. "Mrs. Longacre."

Vera supposed Poppy had given him her parents' names in the car, as Vera realized she had neglected to do so. His propriety took her aback for a few seconds, and she stood silent while she tried to think of what to say next.

"So you're the artist?" Vera's mother continued.

He smiled and inclined his head. "I am."

"Well."

When her mother did not speak further, panic welled in Vera. She turned and waved to Poppy. "Please, do come here. Mother, may I present Poppy Hastings?"

Before Vera's mother could speak, Poppy quickly strode over, her short curls bouncing. "Oh, charmed," Poppy trilled.

Vera's mother's mouth tightened into a small pucker. "How do you do?"

"And those are my children, over there." She pointed briefly to two small girls in matching sailor dresses, then turned back to Vera's mother. "What a lovely home you have."

"Yes, well, the outside, anyway," Vera's mother said in a brisk tone.

"You know, I told Vera that Emil could stay with us, but she said you wouldn't hear of it. Now I see why." Poppy's green eyes widened as she held out her arms to indicate the size of the house.

"Quite," Vera's mother said, and turned to greet Arthur.

"Oh, your mother is lovely," Poppy said under her breath.

"Isn't she?" Vera glanced at Poppy's car, where the driver stood by the door. "I would invite you in for tea, but I'm sure you want to get to your place and get settled before you return for dinner."

"Yes. I guess we should, thank you." Poppy shooed the little girls down the porch, calling good-byes over her shoulder.

Vera's mother walked back to where Vera stood. "Wherever did you find that woman?"

"I didn't find her, Julius Hastings did," Vera said.

"I wonder on what saloon bar she was dancing at the time. 'Charmed' indeed. Are we the only ones left with any manners at all?" Her mother raised her voice back to a normal level and addressed the party. "Let's all go inside, shall we? I'm sure you want to rest and refresh yourselves before tea."

A team of maids in starched white aprons assembled in a row on the porch and led the way into the house. The foyer had a huge vaulted ceiling with a skylight on each side, and warm golden sunshine poured over the lacquered wood floors. On either side, doors led to the dining room and the drawing room, and a sliver of ocean and sand could be seen through the glass doors at the back. Beside the glass doors were the two hallways, one that led to the master suite, and the other to the suite Vera had occupied as a girl, both of which had access to the porch through French doors in the bedroom. Vera and Arthur would take

Vera's childhood suite. Upstairs there were an additional four bedrooms, one of which would be Hallan's. The Litchfields and their boys would occupy the two on the other side of the house for more privacy.

A cold lunch of cheese, fruit, and pâté had been laid out on the table in Vera and Arthur's room under a glass dome, and a card noted that tea would be served at four in the drawing room. Arthur lay down on the small white bed to rest, while Vera changed out of her traveling clothes and into a linen dress. She wished Marguerite were with her, but she had given the girl the weekend off in a fit of generosity. Of course, she knew how to pin her own hair up in the most basic way, but Marguerite had an expert hand. Vera decided against brushing out the style the girl had set that morning, and simply added a silver barrette to the side. She dabbed a wet cloth against her neck, then touched up her powder. Refreshed, she rang the bell for one of the maids and gave instructions for unpacking. She still had a bit of time before tea, so she decided to go for a walk on the beach.

The party at Abide Away was clearly not the only group taking advantage of the last hint of fading summer. As Vera walked, she dodged people in gaily striped bathing costumes and giggling children throwing balls to one another. The sea beyond glinted and glittered in the early afternoon sun, and Vera slipped off her shoes and walked down to the edge to cool her feet. She closed her eyes as the water slipped over her toes, and she briefly entertained the idea of staying on the beach all day, all night, and never going back in to the scene that awaited her.

But her mother would be mortified if she did not return for tea, never mind if she attempted to camp on the beach all night, so Vera turned and walked back toward the house. Abide Away towered over the shoreline, a grim sentry keeping watch over the cheerful bathers under its nose.

Back in her rooms, she found Arthur still asleep. She placed a hand on his shoulder.

"Darling, are you going to tea, or would you like me to wake you for dinner?" she asked.

"Dinner." He rolled over onto his side and pulled the thin blanket up to his ears.

She checked her hair in the mirror and repinned the strands the breeze had blown loose. After another quick dusting of powder on her nose, she went down to the drawing room.

Tea was not the event Vera was expecting. Like Arthur, Hallan and Walter had declined in favor of lunch and rest in their rooms. The Litchfield children were released to play on the lawn, so with only Vera, her mother, and Caroline present, the hour was not unlike the many Vera passed at the Angelus. Since her mother and Caroline were well acquainted, Vera did not have to take the lead. She sat back and watched the beach through the window, occasionally tuning in to what the other two said. Her ears perked up when her mother steered the conversation to the artist.

"What sort of man do you find him to be?" her mother asked.

Caroline's hand rose to her cheek, and she spoke in an almost girlish voice. "Delightful. Fascinating and so intelligent. You're going to love him, Lorna, I'm sure of it."

Vera's mother sipped from a small china cup, painted with violets that matched her eyes. "He seemed well mannered enough earlier. But so many of those artists have a wild streak. You haven't noticed anything like that, have you?"

"Goodness, no," Caroline said. "You'd never know he was in the building, except that he turns up to every occasion we invite him to. Hasn't turned down the first one. So polite." She frowned. "I suppose he has been late a few times, but that's hardly—"

"Vera, dear," her mother said. "If you have something to add to the conversation, please join in. Eavesdropping is not limited to listening through walls, you know."

Vera cleared her throat. "I wouldn't want to interrupt."

"Then don't. But please don't just sit there hovering. Speak if you have something to say."

"I really don't, thank you, Mother."

Her mother drew languid circles in her cup with a tiny spoon. "You have nothing to add about our guest?"

"I don't know much about him myself. Only what Caroline's already told you."

"You don't know where he comes from? Who his family is? Have you spoken to the man at all?"

"I have," Vera said, suppressing a sigh. "He was living in Paris before he came to the city, that's all I know. I'm sure you can find out everything you want to know if you ask him yourself."

"I'm sure I can."

Vera's mother studied her as the grandfather clock ticked away to their left. Under her mother's inquisitive gaze, Vera grew steadily more uncomfortable. Could her mother see something behind her calm demeanor? Did something of her experiences with Hallan show through? At last her mother set her spoon in her saucer and drank the last drops of her tea, satisfied with whatever she had seen.

Vera braced herself for dinner.

« 19 »

Bea didn't bother to knock on Vera's door anymore. She barged in one evening after dinner, a leather portfolio in her hands. Vera sat on the bed, pen poised over a letter to Cliff. She folded it quickly and stuffed it under a textbook, glad that Bea was too enamored with whatever she had in the portfolio to notice.

"Aren't you worried you're going to walk in on me dressing one day?" Vera asked.

"No, you're worried about that." Bea held the portfolio out. "Take a look."

Vera took the folder and opened it. Inside lay two pieces of ivory paper, each with a different letterhead. The typewritten words on each were mostly identical, but the signatures were different.

"'This letter certifies that I give my daughter permission to travel to New Haven, Connecticut, for the weekend of November 22–23. I will arrange for her to be properly chaperoned to and from school,'" Vera read aloud. "Gracious, Bea, this looks exactly like my mother's letterhead. And her signature. How did you manage it?"

Bea sat on the bed. "I swiped a letter from her off your desk. It was murder getting the letters and ink to match up to look like real embossing. I went through three sheets of paper before I stopped punching holes and got the letters raised up the right way."

Vera turned the page to look at the back. "It does look real though."

"I wasn't happy with some of the detail, but . . ." Bea shrugged. "It's good enough. They won't exactly be inspecting it."

Vera wondered at the time and precision it must have required to create the letters. If Bea applied herself half so much to her studies, she'd be at the top of her class. Vera thought of the copy of the *Bon Ton* cover Bea had made for her a month ago. She had an unquestionable skill for reproduction and an eye for detail.

"You're definitely coming now, aren't you?" Bea continued. "Don't tell me I did all that for nothing."

"I suppose I have to," Vera said, a smile breaking out on her face. "This is so exciting."

"Hooray! Oh, we'll have a fabulous time." Bea stood. "I'll send Harry a telegram and tell him when to pick us up. You can give the letter to the dorm matron tonight."

"But won't you need to make an envelope?"

Bea took Vera's letter out of the portfolio and folded it into a square. "There. Tell her your mother put it in with your letter. That way I don't have to try to make it look like it came from the city."

"Genius." Vera shook her head. "But there's so much we haven't thought of. What if Mother telephones while we're away?"

"When has she ever telephoned you at school?"

"That's true. Oh, Bea, I don't know . . ."

Bea held out a hand. "Stop right there. We're not the first to sneak out of the school for a weekend, and we won't be the last. I can promise you that. And when did you ever hear of anyone getting caught? Especially with the precautions we've taken? It will be fine. Try to enjoy it, all right?"

Vera nodded and Bea let herself out, humming as she went. But Vera could not be so cheerful. Doubts wormed their way into her mind as she thought of what would happen if her mother ever found out. To go out for a few hours with college boys was one thing. But two days away left them open to innumerable ways to get caught. And the rules were there for a reason. What if something terrible happened to them? Cliff, Harry, and Gene were harmless, but Vera couldn't count on all the boys at Yale being so benign.

Surely Cliff would keep a protective watch on her, though. Seeing him again would make the risk worth it. Maybe she didn't have to tell him about Arthur during the visit after all. She had thought telling him in person would be preferable, but maybe she should enjoy her time with him and tell him afterward in a well-written letter. Yes, that would give him some fond memories of her, and leave him alone with the news.

Her mother's voice echoed shapeless warnings in Vera's head, years of stern comments piling on top of each other until all she could hear was the disapproving tone. If her mother ever found out that the girls had snuck out to attend a football game with boys she'd never met, Vera would be sunk.

Her stomach squirmed, and she stood up and paced the few feet of floor. She would have to tell Bea that the plan was off. Maybe Bea could find another girl to go. She pictured some other girl with Cliff, crushed into a gang of students cheering the game, and a pang of jealousy went through her. Vera really did want to go. She picked up the folded letter to look again at the impressive "embossing." No one would question the letter's authenticity. She almost believed it was real herself. She set the open letter on the desk, positioning it so she could continue to admire Bea's talents as she returned to her letter to Cliff. Now at least she could give him the good news that he would see her soon.

« 20 »

At seven-thirty p.m. sharp, Vera and Arthur stepped into Abide Away's drawing room for cocktails. Vera had selected a sunny yellow drop-waist dress in honor of the surprise holiday, but she looked odd standing next to Arthur in his staid gray suit. She had managed to talk him into adding a purple pocket square, giving him a little splash of color.

Vera's parents were already in the drawing room, sipping martinis with Caroline and Walter. The Litchfields' children would dine upstairs as, at ten and seven years old, they were still too young to be much company. Just as Vera took her gin and tonic from the waiter, a car door slammed outside, announcing Poppy's arrival. Her nursemaid would be at the cottage with the children while Poppy dined.

She had, at least, restrained herself somewhat in dress. She wore an off-white gown with gold beading and a thin, glittery ribbon in her short curls. A maid showed Poppy into the drawing room, and she thanked Vera's parents for inviting her.

"What a charming room, just charming," she said, admiring a Tiffany lamp. "So restrained. So elegant."

"We find the best things often are, dear," Vera's mother said in an airy tone.

Shoes sounded on the stairs behind Vera, and her pulse quickened. Hallan walked into the drawing room in a raw linen suit, his hair parted and combed as it had been on the night Vera had seen him at the restaurant. She had to admit, he looked very handsome when he made the effort to look presentable.

"Good evening, Mr. Hallan," Vera's mother said, striding across the room to him. "I hope you found your room to your liking?"

"Very much, Mrs. Longacre, thank you. You have a beautiful home here." He smiled. "I'm only sorry I didn't make it to tea."

"Oh, nonsense," Vera's father said, stepping forward. "The tea is for the women anyhow. Would you like a cocktail?"

He slapped a meaty hand on Hallan's back and waved the waiter over. They made an odd pair, the tall, slim, angular artist next to Vera's doughy father. Joseph Longacre was a big man in every way, though there was a bit less of him since his gray hair had thinned on top. But his wide brown eyes had lost none of their intensity as he aged.

"Is the martini how you like it?" he asked Hallan. "Don't be polite about it, now, you can speak up. We'll mix it until it's perfect."

"Just how I like it, truly. So, when did you buy the house, if I may ask?" Hallan said, directing attention away from his drink.

"Buy the house? No, my boy, Lorna and I built this house," Vera's father said. "Got in with the Georgica Association just in time. This was the last of the big lots left."

Poppy sighed. "Julius wanted in with the Georgica Association, but he simply didn't move fast enough. We do love our little cottage, but the beach on this side is without equal."

"The sands are beautiful here," Hallan agreed. "I've never seen sand so white."

"Not a great deal of white sand in England," Vera's mother said, her eyes fixed on Hallan. "Forgive me, I noticed your accent. Tell me, what part of England do you come from?"

Hallan took a sip of his drink before answering. "London."

"I adore London. One of the finest cities in the world. Why, I've been so many times, it's like a second home to me," she said. "Where did you live there?"

"Westminster," he said.

She sniffed. "Lovely area."

"I think so."

A maid stepped in, and Vera realized she was holding her empty drink so tightly her knuckles were white. She could not even recall finishing it. She set the glass on a tray.

"Dinner is served in the dining room," the maid said.

"Thank you, Esther," Vera's mother said. She turned to the rest of the group. "Shall we go in?"

The party went across the hall to the dining room. Vera was not surprised to see the artist's place card to the left of her mother's seat at the head of the table but was dismayed that Arthur was on her mother's right, putting the two men across from each other. Then Vera realized, with some horror, that etiquette would prevent her from being seated by her own husband. She prayed she would be between her father and Walter but saw her own name to the left of Hallan's plate. At least she would be close enough to keep track of her mother's conversation with Hallan even if, like a speeding train, nothing could be done to slow it. She sat, removing her gloves and laying them in her lap. Hallan sat beside her, and his sleeve brushed her arm as he settled in.

Once the party was seated, the waiters began to serve the soup course, a steaming cream chowder with potatoes and flakes of fish. Conversations started in earnest, and Vera's mother turned her attention once more to Hallan.

"So, Westminster, you say? I know a number of families in that neighborhood. I'm surprised I haven't heard the name Hallan before."

"It was only me and my grandmother, and her last name isn't Hallan," he said.

"And what was her name?"

The corners of Hallan's mouth twitched. "You probably haven't heard her name either."

Vera's mother's eyes darkened. "I see. And my daughter tells me you studied art in Paris? Will I have heard of the school?"

"I studied at the Ecole des Beaux-Arts," Hallan said calmly.

Vera drew in a hard breath. "Mother, I told you."

Vera's mother stared at her for a long moment, then lifted her wineglass. "Darling, you haven't touched your soup. Don't you like it?"

"I think it's delicious," Hallan said, lifting a big spoonful.

"So glad to hear it." Vera's mother wrinkled her nose and turned to strike up a conversation with Arthur about his latest building project.

Vera leaned toward Hallan and spoke under her breath. "Don't toy with her like that. She hates it."

"Like mother, like daughter," he said quietly. "You're both so very interested in me."

She rubbed her palms on her skirt, then reached for her drink. "You ought to be more careful with her."

"Do you mean I won't be invited back to the house? Shame. I'd better make the most of tomorrow, then. Are you going out to the beach in the morning?"

"I haven't decided."

"I'd like to join you on the beach, if you go."

"Whatever you like. Caroline will likely let the children go. You'll have someone to play with."

Hallan sucked in a breath through his teeth. "And here I was hoping you'd play with me."

Vera's spoon clattered against her bowl, and heads all around the table swiveled. "So sorry," she said. "Lost my grip."

Poppy frowned. "Are you all right? You look pale."

"Yes, I'm fine." Vera forced a smile.

Arthur pointed at Hallan. "Tell me, when did you move to Paris? I expect after the war, of course. But that wouldn't have given you much time to finish your studies."

Hallan's jaw clenched. "Got there just at the end of the war, actually. Did you serve?"

A smirk flicked across Arthur's lips. "No. Flat feet. And I was needed here. War effort, and all that. You know," Arthur said to Vera's mother, "I haven't even seen any of his paintings. Vera saw some photographs, but I haven't seen anything."

"The photographs were very good. The paintings looked good in them, I mean," Vera said through a constricting throat. Though Arthur had not been part of the conversation between her mother and Hallan, he had certainly been listening to it. He must not have liked what he heard. Now he was gunning for Hallan as well.

"Is that so?" Vera's mother turned to Hallan. "Do tell us about your work."

"Perhaps Vera ought to describe it," Hallan said. "I just paint, but she went to college to study how to talk about art. I'm sure you'd rather hear it in her words. You must love to hear her talk about art."

Arthur waved Vera off before she could speak again. "I'd like to hear how you see what you do. For example, is it real art you do, or that modern sort?"

Hallan locked eyes with him. "I don't know what you mean."

"You know." Arthur offered him a hard, cold smile. "The things they try to pass off as art these days. Even in the paintings, it doesn't look like anything. A bunch of lines, shapes, things a child could do. Is that what you do, or do you paint in the more traditional style?"

"I know not if you would know the difference." Hallan's voice was strained, rigid.

Arthur narrowed his eyes. "You have the oddest way of phrasing things at times, Mr. Hallan, did you know that? Is that the French influence on your speech?"

Vera stood, her gloves dropping out of her lap. "You know, I'm not feeling well after all. Arthur, will you walk me to the room, please?"

"Of course, dear." Arthur held Hallan's gaze a moment longer, though every other eye was on Vera.

As she took Arthur's arm and left the room, she heard Hallan making his apologies as well, attributing his own illness to the extended car travel. She was relieved not to be leaving him alone with her mother, but she could not have stayed for his sake. Besides, she wanted a private word with Arthur.

When the bedroom door closed behind them, she dropped his arm. "Why were you and my mother going after Hallan like that? The whole scene was unpardonably rude, he's a guest."

"He's not my guest. He's a painter, for God's sake, I have no idea why your mother wanted him here in the first place."

"Do you think he's an imposter? If you think that, why not come out and say it?"

"Because I don't care who he is. If he does the work I've hired him for, I'll pay him. If not, I won't. Doesn't matter what the man calls himself. I could hire a vagrant off the street to paint that wall whatever color he likes. If I say he's an artist, those damn biddies in the building will swoon anyway."

"But what if he means to rob someone? What if he's dangerous?"

"Then I'll call the police and have him locked away. Do you honestly think the man is dangerous? Really, Vera, I expected this foolishness from the others, but not from you. Do you really care what he paints on the pool room wall? Or what school he says he's studied at?" Arthur brushed off his shoulder with his hand and straightened his jacket. "Now, if you'll excuse me, I'm going to go finish my dinner."

Before Vera could say anything else, he strode out and slammed the door behind him. She sank onto the bed and took a shaky breath. She had been foolish to encourage Arthur's suspicions, though her questioning likely came more out of anger at herself than any real distrust of Hallan. Of course she did not believe he was dangerous, and his hesitancy to talk about his upbringing could merely be because his family was poor or in disgrace of some kind. Her mother had been playing the game she loved to play with those she did not feel belonged. And Arthur was right. The worst Hallan could do was leave the pool wall unpainted.

But that was not what bothered her most. What bothered her more than any question of his identity or intention was that she could not stop thinking about the look of wonder on his face when he described the portrait in the museum. Or the feel of his breath in her ear as they danced, or the scrawl of the lines on the card he left for her. No, the worst would not be to leave without completing his work. The worst would be if all of it, his captivated gaze at the paintings and at her, turned out to be a lie.

«««●»»»

Vera woke early Saturday morning, but she could not make herself get out of bed right away. Instead, she stared at the whitewashed boards of the ceiling and prayed she had somehow managed to sleep until Monday morning. The wish made her feel like she had when she was a girl, when the driver would drop her off at boarding school in the fall. She always enjoyed greeting her friends, but at night she would lie in bed and wish to be home.

A knock on the door signaled the arrival of the breakfast tray, and she could tarry no longer. She pulled on a dressing gown and opened the door for the maid, who set the tray on the table by the window. Sipping her tea gave Vera a new clarity, and she admitted to herself that she would face the consequences of leaving dinner early the night before. She had pretended to be asleep when Arthur came in around midnight, trailing the smoky smell of her father's favorite cigars. Now, with the morning light dancing in through the curtains, she would have to speak to him.

The bedsprings creaked as he sat up, rubbing his forehead. He turned a blurry gaze on Vera. "Good morning. Feeling better?"

"Lots. Thank you."

"I hope so. Don't want you to have to spend the whole weekend in your room." He stood and crossed to the washbasin.

"No," she said. "But let's not dwell on it, darling. I want us to enjoy our vacation." She smiled. "I thought we might go for a walk in town today. Remember how we used to do that? When we were courting? You'd buy me a Coca-Cola at the soda fountain and tell me about your work."

Arthur patted his face with a cloth. "Yes, that was always nice. Sorry, but I've already agreed to golf with your father today."

"Ah." Her voice faltered ever so slightly. "Just you two?"

"Walter will come, I'm sure."

"And Mr. Hallan? Won't you invite him?"

"We did. Said he doesn't golf. It will be up to you ladies to entertain him," Arthur replied, the corners of his mouth flicking up.

"I see."

As Arthur dressed, Vera toyed with the card announcing tea and dinner times. When he left, she realized she had torn the paper into confetti, and she swept it from the tablecloth into her hand. She rose, deposited the shreds in the bin, and pulled out her own clothes to dress for the day.

Her hand hit a white sporting dress, and inspiration struck. She knew how to occupy Hallan's time, at least for a while, and keep him away from her mother. Croquet. If he did not know how to play, so much the better. Explaining the rules alone would take up plenty of time. Vera rang for the maid and asked that the equipment be set up on the lawn. Whether or not Hallan had any interest in learning or playing croquet mattered very little. He would play if he had any wits about him at all.

Vera pinned her hair into a knot, then tied an orange scarf around her head. She picked up her parasol and headed to the stairs. Caroline stood at the bottom of the stairs, with her two boys.

"Are you coming out to the beach with us?" Caroline asked, her tone a notch too bright.

"Isn't your girl taking the children?" Vera asked.

"She isn't feeling well this morning. And the boys absolutely insist on going down to the shore. So there we are." Caroline gave a strained, toothy smile.

"I see. And have you seen Mr. Hallan this morning? Will he be going with you?"

"He's not golfing with Arthur and Walter?"

"I'm not." Hallan's voice rang through the foyer as he strolled around the corner. "I'd rather not embarrass myself in front of the gentlemen."

"That's fine." Vera stepped toward him so quickly that Hallan's brows leapt. "I'm staying here, too. I was hoping you'd play croquet with me."

"Croquet?" His gaze bounced from Vera to Caroline and back again.

Vera indicated Caroline's basket of supplies. "Caroline is taking the boys to the beach, you see. And since you aren't going to the course, I thought you might like a little fresh air here at the house." Her words tripped over each other in their haste.

"Yes . . . yes, of course. Thank you for thinking of me."

"Wonderful. I've already had the court set up. Have you had breakfast?"

"I have."

Vera nodded toward the door. "You go on, then. I'll be out presently."

Caroline lifted the basket and nudged her boys out the door, calling a good-bye as she left. After a quick backward glance at Vera, Hallan went out, too.

"Where is everyone going?"

Vera turned to find her mother walking in from the hallway leading to her suite. "Good morning, Mother. Caroline's off to the beach with the boys, and Arthur and Daddy left with Walter to go to the club."

"Well, of course I knew where your father was." Her mother's lips pinched together. "They're not taking Mr. Hallan with them, I understand."

"He said he doesn't play golf."

"That doesn't mean he can't go to the club. What sort of man stays at home with the women?"

A few quick answers occurred to Vera, but she kept them to herself. Her mother would not see the humor in any of them. "Don't worry, I'm taking him out for croquet. He'll be entertained."

"I can't say I was worried about his prospects for entertainment, dear. He seems the type to make his own." Vera's mother cocked an eyebrow pointedly, then breezed past Vera. A sigh escaped Vera as her mother turned to go into the library. At least she was not planning to be in the yard with them.

Vera had chosen a flat patch of grass for the course, close enough to the house to see someone at the door, but not within hearing distance. The lawn was still grasshopper green and thick under her feet. Because of the gentle give of the sandy soil, her walk had a slight but perceptible bounce to it that it lacked on the hard marble or wooden floors she usually walked on. Hallan already stood by the court, which a servant had marked off with little cloth flags. He waved as she approached and handed her a mallet.

"Do you know how to play?" she asked.

"Indeed I do." He passed her a mallet and reached into his pocket for a coin. "Shall we flip to see who goes first?"

She nodded. "I'll take heads."

He tossed the coin into the air and slapped it to the back of his hand. Before revealing the coin, he shot her an amused look. "Not too late to change your mind."

Vera pulled a tiny smile, determined to make the next few hours pleasant. "Heads will do fine, thank you."

Hallan lifted his hand. "Heads it is. Would you like to start?"

"I'll go second," she said.

He inclined his head, then walked around her to line up the ball for the first shot. "Last night, did I thank your mother for her invitation to stay this weekend? I can't recall."

Vera batted her mallet back and forth through the grass. "I am sorry about the way my mother and Arthur behaved. If they made you uncomfortable."

"I hope you won't worry about that. I can handle your mother and Arthur." The ball sailed through the first wicket, and Hallan straightened his back. "About our . . . outings together."

"I don't wish to revisit those, if that's quite all right with you."

He sent the second ball rolling past the first one and stepped aside for Vera to line up her shot. "We had a pleasant enough time, didn't we?"

"That isn't the point." Vera tapped her ball with her mallet, but it clanged off the arm of the wicket and skipped to a stop. "And I think you know why it would be inappropriate to have any more similar evenings."

"But I enjoy your company. It seems you enjoy mine. We have interests in common. I don't see what's so inappropriate about any of it."

She turned and cocked her head. "Dancing? Telling me I'm . . . well, saying things you have no business saying? Even you must see what's wrong with that."

He strolled over to his ball near the second wicket. "What, telling you you're beautiful? That's just honesty, Mrs. Bellington."

Vera's face flamed. "I'm afraid if you can't mind your manners, this will be a very short game."

"Why do you always scold me for paying you a compliment? As to the dancing, I thought it was rude to make a lady sit out."

"An unmarried lady, yes."

He tapped the ball and sent it cleanly through the next wicket. "I stand corrected."

Vera crossed her arms. "Will you please promise me that you won't bring those evenings up again?"

"I thought that was only in front of your mother."

"No. I'd rather you didn't talk about them at all."

"If that's what you want," he said.

"It is."

"Then I promise."

They played for a while in silence. The ocean breeze trickled over the lawn, lifting the ends of the scarf in Vera's hair. Hallan took a clear lead, and his smile inched up more with each move toward victory.

A door slammed shut behind them, and she turned to the house. Her mother strode the length of the porch, a maid in tow. Vera prayed her mother would not come out to the lawn and let out a long exhale when her mother stopped at a rocking chair and sat. When Vera turned back, she found Hallan watching her. He dropped his gaze back to the court.

"She didn't want to join us?" he asked, his tone light.

Vera adjusted her scarf. "No, she doesn't care for competition. Of any kind, really."

"She doesn't like games?" He paused. "Odd. But doesn't your father own racehorses?"

"Yes, and she hates them. She'd hate anything with a smell that strong, though. She always complains that Daddy reeks of them."

Hallan turned his attention to his shot once more. "Pardon me for saying so, but it must have been a severe childhood. No games?"

"Well, naturally I was allowed to play games, I was a little girl. She just never liked them herself."

"Ah. And the horses? Were they your only pets?"

"Daddy's horses are hardly pets. They're working animals. Racing is not a game, Mr. Hallan."

A crack sounded as one ball collided with another. "I stand corrected again."

"I did have one pet." Vera glanced back at her mother.

"Did you?"

She smiled. "One summer, a little tabby kitten came nosing around the yard here. I thought she was darling. Had a little white bib, right here." She brushed her chest with her hand. "I convinced the cook to give me some scraps for her, and bit by bit I worked my way closer to her. Near the end of the summer, she let me hold her."

His expression softened. "I must admit, I wouldn't have expected you to be the type to take in strays."

"Oh, I'm sure she was crawling with all manner of nasty things. But to me she looked fluffy and precious. Had a sweet little pink nose." Vera gazed at the garden wall. "When Mother found out, she threw a fit, rightly so. By then it was time to leave anyway. When we came back the next time, the kitten was gone."

He looked into the distance, thinking. "And that was your only pet? The little stray?"

"Well . . . yes."

Hallan stood quiet and still for a few seconds, then shrugged his shoulders and resumed his stance with the mallet. "We had horses, too."

Vera had to clamp her lips together to keep her mouth from falling open. Was Hallan finally willing to talk about himself? "Racehorses?"

"No, riding horses."

"So you can ride, then?"

He shot the ball through the next wicket and laughed. "I can ride a horse, yes."

She wanted to push further, to ask more, but was not sure what direction to go in. "How did you learn to ride?" she asked at last.

"It was easy. Climbed on the back. Kicked the sides." He waved a hand. "Took off. Nothing to it. Made talking to your father yesterday easier, anyhow."

"I'm sure it did. Perhaps this evening my mother will leave you alone, and you'll have another chance to talk to him. He can be more pleasant."

Hallan glanced at her from the corner of his eye before studying the angle of his next shot. "Your father is such an agreeable chap. Not to veer too far from my promise to mind my manners, but it is odd that he doesn't rein your mother in a bit."

Vera gasped out a laugh. "Rein Mother in?"

"I suppose that's not the right expression. Sorry, had horses on my mind." He laughed too. "It does seem like he'd encourage your mother to be a bit friendlier. She's harsh, even to you."

The back of Vera's neck prickled, and she sensed acutely her mother's presence on the porch behind her. "You can't say that. You barely know her. She might be exacting, but that's only because she has high standards. Daddy knows that. If Mother seems harsh, it's only because she wants the best for me. For everyone, really. It's kindly meant, even if it is . . . difficult."

Hallan straightened. "Please, don't mistake me. You said nearly the same thing yourself. Anyway, I only wanted to agree with you that your father is pleasant. I can tell by the way he talks about you that he must have always doted on you."

Vera swallowed. "I'm glad you like talking to Daddy. I'll try to arrange for you to sit nearer to him tonight."

Hallan looked as if he wanted to say something further but stopped himself and leaned on his mallet. "Sorry to say I won't be able to join you this evening. Poppy invited me to dine at her house."

Vera should have been glad at the chance to enjoy her meal without worrying about her mother and Arthur tormenting Hallan, but instead she thought several unpleasant things about Poppy stealing their guest away. "Well. Won't that be nice?"

"That's one thing about Hildegard Hastings. She's always nice. To me, at least." He gestured to the yellow ball. "Your turn."

《《《●》》》

Hallan left in the car Poppy sent for him at around six-thirty. After handily winning the match with Vera, he had thanked her for the afternoon and gone inside to change into dinner clothes. She stayed on the lawn, walking close to the hedges at its perimeter and enjoying the salty breeze. The evening brought with it a brisk reminder that however warm the weekend had been, autumn was on its way soon.

The car carrying Hallan pulled out of the driveway, and the one bearing the other men took its place a few minutes later. Her father and Walter climbed out of the car, both sweaty and red-faced with their hair in wet curls on their foreheads. Arthur emerged, his clothes still as crisp as if he had just dressed. Vera waited until they disappeared into the house before going in.

The group had cocktails in the library, and the men cursed their clubs and scores until the maid came in to announce dinner. Vera was glad to see that her place card was by her father. She thought back to Hallan's suggestion that her father might have a stronger influence over her mother and suppressed a laugh. Her mother could no more be controlled than the weather, and at least Vera's father mitigated the sternness with an occasional dollop of sweetness.

Hallan was right; her father had doted on her all her life, as long as the doting could be done with money. During her childhood, he had been either working or traveling most of the time, so his involvement in decisions about Vera's life had been limited. Her parents' marriage had always seemed more like a business partnership to her. Their roles were carefully delineated, never overlapping, and requiring only a minimum of interaction. Even the house was divided by imaginary lines. The only place her parents' spheres met was the dining room, where they sat at opposite ends of the table to entertain. The arrangement made sense, even if it did not make for a warm home. At least Vera and Arthur slept in the same room from time to time.

If she had been a son, her father might have taken more of an active role in her upbringing. Naturally, he did not have the faintest idea how to prepare a young woman for marriage and householding, let alone for her social obligations. He had resigned himself to his limited role of bringing her trinkets and complimenting her, and Vera was not one to take such kindnesses for granted. Not when she was hard-pressed to find them elsewhere. She took her seat and flashed him a bright smile.

"My dearest." Her father kissed the top of her head before settling into his chair.

"Not your best day on the course, then?" she asked, tilting her head.

He grumbled a couple of unintelligible words under his breath.

"Wouldn't be so bad if that husband of yours didn't show us up every time. I don't know who decided the wretched game should be played by civilized men in the first place."

Arthur, seated at the other end of the table by Vera's mother, leaned over. "Come now, you and Walter did very well for yourselves." He turned to the other diners. "Good bit of wind out there today, made things difficult."

Vera's father only snorted in response. Servants placed bowls of a pale green cream soup in front of each person. Vera's father wrinkled his nose and spoke under his breath to her.

"And now cream of celery? Will the torture never end?"

Vera patted his arm. "Poor Daddy."

"Tell me about your day, lovely. Distract me." He took a drink of his wine. "Did you dance about while little birds sang only for you?"

"Sorry to tell you, that's not how it happened," she said.

"Then I hope you went to the shops and spent all your husband's money. If he's penniless, you can come back home with us where you belong."

"No, no shops today."

"Shame, shame." He winked. "There's always tomorrow."

"I did get some air today. I played croquet out on the lawn."

"All by yourself? Don't tell me your mother played."

She hesitated. "No, I invited Mr. Hallan to play."

"Ah, the artist." He sat back in his chair. "Good fellow. I like a man who'll look you in the eye when he's talking to you."

"Did he tell you he rides?"

"He did. Surprised he knew so much about horses. Said his brother worked with them."

Vera feigned interest in her glass. "Is that right? Which brother, did he say?"

Her father blinked. "Well, he's only got the one, hasn't he?"

"Of course." A thousand questions scrambled to the front of her mind, but she did not ask. Her father would think it odd he knew more than she did, especially since he had only spoken with Hallan for a short while the previous afternoon. But, for some reason, the artist had confided these details in her father when he would talk to no one else. A brother; what else had he revealed?

"I'd have liked to hear more about his painting," her father continued. "But of course your mother had him at the odd end of the table. A man ought to be able to sit where he likes, damn the rules."

"He told you about the painting?" Vera could have bitten her tongue.

"Not the mural, if that's what you're after. Says it's supposed to be a secret. Ah, thank you." Her father inclined his head at the servant who removed the green soup, and rubbed his hands together at the plate of prawns that replaced them. "Smart of him, I'd say."

"And why would you say that?"

"Because you know very well if he even gave a hint, everyone in that building of yours would feel the need to offer their opinion of his plan. Better to be master of your own house." Her father nudged her. "Or master of your own pool room, as the case may be."

Vera did not answer right away. Her father's instincts had proven far sharper than her own; the potential for interference had to be the reason for Hallan's secrecy. She had let her imagination run wild once again. She forced a gulp of her wine down her tight throat.

"I'm sure you'll have a chance to speak with him again tomorrow at Mother's picnic," she said, when she trusted her voice again.

"Wonderful," her father said. "I've got a new mare I wanted to tell him about." He turned to his left. "I'm sorry, Caroline, I've neglected you. How was the water today?"

Vera gazed up the table at where her mother and Arthur sat, leaning toward one another in intense conversation. If her father engaged Hallan in conversation before her mother or Arthur had a chance to pounce, then they might survive the weekend. She brushed away the thought that she ought to invite Hallan to join her on the beach the next day. Playing croquet had been a kindness on her part. If he did not know to avoid her mother and Arthur by now, then Vera certainly could not be expected to save him. He seemed to think he could handle the two of them just fine anyway. She deserved a few moments to herself. Her mind had been spinning since she arrived, and she needed a break from all of them.

« 21 »

Bea and Vera left Yale Field in a swell of students, all cheering and jostling. It didn't seem to matter to any of them that Yale had lost. Even staid Cliff wore a big grin. She couldn't help but admire how it lit up his normally solemn face. His letters had revealed depths of feeling and sentiment that his stoic expression hid the last time they met.

The boys picked them up in town, to hide from any prying eyes at Vassar the fact that there was no proper chaperone in the car. Vera had once again climbed into the backseat with Cliff and Gene, praying nothing about her greetings to Cliff betrayed their more familiar relationship. She was surprised to find she felt totally at ease with him, despite only having met him in person once before. To Vera's further relief, Bea seemed to suspect nothing. The ride to New Haven was similar to their first outing as a group: Bea and Harry teased each other, Gene peppered Vera with questions, and Cliff sat back against the seat, occasionally offering a word or two. Except this time, when Vera rested her hand on the seat, Cliff laid his beside hers. The brush of his fingers sent a tingle through her limbs that lasted far longer than the touch. As he helped her out of the car, he whispered how glad he was to see her. She nodded an agreement, supposing he had kept his end of the correspondence secret from his friends, too.

The game itself had mostly mystified Vera, despite Gene's efforts to explain it to her. She gave up guessing at what the action on the field meant and resigned herself to yelling when the others did, which made for a surprisingly good time. In fact, everything about the game appealed to her. The muddy smell that rose up from the field as the players kicked up hunks of earth. The way some of the boys in the stands tore their hats from their heads and shouted at the players, as though they could be heard at such a distance. Most of all, the way the whole crowd could be united in emotion, cheering one minute, groaning the next. Vera had never before felt so connected to so many people at once.

Vera grabbed Bea's arm. "What's next?"

"I don't know," Bea shouted above the din. "Harry?"

"There's a dance hall in town. A bunch of people are going. What do you think?" he asked.

"Ooh, I saw that place when we were coming in," Vera said. "It's just down the road from the boardinghouse."

"Let's go," Bea said.

The five of them trooped off to Harry's car and headed for town. Gene, Cliff, and Vera took the backseat again, and Bea hopped into the front with Harry.

Gene leaned over Cliff. "Do you dance, Vera?"

"Of course she dances," Bea said. "She probably came into the world with a full dance card."

"Thank you, Bea." Vera rolled her eyes. "Yes, Gene, I love to dance."

"Then I hope you'll save one for me," he said.

"And me," Cliff said.

Her face flushed and she was grateful for the darkness of twilight. "Of course. I'd love to dance with you both."

"Who's going to dance with me while all this is going on?" Bea asked.

"I'll dance with you, if it will make you be quiet," Harry said.

Bea slapped his shoulder. "I can't dance with you. You're practically my brother."

"Then forget I said it," he replied. "I was trying to be nice, you know."

"We'll dance with you, too," Gene said, looking as if his birthday had come early.

Harry pulled up in front of the dance hall, and they all piled out of the car. The two-story building had big plaster columns in front of a brick portico, which Vera guessed was a stab at elegance. She took the arm Cliff offered, hoping she looked appropriately nonchalant, and followed the other three through the doors.

Inside, the hall bounced with the excitement of the people crowded between the pink walls. A man played a jangling piano tune on a stage, and couples ringed him in various states of closeness.

"Say, Cliff, hope you don't mind if I claim the first dance," Gene said, extending a hand to Vera.

"You ought to ask Vera before you ask me," Cliff said.

A bright flush climbed Gene's neck. "Oh. Oh, right. Is that okay with you, Vera?"

She nodded.

"I get second," Cliff said, with a hint of a smile.

Vera took Gene's hand, and they made their way to where the other couples gathered. Over Gene's shoulder, Vera saw Bea and Cliff join them. At first, she felt sorry Harry was left out, until she saw him chatting with a tall blonde at the entrance. She giggled. How could she have worried about someone that confident?

Gene was no elegant dancer, but what he lacked in talent, he made up for in sheer concentrated effort. His face a stern mask, he guided Vera around the floor in such strict adherence to the steps, she wondered if he had written the official dance manual. When the song changed, she smiled and thanked him. Cliff quickly took his place, and Bea led Gene off to dance. Despite the people around them, something about the way Cliff looked down at her made Vera feel like the two of them were very much alone.

"You look beautiful, you know that?" he said. For the first time she'd heard, he had a slight waver in his voice.

"Th-thank you," she said. "I don't really feel dressed for dancing, this is such an old skirt—"

"Well, it's beautiful on you." He dropped his gaze to their feet.

"That's so kind of you. Really."

He met her eyes again. "Can we step off to the side? Just for a second. I've been hoping for a chance to talk to you in private."

She followed him to the edge of the room. Up close, she could see that the building was shabbier than it seemed at first. The walls had cracks and chips where enthusiastic dancers had bumped against them. With her attention focused on a chink of wood grain, Vera didn't notice right away that Cliff was leaning down. His face was within an inch of hers when she startled and jumped back.

"I'm sorry," he said. "I shouldn't spring something like that on you." He ran a hand through his red waves.

"It's all right." She placed a hand on his. "I think you're wonderful, I really do. Your letters . . . I've so enjoyed getting to know you." She hesitated. *Now or never*, she thought. "It's . . . there's something I haven't told you."

His face went slack. "Oh. You've already got a beau, don't you? Sure you do. Stupid to think a girl like you wouldn't."

She swallowed hard. Maybe she ought to lie. If she said her relationship with Arthur wasn't serious, Cliff could kiss her. What would one little kiss really hurt anyway? But she knew if she allowed a kiss, she'd start to think of him as a real possibility, a real choice. He would want her to be his girl, and she would want to say yes. She summoned the courage to be honest. "I do have a beau. Practically a fiancé."

He sighed, turning his gaze to the wall. "I should have known. I didn't mean to put you on the spot." He started to walk back, but she held his arm.

"If I didn't have a beau, it might be different," she said. "I wish I didn't, I wish it didn't have to be like this."

His expression brightened. "Then it doesn't, does it? If he's not your fiancé yet, you still have a choice. You haven't said yes to him." Cliff took Vera's hand. "You could say yes to me."

She looked at Bea, who was oblivious, laughing through a dance with Gene. "We shouldn't talk like this. Not in front of everyone."

He indicated a side door near them. "Come on. We'll go outside."

They stepped into the icy night air. Vera shivered, and Cliff took off his jacket. "I wish I hadn't checked my coat," he said.

"Won't you be cold?" she asked.

"Better than you being cold."

Her stomach dipped. She wanted to go back in. Whatever he was going to say was only going to complicate her plans, she was sure of it. Before she could speak, Cliff began talking with a boyish enthusiasm she'd never heard from him.

"Think of it, Vera. We could see the whole world. Did you read the *National Geographic* article I sent you? About India? The spices, the music, the colors." He caught himself and looked her in the eye. "I want to share it with you. Only you."

"Why me?" Her voice took on an unflattering begging tone.

"Why you?" He pulled back. "Why anyone else? You're beautiful—"

"So you want to have me to look at, is that it?" She knew she was antagonizing him, though she didn't want to, not really. She wanted to make turning him down easier.

His eyes widened. "No! You're smart, and the way you talk about art . . . the way you talk about what you study, about the world. I've read your letters a hundred times each. I want to see the world through your eyes. More than that—I want to give you the world. Not jewelry or furs or whatever that guy is promising you. He's a rich guy, right? I can give you more, because I can give you what you want. You deserve more. You deserve adventure." He stopped, slightly out of breath.

Vera wanted to tell him he was wrong, but her throat tightened on the words. Though she had never imagined a life of travel and adventure before Cliff and his wonderful letters, now a vision of that kind of future began to take shape in her mind. He was right. Jewelry and furs wouldn't be enough for her now, and Arthur couldn't give her more than those empty status symbols. He probably couldn't even conceive of offering a woman the world.

176 « AMBER BROCK

Even if Cliff wasn't wrong, letting go of all her responsibilities right there on the street in New Haven wasn't an option. She knew that much. She couldn't just fall into his arms and promise him everything, no matter how much she may have wanted to. Her heart sank a little at the sobering thought that he was young and infatuated. His promises might only be temporary, and she still had a real future to safeguard.

"How could you possibly know what I want?" Vera said at last, her words as weak as she felt.

Cliff gripped her arms, pulling her close. "If you tell me you love him, I'll leave you alone. I promise."

"I don't love him," she said. "But I have to accept him."

He moved a hand slowly down her arm. He traced her bare fingers, then entwined his fingers with hers. His rough palm pressed against hers, and fire raced through her. She thought of Arthur taking her hand to help her out of his car, the only real contact they'd ever had. Arthur's touch was a duty, a requirement, like everything else about his behavior toward her. Even his proposal was a necessary next step. Cliff's hand on hers was an embrace.

"I could be the one, couldn't I?" he asked quietly. "Not tomorrow, no. When I make something of myself. I'll be worthy of you."

"You're worthy of me now." She squeezed his hand. Though the words surprised her as she said them, she knew they were true. His name and background might make him unworthy to someone like her mother, but his heart made him the kind of man any woman would be lucky to call hers.

"Then you'll think about it? Saying no to him? Waiting for me?"

A giddy laugh burst out of her. "I will. I will think about it."

She knew she would. Even if she didn't have so much to consider, she would probably never be able to stop thinking about this moment, this feeling.

He slid his arms around her waist and lifted her off the ground. "You won't be sorry. You won't. I'll do everything to make sure of it."

When he set her back down, he lifted her chin with his fingertips.

He leaned in. For just a moment, Vera nearly let herself lean in, too. Her better judgment blared out a protest in her head, louder than the voice telling her to give in. Before his lips met hers, she pulled away. She expected him to look hurt or disappointed. Instead, he nodded. He took her hand again and pressed his lips against the back of it. That would have to be enough for both of them. For now.

She fanned herself, stepping away. Despite the cold, her face blazed. Her cheeks ached from a wide smile she couldn't suppress, and she could still feel where his warm lips had touched her hand. "We can't tell anyone. Please. Not yet."

"No, not until you're ready." His toothy grin mirrored her own. He would likely have agreed to anything at that moment.

"We'd better get back inside. If Bea notices we're out here alone, she'll never let me forget it. Oh!" She pulled off his jacket and handed it back to him. "Almost forgot."

He let go of her hand to put his jacket back on. She smoothed her hair, and they snuck back in the door together. As soon as they neared the dance floor, he swept her into his arms and spun her, both of them dizzy with their shared secret.

The five of them danced until Vera was ready to collapse from exhaustion. She didn't realize until she got outside that she'd gone hoarse from shouting over the music and laughing. The boys walked them to the boardinghouse, the five of them one joyful, messy unit on the frozen streets.

Vera caught Bea's eye. They beamed at each other, but an unexpected lump rose in Vera's throat. In only a few months, she had made more happy memories with Bea than with almost any other person in her life, her family included. She had finally found people who cared about her and loved her for who she was, not her name or connections. Certainly Cliff had made that clear, but if Vera had never met Bea, none of what they'd shared would have been hers. Most of all, Bea had given her a certain kind of freedom. A freedom Vera feared she would never know again if she married Arthur.

« 22 »

After breakfast on Sunday morning, Vera had a maid pack a basket with a lunch and blankets to take out to the beach. She dressed in her bathing suit and robe and carried her parasol down to the sand. The Litchfield boys, with their governess, Pauline, accompanied her. Though they laid their blankets a few feet from hers, the boys immediately ran to the water. Pauline trudged after them, leaving Vera on her own.

She watched the boys kick sprays of water at each other and laughed a little under her breath at their puppyish energy. Pauline, eyes pinched against the brightness of the sun, looked less enthralled. She yawned audibly. In Vera's childhood, she had had two governesses, both selected by her mother for their solemn demeanor and unforgiving adherence to the rules. Perhaps this, in addition to her distant husband, had fed Vera's reluctance to have children. Why become a mother and then hand her children off to someone else? Someone who might be loving and concerned, but who might be as indifferent as Pauline was to the Litchfield boys? Yet someone of her position in society would be expected to hire help. Mothering alone was unthinkable. So Vera continued to put it off, in hopes of a solution that was unlikely to come.

Vera had just turned her attention from the boys to her *McClure's* magazine when a basket dropped into the soft sand beside hers. She squinted into the sun to see Hallan standing above her, wearing a black-and-white-striped bathing costume. Why had she actually expected to have a few moments to herself?

"May I join you?" he asked.

She turned back to her magazine. "If you like."

He sat on the sand near her feet. "Lovely weather today."

"Don't you need a blanket to sit on?"

"I've got one in the basket," he said. "The sand feels good, though. Warm."

"Mmm."

"Are you going in the water?" he asked.

"I doubt it." Her robe slipped from her knee, and she pulled it back up to cover her leg.

"What's the fun of going to the beach if you're not going to swim?"

She set the magazine in her lap. "Usually it's very peaceful. Quiet. Nice to read in the sun."

"But you're not in the sun." He pointed to her parasol. "Afraid you'll melt?"

"Will we ever have a conversation where you don't tease me, Mr. Hallan?"

He shook his head. "I expect not."

After a pause, she inhaled deeply. "I hope it hasn't been too unpleasant a trip. I know you were glad to escape another evening with my mother and her questions. To say nothing of Arthur."

"The things they asked me ... they're nothing you haven't asked me."

"That's true. But I hope I've been a little kinder, anyhow."

"At times you are."

She blushed, thinking of their encounters, both at the Angelus and in the city. Had she said anything friendly to him, after he saved her from eating alone? When he took her dancing? She had at least complimented his paintings. She resolved to be less prickly with him. He did love to tease her, but it was harmless, really. Why should she be so offended that he paid her some attention? She certainly did not get enough from her husband.

As if reading her thoughts, Hallan said, "How did you end up married to someone like Arthur? I hope you'll forgive me for saying so, but he doesn't seem like—he's not someone I can picture courting a pretty young girl."

Vera stared at her hands in her lap, taken aback by the question. "We met here, actually."

"On the beach? Arthur in a bathing suit, that's even more difficult to imagine."

She smiled. "No, not on the beach. My father worked with him on some property investments. Father invited him to stay one weekend. Probably with the hope that he would take some interest in me."

"And he did."

"Yes. He was married before, but she died after only a few years." She sighed. "I am a second wife."

"That explains the age difference."

"He visited on the weekends that summer and asked me to marry him later that year." She looked out at the waves. "It all seems so very fast now."

Hallan ran his fingers through the sand. "So, did you come here every summer when you were a child?"

"I did."

"Brothers? Sisters?"

"No, only me."

"Sounds a bit lonely."

They watched as the Litchfield boys splashed in a tide pool, calling to each other about the shells they found. The governess stood ankle deep in the water. A crowd of young people walked down the beach, bumping into one another and laughing. An ache swelled in her chest. She looked at Hallan's profile, the graceful angles of his face. "It can be lonely. Yes."

"I'm going for a swim," Hallan said finally. He stood and offered Vera a sandy hand. "Would you like to go?"

"I shouldn't. I don't have my bathing cap."

"So your hair will get wet." He squinted at her. "Is this like the roof? Do you need some liquid encouragement? I'm afraid I left my flask in my room."

She stood. "If I look a mess at the picnic this afternoon, I blame you."

He laughed and started for the water. After a slight hesitation, she slipped off her robe and followed. All the fuss over short skirts, and she never hesitated for a moment to wear a bathing suit that barely covered her knees. She might as well be in her undergarments. But everyone else on the shore was dressed the same, even the Litchfields' governess. And it was the same suit she had worn for years, without concern. So why did she feel so exposed now?

The water hit her legs and stung with an unexpected coolness. Hallan waded in to his waist, then turned to wave her closer.

"You're going to have to come a little farther out if you want to actually swim," he said.

"It's cold," she cried. "I'm going back."

He struggled back through the water to where she stood and took her hand. "You'll get used to it. Come on."

They waded together out into the ocean, until the water hit their chests. Vera feared she might freeze, as the temperature was far colder than she expected. But she did not want to turn back, not really. She did not want to let go of Hallan's hand.

"It really is too cold. Look at me, are my lips blue?" she asked with a laugh.

He moved closer, inspecting her face with a mock-serious look. "Not yet. But I'll be happy to keep an eye on them for you."

She shivered. He stood only a few inches away, too close. "Let's go back. We can warm up in the sun."

He pulled the hand he held from the water and rubbed it in both of his. Still staring at her fingers, he spoke slowly and deliberately. "You'll be all right. I won't let you freeze."

The hair on her arms rose. She opened her mouth to speak, but could not think what to say. A voice in her head begged her to wrap her arms around him, to kiss the little droplets of salt water from his parted lips. He moved another step closer, but she turned and yanked her hand from his.

"I'm sorry, I have to get out," she called over her shoulder.

"Wait." He splashed behind her, fighting his way through the water. "Wait, is something wrong?"

She went back to her chair and flung on her robe, then rolled the blanket and tossed it in the basket. Hallan caught up to her and stood behind her.

"I'm sorry," she said breathlessly. "I need to get back, you do, too. If we're late for the picnic, Mother will be beside herself."

"I thought it wasn't until two." He picked his watch up from his basket. "It's only eleven."

"Yes, but I've got to change, and—"

He laid a hand on her forearm. "Vera, don't—"

"Please." She looked into his sea-blue eyes, entreating him to understand, hoping he would not make her say it. "Please. Excuse me."

He nodded, and withdrew his hand. "Of course. If you need to go."

"I do."

She fumbled through the rest of packing the basket, grabbed the parasol, and trudged back up to the house. Her heart sank at the thought of what she had been tempted to do. Where had the notion to kiss him come from? She recalled the feeling she had when he first arrived, of the hand on her shoulder holding her back. The sensation had faded so gradually. She only noticed there, on the beach, that it was completely gone.

《《《 ● 》》》

At the house, Vera bathed and put on a mint-green sundress for the picnic. By the time she went out into the garden, the others were already assembled, along with Poppy and her two girls. The little ones ran off to play on the lawn, leaving the adults sitting in a circle in weather-beaten wicker chairs.

Vera noted that Hallan had taken care to choose a seat near her father, away from her mother and Arthur. Of course, that meant Poppy fell into the seat on Hallan's other side and began chattering away. Vera avoided his eyes and found a chair on the other side of the circle. She distracted herself by telling Caroline about the morning at the beach, reporting the boys' excitement at finding a whole conch shell.

A maid poured lemonade and passed watercress sandwiches, but the heat of the day caught up to Vera despite the cool food and drink. Vera's mother engaged Caroline in conversation, leaving Vera on her own. She excused herself to go inside under the pretense of getting her fan. She wanted to get out of the heat, but also to spare herself the possibility of Hallan approaching her. As she walked toward the house, her mother called after her to ask one of the cooks to send out tea.

She found the fan on her dressing table, but lingered a moment, wiping her face down with a wet cloth. After reapplying her powder, she headed back down the hall toward the kitchen to inquire about the tea. Hushed voices coming from an alcove near the library caught her attention. Against her better judgment, she crept down the side hall, careful to stay close to the wall. A man and a woman spoke in low tones. Were Caroline and Walter having a disagreement? No, it was not their voices.

"... terribly romantic. Julius hasn't looked my way in years, but you ... I'm drawn to you ... last night ... so hard to resist ..." Poppy, simpering and girlish.

Vera gritted her teeth. The man had to be Hallan. So, he was flinging himself at all the women in the building, in the hopes that at least one would succumb to his advances? She leaned in but could not hear his response. Hoping their interlude had the two of them focused on each other, she peeked around the corner. Poppy had her arms around his neck, and her cheek was flushed as she gazed into his eyes. Hallan's back was to Vera, but she had seen enough to understand exactly what was going on.

She stormed back down the hall toward her room, where she sat for a few moments to allow her heartbeat to slow. Poppy's interest in Hallan had been plain from the beginning. Why should she be surprised that Poppy would take advantage of the time away from the Angelus to make her move? Vera was more surprised that Hallan would actually take an interest in someone so vapid.

The sound of her steps in the hallway must have alerted them. By the time she got back to the garden, they had both returned. Hallan's friendly look melted at the sight of her expression.

Vera's mother looked up. "Is the tea coming?"

"Oh. Oh, silly me. I went for my fan and completely forgot to ask." Vera held up the fan halfheartedly. "I'll go right back in, Mother."

Her mother gave her a strange look, but nodded.

Hallan stood. "I'll go with you."

"That's not necessary," Vera said, in a stiff, airless tone. "I can manage."

She turned down the garden path. Despite her protests, Hallan followed close behind. She increased her pace, and he jogged up and caught her arm.

"What is wrong with you today?" he asked.

She pulled her arm from his grip and walked through the side door into the house. "Nothing at all. If you'll excuse me, I have to see that the tea is brought out."

He followed, taking off his hat. "Everyone's hot. No one wants tea. Will you please tell me what's going on?"

"I didn't expect you to take such an interest in conversation with Poppy Hastings, that's all. I've never known her to have much of note to say. I can only imagine how much talking you did at her house last night."

He frowned and glanced down the hall. "What—do you mean earlier? Did you see us in the house?"

She leaned in and lowered her voice to a hiss. "Yes, I saw it. And you really should try harder to hide your indiscretions. I don't know what it's like wherever you come from, but here gentlemen discourage the affections of married ladies. No matter how insistent the lady."

His eyes widened. At first, Vera thought he had the good sense to be ashamed of what he had done, but then his features relaxed.

"You thought we were . . ." He shook his head. "Vera, I'm not interested in Poppy Hastings. She threw herself at me."

Vera lifted her chin. "I'd rather not know the details."

He gazed at her, as if trying to work out a riddle. "I . . . I don't believe it. You're jealous."

"Don't be absurd. What's there to be jealous of? She's indecent."

"You are jealous. You don't like seeing me with another woman."

"That's enough. Why should I care what you do?"

A maid turned down the hall toward them, and Hallan pulled Vera into the study. He searched her face with his eyes. "Do you think I could ever feel for Poppy Hastings what I feel for you?"

Vera's face burned and she looked at the floor. She wrapped her arms around her waist, as if she could protect herself outwardly from what was happening in her mind. "You shouldn't say that sort of thing, you sound ridiculous."

"Do I?" He lifted her chin with his fingertips. "But it's true."

"Please. Please, don't say those things."

"Why not?"

She exhaled hard. When she spoke, she could barely hear herself. "Because . . . because I'll begin to believe you."

"Good." He placed a hand on her neck and pulled her close. Just before his lips met hers, he paused, eyes closed, and sighed. His breath on her lips sent a jolt through her whole body, and she kissed him, unable to hold back. His mouth still tasted of the sweet sting of lemonade. She let herself enjoy the feel of his fingers on the back of her neck, his chest pressed against hers, the bright scent of his shaving lotion.

A noise in the hall brought her back to her senses, and she backed away. Without another look at him, she turned and ran back to her room. She locked the door behind her and sat on the bed. Her heart pounded in her temples. What had she done? What if someone had seen?

She had given in. Worse than that, everything about giving in felt right. His lips fit hers, and his touch on her skin had ignited a fire deep within her. Kissing him felt so natural, as if her life had been quietly building to that moment. As if she had been waiting.

She could not see Hallan again. She did not want to see what "after" looked like. If he might be pleased with himself, or disappointed, or bored. The rest of the day would have to be spent in her room. She rang for a maid to send the message to her mother that she would take her dinner there. Her mother would certainly take issue with Vera's odd behavior, but who could worry about that? Once they got back to the Angelus, she would have to tell him that she could not see him anymore. For the moment, she needed the door between them.

When they departed Abide Away early the next morning, Vera was grateful once more that Hallan was traveling in Poppy's car. He left with only a quick glance in Vera's direction. His expression was stormy, and she could only imagine how dinner had gone the night before without her there. She hoped he had the good sense to take his meal in his room. Though surely at least part of the cause of his expression was her disappearing act after their kiss.

She could not even think about that moment of carelessness without sinking into misery. The kiss played out in her mind, over and over again. She tried to will it away, but the memory only grew stronger. How could she make such a mistake? To Hallan she was a plaything, something to be won. He could not possibly care for her, not really.

Arthur asked how she was feeling, but his show of interest in her absence from dinner the night before was easily deflected, and then he read the paper the whole ride back. Vera was left to stare out the window, watching the city quietly rise in the distance. She was surprised Arthur had stayed the whole weekend, rather than going back on Sunday afternoon. Then again, he always seemed to enjoy spending time at Abide Away. She suspected he enjoyed the prospect of Vera inheriting it one day more than anything, as he often mentioned owning a house at the shore but never seemed keen to look into buying one. Another thing for him to be master of, another possession that would secure his position. As they neared the Angelus, the buildings towered over them once more, and she had the unsettling feeling that, instead of standing tall, they were curving above her, threatening collapse.

They arrived at the apartment, and Arthur promptly changed out of his traveling clothes and dressed for work. Vera sat on the bed, half watching, wondering if he would even care what she had done. If she told him, right then, would he even listen? He did not want her; why should he worry that anyone else might? Her husband had never expressed any interest in how she occupied herself during those nights alone. He only ever seemed to care that she looked the part of the society wife in public, not whether she acted it in private.

Vera went downstairs after Arthur left. She was not really concerned that Arthur might find out. What weighed on her now was the need to be sure that Hallan did not count his conquest of her as a victory. She had to make clear to Hallan as soon as possible that he should maintain a respectful distance for the rest of his time at the Angelus. She paced in the library, choosing her words, but she knew she ought not delay too long.

On the elevator down to 2A, her stomach roiled. Not even her best, most practiced cool demeanor would stay in place. When he opened the door, she thought she might have to lean against the wall for support.

His whole body tensed when he saw her. "Vera. Come in, please."

She followed him into the drawing room, where he sat beside her on the couch.

"Mr. Hallan—"

"You're still calling me that? You can call me Emil," he said.

She shook her head. "I don't think that would be appropriate, given the circumstances."

"Given the circumstances? You all really are a strange lot, you know that? You can kiss me, but you can't call me by my first name?"

She glanced around, half by instinct. Still, she would not want his servants hearing and spreading it to any others in the building. "Please. Don't talk about that."

He dropped his eyes. "I understand. In fact, I'm glad you came. I was going to call on you if you hadn't come down."

"I really don't mean to lead you on. I shouldn't have done that. And it can never happen again."

"I know."

Vera had not expected that. "You know what?"

Hallan stood, running a hand through his hair, then began again. "I know," he said. "I was wrong to pursue you the way I did, and I offer my apologies."

Her heart twitched. "Is this about Poppy?"

He laughed dryly. "No, this is certainly not about Poppy. After what happened . . ." He rubbed his forehead. "It was what I wanted. But I understand, you are a married woman, there are certain expectations. This society you're part of. You can't just dally with any poor old sap who falls for you. You told me I was inappropriate, many times. I couldn't make myself listen. I couldn't bear the thought of not being near you, not having a chance. But I was wrong, and I'm sorry."

She stared at him. Why was he being so serious, not teasing her? He was not proud of some victory. This was nothing like the man who asked her to dance or flirted at parties. This was the man she met in the art museum. The one who gave her a book of poetry. She did not know how to respond. Fortunately, he continued in the silence.

"So, there it is. I'll leave you alone, I promise. No more silliness." He breathed deeply. "I could see it in your eyes, the torment. I don't want to put you through that."

Vera stood and took a few slow steps toward him. "You would do that? You'll leave me be, you won't pursue me anymore?"

"I will. I know that's what you want, what you need, so I will."

She covered her mouth, closing her eyes briefly. "I can't believe it."

"Is something else wrong?" he asked.

She opened her eyes. "This isn't just a game to you. I thought—I thought you were only . . . only playing."

He grazed her cheek with his fingertips. "No."

"You truly care. You care what I want, what I need."

"I do."

The dam burst inside her, all of the loneliness and hunger spilling out and flooding her chest. She wrapped her arms around his shoulders and kissed him, loosing the fire running through her veins. He slid his arms around her waist, but leaned back.

"But I thought you couldn't," he said. "I thought you would want—"

"I want you," she said.

His eyes lit up. "Then you have me."

He kissed her neck, then her collarbone, as she closed her eyes once more. A long, shaky sigh escaped her at the feel of his mouth on her skin. She slid her hands under his jacket, pushing it off his shoulders.

"Is anyone home?" she asked.

"Anna doesn't come back until this afternoon. Michael is out," Hallan said. He looked over his shoulder to the hall, then back to her. She nodded. He led her to the bedroom, and shut the door behind them.

She fumbled to undo the buttons on his shirt, but he pulled it off over his head. A sudden nervousness came over her as he stepped around behind her and started unbuttoning her dress. It had been a long while, too long, since a man had seen her undressed. What if he decided when he saw her that he did not want her?

He kissed the back of her neck, and her shoulders relaxed. She let the dress fall to the floor, and stood in her slip and stockings. Thin as she was naturally, she had no need of the binding undergarments other women used to achieve a boyish slenderness.

He touched the loops and curls of her pinned hair. "You always wear it up," he said softly. "Is it very long?"

"Yes. Not terribly fashionable."

He sat on the bed, and she sat beside him. He turned her so he could examine her hair once more.

"How many pins does it take to keep it like that?" he asked.

She laughed softly. "Quite a few."

He leaned in. "Ah. There's one." He gently worked the pin out of her hair, and a curl dropped to her shoulder.

"Don't take it all down." She tried to turn to look at him, but he moved her back into place.

"I want to see how it looks. I imagine it's beautiful. Why do you always wear it up?"

"Only little girls wear their hair down," she said.

"We'll have to keep this between us, then."

He found another pin, and another. She smiled as lock after lock fell across her shoulder and back. Finally, it was all loose, in a thick curtain that hung to her waist. He combed through it with his fingers.

"It's glorious." He pushed the hair aside and kissed her neck. "You're so beautiful, Vera."

She turned to him. "It's been a long time since anyone but you said that to me."

"Then I'll say it every hour, every minute to make up for their mistakes." His lips met hers again, and he pushed the slip's strap from her shoulder. He grazed her now-bare breast with his palm, and a shiver ran up her back.

Her need for him took over, and she took off the slip. He undressed, and they lay down. She reached to cover herself with the blanket, but he pushed it away, and admired her pale, slender form, running his hand over her breast, her stomach, and to the inside of her thigh.

"Are you sure this is what you want?" he breathed.

"More than anything," she said.

He shifted so that he was between her legs, and entered her. The sensation was nearly foreign, and she let out a gasp that turned into a moan. His hair grazed her cheek as they rocked together. The delight of him inside her swelled, expanded, and grew until she could not contain it. Her excitement escaped her as she cried out, louder and louder, and he answered her with astounded groans of his own.

This is right, she thought, *this is right and can never be wrong*.

He whispered in her ear, shapeless words without meaning. They slowed, then stopped, and he rested his head on her shoulder. At last, he moved back over to lie beside her, his hand still idly stroking her cheek.

She laughed, that same sound she had made on the rooftop, from so deep within her she had not known it was still there. He sat up on one elbow.

"I hope nothing is funny," he said, still a bit out of breath.

"Oh, no, no. I'm happy, that's all."

"I'm happy, too."

"Are you?"

His face grew serious. "All I've wanted since the moment I first saw you is this. You, with me. However you wanted me. For you to want me at all."

She pursed her lips. "I'm glad I make such a good first impression."

"But I don't want you thinking it's only because you're beautiful. Though you are." He grinned. "Yes, I thought you were lovely when I first saw you. But it was after we talked in the museum that I knew I was going to fall in love with you."

The shock of the words surprised her, and she wondered why they should feel so powerful. She had been told she was loved. But when? Had Arthur ever once said he loved her? She struggled through the memory of their courtship, wedding, and honeymoon. The first years of their marriage, when he had still seen fit to touch her. She could not recall, though she recalled the time her mother had asserted that "all mothers love their children" in a fit of Christmas cheer one year. Or her father, who told her he loved her in a whisper as he led her down the aisle. But not Arthur. No memory at all of him saying anything of the kind. The closest she had come to love from someone outside her family had to be Bea. There had been more real love in her friendship with Bea than even in Cliff's boyish infatuation. But that bond had been destroyed so quickly, for such foolish reasons. Maybe Arthur had never said he loved her because he could sense, somewhere deep down, that she was not worthy of being loved.

Vera noticed the hint of confusion on Hallan's face at her long silence and stroked his cheek as the fog of memory lifted away. "That's a very romantic thing to say, but you're not in love with me. You've only known me a few weeks. You don't know who I really am."

"I only needed a few moments. The light in your eyes when you look at a painting, or a sculpture . . . I thought, 'Ah, this is a woman I understand. This is a woman who will understand me.'"

A little worry tickled her mind. "But I don't know anything about you. You ought to tell me more—"

"'Given the circumstances'?"

"You love to turn my words back to me, don't you?"

He traced her breastbone. "All right, I will tell you one thing about me every day. And that way you'll keep coming to visit me. I know even if you don't care for me, your curiosity won't let you stay away."

She knew she ought to ask him directly who he really was. Playing some game with him would be childish and foolish. She ought to demand that he tell her everything. But at that moment, she did not want to know the answer. She wanted to enjoy the taste of happiness she had found, if only for the day.

"So, what's my bit of information for today?" she asked.

He leaned over her and kissed her deeply, holding her tight in one arm. Then he whispered in her ear.

"I had never been in the ocean until I went in with you."

« 23 »

Harry drove Bea and Vera back to school on Sunday alone. Vera was disappointed not to see Cliff again, but they couldn't very well have said a proper good-bye in front of their friends. There would be plenty of time for them to talk in the future. She even began composing her next letter to him in her head as they rode back to campus.

The girls carried their suitcases across the quad, kicking up brittle brown leaves as they made their way to their dorm buildings. Vera's mind was still racing from excitement and lack of sleep, and Bea kept up a frenzied recap of the previous day's excursion.

"New Haven was more posh than I thought it'd be, didn't you think? That dance hall was smashing. And the game . . . I think I like football. We'll have to go to another game sometime." Bea sucked in a deep breath of cold air and turned to Vera with a smirk. "And you naughty girl, you kissed Cliff."

"Nearly kissed," Vera corrected her, but could not tame her own smile.

Bea slowed her step. "I'll admit, I didn't think you'd ever go."

"You sure seemed to think so when you were planning it all. Why else go through all the trouble with the letters?"

"But you're so . . . good. I thought you'd end up being too afraid. Ditch me at the last minute, something like that."

Vera elbowed her. "And now you know better. I can be as fearless as you."

"Now I know better." Bea laughed. "But wasn't it everything I said it would be? Aren't you glad you went?"

"I am. But now I need sleep. I've still got an essay to finish." Vera stopped at the front door of her dorm building. "Meet me for supper, all right?"

"Sure. See you then." Bea kissed Vera's cheek, then paused. "You know . . . you're the best friend I've ever had. I know it hasn't been long, but—"

"I feel the same way." Vera pulled Bea into a hug. "Go on, get some sleep."

Vera lugged her suitcase up the stairs to her room. She opened her suitcase but found she didn't have the energy to put anything else away at the moment, so she set it in the corner to deal with later. As she pulled off her coat, she felt something stiff through the lining. She pulled a folded piece of paper from the pocket. A note. She opened the paper to find blocky male handwriting.

Dear Vera,

You're the most incredible gal I've ever met, beau or no beau. Thanks for the best night of my life. Well, so far. If you choose me, there are even better nights ahead. Promise.

Cliff

She smiled and tucked the letter into a book on her desk. Still dressed, she stretched on her bed. The weak winter sunlight peeked in through the curtains, tracing the edges of the decorations on her wall with a faint glow. She blinked in and out of sleep as vivid images from the night before played against her eyelids.

The sound of a drum made her sit up straight. No, not a drum, a knock at her door. She reached for her watch. Bea couldn't be here to get her for dinner; it was only two o'clock in the afternoon. Voices rang in the quad. Had she slept through the night? Was it Monday?

She brushed the wrinkles out of her skirt and went to the door. Hazel Weston, a second-year student who sometimes worked at the reception desk, stood on the other side, her hand poised to knock again. Hazel's mouth, a tight line of concern, sent lightning up Vera's spine.

"Is something wrong?" Vera asked, her voice husky and dim.

"Someone is downstairs to see you," Hazel said.

"Who is it?"

"You'd better just come down." Hazel turned back for the stairs.

Vera stepped over to the mirror, and her eyes landed on the folded note poking out of the book. Had Cliff come to Vassar to see her for some mad reason? She couldn't think of any visitor that would worry the girl on desk duty as much as a boy.

Her hair in place, she raced down the stairs. The last person Vera expected to see sat in a chair in the foyer.

"Vera. Hello." Her mother stood, a tightly controlled tower of rage. "Would you like to tell me what you've been up to this weekend?"

« 24 »

Vera did not even mind attending tea that afternoon at Ida Bloomer's, as she allowed her mind to drift back to her stolen morning with Hallan. Her thoughts overwhelmed her, and she wondered if the other women could see her need for him, crawling like an itch under her skin. But they chatted blithely around her, and since Vera never really contributed much, they did not question her silence. But at last, Ida asked the question she had certainly invited everyone to tea to ask.

"So, how was the trip to Montauk? I was heartbroken not to come, just beside myself," she said, fluttering her lids in a display of her distress.

"I thought it was very hot, even in the evenings, didn't you, Vera?" Caroline said.

Vera snapped her head in Caroline's direction. "Hot. Yes, a bit hot. But the water was cold."

"And how did Mr. Hallan like it?" Ida asked.

"He seemed to enjoy the house," Vera said.

"Oh, Vera. You're so discreet." Poppy looked at Vera over the lip of her teacup.

Vera's mouth went dry. "I'm sorry, I don't know what you mean."

Poppy turned to the others. "There was a very interesting discussion at dinner the first night."

"No one needs to hear about my mother's rudeness," Vera said, each word razor sharp but laced with false friendliness.

"I don't think she was rude at all. She simply wanted to know more about Mr. Hallan." Poppy cast her gaze around the circle once more. "And he wouldn't tell her a thing."

"You find scandal everywhere you look," Caroline scoffed. "He told her he's from London, and specifically from Westminster."

"But wouldn't breathe a word about his family," Poppy continued. "Mrs. Longacre—Vera's mother—said she had never heard of any Hallan family in Westminster, and she knows the city like she was born there. She said so."

Caroline frowned. "That is true."

"Oh, for goodness sakes. She's been to London a couple of times, she doesn't know every soul in town," Vera said.

"But I'm sure she knows all the best families. And he wouldn't give her his grandmother's name, don't you think that's odd?" Poppy focused her full attention on Vera, with an intensity that made Vera ill at ease.

"So then he doesn't come from one of the best families, he never said he did," Vera replied.

"And there was another thing. Something he let slip to me." Poppy calmly stirred her tea, reveling in the attention of the other ladies. A few of them actually leaned forward, straining for her secret.

"Well? What did he tell you?" Caroline asked.

"He's in love with someone."

"That's all?" Vera asked, pressing her hands into her lap to hide her rising concern. "He's a young man, of course he's in love with someone."

Poppy stared at her for a beat too long. "Someone he shouldn't be in love with, I think."

"Ladies, gossip is for the weak-minded. I don't think we need to discuss this any further," Vera said.

The other ladies wilted a bit in their seats, clearly disappointed to be stopped from speculating about the artist's illicit love. Vera was less concerned about that than she was about Poppy's line of thinking. Why was she introducing the idea that Hallan was not who he claimed to the others in the building? She had not liked being spurned. Vera worried now that Poppy might have a mind for revenge.

Chastising Poppy in front of the others would only make Vera look severe, but something had to be said. That evening, before she dressed for dinner, she rode the elevator down to the fifth floor. As the doors slid open, she hesitated, recalling Poppy's pointed look at tea. Vera pushed the image from her mind. Vera had dealt with far more intimidating people than Poppy.

A weary-looking woman in a faded black service dress answered the door and led Vera into the comparatively cramped drawing room. She sat on the sofa and removed her gloves, declining the offer of a drink. Poppy came in a few minutes later, her steps hesitant.

Poppy perched on the edge of the armchair nearest Vera. "How lovely to see you, Vera, I wasn't expecting the pleasure. Did Sophie offer you a drink? She didn't, did she? Honestly, she—"

"She did," Vera said. "Thank you, but no. I don't have long, but I wanted to speak with you about tea today."

Poppy cocked her head. "Oh?"

"I won't mince words—I find gossip tawdry and distasteful. A woman of good breeding avoids it. When she cannot avoid it, she puts it to rest. And, frankly, I didn't appreciate you insinuating what you did about my mother. She had no intention of exposing some secret about Mr. Hallan. She appreciates forthrightness. She fairly demands it. And Mr. Hallan is an ill-mannered man who dodged her questions and toyed with her." Vera clasped her hands on her knee and hoped her stern look masked the thrill she felt at saying his name. "Have I made myself perfectly clear?"

An odd glint sparked in Poppy's eye. "But there is something strange about him, don't you think?"

"It doesn't matter what I think. Speculation is idle. I advise you to avoid it in the future, if you wish to be judged good company in this community."

"It's not speculation that he's in love with some woman. I think it's someone in the building."

Vera had to put a stop to that line of thinking. She let out an exaggerated sigh. "I didn't want to have to bring this up, but . . . do you think your dissatisfaction with Mr. Hallan might have something to do with the discussion the two of you had in Montauk?"

Poppy sucked in a breath. "I'm sure I don't know what you mean."

"I saw you in my mother's house."

"He tried to seduce me," Poppy cried. "I told him I'm not that kind of woman."

"That's not what it sounded like you said at the time."

"How dare you? I love Julius, I would never do something like that."

Vera stood, clutching her gloves. "I'm sorry to upset you. I merely wanted to make plain to you how I feel about gossip."

"You have." Poppy stood, too. "You've made yourself quite clear. And now I think you'd better go."

"Of course. But please. Consider what I've said." Vera left Poppy in the drawing room. In the foyer, she waved off the maid's effort to beat her to the door, and let herself out. She hoped what she said would be enough to stem Poppy's enthusiasm for spreading rumors. She did not like to have to throw the indiscretion in her face, but the situation seemed to require it. Still, the issue was likely far from settled by Vera's reprimand. Poppy might feel she had defense enough with her lie about Hallan's "seduction." There might be nothing that would quiet her now.

《《《●》》》

The next morning, after Arthur left, Vera took the back exit from the penthouse to the stairs. She had decided that the wisest course of action would be to avoid the elevator. Better that the elevator operator not see her regularly stopping at the second floor. People in the building had enough to talk about as it was.

Hallan met her at the door of 2A.

"Not too taxing of a trip I hope," he said, closing the door behind him.

"Are your servants out?"

"I gave them both the morning off. Might as well do that every day, not much for them to do with just me here."

"I tried to talk Ida out of a valet, but she insisted."

He reached for Vera. "You ladies do spoil me so."

She kissed him, drawing back with a little throaty sound of satisfaction. "So?"

"So?"

"I called. What will you tell me about yourself today?"

He tugged on her hand, pulling her down the hall toward and through the bedroom door. "That wasn't exactly the arrangement as I recall it."

"Oh, wasn't it?"

"Look, I'm a gentleman, I'd never insist, but . . ." He sat on the bed and patted the blanket beside him.

She stood over him and ran her hands over his chest. "You're no gentleman, Mr. Hallan."

"I don't suppose you'd start calling me Emil, would you?" He grabbed her waist and pulled her down onto the bed with him, and she squealed. She pushed herself up onto her elbows as her face warmed.

"I wanted to talk to you about—" She paused, unsure how to word her request. "We ought to . . . be careful. When we're . . . together. We should have thought of it the other morning, but that's as much my fault as anything—"

He held up a hand and nodded. "You don't need to worry. I've been to the chemist. The pharmacist. It's taken care of."

She sighed, relieved. "Thank you. That was very thoughtful of you."

"I'm a thoughtful man."

"Speaking of being careful, I think you ought to know, it seems Poppy hasn't taken too kindly to you turning her down," Vera said.

Hallan shrugged. "Who wants to be rejected? I'm sure she doesn't like it. She'll recover."

"You may want to make amends with her. At least be friendly."

"Why are you so concerned?"

Vera untangled herself and sat beside him. "At tea yesterday, she brought up the conversation you had with my mother and Arthur. She seems to be trying to imply you're not who you say you are."

He shook his head. "All of you are so suspicious, just because a man doesn't go around shouting every detail of his life."

"You know very well you've been unusually quiet about yourself. Now it seems Poppy is trying to use that to get some sort of revenge."

He sat up and squinted at Vera's hair, locating a hairpin and pulling it out. "It's of very little concern to all of you where I come from, or who my grandmother was. I'm here to paint."

Vera stood. "Yes, you've said that. But that's just it. It's of concern to me who you are, if we're to continue this . . . this . . ."

He stood and crossed his arms on his chest. There was an amused glint in his eye. "Affair? You can say the word, Vera."

"Yes, all right, this affair." She laid a hand on his forearm. "You must tell me who you are. Please."

"I've told you, I will," he said, his tone softer. He sat on the bed once more, and she allowed him to continue taking down her hair.

"One little bit every day, that's hardly anything." She tilted her head. "So, it was only you and your grandmother, then?"

"No." He cleared his throat. "Me, my grandmother, and my brother. Peter."

"Is Peter still in London? Did he go to Paris with you? How old is he?"

Hallan removed another pin, then sat, turning it over in his thumb and forefinger. "I don't want to play games with you. I hope you'll understand when I say that I can't tell you any more. Not now. It's too painful, and I'm not ready to tell everything. Especially not to you. I'm afraid the hurt will ruin this joy."

Vera studied her hands in her lap. Maybe she had guessed right that night on the street. He must have experienced something too terrible to speak of; so many men had. In her mind, Hallan's past, his childhood, education, and home, floated behind a gray mist that obscured her view. She wanted to know every part of him, to threaten never to see him again unless he told her everything. But she could not be so unkind as to insist that he revisit something horrible just to satisfy her curiosity. So she did not press further.

"Did you tell Poppy you're in love with someone in the building?" she asked.

He chuckled softly. "I'm careless, not foolish. Why? Did she say I did?"

A sour taste rose up the back of Vera's throat. "Not exactly. She added the building part herself. But she said you told her you're in love with someone."

"I thought it would be the kindest way to let her down. When she came after me in Montauk."

"I think you should have found another excuse. Or at least said it was someone from home. She brought it up to the other ladies yesterday."

"Oh, she thought it would be something interesting for them to talk about. I'm sure they're all bored of the usual teatime subjects. Don't worry, Vera." He guided the last pin from her hair and combed through it with his fingers. "There, that's better."

She turned to him, and his calm gaze comforted her a bit. Maybe she was being silly. After all, she had suspected the worst when he would not let anyone see his work in the pool room, but her father's coolheaded assessment made more sense than any of the wild ideas her mind had produced. Her shoulders relaxed. Hallan wrapped an arm around her waist and kissed her, and she abandoned herself again to his body and bed.

《《《●》》》

Hallan dozed beside Vera as she watched the trees sway outside the window. Their leaves would soon begin to darken, and the cooler air meant summer was leaving at last. The heft of Hallan's arm around her waist anchored her, calmed her. She rolled over to face him, and he blinked dreamily.

"I should go," she said.

He pulled her closer. "Never."

She tapped his arm playfully. "But you have to work."

"How do you know that? You haven't seen the pool room. I could be done." He grazed her shoulder with his lips. "It could be a masterpiece."

She unwound herself from his arms. "I'd wager it's not. Done, I mean."

"You're right. You're always right." He propped himself up on one elbow. "Stay. We'll have dinner. We'll fall asleep together."

"What would the servants think if I stayed out all night, with no notice?"

"I doubt very much they would care at all. Though I suppose Arthur might object."

She pulled her slip over her head. "Arthur is in Philadelphia. He won't be back until tomorrow evening. Though I'm not sure he'd notice if he were here."

"That's it then," Hallan cried, sitting upright. "Give your staff the night off, let's bash around your place. I'd love to get a taste of the high life."

"Don't be silly. They would think it was strange, all of them being let off the same evening. They'd have to wonder what I was up to."

"They might. For a minute. Until they started rejoicing at a surprise night off."

Vera could not believe she was actually entertaining the idea. Since she was technically mistress of the house, all servants except Arthur's valet were in her domain, but surely one of them would let slip to Arthur something about their free night. And who would cook? Clean? Refill the decanters and press Vera's clothes? Then again, it was only one night. They would all be back to their tasks in the morning. The very idea was the height of folly, but the thought of an entire evening with Hallan pressed on her. His warmth in her bed. Someone to kiss her good night. A smiling face in the morning.

"All right. You go paint, I'll inform the servants." Vera hooked her earring into her lobe, inwardly pleased at Hallan's widening eyes. "Shall we say sevenish? I'll have Gertrude put out something cold for dinner." She twisted her loose hair into a bun and held out a hand for a pin.

"You're joking with me." He picked up a pin from the bedside table and gave it to her.

"Not a bit."

He leaned forward. "I'll see you at seven."

〈〈〈 ● 〉〉〉

Vera walked back up the stairs to the penthouse with a leaden stomach. She should never have agreed to have Hallan stay the night. Even if the servants could be counted on to keep their free night to themselves, someone from her social circle might pop by. Or someone looking for Arthur. Or her mother. Vera shuddered. Leaving the door unanswered would not be an option. Everyone expected her to be home, or Evans at the very least.

She entered through the kitchen to find Gertrude chopping vegetables. The cook startled at the opening door.

"Madam, is everything all right?" she asked.

"Yes, fine, thank you." Vera steeled herself. She had to get the words out before language failed her entirely. "I'm glad I found you. I'd like you to lay out a cold supper tonight. A good bit, please, I'm fairly famished. And then—well, when that's all done . . . you may have the night to do as you please."

Gertrude frowned. "Madam?"

"I mean you are released for the night. Beginning at five thirty. You are to report back at the usual time in the morning."

The cook stared at the carrot under her knife for a long while. "Yes. Yes, madam, as you like."

"Thank you," Vera said. She strode out of the kitchen into the hallway, where she stopped and took a few deep breaths. When her lightheadedness had passed, she went in search of the other servants to inform them. Though her little speech got easier with each repetition, each person reacted to the news as Gertrude had: with a thoughtful silence and a look of confusion. All except for Evans, who merely nodded and said, "Yes, madam."

Once the job was done, she went to the library to think through solutions to her worst-case scenarios. If Arthur found out, she could simply say she wanted some quiet and solitude. He would think it eccentric, but of all people he would understand the appeal. Unexpected guests would prove more difficult. Though no one but her mother would outwardly question Vera answering her own door, anyone who might come knocking would be appalled to see her do it. But then, it had been ages since anyone dropped by unannounced. Once again, Vera was worrying over a most unlikely occurrence, and she poured herself a cocktail to ease the thoughts out of her mind.

At six o'clock, she walked from room to room. The only sign of anyone was the meal Gertrude had laid out on the table. Some bread, cheese, a little salad. All the food would hold up well until it was time to eat. Evans had brought up a bottle of red and a bottle of sparkling wine, and both sat on the sideboard with a few clean glasses.

Hallan knocked on the kitchen door as instructed at a few minutes after seven. He held out a wrapped parcel with a silver ribbon around it.

"Some chocolates for the hostess," he said.

Vera smiled. "Why, thank you. What a thoughtful caller you are."

"I hope they're the kind you like."

"I like all chocolates." She set the box on the counter and wrapped her arms around his neck. "Are you hungry? I've had dinner laid out, and there's wine. Or we could have a cocktail first, if you'd rather."

He gave her a light kiss on the lips. "I'd love a cocktail and a tour. I want to see all of this place."

She tilted her head. "It's an ordinary home, I'm afraid."

"Then you and I have different definitions of ordinary."

She led him to the library to pour their drinks, then around to each room in turn. Their tour was an uncomfortable reminder of the night she had wandered the house, drinking and contemplating her pretty toys. A new vase had appeared the next day to replace the one she had smashed, and it now stood full of damask roses.

Hallan exulted over the paintings, the Roman statuary, and the rug hanging from the wall. The pieces seemed to come alive for her again, as she imagined seeing them through his eyes. His face was aglow as they sat down in the dining room to their meal.

"What a thing," he said. "To surround yourself with such treasures, to have the means to get whatever you want."

She raised an eyebrow. "After we eat, I'll show you my favorite item."

"It's not any of the ones I've seen? It must be marvelous."

"I think so."

"Is it the crown jewels? A piece of the true cross? The Holy Grail?"

"Don't be clever. It's nothing like that, but it's my favorite all the same."

Hallan took a bite of his bread. He rubbed a hand on the arm of his chair, and a cloud fell over his face. "Is this where Arthur sits?"

"It is. Would you like to sit somewhere else?"

"No." He sat up straighter, leaning forward a bit. "No, this is fine."

After they ate, he rounded the table to her chair and held out his hand.

"What a gentleman," she said with a laugh.

"Let's go see your favorite," he replied.

They went up the stairs to the master suite. She watched as he took in the sight of the brass bed, the enormous windows with their heavy curtains, the plush rug under his feet. He turned to her.

"Is your favorite the bed? Now I am glad to see it."

"Not the bed. In here." She went into the black and white bathroom and gestured to the claw-foot tub. "I found it in France on my honeymoon. I don't know why, but I love it. There are some paintings that would overtake it if I owned them, but . . ." She sighed. "I think it's the most beautiful thing, honestly."

He ran a hand along the glossy white surface. "Porcelain?"

"Yes."

He glanced at her. "May I try it?"

She pulled back. The request was not unpleasant, only unexpected. "I don't see why not."

He handed her his glass and turned on the tap. As he made adjustments to the temperature, Vera brought a chair in from the vanity for herself. She could not help but giggle at him as he undressed and climbed into the tub. He ducked under the water, then came up and smoothed his dripping hair.

"I can see why you like this so much," he said, leaning back with a satisfied sigh.

She balanced her elbow on her knee and cupped her chin in her hand. "I do like this. Very much."

He laughed and closed his eyes. "So this is Mrs. Bellington's life. Warm baths and wine."

"That's part of it. But then when you get out of the bath, you have to go up and down that elevator, a different floor every hour." She swallowed hard and tried to keep her tone light. "This one for tea, that one for dinner . . . ah, and don't forget lunch with Mother."

"If I'm having lunch with Mother, I'm going to need more wine."

"Fortunately, you'll have as much of that as you want." She twisted an earring between her fingers. "May I ask you something? How old are you?"

He looked up at her. "Twenty-eight. Why, how old are you?"

"You shouldn't ask a lady that. It's rude." She dipped her fingers in the water and splashed a few drops on him. "And I'm thirty-one."

"You wear it well." He grinned. "Wouldn't you like to get in with me?"

"I've had a bath already, thank you."

"That wasn't exactly what I had in mind."

She smiled. "Why don't you get out, then?"

He stood, and she handed him a towel. Vera located one of Arthur's robes, and he slid into it. He followed her back into the bedroom and unzipped her dress before lying on the bed. She pulled the dress over her head and stretched out beside him. They lay together in peaceful silence for a while. She put a hand on the warm skin of his chest, felt the muscles expand and contract as he breathed. A lump rose in her throat, and she looked up at him.

"I want things to go back to the way they were." She brushed a damp lock of hair from his temple. "Before you came."

"Why? Were you happy then?" He ran a hand up and down her arm.

"No. But at least I wasn't sure I wanted something else." She sat up and hugged her knees to her chest. "What happens after? Will you disappear?"

He frowned. "There is no after. Why does there have to be an after?"

"Because you'll go, won't you, when the painting is finished? To California, like you said."

"I may." He wrapped an arm around her and pulled her back down to his side. "But for now, we're both here. Isn't that worth wanting, too?"

She placed a hand on his jaw and kissed him. The feel of someone's arms around her in her own bed was almost more joy than she could bear. She lay awake for hours that night, unwilling to surrender a moment to sleep.

« 25 »

Vera hunched over a cold cup of tea in the café. Her mother sat across from her, the steering-wheel-sized table putting insufficient distance between them. The only other people in the café were two elderly women shouting their conversation at each other. Even the waitress had disappeared to the back after bringing Vera and her mother their drinks. At least Vera's humiliation wouldn't have witnesses.

In the car, her mother had taken advantage of Vera's stunned silence to explain that the dean's office had telephoned to ask the name of Vera's chaperone for their records. The deception had unraveled quickly from there.

"I won't bother to ask what you thought you were doing," her mother said. "It's clear you weren't thinking."

"It was all very innocent, Mother, I promise you. We went to the football game at Yale with Bea's cousin and his friends. Nothing happened for you to be ashamed of."

"Then I shouldn't be ashamed that my daughter would lie? Or sneak out overnight with young men of who knows what character? Or forge my signature?"

"I didn't forge your signature." The words came out of Vera's mouth before she considered the ammunition the information would give her mother.

"Then who did?"

Vera sat on her hand to keep from chewing her fingernail. She ran her thumb back and forth under her thigh. "Mother, please, I'm very sorry about the whole thing—"

"I should hope you're sorry. If you aren't by now, you soon will be. Now tell me at once who used my name."

Vera searched for a plausible lie, a person who could have created the letters instead of her or Bea, but nothing came. Her mind might have been weakened by exhaustion. More likely her mother had trained her so well that even her own thoughts conspired against her. There was no point to a lie, however good. Her mother would get the truth from her eventually.

"Bea." Vera concentrated on the tablecloth. "Bea made the letters."

Her mother inhaled deeply. "I can't say I'm surprised. I knew what sort of girl she was the moment I saw her. Has she told you why she ended up at Vassar? Why she left Agnes Scott?"

Vera, her mouth agape, jerked her gaze up to meet her mother's. How had her mother known where Bea went to school in Georgia?

"I did a little digging into her history. I won't be ignorant about who my daughter associates with." Her mother shook her head, jaw clenched. "I should have intervened. But then I never thought you'd go along with one of her schemes. And I thought she'd stay out of trouble here. I'm sure her family thought so, too."

An icy sensation feathered across Vera's scalp. "What did Bea do?"

"So, she didn't tell you? That makes sense. Probably hoping to hitch her wagon to your star and find a good husband before word got out." Her mother's eyes narrowed. "I don't know the details, just that the administration at Agnes Scott asked her to leave. I do know her family made a sizable donation to Vassar to get them to look the other way about her record. She didn't tell you any of this?"

"I knew she left Agnes Scott to come here."

"And that didn't seem odd to you, Vera?"

Vera couldn't say any more. The miserable, sick feeling she'd had since her mother arrived now shared space with a spark of anger. How could she have ignored the blatant warning signs? The donation to Vassar explained Harry's crack about how Bea had spent her family's money. Vera had been so delighted to have an exciting, lively friend, she had not thought to be more cautious. Why? When she knew Bea had no qualms about courting trouble? She'd been cheating, forging letters, who knew what else? Vera had been so sure Bea liked her for who she was. Now it seemed clear Bea had been as attracted to Vera's name and connections as everyone else.

Maybe her mother was wrong, though. She didn't know the details of Bea's disgrace at Agnes Scott. There were plenty of reasons an incoming family might make a donation. And no matter how neatly the idea that Bea needed Vera's friendship to establish herself fit the narrative her mother laid out, it still didn't make sense in Vera's mind. She needed the whole story. She wanted to talk to Bea. For the moment, however, she had to appease her mother, who clearly had a solution to the current problem in mind.

"What should I do?" Vera asked.

Her mother puffed out her chest, resolute. "If she was the one who actually created the letters, then she's the one who should take the blame. You'll simply need to make it clear to the administration that she coerced you into doing this. If you do, you might be able to escape with minimal scandal."

"She didn't coerce me," Vera said, sinking to a new low of misery. "It was our plan together. I can't lie."

Her mother's voice lowered to a hiss. "And then what? If the school formally sanctions you, your father will find out. Would you like that—hmm? And you can forget Arthur ever proposing if he learns you've spent the night with some boy."

Vera shut her eyes tightly against the memory of Cliff's warm hand entwined with hers in the cold evening air. "Not spending the night, nothing like that." Her hope of waiting for Cliff dissolved into nothing. She would have to accept Arthur now, her mother would insist on it.

"And who's to say?" Her mother cocked her head as her voice took on a mocking tone. "You? This girl? Forgive me if I don't find your version of events the most trustworthy at the moment."

"What should I say? Bea made the letters, it's true, but she never forced me to do anything." She didn't want to point out to her mother that Bea didn't have to work that hard to convince her. "How could she have? I had to have permission. They'll know I could see the letter wasn't really from you."

Her mother thought for a moment, then placed a hand on the table. "I'll tell you exactly what to do. You tell them you didn't know I hadn't given permission. You thought she wrote me secretly to surprise you. As far as they know, she lied to you, and this was all her doing. Well, she did lie to you, in a way. She's caused trouble before. Even if she gets out of it this time, which she won't, she'll find a way to ruin herself. She will come to no good. Let them deal with her as they may."

Vera decided to concede a smaller battle to her mother in the hope of winning the larger war. She couldn't lose everything in one blow. She never really had Cliff to begin with, she could see that now. Her last semester at Vassar was an easy sacrifice if it meant a chance at keeping what might be her one true friendship intact. "But you said I'm not coming back to school after Christmas. I've never been in trouble before. If I take the blame, they'd only give me probation. What difference does that make if I'm leaving anyway?"

"The difference is that you are my daughter, and I won't have your name dragged through this girl's mud. She's going down a bad path no matter what. You still have a chance to save your reputation. And you're leaving now, after this matter is settled. No question of that."

Tears stung the corners of Vera's eyes. "I can't do that. I have to do the right thing. I have to tell the truth."

"The right thing is protecting your reputation."

"She's my friend," Vera said, swallowing hard against the last word.

"Anyone who convinces you to take a risk like this is not your friend. If she's not your mother, your father, or your fiancé, then she's nothing to you. Your responsibility lies with us, and you will do as I say. Arguing with me will not change my mind. There is only one way out of this without ruining yourself, and it's my way. You cannot protect this girl. She doesn't care enough to protect herself. You must let her suffer the consequences. Her alone. Am I being clear?"

Vera stared at the thin piece of lemon on the bottom of her cup. A dark pit opened in her chest, sucked in what energy she had, and spread all the way to the tips of her fingers and toes. If she could get to Bea, they could sort it out. She could find out the whole story, make up her own mind. There might still be some way to save their friendship. She just had to think of it. And she had to talk to Bea.

« 26 »

Reluctant as she was for him to go, Vera was glad she had Hallan leave the penthouse before the sun came up. She climbed back into the bed, her head on the pillow he had slept on, and reveled in the warm scent he left behind. The dull sound of a door closing announced the return of the servants, and she stirred from her reverie. She pulled the sheets up to the pillows and plumped one so that the presence of two people in the bed would not be immediately obvious.

Their night together was well timed, as she had lunch with her mother that morning and could not visit his apartment. Vera told him she could come in the afternoon, but he said he planned to paint most of the day. They agreed to meet again Thursday morning. After their conversation in her bed, she almost wanted to tell him to put off the work or delay it by a few hours. Once the painting was finished, he would have no more reason to stay at the Angelus. She knew when the affair began that it would only be temporary, but the thought of him leaving pressed so hard on her chest it took her breath away. She resolved not to dwell on what was to come. Vera had lived thirty years without Hallan. She could do well enough without him when he departed.

Before she went to meet her mother, she and Marguerite reviewed her social calendar for the week. She groaned at a reminder that she and Arthur had been invited to a small dinner party at the Hastings' that evening. Since Julius had been ill, Vera thought Poppy might cancel. But however indisposed Julius was, his condition would apparently not keep Poppy from her plans.

Vera sat through lunch with her mother with a distracted, fuzzy mind. Fortunately, Vera's father had purchased two new racehorses, which meant her mother was in the mood to give a speech about "that man's ridiculous obsession." She went on so long that Vera did not notice right away when the topic changed.

"Vera? Are you listening?" Her mother clinked a spoon down on the tea saucer.

"Hmm? Oh. Yes. I agree completely." Agreeing was always the wisest course of action with her mother.

"I thought you might. You certainly spent enough time in your room. Well, I can hardly blame you. Insufferable company does nothing for my digestion either."

Her room? Vera realized her mother was talking about the trip to Montauk and struggled to refocus her attention. She managed a nod and an "mmm."

"That Hastings woman was beyond belief. But I suppose you must tolerate her because she lives in your building."

Vera pondered a chunk of tomato at the end of her fork. "Poppy is certainly an interesting person."

"Well said." Her mother sniffed. "But that artist character. I hope you know he's set his sights on you."

Vera fumbled with the fork, and gripped it hard to keep from dropping it. "Mother. I can't believe you'd say such a thing."

"Well, darling, I've seen it before. Slick boy like that, in some romantic profession, wends his way into good society and targets a well-to-do woman. Up to no good. He's after money, mark my words."

"You don't really believe that, do you?"

"I know it. I knew it from the moment I laid eyes on him. And he had the indecency to stare at you every time you came into the room, hoping you'd catch that moony expression on his face." Her mother took a sip of tea. "You were right to avoid him. If you ignore him, he'll find some other woman. He'd do better off going after the Hastings woman. My daughter is no fool."

"Well, thank you, Mother." Vera's voice came out a little more hoarse than she would have preferred, but her mother paid no mind.

"You had to know from that accent. It takes a good ear, like mine, but I know he's putting it on. If he's from Westminster, I'm the Queen of Araby. Even if he is from a low family, it simply would not sound like whatever that is meant to be. He could be Irish, though it sounds like something else entirely to me."

"Yes." Vera stared at her plate, what little appetite she had gone. Was Hallan really after her money? She sat up straighter, taking a deep breath. If he was, he would be disappointed. She would never give him a cent.

Her mother's words echoed in her head the whole drive home, as Vera wrestled with the possibility that he was a swindler. The little sound behind his accent, that odd scraping in the back of his throat, had bothered her, too. What if he was not really from London? What if all of his sweetness and declarations of love were some kind of trick to con her out of her money? Her mother had been right about Bea's hidden past. What if she could see through Hallan in the same way?

But his behavior could not be a trick. Her mother was right; if money was his aim, there were easier targets in the building. And he had paid the cab fare the night they had gone out, as well as the bill at the bar. He had never asked her for anything but her companionship. He had been in her home, among all her most precious treasures, and behaved as if she were the greatest of all of them.

Still, she hated that each day brought new doubts about him, new fears. She would demand to know about his life, or she would end the affair for her own good. Even if it hurt her to lose him, to risk her own name and reputation for a lie would be far worse. The affair would have to end sometime, anyway. Why not be the one to take control?

《《《●》》》

Vera and Arthur arrived at Poppy's fifth-floor apartment at eight o'clock, as Poppy had not noted any time for cocktails on the invitation. A rather harried young man, in an ill-fitting suit rented for the occasion, answered the door and led them toward the drawing room.

"Excuse me," Vera said, "but shouldn't we go to the dining room?"

He shrugged. "Everyone's in here. Uh, ma'am."

The crowd threatened to overwhelm the tiny drawing room, as people shoved into corners or stood shoulder to shoulder to fit themselves in. The air was warm and sticky with the heat of bodies and mingling of perfumes and colognes. Poppy stood by the door, a bit wild-eyed. "Vera, Arthur! Welcome. Everyone, Vera and Arthur are here."

"I'm so sorry, Poppy, I didn't know you had a cocktail hour," Vera said, straining to keep her tone polite.

"No, no, I didn't. There's been a—a delay." She clenched her teeth. "It seems the menu was very nearly too much for my mai—my cook. But don't fret, she's nearly got everything together."

Without a word, Arthur left them to go talk to Clarence Bloomer. Vera patted her chignon, trying to think of what to say as Poppy darted nervous looks toward the dining room. Just as Vera opened her mouth to speak, the maid appeared. She was red-faced and sweating, and her starched cap leaned perilously over one side of her head.

"Dinner is served, ma'am," the maid said, holding out an arm in the general direction of the dining room.

Poppy stomped over to the maid. "About time," she hissed. "And it's not 'ma'am.' It's 'madam.' Emily Post says it should be 'madam.'" She turned and painted on a cheerless smile. "Come, everyone. So sorry to keep you waiting."

Bessie Harper, patting her wilting gray curls, fell into step beside Vera. "What a horror. Talking to her maid like that in front of everyone. You know she didn't hire anyone for the evening, except for that boy who answered the door?"

Vera scanned the group. "Where is Julius?"

"Still not well, poor man." Bessie held her elbow to keep her drink from sloshing.

"I'm sorry to hear it. I hope Poppy knew she didn't have to hold the party on our account."

"She was most insistent. When I phoned earlier today she said Julius wanted us all to go on without him. Which, of course, we do." Bessie chuckled. "Even when he's present."

Vera did not answer. She had noticed another absence from the group. "And Mr. Hallan? Won't he join us? He's been at every dinner since he arrived."

Bessie's eyes gleamed. "I asked Poppy about that. You know, ever since the doubts about him began to surface, she said she felt uncomfortable inviting him to our little get-togethers. So she phoned and told him the dinner was off. I told her she was quite right, that it really ought to be just the usual gathering. Looks as though she can barely handle that."

Vera sucked in a short breath. "I see. Ah, excuse me, that's my seat over there."

She fell into the seat with her place card, almost forgetting to take off her gloves. Walter Litchfield and Andrew Keller sat on either side of her, and Arthur sat a few seats away, near the head of the table. As she turned to greet Andrew, she almost gasped. There, hanging above the fireplace, was the fake Vermeer from Fleming's shop. The sight of it transported Vera to the back room of the gallery, down to the acrid smell of turpentine. She knew she should not say anything, but the temptation was too much.

"Poppy, I didn't know you were collecting art these days." Vera smiled up the table.

Poppy's frazzled demeanor faded as she beamed up at the painting. "Yes, do you like it? It's a Verdeer, you know. I saw a letter from the lord who sold it."

"What a find."

"It wasn't cheap, but I adore his work. I had to have it. Don't you love the . . . um. The . . ." Poppy's eyes darted around the canvas as she struggled for words. Vera decided to have mercy on her.

"Yes, the lines. And the use of shadow."

Poppy nodded hard. "Shadow, yes, that's the word I was looking for. Shadow. And the . . . ah . . . well, the colors."

"Mmm. Vermeer is known for his blues, isn't he?"

The door to the dining room swung open, interrupting them. Poppy's maid came out with a tureen of soup. As the woman ladled servings into bowls, Vera glanced up at the painting again. She might have a chance to get close enough to inspect it after dinner. There may be some hint, something in the odd blue color or the brushwork, that would reveal the painting as Bea's handiwork. But what if there was nothing? Would the lack of a sign settle the question at all? Vera would never reach out to Bea, no matter what her level of involvement in the forgery scheme.

No need for a closer look, Vera thought, returning her attention to the bowl of soup in front of her. When she ate her first spoonful, she nearly spit it back out. The broth was ice cold, though it ought to have been served hot. She steeled herself for a very long evening.

The maid appeared again a few minutes later and whisked the soup bowls away, well before the course ought to have been finished. No one complained, least of all Poppy, who likely wanted everyone to forget the untouched portions in front of them as soon as possible. The boy who answered the door had been pressed into service in the dining room, and he brought out a tray of watery salmon mousse. Bessie Harper could not hide the sneer of disgust that temporarily crossed her face. In what must have been an attempt to distract himself from the gelatinous glob of pink paste now trembling in the middle of the table, Andrew Keller turned to Vera.

"So, have you heard anything lately about the mural? How is the artist progressing?" he asked, his thin face aglow with false cheer.

"What? Oh, sorry, I haven't heard anything," Vera said.

"I thought he might be more willing to talk to you, what with your art education and all," Andrew continued.

"We were discussing at tea how he doesn't talk much about anything," Caroline Litchfield said from across the table.

"What do you mean?" Andrew asked.

"Only that no one knows a thing about him, and he was hardly forthcoming in Montauk when Vera's mother asked him about his family," Caroline said. "A perfectly innocent question, and he wouldn't answer."

"Let's not trot that conversation out again," Vera said. It seemed the discussion at tea had been enough to change Caroline's mind about Hallan. "I imagine he doesn't talk about his family because there's nothing to tell."

Walter Litchfield cut in. "You know, I thought he seemed an odd fellow, but I wasn't going to bring it up. Didn't seem to be the popular opinion."

"And the business with the keys," Ida said, with a wag of her finger. "What's he got to hide? If he were really that good, I imagine he'd want everyone to see him work."

"Some artists prefer to finish a work before anyone sees it," Vera said. "My father thought highly of him, and my father is an impeccable judge of character."

"What do we know about Mr. Hallan? Really?" Poppy's voice rang out from the head of the table. "The accent tells us where he's from, at least in the most general sense. He claims to have gone to this school—"

"Clarence's friend knew him personally. I doubt he'd have reason to lie. Don't you agree, Clarence?" Vera reached for her wineglass, bumping Andrew's with her hand and nearly sending its contents onto the tablecloth.

Poppy did not give Clarence time to speak. "We know Clarence's friend wouldn't lie to him, but who's to say Hallan didn't lie in the first place? This job, lots of money. Seems a good enough reason to me."

"But there were paintings," Vera said.

Poppy smirked. "Photos of paintings."

"That's true, very true," Vera said. She realized conceding to Poppy was wiser than embroiling herself further in the argument. "I suppose he's here now, isn't he? He'll either paint or not paint, and it's not as if we have to pay him if the mural isn't complete." She offered a serene smile down the table and was pleased to see more relaxed, calm expressions. "Why should we worry ourselves so much about him?"

Before anyone could respond, the maid burst into the dining room once more. After the maid removed the mousse, she and the boy walked around delivering plates of lamb chops in the tense silence. A few of the women commented on the lovely presentation, despite the fact that each chop sat in a congealed pool of blood, accompanied by a limp sprig of mint and a few warm, dry cucumber slices. Poppy's eyes darkened, and she scrunched down in her chair throughout the equally disastrous fish course, dessert, and cordials.

At last the men excused themselves and went to the library for cigars. The lack of decent food combined with copious amounts of alcohol had left most of them red-faced, with glazed eyes. The women returned to the drawing room, where they sipped sherry. The maid set out small bowls of cashews, and Vera resisted the urge to pour two or three of them straight down her throat. A few of the ladies started a halfhearted game of whist, which fizzled out into a few idle questions about just who designed the first playing cards, anyway. No one seemed to be able to muster up the courage to mention the artist again after Vera's admonition.

Vera had never been so glad to see Arthur appear at a door as she was when he came to take her home. Poppy made a perfunctory protest through puckered lips, then thanked them for coming. The boy opened the front door for them and watched them go through heavy-lidded eyes, the sleeves of his oversized jacket nearly down to his fingertips.

In the elevator, Vera exhaled hard. "What an evening."

"A woman of her means never should have attempted a party like that," Arthur said.

"I quite agree. And such silly gossip at the dinner table."

"I'm tired of hearing about it."

Vera brightened at the idea that Arthur was in agreement with her. "All that speculation about the poor man, when they all fawned over him like schoolgirls when he arrived."

Arthur nodded. "Well, it will all be at rest soon enough."

"What? How?"

"The men all agreed that we've had enough of this nattering. If he won't tell us who he is, we'll find out."

"How do you propose to do that?"

"Walter's agreed to hire a private investigator."

Vera's mouth went dry. "I thought everything was resolved at dinner. Hiring an investigator isn't necessary. Why not just talk to the man?"

The doors opened, and they stepped out into the penthouse hallway. Vera tried hard to keep her steps steady. Arthur opened the door, and Evans appeared to take her gloves. After assuring him that they did not need anything else, Vera followed Arthur up the stairs to the bedroom.

"Arthur? You didn't answer me. Why not talk to Mr. Hallan? I'm sure no one needs to spend good money on an investigator."

Arthur unbuttoned his jacket. "I thought it was foolish, too. But they seemed determined, and what do I care what they do with their money?"

"What do they expect to find out? That he's a fake? Not an artist? His background is immaterial as long as he can paint, you've said that yourself." Vera paced the floor as Arthur dressed for bed.

He chuckled. "Perhaps they'll discover he can't paint."

"Then why don't they break into the pool room? That would settle it once and for all."

"I asked that. They said they want to go about it the proper way. If he's misrepresenting himself, they can have him deported or put in prison rather than giving him the opportunity to run. Or something to that effect."

She threw up her hands. "That's absurd. They're bored. They have nothing better to do than to sit around making up stories about people."

Arthur eyed her wearily. "You're right about that. Don't wear yourself out over how those people entertain themselves. It's nothing to you. Get some sleep."

Vera went into her dressing room and changed into her nightgown. By the time she returned, Arthur had turned off the lamps in the bedroom. In the dark, she tossed under the sheets, unable to sleep.

《《《●》》》

When Vera woke, she brushed powder onto the dark circles under her eyes from her sleepless night and took the stairs down to the second floor. Hallan met her at the door to 2A, but his smile drooped at the sight of her appearance.

"Are you all right?" he asked. "You're not ill, are you?"

"No."

He took a step toward her, but she stepped back. His expression darkened.

"What's the matter? Did Arthur find out?" he asked.

"Goodness, no. And if he did, he most likely wouldn't care, as far as I can tell. But we need to talk."

He led the way to the drawing room. "Do you want a cup of tea?"

"Not now." She inhaled deeply. "Emil, you need to tell me about yourself."

"I told you, I can't. Not now."

"I know. It's something painful for you. But you may have to tell me, and it may have to be now. There was a dinner party last night."

He frowned. "Where?"

"At Poppy's."

"She told me that was canceled." His face went slack. "Oh. I see."

Vera worried the clasp of her watch. "The usual questions about you came up. If you would tell people more about who you are—it doesn't have to be whatever is worrying you so much. Little details, that's all. Your childhood, maybe. Your family. Something simple."

He groaned. "Not this again. Who cares what neighborhood I lived in as a boy, or how many cousins I have?"

"It's not that, and you know it. No one knows anything about you, and they're suspicious."

"About what? Do they think I'm planning to burn the building to the ground?"

"I don't know."

He propped his elbows on his knees and rubbed his mouth. "Fine, I don't care what they say about me. I don't have to tell them anything."

"Then tell me," she cried, standing. "Why are you being so stubborn about this? Why does it have to be such a secret? If anyone can know, shouldn't I?"

He did not answer, but instead rose and crossed to the mantel, facing away from her. She went over and laid her hands on his back.

"They're hiring a private investigator," she said softly.

He glanced over his shoulder. "Let them. They won't find anything."

"Emil."

He finally turned to her and pulled her close. She laid her head on his chest, closing her eyes at the feel of his heart beating. He was real. She could verify that, at least. Beyond that, there were only a few scraps of him, nothing for her to piece together into a full man.

"I want so badly to love you," she said.

"You don't?"

"I don't know enough. You must give me something."

"You said yourself there are things I don't know about you. I love you the way I know you now, isn't that enough?"

Her eyes flew open and she pulled away. "I'll tell you about me. Something I haven't told anyone. But you must do the same."

He dropped his arms and turned again, the struggle plain on his face. She sat on the couch. After slipping off her shoes, she tucked her feet under her. She supported her elbow on the arm of the couch, and held her face in her hand. Perhaps if she gave him a part of herself, he would offer something in return. At first, she did not know what to say. Then she realized: her marriage. She could tell him about Arthur.

"I got married in 1914. Nine years ago now, though it doesn't feel like it could be that long. I had just left college." Bea's face appeared unbidden in Vera's mind, but she brushed it away. She still could not bring herself to unearth that whole fiasco. "For all the good college did me. Sometimes I wonder why I went at all."

Hallan moved to the couch, resting on the edge of the cushion. Vera smiled sadly at him.

"We married in May," she continued. "In my youth and naïveté I thought, Oh, he's just a serious person. He'll warm to me. He must love me, why else would he want to marry me? He was kind enough, treated me well, bought me enough jewelry to open my own shop. But now, you know, I don't think he ever did care for me, only my family's name and what it could do for him in society. And I wanted someone to care for me." She reached for Hallan's hand and squeezed it. "I planned this honeymoon, a grand trip to the capitals of Europe. London, Paris, Madrid, Rome. As soon as we got off the boat, he holed up in the hotel room, reading the financial news. Oh, he took me to dinner, of course. Sent me out shopping with plenty of cash. He was forever writing letters or telegraphing someone in the office, always some urgent matter. I felt like I was a nuisance more than anything.

"And so I did all those things I thought would be so lovely and romantic. I toured the Louvre, the Coliseum, standing close to families so people wouldn't know I was alone. I stood in the Prado, in front of my favorite painting in the world, and cried. I'm sure people thought I was a passionate soul." She sniffled. "But I realized, standing there, that I was at the edge of the loneliest precipice of my life."

Hallan gave her his handkerchief, and she wiped her eyes.

"I have so much, I feel ungrateful," she continued. "How can I be so sad when there's so much tragedy I'm not living?"

He considered this. "You're living the tragedy you know."

"I feel like there's this other woman I should have been. Almost was. Someone vibrant and happy. And she starved."

He reached up and stroked her hair. "She's still in there. I see her."

Vera looked at him expectantly, and he withdrew his hand. He sat in silence, the muscles of his jaw tense, opening his mouth once or twice before beginning.

"I . . . my father died when my brother and I were very young. Peter—my brother—he was older. I was a baby, so I never knew Papa. My mother . . . now, I did know her. When she got sick, Grandmother came to take care of us. I was about five then." His eyes lit up. "Grandmother was wonderful. She's the reason I came to love art. Part of the reason. And Peter. He's my best friend."

"You left them behind? Are they in Paris?"

"Peter is in France, but not Paris. Grandmother is in London, but . . . well, I don't write her like I should."

She sighed. "It doesn't sound like there's anything in your past dark enough to justify worrying the residents so."

"There's something dark in everyone's past," he said.

Vera thought of the wreckage of her friendship with Bea, the only person other than Hallan to see that woman who might have been. For all Vera's sadness at having lost her friend, she was almost as sad to have lost that piece of herself.

The clock on the mantel chimed, and he stood.

"Where are you going?" she asked.

"I need to work. If your friends are forming a mob, I won't be welcome long."

"But I'll tell them there's nothing to worry about."

"Do you think they'll believe you?" He smiled. "Don't worry. And come earlier tomorrow, all right?"

"All right," she said vaguely.

He saw her to the door, kissing her before opening it. "I want to get the painting done before they break down the door or some other such madness. No one can see it half finished."

She nodded and headed for the stairwell. Taking the steps slowly, she wondered over their exchange. He seemed to be telling the truth about his family, but there was so much he did not say. And, despite her assertions to the contrary, she felt she was falling more in love with him even though she knew so little.

《《《 ● 》》》

The next morning, Vera went down to the dining room as the first glimmer of dawn peeked over the trees in the park. She would not have guessed Arthur had been home at some point, were it not for the newspaper at his place setting, folded neatly beside an empty coffee cup. She debated ringing to have her own breakfast brought in but decided she would rather not eat with only his remnants for company. She rounded the table and caught sight of a headline that sent an icy bolt through her: SUSPECTED HEAD OF ART FORGERY RING ARRESTED. Her hand shook as she lifted the paper. She scanned the article for the most important details. *A man calling himself Michael Fleming . . . victims among the city's elite . . . arrested at his gallery . . .*

No mention of Bea. No mention of anyone else, except to say that the ongoing investigation would likely turn up accomplices. Of course there would be accomplices. A memory of the *Bon Ton* cover Bea had re-created for her surfaced again. How the colors had matched exactly. And Bea had copied her mother's letterhead and signature so perfectly, even going so far as to replicate the embossing. Perhaps she had spent the decade since their college days perfecting her technique.

Bea would be discovered and arrested, no doubt about that. Vera sank into a chair and set the newspaper on the table. If only . . . but there was no sense thinking of "if"s. Bea's choices were her own. Her ruin would be, too. Vera wished she could believe that Bea was only a secretary, but the evidence left no question. If Vera was honest, there had never been any question to begin with. There was only one good reason Bea would be working in that gallery among forged paintings. Vera only hoped that she was smart enough not to get caught. She had imagined so many exciting lives for Bea over the years; but here was proof that Bea had simply taken too many wrong turns, too many risks. Vera had to stop blaming herself. Some people were born to turn out bad, and nothing anyone could do would change that.

« 27 »

Vera's plan to find Bea and talk the whole mess out had failed. After they left the café, her mother had insisted on staying by her side until Vera's appointment with the dean, Miss McCaleb, on Monday afternoon. She hadn't even been allowed to sleep in her dorm. She'd stayed with her mother in the hotel that night. That morning, her mother agreed that Vera needed to go to her room to get a change of clothes, although they went together for that, too.

A small part of Vera held out hope that Bea might be sitting on her bed, waiting for her when they arrived. Her mother might not permit them to have a full conversation, but Vera could at least say something that would help make sense of the situation. A few steps ahead of her mother, Vera swung the door open, but the bed was empty. Her heart sank until she heard a rustle under her foot. She scooped up the paper and put it inside her coat before her mother saw.

Back at the hotel, her mother freshened up for lunch. "Aren't you coming down?" she asked.

"I'm sorry, Mother. I have a headache. I think I'd better rest."

Her mother looked her over. "Whatever you like. But I've got the whole staff looking out, and they know not to allow any telephone calls from this room."

Vera held in a sigh. "I'm not going to try anything. I know better than that."

Her mother nodded. As soon as the door closed, Vera pulled the letter from her coat. The grand flourishes of Bea's handwriting covered the front and back of the page.

> Vera,
>
> I'd hoped to see you, but I guess you're with your mother, and I'll bet she's angry. My mother almost didn't let me out of her sight long enough for me to write this.
>
> I'm in real trouble. I thought it would only be probation. I've known girls who snuck out. That's how I got all the test answers and essays—I forged letters for a few of them. I should have told you, and I'm sorry. But the girls who got caught never got more than probation.
>
> And it's worse—they've found out about the cheating. Professor Harrison figured it out from the test last week. And there's something I never told you about Agnes Scott. I've been in trouble before. I would have told you about it, but I didn't want you to think less of me. It's silly, because I know you're my true friend, and I know you'll understand.
>
> There was an art professor at Agnes Scott, Professor Lewis. She thought I had talent, thought I should do more with my art. Just like you, she thought I should eventually go on to a studio program. She had studied in Paris and Chicago, she knew what she was talking about. The school wouldn't let us use nude models, but she mentioned that someday I'd have to work with nudes if I wanted a full art education. You know me—I couldn't resist. I didn't want to wait until I was in Paris or somewhere, surrounded by more experienced artists. I didn't want to look like a fool who didn't know anything. I dogged Professor Lewis until

she gave me the contact information of a model I could
practice with. A male model.

I arranged to meet with him after hours in one of the
studios. I don't know why I didn't go off campus, that
would have been the smart thing to do. I thought my
roommate was asleep, but when she saw me leave so late,
she went to the dorm matron. Sure enough, when she
walked in, there I was alone in a classroom with a naked
man. You can imagine what everyone thought, and I
couldn't bring Professor Lewis into it. I didn't want to
get her in trouble, too. I tried to explain, but I know how
fake it must have sounded. The school agreed to keep it
quiet if my parents took me out. I'm sure there was money
involved, too.

I wanted to tell you everything. Now that I've come
clean, I hope you'll forgive me for not telling you sooner. It
wasn't what they thought it was, but it was enough to make
my family send me here. I don't know what they'll do if I
get expelled from Vassar, too. My father might throw me
out when he finds out I'm in trouble again.

Maybe if you say something on my behalf, make it look
better than it is, the school might reconsider. After all,
you always follow the rules, and you're a model student.
And your family is so respected—they'd listen to you. It's
the only thing I can think of, and I'm desperate. This was
supposed to be a fresh start for me, and now I've spoiled it.

Please help me any way you can think of. You're my dear
and loving friend, and always will be, no matter what.

Love,
B.

If Vera didn't have a headache before reading the letter, she had
a fierce one after. If she did what her mother asked, Bea would be

expelled, which would cast an indelible shadow over her entire future. Even though Vera was frustrated Bea hadn't trusted her with the real reason for her transfer to Vassar, Vera knew Bea well enough to believe her version of the story. She didn't deserve to be punished for simply wanting to learn more about art, even if she had foolishly decided to involve a nude male model in her efforts. It was a youthful mistake, not a serious transgression. But if Vera did what Bea wanted, Vera's own prospects would be damaged, and not just with Arthur. The gossips of high society would never stop passing around the story about the Longacres' only daughter traipsing around unchaperoned with boys overnight. The tale would only grow worse as it reached the ears of any potential suitor, and Cliff, the one man who wouldn't hold it against her, would never be an acceptable choice now. He had only ever been a childish dream anyway.

What could she even say that would make things better for Bea? The facts told the complete story. They snuck out. They spent the night away and went out with boys without chaperones. Bea alone had faked the letters. She was a cheater who had once been caught alone in a room with a nude man. Vera could not dress any of it up to make what happened look less like the truth. Still, Vera couldn't stand the idea of saving herself while letting her friend suffer. Bea loved her, really loved her, without wanting anything more from her than her friendship. That was clear now.

The impossible choice tore at her. She could not satisfy both her mother and her conscience. She only had an hour to decide before her meeting with the dean.

« 28 »

Vera and Hallan continued to meet in the mornings, and he left his apartment after she did each time. He said he was working, and wanted to complete the job as soon as possible, given the increasingly hostile environment in the building. She had to admit that he was right about that. Every tea, luncheon, card game, and dinner she went to was consumed with talk of who Hallan might really be. Vera gave up defending him, not wishing to draw suspicions to herself. She hoped the men had forgotten their drunken decision to hire an investigator, but as she left one Wednesday to meet her mother for lunch, she discovered they had not forgotten a thing.

She got off the elevator on the ground floor, and her shoes clicked across the marble tiles as she made her way to the glass doors. Before she reached the entrance, the doorman let Clarence Bloomer in, along with a man Vera did not recognize.

"Vera," Clarence called across the lobby. "Do you have a moment? I'd like you to meet Mr. Stanton."

Mr. Stanton removed his bowler hat and nodded at her. He had a sturdy frame and wide, sad-dog eyes that made Vera feel she ought to rub his back and say soothing things.

"Mr. Stanton, is it? How do you do?" she said, with a discreet glance at her watch to be sure she was not running late for lunch.

"This is Mrs. Arthur Bellington, the wife of the building's owner and designer," Clarence said.

"Ah. So nice to meet you." Stanton took in the high ceilings of the lobby. "It's a grand building, just grand."

Clarence lowered his voice. "Mr. Stanton is the investigator I've hired to look into our little mystery."

Heat rose in Vera's face. "You're honestly going through with that? Forgive me, Mr. Stanton, I'm sure you do wonderful work. But really, Clarence. This is ludicrous."

"Well. Humph. We'll see about that, won't we? Come on, Stanton. We ought to get upstairs so we can talk more in private." Clarence strode toward the elevator.

"Yes. Right away." Stanton turned to Vera and spoke in a low tone. "If you're worrying about a scandal in your building, I wouldn't, Mrs. Bellington. In my line of work, I find most people prefer to see ghosts where there are none."

"Oh. Yes. Well, thank you."

He inclined his head again and followed Clarence to the elevator.

"Mrs. Bellington?"

Vera turned. The doorman stood holding the door open.

"Your car's here," he continued.

She hesitated, then left the building.

〈〈〈●〉〉〉

All through lunch with her mother and the evening that followed, Vera feared her nerves might jitter right out of her head. The investigator was here; he was right in the building, and he was on the hunt. What might he find out? And how quickly? If Hallan was not the man he said, would she want to know who he really was?

Alone in her bed that night, she sat up in the darkness, hugging her knees to her chest and trying not to think of what awful things she might learn. At last, she threw on a simple dress and went down the stairs to his apartment. She knew she should not wake him in the middle of the night. Worse still to wake his servants and have them talking. But she had to see him. Nothing else would suffice.

She had to knock twice before she got an answer, and even then it took five full minutes. The valet came to the door, bleary-eyed and blinking.

"And who should I tell him is calling?" the man asked.

"Just tell him someone's at the door, please. I believe he'll understand." Vera had to credit Ida's choice in servants. The man was a professional who asked the right thing, even at three o'clock in the morning.

At last Hallan appeared. His eyes widened and his mouth dropped. He rushed to Vera, leading her in.

"Thank you, Michael, that will be all." Hallan waited for the valet to leave. "Good Lord, Vera, what's the matter?"

Panic made her words tremble. "He's here. The private investigator. I've met him."

Hallan slumped against the wall, pinching the bridge of his nose. "Is that all? I told you, there's nothing to find."

Vera shook all over, her nervous energy getting the better of her at last. "Who are you? You must tell me everything. You must. I'll find out anyway."

Hallan grabbed her shoulders. "Calm down. Please. Come on, let's go talk." He took her hand and started for the bedroom, but she tore her hand away. "We can't talk in the living room," he said. "It's too close to the servants' rooms. Come with me."

She followed him to the bedroom, where he closed the door. He pulled a chair from the corner, and Vera sat. If she touched him, she might lose her resolve.

"Who are you, really? Why won't you tell me anything?" she asked in a whisper.

He sighed. "I can't."

"Are you a crook? Did you come here for money?"

"I came here for money for the work I'm doing. I would never steal."

"Then you're really working?"

"I am. Of course I am." He held up a hand, paint around the edges of his nails.

She sat silent, less terrified of the question she was about to ask than of its answer. "It's not just some painful memory, is it? You do have a secret."

He stared straight ahead. "Yes."

Vera felt as if someone had made a tiny hole in her, and everything inside was draining slowly away.

"Tell me. Tell me who you are," she said.

"I told you, I can't."

"You ought to leave. Get out of the city. When they find out, if it's bad enough, they'll throw you in prison. And that's not the worst of it. These are powerful men with enough money, friends, and time to make sure you regret coming here."

He shook his head. "I have to finish the job first."

"Why don't you have any work in the apartment?"

He looked at her askance. "Why would I have work in the apartment? I'm not painting a mural in here."

"You have to show it to me. If you're really painting, I want to see it."

He rubbed his eyes. "I don't want to show it to anyone until it's done. But you'll be the first, all right? Is that enough?"

"Enough?" She stood and crossed her arms over her chest. "Emil, you lied to me. Whatever the truth is, it must be terrible. Am I wrong?"

"It's not bad in the way you think. You won't hate me, I swear it. I will tell you everything when the work is done. And it will all make sense. Please. Believe me."

She dropped her eyes to the floor. "You know we can't see each other anymore."

He stood and crossed to her, laying a hand on her arm. "Vera, darling, nothing has changed, has it? I'm still the man I was. You know now there's something I haven't told you about myself, but that's true of everyone you know, I'd wager. Arthur . . . even your mother. Everyone has secrets. And I will tell you. Later."

Her shoulders drooped. He was right. She had withheld her secrets from him, for fear of what he would think. But she could not carry on with this man and whatever he was hiding. To do so would be too reckless. Even if Arthur would not be jealous, he would certainly make her sorry she embarrassed him. The other women would drop her from society. And her mother . . . no telling what her mother would do. But worst of all would be letting Hallan play her for a fool. She balled her hands into fists and gritted her teeth.

"No," she said. "I can't continue what we shouldn't have started in the first place."

He took her hand, easing the fingers from their clench. "I told you before, you've seen my art. That's the most important thing. All you need to know about me is in those paintings, my whole soul, everything I am. And I will tell you all those details you seem to feel are so important. I will. But I want you to see what I'm working on first. When you see that, it won't matter what I tell you."

"How can you say that? How can you be sure?"

"I just know it." A sad smile crossed his lips. "You love something about me, don't you? I know you do. Trust me now. You don't have to come here anymore, you don't even have to look at me if you don't want to. But allow me to show you the painting when it's done. Then I'll tell you everything."

She thought of the pang she felt when she first saw the photos of his paintings. Of the irresistible pull deep within her since then. She took a step back. "I'd better go. I don't want your servants telling everyone there was a woman here all night."

He nodded. "If that's what you want."

Despite all the objections of her rational mind, it was not what she wanted. She tried to force her feet to carry her to the door, but instead she threw herself into his arms. He kissed her, as though his lips could erase all her fears and doubts. There was something, some part of him she had glimpsed, that insisted he was who she knew him to be. He gave her something she needed, something she had not had for a long time. But he was also pulling her closer to a choice she had been faced with once before, between the demands of her heart and the obligations of her life. She did not want to be tempted by the same mistake again, but she could no longer see clearly which choice was right.

〈〈〈●〉〉〉

Before Vera left Hallan's apartment, she agreed to come back the next morning, when he could send his servants out. She went home, slept a few hours, and returned early. This time, she made no protest. Nearly without words, they went into the bedroom and made love. Her exhaustion after her sleepless night gave it the cloudy feel of a dream, and afterward she lay in his arms, her eyelids falling closed every once in a while as she dipped in and out of sleep.

His voice woke her. "I want to be with you forever. We'll go away together. When you leave Arthur . . ."

She rolled over onto her side. "I won't leave Arthur."

"I want you to talk as though you will. Just talk." Hallan ran his fingers up her arm.

"Don't be silly. I can't," she mumbled.

She drifted off again. When she woke, Hallan was dressing.

"I didn't want to wake you," he said, pulling on his suspenders, "but I need to go to work."

"Can we have a cup of tea first?" she asked.

"If you like. Anna's not here, of course, but I think she keeps it in the cabinet over the sink. The kettle is on the stove. Go on in, I'll be right there."

Vera buttoned the front of her dress and went to the kitchen. After opening a few cabinets, she found the tin of tea and set it on the table. The kettle sat on a burner on the stove, and she inspected the setup carefully before sitting in the chair by the window. Hallan came in a few minutes later and looked around questioningly.

"Did you put the tea on?" he asked.

She had hoped he would not ask. She feigned ignorance. "Put it on?"

"Yes. You didn't start the water boiling?"

"I didn't know you wanted me to."

"You wanted tea. I thought you'd make it."

"It's not my apartment."

He stared at her. "You don't know how to make tea, do you?"

She drew herself up. "I know how to make tea, for goodness sakes. It's the stove. I've never used one like that, that model. I didn't want to make a mistake lighting it. And the portions . . ."

He cast a sidelong glance at her but did not press the matter. Instead, he filled the kettle and set the water to boil. When the kettle whistled, he poured a cup for her but did not take one himself. She drank, embarrassed at her helplessness.

After she finished her tea, they kissed and left the apartment. She went upstairs, considering an idea that had come to her in the fog between sleeping and waking that morning.

《《《●》》》

Vera sat in the library with a newspaper spread over the desk. She scanned the headlines, but like yesterday and the day before, she could not find any mention of Fleming or the art forgery investigation. A voice in her head nagged her, whispered that she ought to try to find and help Bea. Vera's good judgment always prevailed over the thought, however. Attaching herself to Bea's disgrace would do nothing to help if she had actually forged paintings, but it would connect Vera to a criminal. And how would she even find her now? Surely Bea had the good sense to get out of the city.

The door creaked open behind her. She nearly jumped out of her skin at the interruption.

"Yes, Evans?"

"Mr. Stanton is here to see you," Evans said.

Vera refolded the newspapers and sat on the couch. "Thank you. Please, show him in."

Stanton came in and handed his bowler to Evans, who left the two of them to talk. Vera indicated the chair closest to her, and Stanton sat, adjusting the lapels of his brown wool suit.

"Thank you for coming on such short notice," she said.

"I was lucky enough to be available." He smiled, but the sadness in his eyes lingered.

"Would you like something to drink?" She rose and went to the little cart that held the liquor decanters.

"A glass of port would be very nice, thank you."

Vera poured Stanton's drink, then sat on the couch again. She had expected to feel nervous, but something about Stanton's worn-leather voice put her at ease. "You must be wondering why I asked you here."

"I believe I can make a guess."

She smoothed her skirt over her knees. "Well, naturally I wanted to find out how the investigation is going. If you've discovered anything. As the wife of the building's owner, it's critical that I know as much as possible about what happens in our home."

Stanton studied the glass in his hand. "Naturally. Although I'm afraid I'm bound to Mr. Bloomer. You understand, he's the man who hired me. I'm sure he'll be good enough to share my findings with you, when I have them."

"I'm sure he will," Vera said, her back tensing.

When he spoke again, his voice was softer. "Mrs. Bellington, I hope you'll forgive me for saying so, but you seem to have a singular interest in this case. Is something troubling you beyond your concern for the others in the building?"

Stanton's weary, elder-brother manner made her want to unburden herself, as if she could tell him everything and he would pat her head and say things would work out all right in the end. That confessorial air probably came in handy when he was trying to get information. She resisted the urge to spill everything, but decided to cut to the chase. There was no point in trying to hide her true intentions.

"I want you to come to me first with anything you find about Mr. Hallan," she said. "I'll pay whatever you ask. And you can still tell Clarence Bloomer, of course. But, if you agree, I'd like to know before anyone else."

Stanton considered this. "That would be unusual. When I have an agreement with a client, he's always the first to know what I turn up."

She offered a small smile. "Think of me as a new client, then. I would also like to know about Mr. Hallan. I just want to know sooner. I'm not asking you to deceive Clarence, or anyone else. And, as I said, I'll pay you whatever you think is fair for this type of request."

"All right. I suppose there's no harm in it, as long as I honor my agreement with Mr. Bloomer." Stanton drained the last of his port.

"So have you? Found anything, I mean?"

"Nothing yet. My contacts in Europe should get back to me in the next week or so." Stanton glanced at her out of the corner of his eye. "Until then, I'm interviewing people around here. Neighbors, servants . . . that sort of thing."

Servants. She cursed her own carelessness. Hallan's servants had seen her come to the apartment in the middle of the night. And they likely knew Hallan was entertaining a woman by the frequency of their mornings off, to say nothing of any hints of her presence left after her departure. How much could a whiff of perfume or a lipstick smudge on a glass tell them? If Stanton had not already spoken to them, he would soon enough. Vera stood quickly, and Stanton rose beside her.

"Yes," she said. "Well. We'll keep this little arrangement to ourselves, shall we? And please, do let Evans know how much I owe you for this. I'll have the money to you as soon as possible."

Stanton held out a hand to her. She hesitantly placed her hand in his.

"I pride myself on the ability to read people, Mrs. Bellington. To see through the person someone presents to the world, down to his truest intention and feeling. You'd be surprised how much most people give away, despite the masks they wear." The corners of his mouth rose once more, and he gently squeezed her fingers. "So much goes on beneath the surface, and so few people are inclined to look."

Vera's shoulders tensed. "I suppose I don't have to maintain any pretense with you, in that case."

"It likely wouldn't do you any good," he said. He took a step toward the door, then stopped, meeting her eyes once more. "I wonder . . . I wonder if you might consider that knowledge of Mr. Hallan's past won't be an answer to the question you really have?"

She thought for a moment. "I don't understand."

"Mr. Bloomer's interest in Mr. Hallan reveals a lot about him. As does, I would say, your own interest. I don't mean to cause offense. May I speak plainly?"

Vera considered how rarely anyone she knew did. She nodded.

"From what I've seen in my work, other cases, I'd surmise that Mr. Hallan is making you question yourself rather more than you're questioning him." He bowed his head to her. "Good evening, Mrs. Bellington."

《《《●》》》

The women of the Angelus building lacked imagination. They knew of one way and one way only to welcome a new acquaintance into their social circle, and that was for one of them to host a dinner party. Despite his status as a temporary employee, Ida Bloomer had decided that Stanton merited a dinner in his honor. Vera thought they might want to keep Stanton's engagement a secret from Hallan, but as with most things, they were determined to flaunt the detective. She considered wryly that they probably took great delight in being the first building on the block to have need of one.

The chosen evening fell a week after the investigator came to speak to Vera in the penthouse. Vera braved the event alone, as Arthur had a late meeting. She thought being seated by Stanton at the table would give her the opportunity to speak more with him, but learning more about him seemed to be everyone's goal. The brisk conversation meant she could not get his attention, though she was only a few inches away.

"Tell me," Ida said, waving a fork at the detective. "How does a man find himself in your line of work, Mr. Stanton?"

He set down his cup. "I was a police officer in Concord for a few years but had to leave the force because of an injury." He touched the right side of his rib cage. "I knew I wanted to continue with detective work, and this seemed to be the wisest way to do so."

Andrew Keller leaned over Vera to get Stanton's attention. "Do you mind, may I see your license?"

"Is this an official inquiry?" Stanton said, his tone playful.

Andrew laughed. He pointed his index fingers at Stanton. "Stick 'em up! Isn't that what you say?"

"No, it isn't." Stanton reached into his breast pocket and produced a small white card. He turned with a smile to answer Andrew's baffled silence. "At least, not anymore."

Andrew's grin returned. "Oh. Oh, no, not anymore."

Stanton passed the card in front of Vera, and she caught sight of a seal and a scratchy signature. Andrew took the card, his mouth wide in something approaching awe.

"It must be simply thrilling," Caroline Litchfield said. "Following dangerous men all over the city, at all hours of the night."

Bessie Harper snorted. "Didn't know that was your idea of a thrill, Caroline."

Caroline ignored the comment, and Stanton shook his head, his weary eyes still friendly. "I'm afraid I don't do much surveillance. Most of the job is writing letters, checking files, that sort of thing."

This answer deflated Caroline a bit. She clearly preferred her version of Stanton's life. "Then you don't ever have to follow anyone?"

"Well, you don't expect me to reveal all my methods, do you?" He glanced around at the others and lowered his voice. "Trade secrets, you know."

The ladies tittered and the men grumbled their approval. Martha Keller tilted her head, nearly batting her eyelids at the detective.

"Then I suppose you can't tell us anything you've found about the artist?" she asked. "You must know something by now."

Stanton shook his head. "Nothing I can say. But when I find something, I'm sure it will get around soon enough." He turned to Ida. "I understand you're on the opera board. That must be fascinating work. Will you tell me about that?"

Ida's cheeks reddened like a schoolgirl's, and she launched into an exhaustive description of her duties. Vera watched Stanton out of the corner of her eye. She could not help but notice that he, like Hallan, could expertly turn a conversation away from himself.

When they finished the meal, the men adjourned to their cigars, and the ladies to their cordials and chatter. Without Arthur to collect her, Vera would have to disentangle herself at the appropriate time. Fortunately, the other women were engrossed in a conversation about the investigator that she was not part of, and she was able to leave after only a few good-byes.

She rang for the elevator. Before the car arrived, a voice rang out down the hall.

"Mrs. Bellington." Stanton waved and walked toward her. He had a slight hitch in his walk she had not noticed before, and she thought of him laying a hand on his side at dinner.

"Mr. Stanton. Did you enjoy the party?"

"I did. Mrs. Bloomer is quite a hostess."

"She is that. You're not having cigars with the others?"

"No, I don't smoke. Besides, I have an early morning." The elevator doors slid open, and Stanton gestured for Vera to enter. "I wonder, would you mind riding down and walking me out?"

She hesitated. "Surely you don't need help finding your way out?"

He smiled, but his eyes held hers in a firm gaze. "No, it's not that. It's so clear out, I thought we might go for a walk. Have a quick chat?"

"Oh. Oh, yes, of course. Let's." She stepped onto the elevator, avoiding the operator's eyes. The doors closed, and they rode together to the lobby.

When they walked into the night air, the autumn chill bit through Vera's silk gown, and she flinched. Stanton noticed and draped his coat around her shoulders. They fell into an easy stroll down the sidewalk.

"Thank you," she said. "So, you have information already?"

"I do. But not the information you've paid me for. I'm still waiting on word from my contacts in Europe." He scratched the dark stubble on his cheek.

"Then why did you want to talk to—" She stopped short and clamped her mouth shut.

He nodded. "I thought it prudent to advise you."

Her heart dropped. "You know."

"Yes, I know."

"How?"

"Because knowing is my business. It's my livelihood." He looked across the street. "You had to realize I'd find out sooner or later."

She pulled his coat tighter around her. "Was it the servants? Mine or his?"

"As I said at dinner, best not to reveal too many trade secrets."

She let out a bitter laugh. "Dinner. Wait until Clarence Bloomer hears about this."

"That's not the information he paid me for, either. He wants to know who Hallan is, not how he spends his time in New York. I don't see any reason to tell him."

She shivered. "Why should they care? It's all nonsense. They have nothing better to do than invent scandals."

"Forgive me, but you said I can speak plainly with you, and I will. They may have invented a scandal in Mr. Hallan's past. I don't know yet if their concerns are valid on that point. But the relationship you have with him will be a scandal, and it will cause you grief. If you continue to see him, someone will find out."

She lifted her chin. "Don't be ridiculous. I don't plan to continue with him. I know I told you to speak frankly with me, but I think you're speaking a little too frankly about things you don't understand."

Despite her haughtiness, his words never lost their fatherly warmth. "On the contrary, I only speak this frankly about things I do understand. I've seen this more times than you can imagine, and it never ends well for the wife. No matter what her role in the whole scenario. I want you to consider the possible outcomes, and start settling yourself to achieve the one that benefits you most."

She took in a deep breath, then exhaled slowly through pursed lips. "Why are you telling me this?"

"Because there's something about you that's thoughtful. You're an intelligent person. You could be just another woman in another ill-conceived love affair, or you could take care of yourself first. I strongly advise you to begin to think now about how you want all this to end. If it's an escape you're after, some kind of change, there are better choices you could make."

She did not answer right away. When she finally spoke, her voice was unsteady. "It will end, of course. I plan to end it. I'm not a fool."

"No. No, you're not." He lifted a hand in the direction of the entrance. "I've kept you out here long enough. Let's get you inside."

He walked with her back into the lobby. With some reluctance, she handed him his coat. She had enjoyed its soft, warm comfort. The weight of it had been a bit like having Stanton's arm around her shoulder. She worried she might drift away without it.

"Thank you again," she said.

"It was my pleasure." He tipped his hat. "I'll be in touch. Most likely very soon. Good night, Mrs. Bellington."

Vera's conversation with Stanton shook her. The problem was not that he knew about the affair. He was a savvy man, and he did not seem to think any less of her, as his kindness had proven. She was more bothered by the fact that having an open conversation with someone about her relationship with Hallan confirmed it. Now their trysts were fact, instead of some daydream she could brush away.

The morning after the dinner party, even the spacious penthouse stifled her. She went out for a walk, something she hardly ever did. With no particular destination in mind, she walked down Park Avenue, brushing past men carrying briefcases and secretaries tapping along the concrete in high heels. The cool breeze lifted Vera's spirits, and her head began to clear.

She turned a corner and nearly bumped into a woman who was attempting to walk while reading a newspaper. Vera opened her mouth to excuse herself, but her jaw clamped shut when the newspaper lowered and she saw the woman's face.

For a moment, both women paused. Vera assumed Bea was trying to make the same decision she was. Would they walk on, as they had done every other time they had seen each other in the city, or would they finally speak? Bea took a step to go around, but Vera held up her hand.

"Ah." Bea tucked the newspaper under her arm. "So you want to talk, do you? After so long. I'd ask about your health, but the truth is, I don't much care."

Vera nearly took her at her word and let her go, but the slight catch in Bea's voice held her there. "We'll leave the niceties out of it, then." She glanced over her shoulder. The Angelus building was still in sight. "What are you doing in this part of town?"

Bea's lowered lids suggested she was not impressed. "You mean your part of town? I'm meeting a friend. Other people live around here too, you know."

"So you knew I was living at the Angelus?"

"Fleming couldn't shut up about his high-class visitor. I pieced it together."

Vera stepped closer to the nearest building, out of the way of the passing crowd. She lowered her voice. "I saw the news about him. The arrest."

Bea laughed. "Fleming? He'll be fine."

"And you?"

"Don't you know me at all? I'm already fine."

"Why are you still in the city? Aren't the police looking for you?"

"No. They're looking for Bea Stillman." Bea paused to let the meaning sink in. Her eyes gleamed with defiance. "So this is what became of Vera Longacre. You married Arthur and got everything you wanted. Is it? What you wanted? Ever wish *you* got a new name?"

Vera could hear the questions behind the one Bea asked. *Was it worth it? What you did to me?* She threw her shoulders back. "You lied to me."

"I didn't lie to you. I just didn't tell you everything. There's a difference. I deserved a new start." Bea's grin was a flash of the girl from ten years ago. "Now I can get one whenever I like. As a matter of fact, I am leaving the city. Soon. But I'm so glad we had the chance to catch up. Now, if you'll excuse me, I really don't want to take up any more of your valuable time."

Vera held Bea's gaze. A sudden urge to say everything she would have said on that awful day at Vassar seized her, and she could not move. Bea watched her, studying Vera's face as she struggled. Vera willed the apology to come, but it would not. She wanted to say she had been wrong. She needed to confess. She craved forgiveness, even if she did not deserve it.

Instead, she said, "I had to. You know I had to."

"Hmph. You 'had to.'" Bea cocked her head. "That man I saw you with at the movie theater. I know that wasn't Arthur." She flicked the newspaper. "Society pages. You and Arthur are all over them, and I've never seen that man with you once."

Vera shook her head. "No."

"So? Is that man ruining your life, or saving it?"

"I . . ." Vera swallowed hard. "I don't know."

Bea's tight smile was somewhere between amusement and pity. "I hope someday you'll realize you don't always 'have to.' Good-bye, Vera."

Vera stood on the corner, unable to watch Bea walk away.

« 29 »

Double-cross. One of those vulgar slang terms she would have chided Bea for using. The word would never pass her lips, especially not now, in the heart of the very act. The proper term to use would be *betray*. Her mother's euphemism for it would be *preservation*. Preserving one's own reputation. Slang, proper, or euphemistic, all versions of the concept applied to Vera's presence in the dean's office.

The kindness of the slender, white-haired woman's eyes did nothing to calm Vera's shaking hands. Two cups of tea sat, untouched, on the table between them. Vera gripped the arms of her chair, grateful that her mother had not been allowed to sit in the office while the meeting took place. Her mother's gloating presence would make the lie harder to say.

"If you could, I'd like you to tell me in your own words what happened." Miss McCaleb even smiled, but Vera couldn't return the gesture.

"I didn't know Bea made the letters. She told me she'd written to my mother in secret, to surprise me. I thought we had permission." Vera intoned the words she'd rehearsed in her head in a dull voice. The lie scraped her throat as it came out, but she could not reach for the tea. She didn't deserve comfort.

"Where did you stay in New Haven?"

"She had a friend at a ladies' boardinghouse. Otherwise I would have asked to come straight back. I would have known. It all seemed right."

"Then what did you say when you saw there was no chaperone?" Miss McCaleb asked.

"I knew it was strange, but she said the school had approved her cousin as chaperone. I thought since he was her family it must have been a special case. And we were staying with ladies . . ." Exhaustion washed over her. She wanted the conversation to be over. She battled the lump in her throat and put the appropriate level of pleading into her voice. "Bea lied, that's all. She tricked me. I promise. I would never knowingly disobey the school's rules. Or my mother's."

Miss McCaleb scanned the papers on her desk, then removed her reading glasses. "I want to set your mind at ease. Obviously I can't discuss another student's discipline, but I can say your record these past few years speaks for itself, just as Miss Stillman's speaks for her. This incident has also brought to light some information about her behavior at her previous school . . . but I won't trouble you with that. We have a very clear picture of Beatrice Stillman. After hearing your two versions of the story, I don't think you have anything to worry about. I'll have my official determination tomorrow morning." She tilted her head sympathetically. "But please, Miss Longacre, do be careful in the future about whom you choose as a friend."

Miss McCaleb said a few more things, Vera's mother came in, fears were assuaged, and final pleasantries exchanged. But Vera heard none of it. Nothing after the word *friend*. She lay in bed that night, staring at the blank darkness of the hotel room. *Friend* rang in her head, again and again, silly and empty. Vera couldn't give a thought to whether or not she was a true friend. Not when everything confirmed she wasn't even a good person. Oh, she was a very good Longacre. She'd make a good wife to Arthur, too. A good member of the society to which she was born. But a good person?

No, she thought. *I made my choice.*

« 30 »

As the days passed, Vera grew more and more agitated at the thought that, at any moment, news might be traveling across the Atlantic from Stanton's sources. News she did not want to hear. Despite the detective's warnings that her secret would come out, she continued to visit Hallan in the mornings. She could not keep herself away. Stanton was correct to say she could not go on as she had forever, but when she was in Hallan's arms, the need to end the affair never felt as urgent as she knew it should. She tried to forget the awkward interaction with Bea on the street, but every look at Hallan's face reminded her of Bea's question: *Is that man ruining your life, or saving it?* Vera feared the answer was "both."

She kept up some of her social schedule in the afternoons and evenings, though she declined as many invitations as she accepted. In her absence, something about the teas and card games began to change, so that when she joined them again everything was slightly off. The strangeness eased in like a fog, covering everything before Vera quite noticed it was there. The other women grew colder, their conversations distilled down to talk of the weather or the ballet. At last, she realized they were waiting to really talk until she was not there. They wanted to talk about Hallan, and she was in the way.

She had not been back from Hallan's long enough to take off her hat one morning when a knock sounded at the door. Evans looked at her questioningly.

"I wasn't expecting anyone. Go ahead, though," she said.

He opened the door to reveal Poppy, who breezed right by without acknowledging him.

"Vera, good, you're home," she said airily. "Do you have a moment? I'd like to speak to you."

"Of course. Evans there can take your gloves, if you like." Vera stared pointedly at the man closing the door.

"Oh. Here." Poppy yanked her gloves off and held them out to the side, waiting silently until he took them.

"Well," Vera said. "Won't you come into the drawing room? I was just going to call for a cup of tea. Would you like something?"

"No, thank you," Poppy said. "I can't stay long."

She followed Vera into the drawing room and sat on the couch. Vera sat on a chair, more comfortable with the coffee table between them as a buffer.

"To what do I owe the pleasure of this unexpected visit?" Vera said.

Poppy looked her up and down. "You can save the pleasantries, Vera. You don't need them with me anymore."

Vera clenched her teeth. "Oh? How's that?"

"I've found out something very interesting about you."

"Did you?"

"Yes." A slow, snakelike smile crept across Poppy's face. "It seems the perfect Vera can make mistakes. You see, I know what you've been up to with the artist."

A pleasant calm washed over Vera. The fear of this moment had plagued her, but she had not once imagined Poppy Hastings would be the one to confront her. Any dread she had was replaced with the usual certainty that she need not fear this woman. She gave a cold smile, and Poppy's smug look wavered.

"How did you find out?" Vera asked.

Poppy sat up a little straighter. "My maid spoke to his maid. I guess they're friends, and they were in my kitchen talking. His maid said something about a woman coming around a lot. Big secret, he always gives her and his valet mornings off. Said the valet told her it was someone in the building, dark hair, very posh." She sniffed. "Are you going to try to deny it now?"

Vera had prepared several plausible denials for just this sort of occasion, but she would not dignify Poppy's pathetic attempt to frighten her. The woman would not leave Vera's home victorious over her, not for any reason. She kept her tone light and comfortable. "No. I won't deny it."

Poppy's eyes widened, and she cleared her throat. "Well. Good. Because I knew anyway. You were so wary of him when he got here, then all of a sudden you were defending him. Wouldn't let anyone say a word against him. And I saw how angry you were when he . . . well, after the incident in Montauk. When he tried to seduce me. And then he ran after you to console you."

Vera folded her arms on her chest. "Aren't you clever? And tell me, what do you plan to do with this information? I assume you'll tell Arthur. Were you going to phone him, or just drop an anonymous note in the post?"

Poppy opened and closed her mouth a few times before she could get any words out. "I will. I will tell Arthur. Unless you agree to a few things."

"Oh, so it's blackmail. All right, let's hear your demands."

Poppy's eyes narrowed. "I want what you have."

"I beg your pardon?"

"You're the one the other ladies look to. They listen to you. Respect you. And now, I want you to respect me. Whenever there's a decision to be made among us, you will defer to me." Poppy pointed at Vera. "And I won't have you chastising me anymore, either. In public or in private."

Vera felt a little twinge in her heart at how pitiful the terms were.

254 « AMBER BROCK

"Respect is something earned, Poppy. It cannot be gifted or trans-
ferred."

"You'll figure out a way, or I'll tell your little secret to anyone who
will listen."

"And you'll still be a gossip."

Poppy stood. "You think you're better than me, don't you? Just because you live in the penthouse, and I live on the fifth floor."

"This isn't about money. There are plenty of vulgar people with lots
of money."

"Are you calling me vulgar?"

Vera rose from her chair and took a few slow steps toward Poppy.
"I think you are a rude woman. And ungrateful. I think you are a little
girl playing dress-up, and that nothing will ever be enough. You want
to take my place? Take it. It won't be enough. There will always be
some prize out of reach, some penthouse above a woman like you."

Poppy's nostrils flared, and she clutched her purse so hard her
knuckles turned white. "How dare you talk to me like that? When I
know what I do?"

Vera leaned in. "Because I'm not afraid of you. Tell Arthur, if it will
make you feel better. Much good may it do you. I'd be surprised if he
wasn't more annoyed that you'd bothered him."

Poppy started to tremble. "I will tell him. I will! I'll tell everyone.
I'll give you some time to think it over, because once you realize what
this means, I'm sure you'll see things my way. I can ruin you."

She stormed toward the door and slammed it behind her. Alone
once more, Vera sat in the nearest chair, drawing in a deep breath.
Why had she made no attempt to deny the affair? She could have at
least bought herself a little more time. But she could not let Poppy
dominate her. Vera could not conceive of a moment so dark that she
would yield to a callow gold digger. Daring her to tell provided a moment of welcome amusement, but now that Poppy's flustered expression was no longer in view, Vera regretted her choice to admit so easily
to the affair. She did not really believe Poppy would tell Arthur, at least

not directly. He intimidated her too much for her to march up with news of his wife's infidelity. She would, however, take great pleasure in telling the other women as soon as it became apparent that Vera had no intention of deferring to her. That was what Poppy really wanted, and she would give it time to happen. Still, the news would get to Arthur one way or another, and he would make sure her mother knew. Then she would really have to answer for the affair, and they would certainly see to it that Hallan suffered, too. The only question left now was not if, but when.

《《《 ● 》》》

As Vera predicted, Poppy did not seem to rush to make good on her threat to tell Arthur about Vera and Hallan. Arthur came home from work relatively early the next few evenings, and even dined with Vera twice without saying a word. It occurred to Vera that Poppy had evidence enough to satisfy herself and the other ladies, but maybe not enough to present to Vera's husband as damning proof. The word of a maid and speculation from Poppy would never rattle Arthur. But apparently she had been true to her word about giving Vera time to concede, as no one else acted as if they knew about the affair either. The other women continued to invite her to social events and were cordial as ever in their interactions.

Though Vera knew she was tempting fate, she continued to visit Hallan. She knew she ought to stop. Every night she convinced herself she would not go back, and every morning her feet led her to his door.

One morning she rolled over, tangling herself in the sheets as he sat up beside her. "You've given up telling me things, do you realize that?" she asked.

Hallan toyed with a lock of her hair. "You're too clever as it is. Any more information would ruin you."

She sat up on one elbow. "Believe me, I know by now you're not going tell me anything of consequence. We've talked about art, poetry, music . . . but not you."

He held up his hands. "That is me. Those are the things I care about."

She sighed and lay on her back. "Poppy knows about us. I should have told you. She visited me the other day. Seems your maid has a loose tongue."

"You don't seem worried."

"I ought to be." She studied the white metal tiles of the ceiling. "Stanton knows, too."

"Who?"

"The private investigator."

"Anyone else?"

"Probably. Soon everyone will, at this rate."

"I hope Arthur's next. Then you can leave with me."

She swatted his arm. "I've told you, that's not going to happen."

"But it could. If you wanted to, you could go."

"I'd need a better reason than that." She lifted her slip from the chair and dressed as Hallan prepared to leave to work.

When Vera came in from Hallan's, Evans surprised her with the news that she had a caller in the drawing room. She went in to find Stanton sitting on the couch, drinking a cup of coffee. A stack of folded pages sat on the table beside him. On seeing Vera, Stanton put his cup on the table and rose.

"Mr. Stanton," she said. "So good of you to come."

He nodded. "Mrs. Bellington."

"Please, sit. I assume you have news for me?"

He took the papers from the table, and her heart began to drum against her ribs. Her head swam, and she sat. Before he spoke, he flipped through them, as if to remind himself of their contents. He looked up and met her gaze.

"Are you sure you want to know?" he asked.

"Y-yes," she said, her voice small and wispy.

He sighed. "I had my contact comb through records in Paris. He telegraphed and wrote to associates in London. He was very thorough. Birth records, hospitals, police precincts, prisons. He visited the school Mr. Hallan says he attended. All of it pointed to the same answer."

"And what's that?" Vera's nails dug into her palms in an effort to keep her hands from shaking.

"There is no Emil Hallan."

For a moment, Vera sat unblinking. That could not be true. She had held Hallan's hand in the ocean. She kissed him. She felt his heartbeat close to hers. He told her about how he chose the colors, how art was supposed to make you feel human. He gave her poetry. She had wondered if he might be a criminal of the worst kind. She could never have imagined that he might not exist at all. One word escaped her, more a whimper than a word. "What?"

"There were no records of any man by that name in London or Paris. No one by that name at the Ecole des Beaux-Arts."

Her hand flew to her mouth. "Well, who is he then?"

"That I don't know. I'm still working to match his description, but that could take a very long time." He leaned forward and spoke in a low voice. "Long enough for him to leave before I find it, I'm afraid. Do you understand?"

Vera nodded. She drew in a few labored breaths. He was not Emil Hallan. Or, if he was, he had not gone to the Ecole des Beaux-Arts in Paris. Nor had he been born in London. Her stomach twisted.

Who was he?

"I do know one thing for certain," Stanton said, with a slight hesitation.

"O-oh?"

He rubbed his chin. "You paid for his passage from Paris, correct? On the *Leviathan*?"

"We did."

"I spoke with several attendants on the *Leviathan*. Mr. Hallan's stateroom was never occupied."

"What do you mean, never occupied?"

"Just that. The room never needed cleaning, he never came for his meals . . . no one was in his room."

She closed her eyes tightly. "That's impossible. We picked him up from the docks. He had his trunk."

"He found some other way to get to the States, then. But my sources all agree. His room was empty."

She could not listen to any more. Her knees wobbled as she rushed to stand. "Thank you, Mr. Stanton, you've been very helpful. Will you go to Clarence Bloomer right away?"

"No, I thought I would try to find more information before I concluded my report. I doubt this will be enough to satisfy him. He'll want to know who this man is. When I find out more, would you like me to contact you first again?"

"No, thank you. This is quite enough." She stuck out a hand, and he stood and shook it.

"If you're certain," he said.

"I am. Thank you again."

The detective closed the door, and Vera covered her face with her hands. Her heart had frozen, as if it had stopped beating entirely. When she could feel it pulsing again, it gulped and stuttered. Hallan was not Hallan. All the fears she had about him lying surged forward again. She stood and headed out the door, unable to bear her own silence a moment longer.

Vera raced down the stairs to Hallan's apartment as soon as the front door closed behind Stanton, the beads on her dress shimmying and shushing as she ran. She stood outside the door to 2A to catch her breath, then knocked. Hallan's valet answered.

"Is Mr. Hallan in?" she asked. "I need to speak to him."

"I'm sorry, madam, he's not."

"Then I'll wait."

He frowned. "I'm sorry, it may be quite some time. He usually doesn't come upstairs from working until very late at night. Shall I go down and tell him you're here?"

"Yes, please, will you?"

The valet stepped aside so Vera could enter. "Let me show you to the drawing room."

"No need. I know where it is. Thank you for fetching him."

The valet left, and Vera went into the drawing room. Too anxious to sit, she paced in front of the mantel. As she waited, she mentally prepared what she wanted to say. The maid came in to offer a drink, and Vera gratefully requested a gin and tonic. She had just hit the bottom of the glass when she heard the front door open.

Hallan strode into the room. His face, shirt, and arms were flecked with pale blue paint. Even his hair had dots of paint here and there.

"What's the matter?" he asked, a little out of breath.

She swallowed hard. "I found out something today that I want you to explain to me."

His face went slack. He sat and took a deep breath. "All right. If I can."

"I spoke to the private investigator. He said he's searched all over London and Paris. The art school included. He says there is no record of anyone named Emil Hallan."

He rubbed his forehead, his eyes squeezed shut. "I said he wouldn't find anything, didn't I?"

"Then that isn't your name? I don't even know your real name?"

"No."

The word shattered her last hope. Her knees buckled, and she sat in a chair. "Oh God."

"What does it matter? It's only a name."

"It's not 'only a name,'" she cried. "I let you into my home, into my bed, and I don't even know who you are. None of it's true, you didn't study at that school—"

"I admit it." His voice was firm. "I didn't study at the Ecole des Beaux-Arts."

She lifted her head. Finally, some truth from his own mouth. "Did you study art at all?"

"I did."

"I suppose it would be pointless to ask your real name."

"My first name is Emil, that's true. It's only my last name you don't know." He stared out the window. "Last names only matter to people like you."

She let out a harsh laugh. "People like me? Honest people? People with nothing to hide?"

"People at the top. It's your calling card, your invitation. The way to show you belong and keep other people out. Believe me, my last name is of no use to you." He pointed at her. "And you hide plenty, by the way."

"Don't you dare act as though what I've done is the same as what you've done. You lied about everything. He said you weren't on the boat. How did you even get here?"

Hallan did not answer, though she half hoped he would. He had told her a little something. Maybe she could make him open the gates if she found the right question. She stared at him for a moment before continuing. "You could be anyone. What is it, do you have a wife you're running from?"

"No."

"Children?"

"No."

"Some horrible crime? You could be a murderer for all I know."

He pressed a fist to his mouth. When he spoke it was so low she could barely hear, as if each word pained him. "I am not a murderer."

"How would I know that? Why should I believe you?"

He moved to the couch beside her. "Because you know me. You do. I know you care for me. And you've waited this long . . . let me finish the painting, and then I'll tell you everything."

She cursed herself. Despite everything, all her fears and concerns, she still felt drawn to him, more each day. She wanted to believe him. To hear his story, see his painting. And she wanted him to be safe. He lied, yes, but he could never be dangerous. She laid a hand on his knee. "The investigator is still looking for more information about you, and he'll find it. Why don't you go now? While you still can?"

"I'm going to finish the painting first."

"Forget the painting! What does that matter?"

He stared ahead, his eyes fixed and resolute. "I have to finish the painting before I leave. It's nearly done. Then I'll go. And I want you to come with me."

Vera stood. When he had made the offer before, she had enjoyed hearing him say the words. Now the idea turned her stomach to lead. "I can't leave with you. I don't know you."

He rose and took a tentative step toward her. "Yes, you do. Please, Vera. Think about it. What do you have here?"

"A home, a husband, my family—"

"And it's suffocating you. They're going to drain you until there's nothing left but a shell. If you leave, you have a chance to be that woman you said you ought to have been. You'll have a chance at a real life. Why does this have to be tied up in the past? Why can't it be about the future?"

She shook her head. "There is no future. Not with you. This is absurd."

"I'm only asking you to think about it. And I'll show you the painting and tell you everything. Then you can decide. But I want to be with you. I want to take you out of this place."

The floor spun beneath her. "I—I have to go. I can't . . . I've got to go."

He nodded. "Go. But think about it."

《《《 ● 》》》

Ridiculous. Hallan's proposal was ridiculous. She could not run away, least of all with a man about whom she knew nothing, someone who lied to her right from the start. And they had nothing. She had no money of her own, and who knew if Hallan could get a job? Where would they go? The whole idea was lunacy.

Then why did she keep picturing them on a train? Why could she clearly see them, side by side on a rattling train car, speeding toward a new life? Why could she not stop herself from thinking which of her belongings she would take with her, and what she would leave behind? Something inside her begged her to take the elevator down one final time and never come back.

As pervasive as thoughts of Hallan were, Vera could not help but think of Bea, too. Did she have to invent elaborate lies to hide her disgrace, as Hallan did? Vera's confession ten years before might have set Bea off on the path that led to forgery. Vera could choose the train, choose the new life. Bea had been forced. In the moments when Vera was most honest, she had to acknowledge that the speed with which she had forgiven herself for the way she had treated Bea years ago diminished her. Thinking of it made her feel small, almost pathetic.

With Hallan, at least, Vera could console herself that she could say good-bye to him before he left. And she would. If they parted for good, it would not be in the confused silence that had separated her and Bea, her and Cliff. Vera had heard shortly after returning from Vassar that Bea was expelled. Vera had tried to find out more, but soon the stream of gossip dried up. She could not inquire too insistently, lest her mother get word. Vera assumed Bea's family had taken her home to Atlanta, until she first spotted Bea on the street in the city years later. They had been robbed of a chance to say even the simplest good-bye. Their encounter on the street was hardly an ideal final conversation. Vera would not allow that to happen between her and Hallan.

The thoughts and questions muddied her mind as she moved in a daze through her daily life. She assumed Hallan continued to paint, but for the next few days she was at last able to stay away from his apartment, and he left her alone. The loss of him in her day was palpable. A gnawing hunger opened up inside her and never let her forget him. She hoped he would finish soon and go, and she could attempt to return to her life as it had been.

Arthur still seemed to know nothing about the affair. If anything, he became more pleasant than he had been in a long while. He dined at home more often, struck up lively conversations with her instead of keeping his nose in the financial news, and went out of his way to compliment her. Once he even planned a full evening out, complete with dinner and a play, perhaps finally making good on his promise after he failed to meet her at the Ritz. His behavior, while friendlier, was still not exactly loving, but Vera had more hope than ever they could get there if she just tried a little harder.

Even the cold shoulder Poppy turned to her when they entered the Litchfields' apartment for a dinner party one evening did not extend to the other women. Ida Bloomer greeted Vera like a long-lost sister and admonished her for not attending the ballet with them a few evenings before.

"We missed you terribly, dear," Ida said. "Though I hope it wasn't because you were ill again. Poor darling, to have health troubles, young as you are."

"Everything is fine now, thank you. And I certainly plan to be at your luncheon tomorrow." Vera smiled.

"Oh, wonderful. It hasn't been the same without you."

The maid came in to announce dinner, and Ida took Vera's arm as they went to the dining room. Vera noted with some satisfaction that her place card sat at the top of the table, as near Caroline's seat as she could be. Even with her recent absences, she still retained her status in the building. Perhaps it had even been heightened. They had been distant when the artist was the hot subject of discussion, but when she avoided them, their interest in her seemed to have revived. Yes, she could fall back into the rhythm of her life as if the artist had never existed.

She was chatting with Kenneth Harper about his new car when something Arthur said to Caroline caught her attention.

". . . and so I'll be in Philadelphia for a week, then it's on to Boston," he said. "Not to mention late nights at the office, too many of those to count. Vera will have to attend these things without an escort for a good while."

Vera's throat tightened. Another one of his extended "business" trips. He hadn't had one in a while. Now Vera wondered if the pleasantness that had passed between them the last few days was his way of placating her in advance of this news.

The trips had started shortly after they were married. He claimed there was the need to visit a lot of building sites, shake a lot of important hands. She had been terribly proud of her busy husband. Then, a little over two years into their marriage, she got a phone call from the Tiffany store. A clerk named Mr. Blake cheerfully reported that the pocket watch Arthur had ordered was ready early. Of course, Arthur could still pick it up on the agreed-upon date, but the clerk thought the client might like it delivered to the Plaza instead. Mr. Bellington had mentioned he was staying there, Mr. Blake explained, but then an assistant noticed that the home number on Arthur's profile card was in the city. The clerk thought he ought to phone Mr. Bellington's home in case he misheard. Confusion had given way to the sinking realization that although Vera's husband might indeed be in a room at the Plaza, whoever was staying in the room with him was not his wife. More than that, Arthur was supposed to be in Baltimore. She called the hotel and asked if Mr. Bellington was still there. The man at the desk offered to put her through, and she hung up before anyone could answer. Though Vera never mentioned it to Arthur, that afternoon was the beginning of her understanding that business was typically not what kept him away from home overnight. One night at a time was bad enough. But the extended weeks holed up with some unknown lover hurt the worst.

Hallan had been right. How well she knew someone did not matter. Everyone hid something. She had her own horrible secrets, too. She had sacrificed a friend to save herself, and for what? To be disdained by her husband? To become the queen of meaningless social rituals? To be a good girl but a bad person?

Vera slammed her fork down on her plate. Silence overtook the table as every head turned to her. Arthur's eyes narrowed.

"What in the world is the matter?" he asked.

"You're taking a trip? For several weeks?"

"It's business. I've done it a million times."

"I'm a little surprised, that's all. You didn't mention it."

Arthur locked his gaze on Vera's. "I didn't think it would inconvenience you. You'll do perfectly well without me, you always do."

"Well, it's an awful lot of 'business,' isn't it?"

"What are you saying?"

Everyone at the table seemed to be holding in a breath waiting for Vera's response. Even Bessie Harper sat silent, her mouth agape. Instead of answering Arthur, Vera turned to Poppy, who nearly leapt out of her seat.

Vera's tone lit up with false brightness. "I'm so sorry, this isn't appropriate dinner talk, is it? Perhaps Poppy should choose the topic of conversation. What is refined society discussing these days, Mrs. Hastings?"

Poppy glanced around the table, wordlessly imploring the other guests for help, but they focused on their plates or the wall. Her brow wrinkled, then smoothed again as a light of inspiration came over her face.

"You poor dear, you're obviously not feeling well. A few too many . . . exertions of late, hmm?" Poppy flicked her gaze at Arthur.

Vera leaned in. The brightness leached out of her words and venom took its place. "You always know just what to say to make an impression. How right you were to demand that I defer to you in social matters."

"I don't know what you're talking about." Poppy let out a watery laugh.

"Come now, no need to be so modest. You set your sights on what you wanted, and you got it. I applaud you." Vera snatched her napkin off her lap and tossed it onto her plate. She stood and gestured to her chair. "And here's my seat, if you want to take it. You can even have my place card. Call yourself by my name for all I care. May it bring you all

the warmth and satisfaction it has brought me. Excuse me, everyone."
Gloves clenched in her hands, Vera stormed from the room. She heard
Arthur making hasty apologies behind her, but she could not slow her
step. He caught up with her at the elevator and grabbed her arm.

"What was that hysterical display about?" His voice was low and
threatening, his face an inch from hers.

She drew herself up. "I think you know very well."

"You'd be surprised what I know."

She turned to him, eyes widening. The elevator doors slid open
with a slight creak. He pulled her on, and they rode up without a word
to each other. When they reached the penthouse, he kept his grip on
her arm and took her into the library. After letting go of her, he poured
them each a glass of bourbon.

"Sit," he said, holding a drink out to her. "We need to have a little
chat."

She lowered herself gingerly into a chair. "Arthur—"

"No. I'm going to talk first. How dare you act like that? What I do
is none of your business, and I'm certainly not going to discuss it with
you at the goddamned Litchfields' dinner table."

She took a shaky drink from her glass. "For ten years I've been a
good wife to you, and you throw it in my face."

He sneered. "At least I don't bring them to the building."

"So you know."

"Of course I know."

"Poppy told you?"

"She did. Stupid woman. But I knew anyway, do you think I'm
blind? The way you two carried on in Montauk. I knew he wanted you,
and I knew you'd give in eventually. You're the sort." He took a swallow of his drink. "Overly romantic. I thought you'd outgrow it."

"If you'd loved me, I wouldn't have gone near him." Vera choked
on the words. "But you don't. You never did. You've been carrying on,
meeting women in hotels since we first married, what did you expect
of me?"

His eyes narrowed. "I expect you to tolerate it."

Her face burned. "Why did you marry me if you don't love me?"

"Because you were the best choice." He shook his head slightly, as if her question made no sense. "The only choice. I knew you would represent me well in society, that you could host a dinner party and serve on some charity board somewhere. At least, I thought all that was true. I thought with your family, your breeding, you'd know how to conduct yourself. But you've proven you're just another silly damned woman."

"But you've been so warm lately." She turned away when he winced. "Things have been so nice between us. If you knew, why would you act that way?"

He swallowed a gulp of liquor and rubbed his temple. His lips parted, but he hesitated. The words seemed to crawl from his throat. "It was a relief, to be honest."

"You weren't angry at all?"

"I thought . . ." He heaved a sigh. Vera noticed deep pockets under his eyes. Under the lamp's harsh electric shine, he looked a decade older. "I thought you'd finally figured out how to survive it. How to make it work." His mouth set in a bitter line. "But you hadn't. You still want this impossible thing."

The jeweler's voice rang in her head again as he read the initials engraved on the pocket watch. Initials that were neither hers nor Arthur's. A pocket watch. Not a necklace, or a brooch, or earrings. The truth about Vera's husband suddenly flashed before her, a truth she had carelessly dismissed time and time again. Like a dust mote passing into a beam of light, a new understanding of his indifference came into view, then slipped into shadow and was gone once more. Hallan had said Vera was living the tragedy she knew. She had not grasped that there was tragedy enough to go around. What if, all this time, Arthur had been living his? What if Vera, willfully blind to it, had made his reality sadder still?

She stared at the rug so long the pattern became a noisy jumble of colors and angles. Arthur seemed content to sip his drink in the silence. She knew at last the battle was over. Any further fighting for his affection would be as futile as all her previous efforts had proven to be.

"I'm leaving you," she said.

He snorted. "That's not the solution you think it is."

"I am. I'm leaving."

"What, are you going with him? You think he can provide for you? You can't provide for yourself, that much is certain."

"Maybe with him. Maybe not." She stood and placed her empty glass on the table beside Arthur. "But I'm not staying here."

He shook his head. "You'll regret it."

"Possibly."

She left the library, shutting the door behind her. The unexpected honesty of the conversation left her drained. She took a few steps up the stairs but grew dizzy, and she sat on the landing halfway up. Her hope, misguided though it was, had kept her fighting for the life she thought was possible. The marriage she wanted that might have made the penthouse a home. She looked over the foyer, her eyes lingering on the closed door of the library. The familiar rooms became the landscape of a foreign country, harsher and colder than any journey into new territory could ever be.

Her energy restored somewhat by her brief rest, she continued up to her room. Vera tossed in the bed for a bit, as the familiar twitch of insomnia agitated her muscles. Giving up, she turned on the lamp on the nightstand. She certainly did not have to worry about Arthur joining her that night, so no need to worry about the light bothering him. Inside the nightstand's drawer, she found the little book of Hopkins poetry Hallan had given her. She flipped through its pages, taking note of poems he had marked and reading the words he had penciled in its margins. The sight of his handwriting reminded her of what she was capable of, what she had the strength to do, and its reassurance brought with it the heavy comfort of sleep at last.

« 31 »

The next morning, Marguerite tapped Vera's shoulder, waking her. Vera blinked in the morning sunlight streaming through the drawn curtains. As she had expected, Arthur's side of the bed was still neat and smooth.

"Madam," Marguerite said with a slight waver, "your mother is here."

Vera bolted up, now wide awake. "Did she say what she wants?"

"No, madam. Shall I ask her?"

"No need. Is my dress laid out?"

"It is." The maid wrung her hands and glanced around the room, as though she were the one about to be castigated.

"Tell her I'll be right down."

Vera threw on her dress and brushed her hair, winding it into a plain knot at the base of her neck. She knew better than to keep her mother waiting too long. A few minutes later, she sat in the drawing room, her mother's eagle glare pinning her in the chair.

"Would you like some tea?" Vera asked.

"Let's not waste time," her mother said. "I hope you know why I'm here."

"I imagine you've spoken to Arthur."

Her mother's lips flattened into a thin line. "I have. He says you've threatened to leave him. For the artist, I assume?"

Vera struggled for a way to explain her thoughts to her mother, but nothing she could say would make sense to a woman like her. Instead, she stared at her hands, crossed in her lap.

"Right," her mother continued, "let's get one thing straight. This is not a fairy tale, and you are not some princess in a tower to be rescued. You have responsibilities. To your father and to me, who raised you better than this. To your husband, who gives you an exquisite home. And to your society. Honestly, Vera, what would people think?"

"I don't know," Vera said softly.

"Oh yes, you do. I want to be perfectly clear. If you continue this affair, your husband has every right to cast you aside without a penny." Her mother thrust out an arm, as if physically trying to toss Vera aside.

Vera looked up. "But why should I be the only one punished? He's carried on all over town, with God knows who, God knows how many."

"Of course he has, that's his right." Her voice lifted on the final word, as though Vera's objections baffled her. Vera weighed the matter-of-factness of the statement. Had her mother looked the other way at her father's indiscretions? Was that what her mother had been trying to warn her about all those years ago by the lake? Did her mother know what Vera was getting into with her marriage to Arthur? Had she known what Arthur was struggling with? How impossible his needs would make their marriage?

"You knew?" Vera asked slowly.

"What really matters is that you knew. I told you marriage to him wouldn't be bliss. But no matter what your husband does or does not do, you must conduct yourself like a lady. That does not include falling into bed with whomever happens by."

"He's not someone who 'happened by'—"

Her mother held up a hand. "I am not interested in the numerous admirable qualities you believe you've found in that man. I am merely telling you that you will not see him anymore. Nor will you speak to your husband as you have. It is unacceptable, and I will not tolerate it."

"Mother, I'm not a child—"

"But you are a child." Her mother's voice grew cold. "I cannot believe we're having this discussion again, after that business at college. Did you learn nothing? How many times will I have to rescue you from your own foolishness? You are absolutely a child. You're still behaving like one."

"Please, I don't want to talk about what happened back then—"

"But it's the same thing all over again. You didn't think then, and you're not thinking now. You say you're leaving. What do you think it will be like, hmm? Can you launder a sheet? Can you cook a meal? You don't even dress your own hair. Look at it this morning, it's a mess, you must have done it yourself. You think this man will take care of you? Do you have any concept of what kind of income is required for a life like this?"

Vera's arms and legs suddenly felt very heavy. Her mother was right. She had not thought it out. Her experience in looking after herself was limited to personal care and the occasional mending of stockings at college. Even there she had someone to clean, someone to cook. She could not even light the stove for tea. How would she survive? And the only thing she knew for certain about Hallan was that he had lied. She did not even know his real name. What if she did leave with Hallan, and he abandoned her? Or worse?

Her mother leaned in and, as though reading her mind, said, "If you leave Arthur, you will be on your own. Your father and I will see to it that you are cut from the will, and we'll certainly offer you no assistance while we're alive. Any correspondence from you will be destroyed unread. Do you understand me? You will have nothing."

Daddy. She would never be able to contact her beloved father again. Her mother would see to that, and he knew better than anyone not to fight Lorna Longacre. Vera closed her eyes briefly then nodded. "Yes, Mother. I understand."

Her mother stood. "Good. I'll see you at lunch on Wednesday. And no more of this madness, please. It gives me a headache." She glared down at Vera. "Well? Show me out."

Tears threatened as Vera walked her mother to the door. She assumed she would need to apologize to Arthur. Her mother would not have it any other way. She had kept Vera from making a mess of her life once before. To see her standing on the brink of disaster again had clearly reopened the old wound. Behind her mother's stony glare had been a flicker of something like regret. Not for Vera's situation, but for her own. Her mother had worked tirelessly for thirty years to mold Vera into the perfect society wife. Vera's failure meant her mother had failed, too.

Then Hallan's heaven-blue eyes replaced the image of her mother's, and his words came back to her: *Names only matter to people like you.* The gatekeepers of culture, the very soldiers of civilization, to hear her mother tell it. Vera had spent her whole life locked behind those gates and protected from herself. Hanging from the wall like a painting in a museum, lit with perfectly angled yellow lights. Dusted. Admired from time to time. Valuable, beautiful, and untouched.

Now the terms were clear, etched in sharp relief by her mother. This was no scandal about college-girl carelessness. If Vera left, she left it all behind. The money, the husband, the mother, the father, and her name. Most of all, the security. The end result was indisputable: she could not leave. She got up and went to the library to compose a note to Hallan. She had promised herself she would say good-bye, after all.

《《《●》》》

Vera heard the front door open when Arthur arrived home from work shortly before the dinner hour. She had asked Evans to send him to the library, and she presented him with a martini when he walked in.

"I hope you had a pleasant day," she said.

"You spoke to your mother, did you?"

"I did."

He settled in the large leather chair by the fireplace, crossing his long legs. "Good. I hope she talked some sense into you."

Vera tugged on her earring. "Yes, well. I hope we can forget about it. I know I'd very much like to."

Arthur gave her a tight smile. "Forgotten."

"Thank you."

"And, until this little episode, you have been a commendable wife."

Commendable. As though he were thanking her for her service. "I'm glad to hear it."

He lit a cigar and rolled it thoughtfully in his fingers. "We so rarely get what we want in life. It's important to be content with what one does have, instead of worrying about what one doesn't."

"I agree."

"People like your artist . . . they contribute nothing. I knew you'd see it, sooner or later. You're a smart girl, for the most part. You'd never have been satisfied with a man like that."

"No, I suppose not."

"Of course not. They're all layabouts, those artist types, flitting from one place to the next with no obligation. If he were a serious man he'd have a job, a home. Instead he's living on the handouts from his betters. I'd bet he hasn't done a thing in that pool room. He'll probably take off one day and we'll never hear another word about him." Arthur took a drag on the cigar. "Did that detective ever find anything on him?"

Stanton's careworn but kindly expression rose to her mind. He would be pleased she had made the right decision. Of course, she could not tell Arthur what she knew; it would only make her look more foolish. "I don't think he's told Clarence anything," she said.

"Well, doesn't matter to me anyway." Arthur sipped from his glass. "Perfect martini, well done."

Vera stood, smoothing out her skirt. "Shall we see if Gertrude has dinner ready?"

"Excellent idea."

Arthur stood and walked out of the library, and Vera followed in the haze of smoke from the cigar. The years of dinners, with him, with the others, and alone, stretched out before her, empty and hollow. She hoped she could numb herself enough to endure them all, knowing now how large the hole in her life really was.

《《《 ● 》》》

Marguerite came into the dining room early the next morning while Vera was finishing her breakfast. Arthur had already left for work, and Vera was planning to go out early to get in a little shopping before lunch with her mother. After the excitement of the past few days, she wanted nothing so much as to get back into her routine. But Marguerite's troubled expression meant something was likely about to prevent that.

"Madam? Excuse me, you have a visitor."

"Who is it?"

The maid paused. "It's Mr. Hallan."

Vera's pulse drummed in her temple. She stood and threw her napkin on the table. She stormed to the entryway, but Evans pointed her to the library.

"Evans," Vera said, her voice strained. "Mr. Hallan is not welcome here. If he returns in the future, please send him away. And he's not allowed to leave any notes."

Evans bowed slightly. "Madam, I'm terribly sorry, I didn't know."

"No, it's my fault. I ought to have told you. I'll deal with him for now."

She walked into the library, where Hallan was waiting. The note she had sent him to say good-bye was crumpled in his hand, and there were dark circles under his eyes. His skin was ashen, his hair tousled and flecked with paint.

"Goodness," she said. "You look awful."

"I was up all night." His eyes shone, the note temporarily forgotten. "I finished it. I finished the painting."

A thrill ran through her, but she spoke calmly. "That's very nice. I hope you'll take your payment and be on your way."

"Oh, no," he said. "I'm not going anywhere until you see it. You think this little note was enough to keep me from you?" He crossed to her and pulled her into his arms. Her lips burned for the touch of his, but she slipped away.

"Not in my home. Not anywhere, never again. I tried to make that clear." She lifted her chin. "I think you'd better leave, Mr. Hallan."

He barked out a laugh. "Yes, I know, I read the note." He held the paper up. "'Dear Mr. Hallan'—so we're back to that, are we? 'I have come to an important decision regarding our friendship. It is with a heavy heart that I must ask you to cease all communication with me—'"

Vera pressed a hand to her stomach. "Stop, please stop."

His expression softened, and he dropped the note on the table. "Come with me. You must see it."

She straightened her back, jaw set. "I want to know the truth first. Everything. About who you are. If you want me to look at your painting, you'll have to tell me." She sat on the couch and motioned for him to join her.

"Can anyone hear us?" he asked.

"There's no one here but the servants, and I imagine most of them are on the other side of the house."

"May I lock the door?"

She nodded. He closed the door, then turned the key and removed it from the lock. After placing it on the table, he sat on the couch beside Vera.

"I don't know where to begin," he said. His eyes took on a distant look, as if reaching into his memory.

"You could start with your real name," she said in a gentle tone. "Or where you're really from. Or why you have the need to hide all these things in the first place."

He clenched his jaw, letting out a long, steady breath. "I'm German. I was born and raised in Leipzig."

She furrowed her brow. "German? But your accent?"

"My grandmother was from London. My mother, her daughter, moved to Germany and married there. What I told you about my family was true. My grandmother came to help when my mother was ill. After my mother died, my grandmother stayed to raise us. Her German was poor and never improved, so Peter and I spoke English at home from a young age. The man she worked for was from London—Westminster—so we spoke English with him, too. Peter always spoke with a German accent, maybe because he was older when he learned, but I was able to speak both languages like a native."

Vera sat back against the couch cushion. Surely something as benign as his nationality was not his secret. "So you're German. Is that all? Why should that matter?"

"You know why it matters."

"You fought in the war, I assume."

"More than that." He rubbed his hands together, then glanced at her. "I want to explain it, from the beginning, so that you understand."

"All right. Wherever you'd like to start."

He thought for a moment. "My grandmother was a lady's maid to the wife of an art collector and professor from Westminster. He came to the art academy in Leipzig shortly after my grandmother moved there to care for us, and she went to work for him then." Hallan smiled faintly. "I loved his house. Huge, sunny place, full of paintings and sculpture, beautiful pieces. One day—I was young, I must have only been seven or eight—he found me staring at one of the paintings. He asked if I painted, and I told him I'd never tried. So he gave me a set of paints and some brushes. He encouraged me, and when I was old enough, he paid my tuition at the art academy. I started there when I was fourteen."

"He sounds like a wonderful man," Vera said. "He must have thought a lot of your work."

"He thought I had promise, anyway."

"What was his name?"

"Allen. James Allen."

She tilted her head in thought. "So that's where you got the name Hallan."

"Yes. He took a special interest in me, and in Peter. I suspect it's because he and his wife had a child, but the boy died in infancy, and they never had any other children."

"Is Peter an artist, too?"

"No, even from a young age he favored being outdoors, working with his hands."

Vera considered this. "So you were studying art when the war broke out? Were you called to action right away?"

Hallan shook his head. "I was so grateful. So stupidly grateful. Neither Peter nor I was called up in the beginning. I really began to believe the war would end quickly, and we wouldn't have to go. But then, after that first year, things got worse. The German army struggled. They started calling up draft years earlier and earlier. Peter wasn't supposed to be called up until 1916, but he got his letter in 1915." He cleared his throat. "I knew it wouldn't be long for me after that, and I was right. I should have had until 1917, but they called me up in the spring of 1916. Fortunately, after about six months or so, I was able to join Peter's division."

"You were together?"

"We were both in France, you see." He covered his face with his hands and spoke in a dry whisper. "God, it was awful. You can't even imagine it. That smell of earth and blood and explosives. Men torn apart, just an arm left, or some gruesome mound of flesh that used to be human. Someone with a name, with thoughts and desires, with a family and friends."

Hallan placed his hands on his knees, and Vera covered one with her own. He jumped at her touch, as if he had forgotten she was sitting there.

"But that . . ." he continued, "that was different. That was war. I might have been able to move on, I might have been able to go on and live my life. But then we got the orders to move back. Strategic, they called it. Not a retreat. We were to destroy everything in the towns we left behind." He turned to her. When he spoke again, his voice was strangled with exhaustion and emotion. "The top command, they said to destroy—they meant wells, trees, crops . . . things like that. But my commander was a cruel man. He had the devil in his eyes. And we had to do as we were told, dump refuse in the wells, burn barns, blow up roads. But he wanted more.

"He shot horses, though he knew we could have used them or left them behind. He burned coops with the chickens boarded up in them. They died screaming. The men who lived in these towns had left, for fear of being taken prisoner or killed to weaken the French. But they left behind women and children. And, finally, killing animals was not enough for this man, our commander. He sought bigger prey."

He halted, and a cold chill ran up the back of Vera's neck. She did not want him to continue. Had he been made to kill an innocent civilian? He shut his eyes tightly and struggled to finish his story. The blood had drained from his face.

"He kicked open the door to a house and found an old woman in it. The poor woman was confined to a chair, and she was alone. He called Peter over and told him to shoot her. Peter refused. The commander asked why, said she was no good to anyone. Peter refused once more. And then . . . I could not stop it. It was too fast." Hallan gasped out a sob. "The commander took Peter's gun from him and shot him in the head."

"Oh my God," she said. Her fingertips tingled and dizziness washed over her.

He turned to her, eyes wild and ringed with red. "Vera, I tell you all these things I have never told another living soul. I tell you because you must understand what I did next."

Her mouth and throat were dry. She stared at the floor, unable to look at him. "Did you kill him?"

"No. I should have. I should have shot him where he stood. No. What I did was worse." He swallowed hard. "I ran."

"You deserted."

He nodded.

She sighed with relief. "Oh, Emil, I think anyone would understand that."

"Not anyone. I saw them line up the deserters and pick them off without a second thought. You ran, you died. Even now, if they find you, you're off to the gallows."

"But . . . then . . . how did you get out?"

"I knew of a friend Mr. Allen had in Paris. An instructor at the Ecole des Beaux-Arts. I thought if I could make it to Paris, I would be safe. I knew we were somewhere near Arras, a few days' walk at least. I broke into a store at night and took clothes so my uniform would not give me away immediately. I hid well, I was never seen. I slept in barns, in ditches, wherever I could conceal myself, during the day. I ate whatever I could find, though sometimes that was only an egg stolen from a nest, or scraps from a trash heap. I walked, I don't know how many nights, until I was in Paris. I found the school, and Mr. Allen's friend, Mr. LeBlanc, took me in. We sent Mr. Allen a telegram, and he sent a good deal of money for my expenses. I can never . . . I owe him everything." He took a few deep breaths to calm himself. "Mr. LeBlanc convinced me to start painting again. I studied with him, in his home. Even after the war ended, I was too afraid to leave. I had to wait until I could come to America. And I wanted to keep studying. I worked odd jobs, and saved up."

"And that's why you weren't on the ship. You were already here, in the city," she said, the pieces falling into place in her mind.

"Yes. A friend told me about the job here in the building, and I knew it had to be enough money for me to finally go out west. I sent the letter to Clarence through Mr. LeBlanc, so the postmarks would be correct. On the day the ship was to arrive, I went out to the dock and waited. But my paintings, the photos you saw—those were real. The mural wasn't mine, but I expect you knew that already."

Vera let the story sink in. "So your plan was to paint the mural and then use the money to start over. Change your name again."

"Yes. I already have new papers. Your investigator might reveal me, and then I'm sure I'll have a one-way ticket back to Germany."

"But none of that can possibly matter," she said. "I read a story in the newspaper, back when the war was on, about a German deserter who escaped to America. He was treated kindly. You deserted, yes. But you deserted our enemy. The men in this building won't be in a rush to turn you in."

Hallan laughed bitterly. "They might have been friends to me during the war, but the war is over. I heard Clarence Bloomer's opinion of Germans. He would happily give me up for nothing more than the pleasure in knowing he had gotten rid of me. As for the others, the opinion of me in this building has soured, to say the least. They'd have me on the next boat back in chains."

"It wouldn't be that simple, would it? They may not like you, but I doubt they want you dead." She looked up at him, going over his words in her mind. His crime, his flight . . . elements of the story made sense, fit neatly. But her rational mind protested at the way the parts came together to form a whole. Something was missing.

He wasn't on the boat. He was already in the city. Before he knew about the mural, he was in the city.

She stood and whirled to face him. "You were already here. There's still something you haven't told me. There's more, isn't there?"

He rubbed his eyes and sank back into the cushions of the couch. "Vera . . ."

She perched on a chair across from him and folded her hands on her knees. "I think you'd better finish your story."

« 32 »

"Well?" Vera continued. "I want to hear the rest. You weren't on the ship. You came to the States before you'd even heard of the mural. If that wasn't what brought you here, what did?"

Hallan sat up, but his shoulders still drooped. "Please, come see the painting first. I don't want to tell you before you see the painting."

"The painting, the painting." She shook her head. "If the rest of the story is that awful, do you really believe the painting will make everything all right?"

"It's not that. I want you to see what I can do before I tell you what I've done."

"I saw the photographs. Unless those were someone else's paintings, I know what you can do."

A faint light appeared in the back of Hallan's eyes. "Those paintings . . . those were mine."

"The ones you painted after the war."

He nodded. "And the war was in them. But now, at last, I'm able to paint again like I used to. With color. With light."

She paused. "And I'm glad. I really am."

He stared at his hands. "I never wanted you to think—when I tell you what I did, who I am, I want you to know . . ." He met her gaze. "I want you to know those were real."

"All right. I know. Tell me the rest. What were you doing in the city?"

Hallan heaved a sigh. "In Paris, a man visited the school. He happened to see a work of mine Mr. LeBlanc had on display. He found my name, found me, and offered me a job. It seemed like the solution to all my problems—work, free passage to New York, papers. And money. I knew it was wrong, but I wanted to get away more than I wanted to do the right thing." He snorted. "I guess that's a pattern of mine, isn't it?"

"What did this man want you to do?" Vera could not imagine— theft? Something darker? Why seek out a painter? The answer hit her squarely in the chest as Hallan's earlier words came back to her. *My paintings, the photos you saw—those were real. The mural wasn't mine, but I expect you knew that already.* She bit her lips together, phrasing her question. "How did you know? That I would know the mural wasn't yours. Why did you say that?"

He looked up at her. His whole face relaxed with the relief of the truth. "The day we met on the docks . . . that wasn't the first time I saw you. It was Fleming who came to me in Paris. I painted for him. I saw you in the gallery. In the back room, when you came to look at the Vermeer."

Heat and cold rushed through her chest. "You were there?"

"He bought me a ticket to the States, said he'd pay me a commission after the fare was paid off. I only cared about getting away. Away from the war, the terrible memories, the nightmares. And he had a good plan. He knew there were people, rich people, looking to buy class. He's not the first to take advantage of that, he won't be the last." Hallan shook his head with a laugh. "I saw pretty quickly that he had no intention of paying me much. Every time I mentioned it, he said I was still working off my ticket. I knew I had to find another plan. A friend from the gallery told me about the job here, so I acted. Besides—"

"You knew I was here." Snippets of her conversation with Fleming came back to her. *The Angelus Bellingtons. Arthur is my husband.* Bea had said Fleming could not help but brag about his important guest. "Were you looking for me?"

He shrugged. "After I saw you . . . well, I was desperate to talk to you, had to know how you knew the painting was forged. Never dreamed anyone would be able to tell. I needed to meet you. The job was a happy coincidence. I needed money, too."

She thought of Bea greeting her in Fleming's gallery. The *Bon Ton* cover. The letters. "But you can't be the forger. I know who it was. It wasn't you."

He leaned back. "What? I can assure you, I painted the Vermeer, along with others."

"But it had to have been Bea. I saw her there, in Fleming's gallery. She was . . ." Vera paused. "We were friends, long ago."

Hallan turned to her. "Bea? No, she had nothing to do with the paintings. She provided letters, documents, things like that. I didn't realize you knew her. Why would you think it was her? Does she paint?"

Vera cast about for an answer. "She . . . she drew. But she and I aren't in touch anymore."

"She never said she knew you. She was the one who made the papers to get me into the States, and she made the ones I'm taking to California. Couldn't tell them from the real thing. She's the one who found out about the job here and encouraged me to send the letter to Clarence through Mr. LeBlanc, so it would come from France. She's clever. When we saw her at the Rialto, I was afraid she'd speak to me, and you'd put the pieces together. Me and the Vermeer."

"How did she find out about the job?"

"She saw I was curious about you after you came into the gallery. She said she'd find out more about you. Though I guess she didn't have to dig far, if you knew each other." He frowned. "Strange she wouldn't just tell me that, though. She even met me for lunch a few times, to see how I was getting along here. Sweet of her, really."

"As I said, she and I hadn't seen in each other in a long time." Vera could not continue. Her thoughts churned at the explosion of new information the past few minutes had yielded. She expected to feel renewed fury at the confirmation that Bea had not given up the tricks that had caused them both such misery years ago. Instead, a reluctant respect overcame the anger. After all, Bea had used her gifts to find a way out of her disgrace. She had not been satisfied with being shipped home after Vassar, hanging her head, and marrying someone her mother deemed appropriate. She had carved out a life for herself, while Vera had quietly given in. Bea had taken the braver path. Vera could not begrudge her that. By the time they had spoken, Bea had already created a new identity, one that would keep her safe from prison. That's why she had not been afraid. Bea created her solutions before she had a problem. She would never be trapped, she would never cower. Vera realized her mother had been entirely wrong. Bea's boldness was not her undoing. It protected her.

And, with that same unstoppable audacity, Bea had helped Hallan get the job at the Angelus, precisely because Vera would be there. She could not doubt that. They had not been friends long, but Bea knew Vera almost better than she knew herself. Bea knew Vera would be drawn to him, and she clearly already knew he was intrigued by Vera. Did she send him in hopes of ruining Vera? Or did she see the loneliness of Vera's situation, know at last what desperation came with the gilded life they had both wanted?

That was why Bea had asked about Hallan when they collided on the street, why she had been near the building at all that day. She had checked in with him. She wanted to know how her plan was working out. As much as Bea might want to see Vera ruined, they had cared for each other once. Some vestige of that connection must have told Bea that the artist was not just the man who might destroy Vera's carefully constructed life. Hallan was also a man she could love. A man who could see through to the real Vera.

Hallan, the forger. Everything made sense now. She could see every detail.

"So it was you," she said, breaking the silence and turning back to him. The distraction of Bea had kept her from piecing it together, but she realized a clue had been there all along, under his nails, in his hair, flecked on his arms. The blue. The light sky blue. Not Vermeer's blue, but Hallan's. The color had not been a mistake, but a signature.

Hallan's voice broke into her thoughts. "I knew you could spot a fake. I didn't want you to see one in me," he said. "I forged those paintings, but I'm not a fraud. I'm the man you know, even if you know me by another name."

"Fleming's been arrested," she said.

"I know. He didn't know I'd gotten this job—I left without telling him I was going, and Bea's probably gone by now, too—"

"I'm sure she's not 'Bea' anymore," Vera said.

Hallan nodded an agreement. "But I'm sure he'll tell them I made the paintings. He only sold them. They'll want to know who painted them. It's only a matter of time until the authorities track me down, I know it."

And then arrest, jail time, possible extradition. The consequences were obvious; he did not have to name them. The forgeries being exposed would certainly have embarrassed some of the wealthiest families in the area, compounding the problem. With Stanton working from one end and the police from the other, the clock had only accelerated. And the risk of finishing the mural seemed to swell far beyond any possible gain from it.

"Then why did you stay when they hired the private investigator?" Vera asked. "Surely you knew he'd make the connection sooner or later."

He crossed to her, grasped her hands, and lifted them to his lips. "Because of you. I planned to paint this thing, maybe slap up some silly pattern, collect the money, and go. My plan was always to move on as soon as possible, to go to California. I didn't expect to fall in love with you. But I did." He pulled her to her feet. "And now that I've told you everything, you must see what I've made for you. That I'm no fraud. And then I want to go together, start a new life."

She shook her head, tears welling in her eyes. "I . . . I can't go. I explained it to you—"

"I know, I know, in that letter. I know Arthur and your mother and probably every other person under this roof has told you why you must stay. But if you stay here, you will never be that woman you were supposed to be. I know her. She deserves to be free." He stepped in closer, wrapping his arms around her waist. "I'm sorry. Sorry I lied, especially to you. Sorry I didn't tell you the real reason I fell in love with you."

She searched his face. "You said it was the art."

"It was, but it was more than that. It was because you knew. You cared if the painting was real, you could see that it wasn't. I knew there was a fire inside you, even if it was only flickering. On the docks, when you first saw me, you looked at me like I was water in the desert. That's why I pushed to speak with you from my first day in the building. I had to find out who you were, what made you different from the rest. I saw in you someone who knows what it's like to need to be free. I vowed to free you. You're right, I should have been gone by now. Falling in love with you changed everything. This job, this plan was going to be the easy way out."

Vera cast her eyes down. "There is no easy way out."

"No. But there is a way out. It may not be easy. But there's a way."

She gazed into his blue-green eyes, and saw the sky. What had been a firm decision the night before, almost the moment before, melted at the edges. She began to doubt.

"Take me to the painting," she said.

His weary face brightened. He unlocked the door and started for the front entrance, but she held him back.

"No," she said. "This way."

They went through the kitchen to the stairwell door, leaving the confused cook behind them. Together, Hallan and Vera raced down the stairs, both a little giddy and overwhelmed. They arrived at the pool level under the lobby out of breath. He took a key from his pocket, then turned.

"Close your eyes."

Vera closed them, and let him lead her by the hand into the pool room. The pool had been drained while he was there, but the sting of chemicals still hung in the air, winding around the thick smell of new paint. Her shoes echoed on the tile as he took her shoulders and guided her into position.

"All right. Open them."

She opened her eyes and gasped. The painting took up the entire wall, one full story floor to ceiling. A few warm tears slid down her cheeks. She turned and kissed him fiercely.

"You see?" he said when they parted. "That's the woman you can be."

And it was.

⟪⟨● ⟩⟫

Hallan left the elevator on the second floor to pack a suitcase. Vera rode the rest of the way to the penthouse, her insides roiling. Only this morning, she had been ready to let go of the girlish hope of leaving with the artist, despite the emptiness of the years before her if she stayed in the Angelus. She stood to lose too much. But he had been right. When she saw the painting, her resolve vanished, and her world tumbled into uncertainty once more.

Now she had to decide, and she had little time to deliberate. Before they left the pool room, Hallan told her he would leave within the hour. He still wanted her to come, but going with him would mean accompanying a fugitive. She knew what she wanted to do and what she should do, and could not find any parts of the two that intersected. They could not be reconciled. Happiness or security. But not both. And maybe neither.

Evans met her at the door of the penthouse. "Madam, I didn't know you had gone out."

"Just downstairs. Did my husband tell you what time he's coming home this evening?"

"He has a dinner meeting. He won't be home until late, I believe."

She checked her watch. "Thank you. Will you fetch my suitcase?"

If he felt any surprise at this request, he concealed it. "Should I bring it to your room?"

"Yes, thank you. Oh, and phone my mother, please. Tell her I won't be coming to lunch."

He inclined his head. "Would you like me to give her a reason, madam?"

"Yes." Vera paused. "Tell her I'm not hungry."

Vera went to her dressing room. Her dresses hung in an orderly rainbow, her hats stacked in boxes, her shoes lined up like a little row of sentinels. The variety paralyzed her. What would she pack? She did not even know where in California he planned to go. And the weather grew cooler every day. Her furs were in storage, her coats in the coat closet downstairs.

A sound in the bedroom startled her. She peeked out of the dressing room to see Evans setting up the suitcase on its stand. When he left, she went and stood over it. The suitcase gaped at her, a jaw dropped in surprise at the extraordinary circumstance of its use. When she thought of how much she required—gloves, stockings, slips, dresses, hats, and shoes—she felt like gaping herself. The suitcase did not look like it could ever hold enough.

How could she think of leaving her life behind? Helping to carry this man's secrets as he lived the rest of his life in the shadow of possible arrest, of extradition? Running to places unknown, with no plan ahead of them? She might be in trouble herself if she helped him. More was on the line now than disgrace and her mother's disappointment.

And if he left her? Hallan might abandon her at the first train stop, or slip the rings from her fingers while she slept. Her mother had vowed Vera would not get a cent if she attempted to leave. She would truly be alone. But she had to choose, and she had to choose now: the Angelus or Emil Hallan. The husband who had never cared for her, or the stranger who did.

An object on the nightstand caught her eye. The book of poems had given her such comfort only a few nights earlier, though the feeling now seemed years in the past. Vera lifted the book and ran her thumb lightly over the leather cover. She thought back to the moment Hallan had given it to her, when she wept with confusion and shame over her reaction to the monster in the film and the vase on its narrow stand. She walked over to the window, book still in hand, and looked down at the city streets below. The view was not so different from the hunchback's vantage point atop the cathedral. Only where were the sneering, jeering crowds below?

A thought crept into her mind—at first a small spark, growing to a steady, focused beam that held her attention. In her mind, the vase she had smashed leapt from the floor, its shards reassembling themselves. The vase became whole again in her hand. The woman from that night, so heartsick and lost, had vanished. The woman she had become could stand in front of an open suitcase and not fear where it might take her.

She did not have to choose Hallan. The private detective's solemn voice rang in her head.

There is no Emil Hallan.

She wanted to go with the artist, yes. And she would. But more than that, she would just *go*. If at some later time their happiness together departed, she could still find happiness in the promise of not being Arthur's wife or Mr. and Mrs. Joseph Longacre's daughter. Even the idea of leaving her father behind forever was less daunting. Though he indulged her with gifts, he had never given her anything of substance. He had not even given her the warm advice that Stanton, a man who had known her only a few weeks, had been more than happy to offer. If he was truly weak enough to let her mother sever their bond, he may not be worth cherishing after all.

The thought of being alone, even at some small-town train station, did not frighten her anymore. She was smart, and she could make her way. Her whole life had been regimented, planned, and divided into squares on a calendar. She had observed the strict customs of the religion of propriety, and for what? What meaning did it give her life to know the exact colors that could be worn at a small dinner before six p.m., or the exact way to greet an ambassador's wife? What had she gained when she betrayed Bea years ago? What, truly, would be the purpose of continuing on inside the Angelus building?

But it was not too late. Vera had time to give her life meaning. She had time to become a woman of value. She could learn how to mend a stocking and wash linens and make her own tea. How to breathe. How to be someone of worth and merit outside of the building's walls. She had never been the woman her mother spent decades shaping her to be. She had been playing a role all her life, and being good at it was no excuse for giving in to it.

Leaving was not the answer. It was the question: Who could she become? What opportunities awaited her?

The artist did not have to free her.

She could free herself.

EPILOGUE

The day after Vera left, Arthur returned home to two letters and a paper-wrapped parcel. The first letter, attached to the parcel, was from Mr. Hallan, who asked that Arthur and the other gentlemen of the building review his work. The keys they had given him were enclosed in the parcel, still on the ring. Should they find the painting suitable, he continued, they could send the promised payment to a Mr. James Allen in London, who would look after it for Hallan. Given the circumstances of his departure, however, he would understand if they chose not to pay. He closed the letter with thanks for the opportunity and hospitality, and fondest wishes for Arthur's continued success. Vera's note to Arthur was rather terser than Hallan's. It said only:

> *Dear Arthur,*
> *I did not want to leave you without a word of good-bye.*
> *You gave me a good life, even if it wasn't the life either of us*
> *wanted. I hope there are better days ahead for us both.*

Arthur asked Marguerite to look through Vera's things, and the girl, her eyes full of tears, confirmed that some of the things in the closet were missing. When Arthur inspected the jewelry box, he noted with some approval that Vera had not taken any pieces he had given her, tactfully avoiding any question of theft. She had even left her wedding ring, placed carefully on his bedside table. Beside it, she had laid her thin silver watch. Only the pieces she had owned before their marriage, the ones that truly belonged to her, were missing. One of the rings and two brooches would later turn up at a Manhattan jeweler's shop. The shop's owner complained that he bought the pieces at rather a higher price than he thought fair. But, he insisted in his defense, the woman who sold them was a formidable negotiator, and they really were such exquisite pieces.

The men of the building took the elevator down to the pool level together that evening. Arthur opened the door to reveal Hallan's prized mural. He had painted the building's four golden angel statues against a pale blue background, with the city skyline below. Three of the statues stood as they did on the roof, wings folded in and arms over their chests, gazes locked on the building below. The statue closest to the viewer, however, perched on one foot on the corner. Her other leg was still in motion, as if she had been running toward the ledge and had been caught at the moment of takeoff. Her wings extended beside her, a few shining feathers fluttering loose. She stretched her long arms out, reaching for the horizon. And on her face, which everyone agreed looked vaguely familiar, was a radiant smile. If the men had thought to go to the other side of the pool to inspect the painting more closely, they might have noticed the faintest dusting of freckles across the bridge of her nose. But they did not think to do that, and so did not notice.

Below the painting was an inscription. Borrowed from the portrait of Giovanna Tornabuoni by Ghirlandaio and translated from the Latin, it read:

Art, couldst thou but portray character and the
mind, then there would be in all the world no picture
more beautiful than this.

"What do you think?" asked Clarence Bloomer.

"What's it supposed to be?" said Andrew Keller.

"The women will love it, anyway," said Kenneth Harper.

Arthur took a long drag on his cigar and stared at the painting. He turned to go, then tossed a final thought over his shoulder before he turned the corner into the hallway.

"Pay the man. And hire someone to paint over the damn thing."

《《《 ● 》》》

Mr. Stanton received a letter in his office a few days after Vera's disappearance.

> Dear Mr. Stanton,
>
> I'm sure by now you must have heard that I left the Angelus building to make a new home elsewhere. I would be remiss, however, if I left New York without expressing my gratitude to you for your invaluable advice. I took your words to heart, thought through my options, and made a choice.
>
> In a few weeks or months, my husband and mother will likely come to you to investigate my whereabouts. They will want to be thorough and follow all the proper procedures to have me declared legally dead. I beg you, friend—allow them to come to the conclusion they prefer. Let them do what they must to record publicly what I myself have lately discovered: there is no Vera Bellington.
>
> I'd like you to find a woman who used to go by the name Bea Stillman. She's originally from Atlanta and may still be in contact with her family there. If anyone can find her, I know you can. I've enclosed a sum that I hope will be sufficient to cover your time. When you find her, please give her the enclosed letter. It contains some long overdue

words of apology. If she wishes to contact me, please give
her the address below, care of Mr. James Allen.
 Knowing you has been my pleasure, if only because I
know of at least one more kindhearted man in the world. I
wish you all the best in life.

After reading the letter, Stanton studied the envelope included with it. The outside had "Bea" printed on it and gave no clue as to its contents. The flap of the envelope was not sealed, only tucked under, but he did not look inside. Some words belonged only to the two people connected by them. They were not his to share. He placed both letters in the top drawer of his desk, then lifted the telephone to begin making inquiries about where to find Bea Stillman.

《《《●》》》

Around that time, a certain Mr. and Mrs. Emil Frye took a bungalow in the Hollywood Hills. Mr. Frye found employment painting set backdrops at a movie studio, although he did receive a nice little windfall shortly before arriving in California. The money allowed Mrs. Frye to keep house instead of seeking work. As a housewarming gift, he bought her a set of brushes and her own paints. She learned to cook slowly, after more than a few burned meals and ruined pans. Mr. Frye never seemed to mind.

About three months after they moved in, papers arrived via Mr. Allen in London. The documents established Mrs. Frye as a resident of California, and they matched her husband's perfectly. Enclosed with them was a letter expressing the sender's happiness that Mrs. Frye's life had, in fact, been saved. Below the unfamiliar name in the looping, swirling letters of the signature was an address that allowed the hope of new friendship.

Mr. Frye bought a car and taught Mrs. Frye how to drive it. On weekends they would take the little coupe into Los Angeles to visit galleries and museums. He joined the Painters' and Sculptors' Club of Los Angeles in the hope of someday exhibiting his own work. They visited with neighbors for the occasional dinner or cocktail, although they seemed to prefer each other's company more than anything. Most evenings, they sat on the porch together and watched the sun set.

Every so often she would take the car out on her own. She'd drive the twisting roads by the ocean with the car's top down and the salty breeze lifting the ends of her hair. She liked to get out of the car, to walk barefoot on the sand. No etiquette to follow. No schedules. No obligations, not even to him. Only the great golden sun and open sky.

ACKNOWLEDGMENTS

There are many, many people who have invested their time, creativity, and energy into making this novel one I am proud to have created.

Without the guidance of my gifted agent, Stefanie Lieberman, this novel would not have been half what it is. The warm thanks I offer her here is nothing close to what I owe her, but I'll offer it just the same.

I'm eternally grateful to Hilary Rubin Teeman at Crown for her support and vision for this book. Thanks also to Lauren Kuhn, Kayleigh George, Rose Fox, and the rest of the Crown team for their help, support, and creative energy. Thank you to Norman Watkins, Ada Yonenaka, Song Hee Kim, and Elena Giavaldi for making the book even more of a joy to behold.

My love and thanks to the friends who have been roped into service as readers and have accompanied me through highs, lows, and many drafts. One person in particular has rooted for Vera and Hallan from the start. Diana Overbey, you are a million in one.

To my wonderful family—Mom, Frank, Dad, Liz, and James— thank you for never laughing at my notebooks filled with scribbles. I love you all.

Finally, without the patience and gifted reading of my loving husband, Bailey, truly none of this would be possible. I'm a better writer and person for having you in my life.

ABOUT THE AUTHOR

AMBER BROCK teaches British literature at an all-girls school in Atlanta. She holds an MA from the University of Georgia and lives in Smyrna with her husband, also an English teacher, and their three rescue dogs.

A FINE IMITATION

ESSAYS,
READER'S GUIDES,
AND MORE

A Reader's Guide

Dear Reader,

It's my pleasure to present my novel, *A Fine Imitation*. The 1920s, a decade rife with contradictions and change, seemed to be the perfect backdrop for a woman wrestling with who she was and who she wanted to be. To help you get to know Vera Bellington and her surroundings, I've compiled some recommendations for browsing, reading, listening, and sipping. Use the signature cocktail recipes to ignore Prohibition in style, brush up on poetry and fine art, and let the sounds of the early twentieth century take you back in time.

I hope you enjoy Vera's journey.

Sincerely,
Amber Brock

Questions and Topics for Discussion

1. Visual art plays a huge role in *A Fine Imitation*. In her college years, Vera explains why she studies art, saying, "Even when it's ugly or sad, it's beautiful." Why might she feel this way? Do you agree with her assessment?

2. The novel explores some of the tension between classical and modern art. The tenants of the Angelus mock modern art, while Hallan declares that the newly emerging cinema is just another form of art. Is one form of art more legitimate than another? How does a style of expression become a true art form?

3. The names Longacre and Bellington come with certain rights and many obligations for Vera. Bea refuses to be called Beatrice. Hallan's name is the subject of doubt and speculation. Even Poppy's name holds a secret. How do names affect the ways in which the characters define who they are? How do their names affect the way other characters view them?

4. Vera enjoys obvious privilege thanks to her

status and wealth. Why, then, is she still miserable? How do you interpret Hallan's claim that Vera is living the tragedy she knows? Do you agree or disagree?

5. Vera's mother makes clear that she doesn't approve of Vera attending college. Why might Vera have wanted to go to school, knowing she would never use her education in a profession? Given the heartbreak that her time at Vassar leads to, would Vera have been happier if she hadn't gone?

6. Vera's breakthrough comes when she realizes she has the power to make her own choices about her life. Which of Vera's choices do you agree were right for her? In which moments would you have done something differently?

7. Each character is the protagonist of his or her own story. How does this novel change when told from Hallan's point of view? Arthur's? Lorna's? Bea's?

8. What role does the Angelus building play in Vera's life? What does it represent to her? To others?

9. Vera struggles to understand why *The Hunchback of Notre Dame* affects her so strongly. How do you interpret her reaction to the movie? Why do you think she claims it's the monster that upsets her? Is that really what makes her so emotional in that moment?

10. Much of the conflict in the novel comes from the secrets the characters keep. Are there times when keeping a secret is someone's right? Are there times when others have a right to know?

Recommended Viewing

Las meninas, **Diego de Velázquez (Museo del Prado)**

When Vera tells Hallan about standing in front of her favorite painting in the Prado and crying, this is the painting she means. Vera studied the Spanish masters in her time at Vassar College, a group that includes Velázquez, Goya, and El Greco. *Las meninas* is a riddle of a painting that plays with the concept of perspective and questions the viewer's role in the observation and even creation of art. Vera would have loved that idea, as well as identifying with the featured princess's privileged position.

Portrait of Giovanna Tornabuoni, **Domenico Ghirlandaio (Thyssen-Bornemisza Museum)**

This is the painting Vera and Hallan admire in the Metropolitan Museum of Art. On loan to the Met in 1923, this striking portrait lives in Spain these days. Giovanna herself was a legendary beauty inside and out, inspiring Ghirlandaio's addition of the Latin inscription behind her.

Woman in Blue Reading a Letter,
Johannes Vermeer (Rijksmuseum)
This is the painting that inspired my description of
the painting Vera suspects is forged. Vermeer's paintings often depicted moments of quiet domesticity,
and his signature blue has pride of place here. I visited the National Gallery in London while studying
Vermeer for this book and discovered that I can now
spot his blue from across a very crowded gallery.

The Music Lesson, **Johannes Vermeer**
(Royal Collection, St. James's Palace)
This painting is the subject of *Tim's Vermeer,* a fascinating documentary I watched as part of my Vermeer research. While Tim's theory that Vermeer was
a technical genius as well as an artist may be up for
debate, I think Hallan would have liked the idea that
mental application is as valuable as inborn talent.

The Expulsion of Adam and Eve from Paradise,
Benjamin West (National Gallery, Washington, DC)
This is absolutely a neoclassical painting Bea would
have taken issue with. In fact, this is the painting
I imagined her pointing to in Vera's textbook when
delivering her diatribe against the neoclassicists. In
fairness to the painting's inherent sense of drama, it
is a dire situation the subject finds herself in.

Madame X, **John Singer Sargent (Metropolitan
Museum of Art)**
This portrait of Virginie Amélie Avegno Gautreau
inspired my description of the painting of Vera that

hangs in her home. The original painting featured Madam Gautreau with a bare shoulder. It caused such a scandal when exhibited in Paris that Sargent had to retouch it to return the strap to its "proper" place. Sargent's ability to infuse his subjects with life is difficult to appreciate without seeing them in person.

La familia de Carlos IV, Francisco de Goya (Museo del Prado)

This is another painting Vera would have made time for in her tour of the Prado. Though I can't imagine she would have much interest in Goya's more famous *Pinturas negras (Black Paintings),* she would have appreciated how *Las meninas* inspired the composition of this painting. Before entering a prolonged period of mental illness and other struggles, Goya was a court painter, and his work had a much more traditional style. However, his future propensity for darker themes can be seen here—at first intimate, this painting has a suffocating quality on longer viewing.

Fountain, Marcel Duchamp (various installations, including the Tate Modern)

I would be remiss if I didn't include this piece, which the inhabitants of the Angelus building hold up as an example of the foolishness of modern art. I'd argue that the brilliance of this piece is in the conversations it inspires about how to define art, which is very much in keeping with the spirit of a lot of unique works such as this one.

Recommended Reading

"Spring and Fall," Gerard Manley Hopkins
I adore Hopkins, so I couldn't resist the urge to make him a favorite of one of my characters as well. This poem is as delicately structured and as deceptively strong as a birdcage. Though it's only referenced in the novel with a brief quote, this poem seemed the perfect one to guide Vera into a better understanding of herself and the nature of life's tragedies.

"She Walks in Beauty," Lord Byron
Hallan rejects Byron, but he can quote this poem! As simple, elegant, and lovely as the woman it describes, this poem remains a bit too superficial for Hallan's taste (and mine). An excellent counterpoint to this poem is Wordsworth's "She was a Phantom of Delight," which paints a fuller image of a woman as a complete person.

"Far West," Pedro Salinas

I've never found a satisfactory translation of this poem in English (though the title is always in English). Though the poem was published in 1929, it describes the speaker's first encounter with—and wonder at—the marvels of early cinema. He marvels at film's ability to bring a wind from eight thousand kilometers away. He can see the breeze, but not feel it. Hallan would very much agree with the representation of film's artistic capabilities.

"The Red Poppy," Louise Glück

Though the title unfortunately contains the name of one of Vera's antagonists, this poem's meaning would have resonated deeply with Vera. I nearly used the line "I speak / because I am shattered" as the epigraph for my novel but went with an equally appropriate quote from Charles Mackay instead.

"The Lady of Shalott," Alfred, Lord Tennyson

Though Vera wouldn't care much for the pre-Raphaelite paintings depicting the subject of this poem, she couldn't help but feel empathy for the poem's subject. Vera must have read this growing up and must have feared incurring her own curse if she attempted to escape her "tower."

Recommended Listening

1913

"You Made Me Love You," Al Jolson

Part of Vera longs for the helpless kind of love described in this song, especially in her youth. In her college days, she wouldn't have had a clue just how hard she'd have to fight her own feelings in the future.

"The Angelus" from *Sweethearts*

I couldn't resist including this! I didn't stumble on this song until well after the novel was published, so it was not the reason I called Vera's building the Angelus. Happy (and strange) coincidence.

"Don't Blame It All on Broadway," The Peerless Quartet

The fact that this cautionary tale is sung by a barbershop quartet gives it a quaint feel. Vera would have agreed with the notion that one is in charge of one's own destiny (or downfall), while Bea likely would have been intrigued by the suggestions of vice available to her in the city.

"Say 'Au Revoir' But Not 'Goodbye',"
Will Oakland
Sad as it is to say, I can imagine Vera listening to this and longing for her sweet college romance with Cliff. I like the use of French in the song, which would certainly bring to her mind his wanderlust.

"They've Got Me Doing It Now," Eddie Weston

I like to think Vera would have enjoyed this bouncy ragtime tune but would never let her mother catch her listening.

1923

"Three O'Clock in the Morning,"
Paul Whiteman
Though I don't name the song in the novel, this is the one I imagine Vera and Hallan dancing to in the speakeasy. It's the perfect blend for the two of them—it was a popular tune, but still with a classic waltz rhythm.

"Si, mi chiamano Mimi" from *La bohème*
Another song I didn't name that features prominently in an emotional scene. This is the aria I imagine Vera listening to in one of her most despondent and confused moments after going to the movies with Hallan.

"What'll I Do?" Irving Berlin

This gorgeous lament about lost love would resonate with Vera as she wrestled with whether or not to give in to her feelings for Hallan. If she doesn't, what could she be missing out on? Definitely a question that bothers her.

"A Pretty Girl Is Like a Melody," Irving Berlin

This song was a popular part of the Ziegfeld Follies shows. The teasing, flirty tone reminds me a lot of Hallan's conversational style (at least with the ladies).

"Nobody Knows You When You're Down and Out," Jimmy Cox

Vera nearly ruins herself twice. The consequences of giving up a life of wealth and comfort, expressed so sorrowfully in this song, are always on her mind.

Recommended Drinking

If you're an Arthur:

THE ARTHURIAN MANHATTAN

2 oz. whiskey
1 oz. sweet vermouth
Dash bitters
1 or 2 black cherries
Orange peel

Add ice and liquid ingredients to a cocktail shaker. Pit the black cherries and smash them along with orange peel in the bottom of a glass. Strain the liquids into the glass.

The deeper, more complex flavor of black cherries suits Arthur better than the sweet maraschino cherries typically used in this cocktail.

If you're a Vera:

SUMMERS AT THE SHORE

¼ cucumber, seeded and sliced (more or less depend-
ing on how much you like the taste)
3 or 4 large blackberries
2 oz. gin
6 oz. club soda

Place cucumber slices and blackberries in the bottom
of a cup and press with a spoon to release the juices.
Top with ice, gin, and club soda. Garnish with an
additional cucumber slice.

Vera's gin would have been imported from the UK by
way of Canada. She would definitely insist on Tan-
queray, though Hendrick's tastes great in a cucumber cocktail.

If you're a Hallan:

AMERICANO (ORIGINALLY KNOWN AS A MILANO-
TURINO)

1½ oz. Campari
1½ oz. sweet vermouth
3 oz. soda water
1 orange slice

Pour Campari and vermouth over ice in a glass. Top
with soda and garnish with the orange slice.

The red color of this drink and its European-to-
American transition make it a natural fit for Hallan.

If you're a Bea:

HONEY JULEP

8 mint leaves
¼ oz. simple syrup
2 oz. bourbon
¼ oz. wildflower honey

Crush six mint leaves in a glass with simple syrup and a splash of water. Fill glass with crushed ice then pour in bourbon. Drizzle with honey and garnish with additional mint leaves.

Like Bea, this drink is sparkling and Southern. She'd approve of the sweetness . . . to balance out her sass.

If you're a Lorna:

FORD COCKTAIL

(adapted from *Modern American Drinks* by George J. Kappeler)

3 dashes Benedictine
3 dashes orange bitters
½ oz. jigger gin
½ oz. jigger French vermouth
Orange peel

Pour liquid ingredients into a shaker and shake. Strain into a glass over shaved or chipped ice. Garnish with orange peel.

Lorna would never drive herself, but she would have accepted being "behind the wheel" of this Gilded Age cocktail.